The Zoo Revisited

BOOK THREE

Dramatic revelations in the race to locate hidden wealth on the Kenyan coast

BOOK 3 in The Zoo Trilogy by

KEITH MAURICE BROWN

. . . golden joys

I speak of Africa and golden joys.

William Shakespeare, Henry IV Part 2

The Zoo Revisited

This novel builds on the earlier adventures of Brett James in Kenya. It is a fictional narrative, weaving together fragments of conversations, memories of raw experiences, and the perceptive observations of knowledgeable people.

Did any of this really happen? Perhaps a more pertinent question might be: could it have happened?

The opinions expressed in this novel are the author's alone.

Poem in Epilogue: 'You are alive' by Pauline W.

The author's artwork used in this trilogy was painted in Kenya during the 1980s.

Tellwell Talent
www.tellwell.ca

ISBN
978-0-2288-5139-4 (Paperback)
978-0-2288-5140-0 (eBook)

Dedication

To the reader who is willing to consider the timeless truths that are woven into the drama of this novel. Those ideas are revealed through the imagined conversations in the story.

Appreciation

It is with deep gratitude that I recall the friendship of one individual in particular: Lay Canon Wilfred Nderitu Gichuki.

He is gifted and sincere; a brother on the journey of life.
In the late 1970s, when he was Principal of an Institute of Technology, he graciously described to me – a results-oriented, achievement-driven newcomer – the benefits of how things were done in Kenya. He patiently took the trouble to demonstrate that, for the amiable Kenyans, deep relationships are more significant than mere accomplishments.

Contents

Acknowledgements

The editorial advice, insights, and critical input from Pauline W, Laura W, Linda Whittome, and Elizabeth WB were invaluable. Their commitment through countless hours of careful review is very much appreciated.

I am thankful for the advice and support of many friends. The following people provided encouragement and valuable information from their own areas of interest and expertise: David Anonby, Jim Barber, Richard Cavalier, Ken Curry, Sue De Vries, Marion Fuller, Randy Hoffmann, Marie Jordan-Knox, Peter Mitchell, John Potts, Meta Smith, Cliff Warwick, Paul WB, and Richard W.

However, they bear no responsibility for the words or opinions in this final story in the trilogy.

Introduction to The Zoo

The Zoo is a fictional, cross-cultural, multi-religious community on the Kenyan coast, located on a peninsula projecting into the Indian Ocean. It lies north of Malindi and just south of a small town called Mwakindini.

Before establishing the Zoo, Henry and Louise Emerson had noticed that relationships were peaceful when different communities and subgroups lived in their own areas; and there was contentment and community spirit when they joined together in mutually supportive activities. Henry likened this to a zoo where the animals are grouped by kind, in individual cages if necessary, but with a central control to provide protection, care, and the essentials for healthy and happy lives.

The unique layout of the Zoo – and its management – reflect Henry's original ideas and enable people to live in their individual groups if they wish. The dwelling units are jokingly called 'cages' and are deliberately kept small in order to encourage residents to use the common areas for as many occasions as they can: entertainment, meetings, dining, and social events.

The eastern half of the peninsula is separated from the residential area by an impenetrable wall. It was designed to protect the natural environment within this reserve and ensure that Henry Emerson's research projects were undisturbed. During Brett James' first stay at the Zoo, from 1984 to 1987, he was unable to resist secretively scaling the wall to explore the mysteries of the forbidden area. This resulted in a severe response from the leaders who were obviously hiding illegal activities on the isolated headland. Unknown forces arranged an attack on Brett to warn him against investigating further.

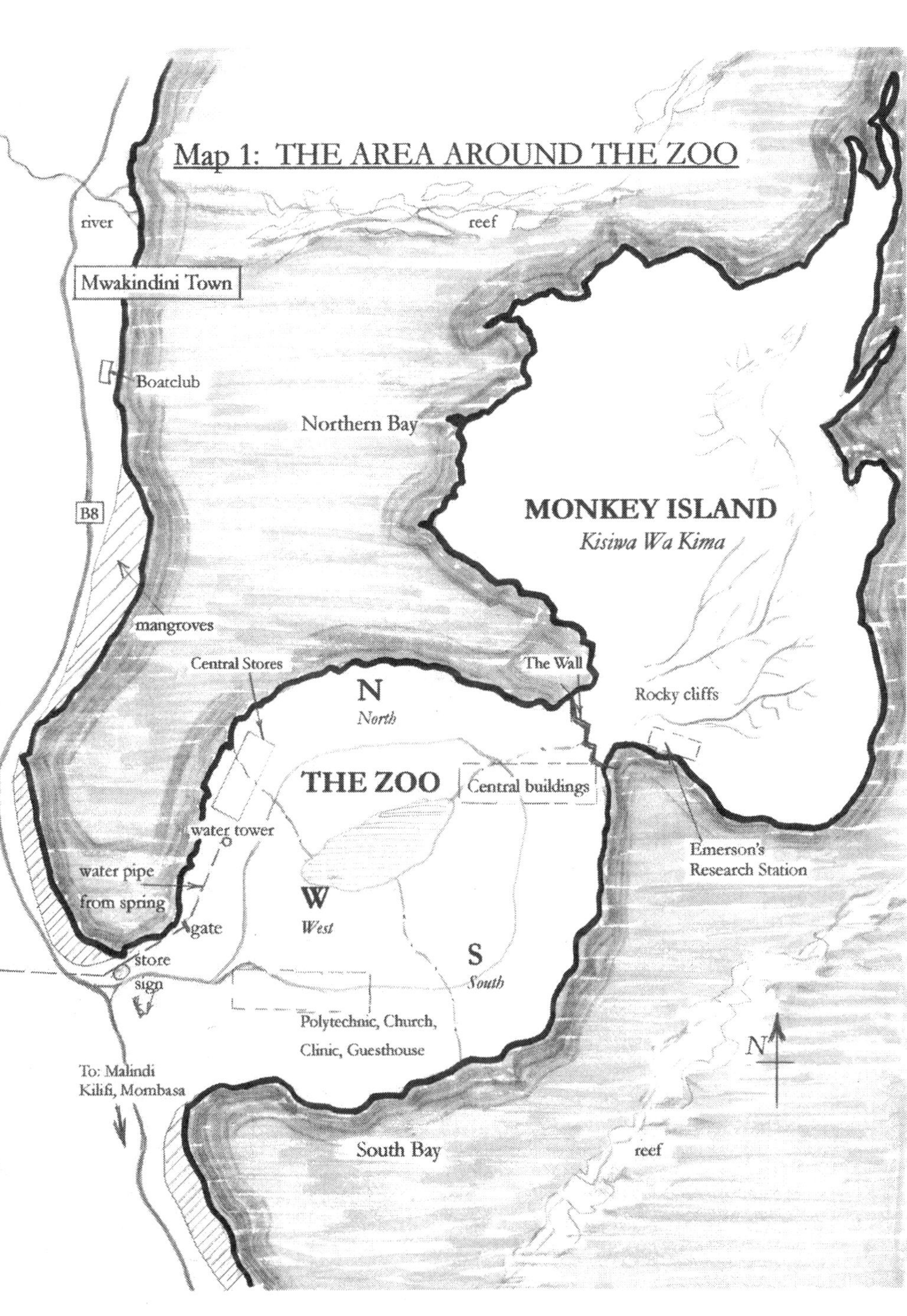
Map 1: THE AREA AROUND THE ZOO
river
reef
Mwakindini Town
Boatclub
Northern Bay
B8
MONKEY ISLAND
Kisiwa Wa Kima
mangroves
Central Stores
The Wall
N
North
Rocky cliffs
THE ZOO
Central buildings
water tower
Emerson's
Research Station
water pipe
from spring
W
West
gate
store
S
sign
South
Polytechnic, Church,
Clinic, Guesthouse
N
To: Malindi
Kilifi, Mombasa
South Bay
reef

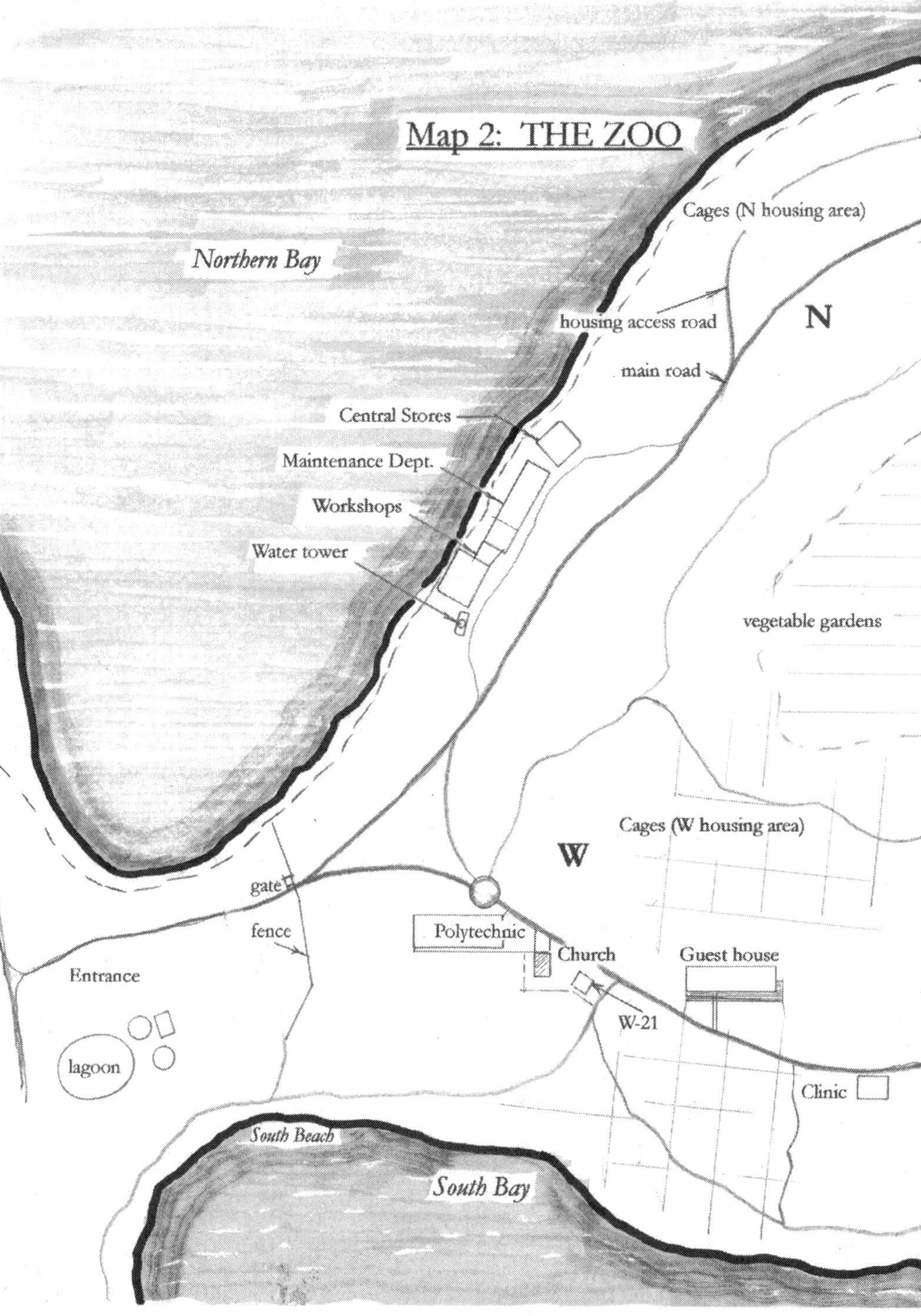
Map 2: THE ZOO
Northern Bay
Cages (N housing area)
housing access road
N
main road
Central Stores
Maintenance Dept.
Workshops
Water tower
vegetable gardens
Cages (W housing area)
W
gate
fence
Polytechnic
Church
Guest house
Entrance
W-21
lagoon
Clinic
South Beach
South Bay

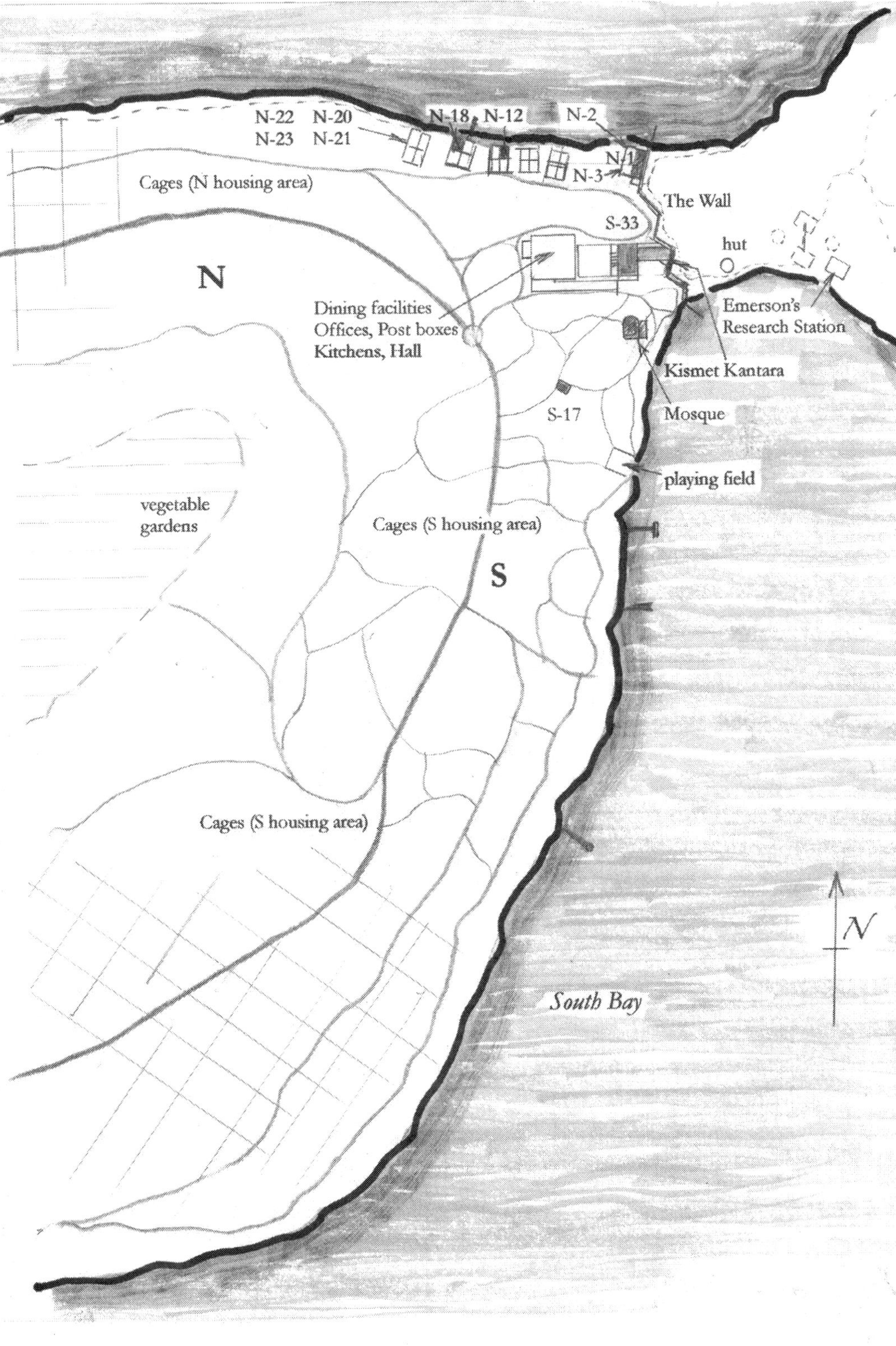

N-22
N-20
N-23
N-21
N-18
N-12
N-2
N-1
N-3
Cages (N housing area)
The Wall
S-33
hut
N
Dining facilities
Offices, Post boxes
Kitchens, Hall
Emerson's
Research Station
Kismet Kantara
Mosque
S-17
playing field
vegetable
gardens
Cages (S housing area)
S
Cages (S housing area)
N
South Bay

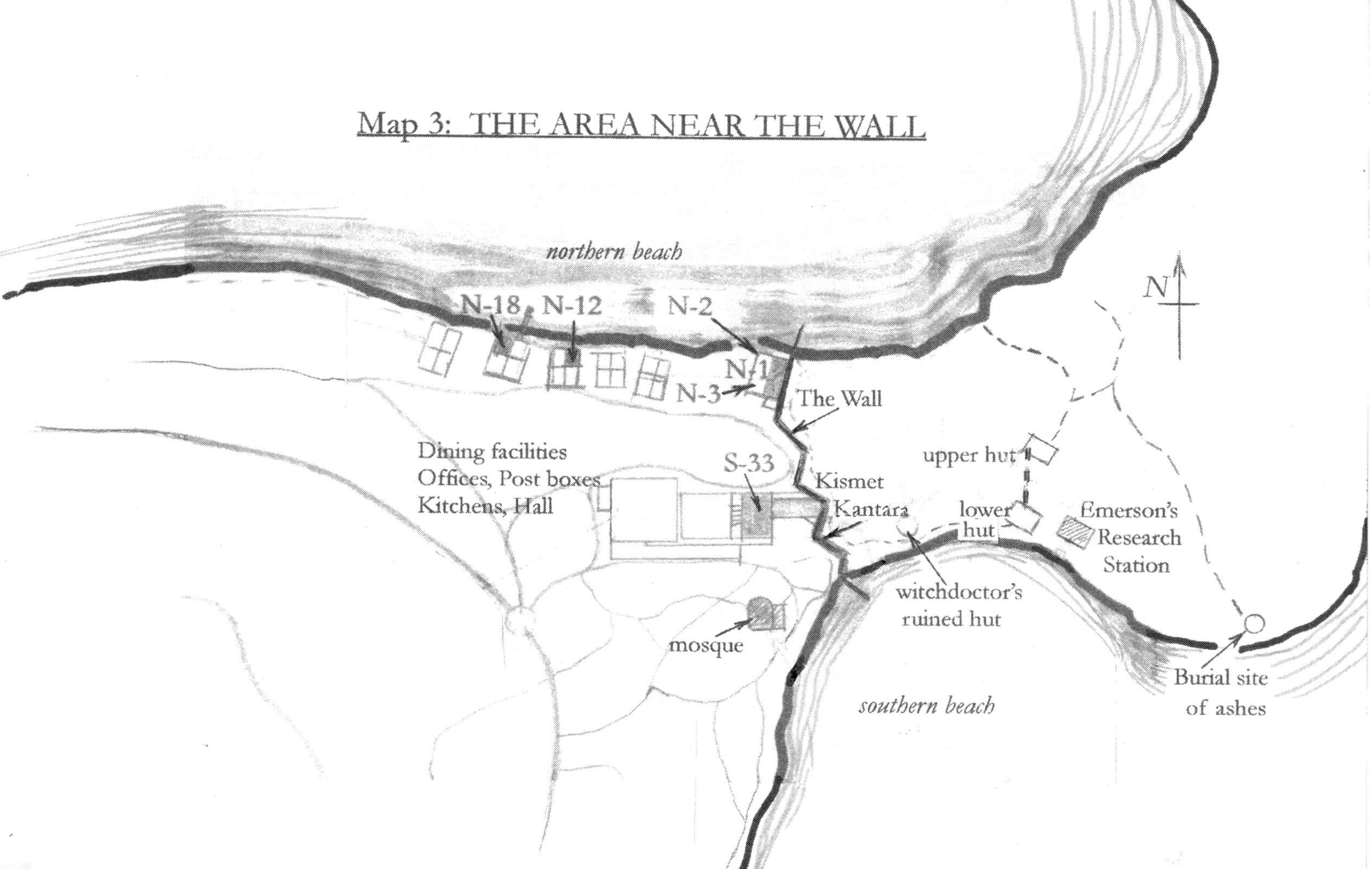
Map 3: THE AREA NEAR THE WALL
northern beach
N
N-18
N-12
N-2
N-1
N-3
The Wall
Dining facilities
Offices, Post boxes
Kitchens, Hall
S-33
Kismet
Kantara
upper hut
lower
hut
Emerson's
Research
Station
witchdoctor's
ruined hut
mosque
southern beach
Burial site
of ashes

The characters in the story (by location and relationship)

<u>In England</u>
Brett: Bretton Morris James, mechanical engineer, teacher
Jane James (formerly Jane Colburn): Brett's wife, Caversham
Tony Colburn (deceased): Jane's late husband
Miles Tiffin Jolly: retired colonial administrator, Bristol (former Zoo resident)
Tom: care home resident, Bristol
Vi: Violet Ridge-Taylor, Sambrook, (former Zoo resident)
Thomas Ridge-Taylor (deceased): former Brigadier, Vi's late husband (former Zoo resident)
Julie Lancaster: Peter Lancaster's daughter in Tenterden

<u>From America</u>
Kelsey McNeil: American anthropologist, Savannah, Georgia
Shane Carson: marine biologist from Galveston, Texas

<u>In Germany</u>
Karl Bergmann (deceased): Henry's former friend in Ulm

<u>In Australia</u>
Alan Emerson: Louise's son in Perth

<u>In Nairobi, Kenya</u>
Allistair Matherton: lawyer, son in Matherton & Son
Geoffrey Matherton: lawyer, father in Matherton & Son
Jim Gossard: retired optician
Mary Gossard: Jim's wife, retired teacher
Mzee Kamau: injured old man
Bishop Wilfred Onyango: Church of the Province of Kenya (CPK)

<u>In Mombasa, Kenya</u>
Dr. John Phillips: Resource Data Imaging
Moshi: Ahmed Nasir, the mysterious criminal boss

In Malindi, Kenya
Ponda: Police Inspector
Ochieng: Police Detective

In Mwakindini, Kenya
Kinyanjui: Police Senior Sergeant
Kuvanza: thug

In The Zoo, near Mwakindini, Kenya:

The south housing area, near the eastern wall, beside the Muslim sector
Louise Emerson: retired nurse
Henry Emerson (deceased): aka Heinrick, Zoo founder, Louise's late husband
Shafiqah: Louise's maid, with medical skills
Fatima: Louise's maid, with linguistic skills
Mjuhgiuna: Louise's elderly manservant
Faiz: Imam at The Zoo
Mzee: fearful and resentful old man, living beside the wall in Muslim sector
Iha: Mzee's dishonest younger son

The west housing area, by the south bay
Steve: Reverend Steven Brandon, Anglican priest, CPK
Coreene Brandon: Steve's wife, expert on world religions
Ruth, Andrew, and Graham: Steve and Coreene Brandon's children
Khadijah: housekeeper in guesthouse at The Zoo
Simion Katana: The Zoo director, former principal of polytechnic
Hamud Sita: The Zoo accountant
Boniface Chengo (deceased): former Executive Officer at The Zoo

The north housing area, by the northern beach
Len: Leonard Moore, retired water engineer
Marie-Anne Moore: Len Moore's wife
Larry Smythe: plumber, manager of the Energy Conservation Centre
Hamisi: Kenyan fisherman on north shore of The Zoo
Peter Lancaster (deceased): former Major and intelligence officer

Part One

THE RETURN

The fictional characters introduced in Part One (in order of mention)

Brett: Bretton Morris James, mechanical engineer, teacher
Jane James (formerly Jane Colburn): Brett's wife, Caversham, UK
Miles Tiffin Jolly: retired colonial administrator, Bristol, UK
Kelsey McNeil: American anthropologist, Savannah, Georgia, USA
Tom: care home resident, Bristol
Allistair Matherton: lawyer, son in Matherton & Son, Nairobi, Kenya
Tony Colburn (deceased): Jane's late husband, UK
Louise Emerson: retired nurse, The Zoo, Kenya
Mzee Kamau: injured old man in Nairobi
Peter Lancaster (deceased): former Major and intelligence officer
Moshi: Ahmed Nasir, the mysterious criminal boss, Kenya
Henry Emerson (deceased): aka Heinrick, Zoo founder, Louise's late husband
Julie Lancaster: Peter's daughter in Tenterden, UK
Steve: Reverend Steven Brandon, Anglican priest, CPK
Vi: Violet Ridge-Taylor, Sambrook, UK (former Zoo resident)
Thomas Ridge-Taylor (deceased): former Brigadier, Vi's late husband
Ponda: Police Inspector from Malindi, Kenya
Jim Gossard: Brett's friend in Nairobi, retired optician
Dr. John Phillips: Resource Data Imaging, Mombasa, Kenya
Geoffrey Matherton: lawyer, father in Matherton & Son, Nairobi
Mary Gossard: Jim's wife, Brett's friend in Nairobi, retired teacher
Coreene Brandon: Steve's wife, expert on world religions, The Zoo
Len: Leonard Moore, retired water engineer, The Zoo
Bishop Wilfred Onyango: CPK, Nairobi
Larry Smythe: plumber, manager of the Energy Conservation Centre, The Zoo
Shafiqah: Louise's maid, with medical skills, The Zoo
Mjuhgiuna: Louise's manservant, The Zoo
Alan Emerson: Louise's son in Australia

1

Miles' final words that night were, "Go to Nairobi. See Matherton. Give him the code. See Matherton...."

Brett and Jane were completely lost in Bristol. She said, "I can't believe this! We've passed that supermarket twice. We're going around in circles."

"I'm sorry. I missed the turning back there," said Brett. "We could have avoided all this traffic in the town centre." As newlyweds, they were reluctant to blame each other, although they both felt inwardly that it was the other person's fault. They had yet to learn the nuanced ways to subtly direct accusations towards their spouse that older married couples have refined. "My fault," said Brett graciously.

"No, I shouldn't have distracted you just before that junction where we had to turn north," Jane responded sweetly. They continued driving slowly, hoping to see a sign that would confirm they were heading north. The Saturday lunchtime traffic was awful.

"I should have known. I found the turnoff successfully last time I drove over here to visit Miles," he said.

"And I wasn't navigating! We'd better stop and ask for directions."

"No, not necessary. My unswerving instinct and unfailing sense of direction will get us out of this. Which direction is the sun?"

"This is England. There *is* no sun! I suppose that's how you found your way around in Kenya, following the sun?" she asked.

"Not for north or south. The sun always appeared to be shining directly overhead! I told you, my unswerving–"

"...sense of direction and unfailing instinct – or whatever it was!"

"Let's try that road," he suggested.

While Brett followed his instincts, Jane looked for a map in the glove compartment. She noticed a sheet of paper. She read aloud the message.

"Miles Jolly is very ill. If you want to see him, I suggest you come soon. Here is the address...."

Brett told her, "I know the place. That note was from the care home, right?"

"Yes, they phoned the church number."

"I gave Miles several phone numbers, including that of the church," said Brett.

"Let's get him some flowers," she suggested. They found a florist and Jane spotted some carnations – red, pink, and white. "Did carnations grow in Kenya?"

"Everything grows in Kenya! Except apples." As they left the shop, he said, "Carnations are my favourite flower, actually."

"Are they? I didn't know that. They last a long time."

"Your favourites are freesias, right?"

"Yes," Jane smiled.

The florist had confirmed they were on the right road, so they made their way north until Brett recognized the route. Within twenty minutes, they arrived at the home where Miles was staying. At the reception desk they asked to see him.

The lady said, "Mr. Jolly? Sorry, he's not here. He was taken to hospital this morning. Would you like to see his room? He won't mind, I'm sure. You must be his friend from Africa or wherever. Am I right?" As they walked, several faces appeared at doors along the hallway.

They entered the room. It was small and tidy. Brett remembered it from his first visit with Miles. The window looked onto green lawns with well-trimmed flower beds. The early September colours that year of 1989 were continuing in their glory. Brett looked at the painting he did of the Kenyan coast.

As he straightened it, Jane said, "That's nice. Miles must have enjoyed having that here." She looked around and saw a pile of cassette tapes and a player. A few titles indicted Miles' appreciation for opera. "I feel as though I'm intruding...."

"Please don't feel that. Miles would be happy to know you're here," the receptionist told her.

Jane noticed a photo of a young lady in a picture frame.

"Ah, that's Kelsey McNeil," said Brett. Jane lifted the photo and studied it.

"She has lovely eyes."

"Yes," Brett said. Jane carefully replaced the frame. "Miles is fond of her. He feels she's a distant relative – a kind of niece. She understands him." He glanced towards the garden. "Few people do."

They heard a neighbour's voice at the door.

"He spoke about you. Both of you."

Jane was still clutching the flowers. "Really? Can we visit him in hospital?"

"I don't see why not," said the neighbour. "I'm Tom, by the way." They shook hands. "Miles is a decent bloke. Great sense of humour. I hope he'll be okay."

As the four of them walked back along the corridor, Tom said, "You know, it's funny, you visiting him like this. I mean, he had no visitors, and – blow me – you two turn up just as he's gone!" They reached the entrance. Tom suddenly said, "Hang on, I tell a lie! He did have a visit from a hefty fellow. Dark skin – he looked African. Stayed about an hour. Talked loud in a language I couldn't understand. Mixed with some English. Shouting and goings-on, you know. Sounded like a row, arguing and all. The fellow left in a huff. Spoke to no one else."

They located the hospital and found Miles in a double room. A nurse directed them inside.

She whispered, "He may not pull through this one. He was pretty weak when he arrived. To be honest, the ambulance attendants didn't think he'd make it here. Still, we're doing our best. He's mildly medicated, so if he can talk – here, go in – even if he does speak, he may not make a lot of sense."

"Thank you," said Jane.

"That's alright, Miss. Take your time. There's a bathroom here and a snack bar downstairs. See that buzzer? That'll get one of us if anything happens."

Brett walked over to the bed and was horrified at what he saw. He almost did not recognize Miles. His normally chubby features were sallow and drawn; his rubicund complexion gone. The haggard face was as white as the sheet he lay on. His sun-induced freckles were prominent but his eye sockets had a kohl-smudged tinge. Brett and Jane positioned two chairs and looked at each other. Both, in their own way, thought, *Now what?*

But Miles – the old trickster – had a surprise for them. The scrape of furniture caused him to open his eyes. Immediately, he recognized Brett and twitched his cheeks in an attempt at a smile. Brett hugged him gently and asked how he was. Miles said nothing but nodded slowly. Then he noticed Jane.

He was awake now and managed to say, "You must be...Jane. So nice meet you, dear." He tried to push himself up on the pillow but the effort defeated him. His attempt to raise a hand to shake Jane's also failed. They spoke to him about their journey and asked if they could do anything to help. Jane laid the flowers on the bedside table. They were both unsure what to say, not knowing how much Miles could understand. Again, he surprised them, "Those flowers are lovely, thank you. This is no way...for me to receive visitors. Sorry. You came all this way...." He lost his line of thought.

After half an hour, Jane went to find a drink and a vase for the flowers. Outside, she met a male nurse. Jane asked him to be brutally honest, and tell her how Miles really was.

"I was a minister's wife. I have dealt with...these situations," she explained. It was clear that Miles was not expected to last long as he was unable to swallow and his breathing was extremely difficult.

"We have oxygen if he requires it," he told Jane. The nurse confided that Miles' heart was at the point of failure. "Congenital disease and a long battle with a deep-seated bacterial infection have weakened him. Just take the time with your friend, as you need."

It was a long vigil. They alternated sitting at the bedside, having a snack, walking about, and reading. They read aloud Psalms 51 and 139 from the Bible in the bedside-cabinet drawer. There was no reaction from Miles.

Jane read again from Psalm 51, "The sacrifices of God are a broken spirit; a broken and contrite heart, O God, you will not despise." Nursing staff came and went. Everyone was kind and attentive.

As darkness fell outside, again Brett lifted the Bible and began to read Psalm 23.

"The Lord is my shepherd–"

Miles' thin voice said, "...I shall not want. I remember that from...from my childhood. What does the rest say?" Brett was delighted to read the remainder of the psalm and asked how Miles felt.

"Fine. Fine. That's what they...say...in Kenya when things are...really bad. Right?"

"Is it bad?"

Miles nodded. "Can't swallow or breathe."

"Shall I call the nurse? Would oxygen help?" asked Brett reaching towards the buzzer.

"No, no. Don't...trouble them. They have...ill patients...to look after."

At that moment, Tom from the care home appeared at the door. He came over to the bed and touched Miles' arm. There was no reaction. Miles was asleep again. They stepped outside.

The nurse whispered to them, "Just a word to the wise...be careful what you say around him. Hearing is often the last faculty to go. He may be listening, even if he appears to be unconscious. Alright?"

Brett nodded, "Thank you."

She said, "Hope you don't mind my mentioning it," and she left them.

"Over the months, he was asking good questions. Obviously searching for...answers," said Tom. "I'm a Christian and I tried to help him understand as best I could."

"Thank you," said Jane.

"Another chap – the supervisor – also spoke with him a lot, I know."

"Do you think he's made a commitment?"

"Hard to tell. You know Miles better than I do, I expect. Apparently, he had several Christian friends in Kenya but he always resisted their invitations to join in their fellowship. That's how he described it, anyway."

They returned to the room but Miles was unresponsive. After a while, Tom left, saying, "If he wakes, tell him I sent my best wishes. And several of us will be praying."

Jane was looking tired. They went to the canteen and had a light supper, wondering what to do.

"I'd like to stay with him," stated Brett.

"But we have to get back. I'm speaking in church tomorrow morning."

"Would you mind driving back on your own? It's about a two-hour journey."

"I can do that. I don't want to let them down. What will you do?"

"I'll stay here. I can catch the train back to Caversham."

"But you have no spare clothes or toothbrush or anything–"

"Just like on safari again! Miles will like that."

"Poor old chap, he's all on his own. It would be good if you could stay with him."

Later, Brett saw Jane off and returned to the ward. It was 9:30pm. Entering the room, he sensed that Miles was not far from death. He studied his colourless face. His lips were grey. Then, amazingly, Miles opened his eyes briefly. They were an ilmenite black in his white face. He closed them again. Disrespectfully, Brett thought, *He already looks like a corpse. How long does he have? Is there anything meaningful I can say?*

Brett was wondering about the wisdom of letting Jane drive home on her own, when Miles interrupted his thoughts.

"I haven't got long. I'm dying, Brett."

"It's alright, my friend, I'm here. Tom was too. He sends his best–"

"When I die…it won't be long…the legal beagle has instructions. Some gifts for you. Also Kelsey."

"Thank you. Just rest now, Miles."

"Is Kelsey here?"

"No, she's in America."

"Oh yes, my American daughter."

"Your daughter?"

"Or is she my niece? Yes, my American niece." He closed his eyes and was silent for two whole minutes. "There is…something for her too." After a long pause, Miles said, "Thank you for coming, Brett. Thank you." His voice faded and he muttered, "Kelsey is a niece, yes, a niece. She understood me." He opened his eyes and spoke clearly: "I have no family. You two are my family."

Brett made an appreciative remark. Miles did not seem to hear. His voice was clear but Brett was not sure if the words made sense. Miles was agitated.

"Go to mnna…ther..ton.," Miles mumbled.

"Matter Town?"

Miles shook his head, "Math…er…erton."

"Matherton?"

"Mmm…"

"Matherton? In Nairobi?"

"Yes, he…will know…. He knows…." Brett was frustrated. It was so difficult to understand. "There's a code…my initials," Miles whispered, almost inaudibly.

"Your initials?" Brett was surprised as Miles reached his hand across and grasped his wrist. Brett noticed the bruises on his hand from earlier intravenous drips.

"MTJ. Miles Tiffin Jolly. Got it?"

"MTJ?"

"Remember the code," Miles rasped.

"MTJ?"

Talking was becoming a burden. "Ugh, ugh…no, each letter…a number."

The nurse entered and checked Miles, taking blood pressure measurements and recording them on the chart at the foot of the bed.

As she repositioned the flowers, she told Brett, "You can rest in that spare bed if you like."

"Can I? Oh that's very kind of you."

"Make yourself comfortable. It's empty at the moment. Stay dressed, but you should be able to get some sleep." As she spoke, she was absentmindedly adjusting the crisp sheets and then gently tapped the intravenous drip tube. "You might as well get some rest. Then you can be with Mr. Jolly – as long as you wish." She glanced at her watch, then the chart again, and left them.

Brett pressured him, "A number? Each letter a number? What number?"

With eyes closed, Miles spoke clearly: "The letter in the...alphabet. M. Its number...."

"Its place in the alphabet?" Miles nodded, almost imperceptibly. Brett used his fingers to count, A, B, C....

"Thirteen."

Miles nodded, "Yes." With considerable effort, he asked, "T?"

Brett continued counting. "21."

Miles groaned, "Nu, ugh."

Brett tried again, "20."

"Yes. My name, MTJ...."

Brett started to count again, "A, B, C, D, E, F, G, H, I, J. Ten."

Miles grunted, "MTJ. 13, 20, 10."

"13, 20, 10. A code?" Miles relaxed and his hand flopped on the sheet. "There is a gift for you. A wedding present. For you and Kelsey."

"Kelsey?"

"Eh?"

"You mean Jane."

"Yes, Jane. You and Jane." His final words that night were, "Go to Nairobi. See Matherton...give him...the code. See Matherton...."

After ten minutes, Brett saw that Miles was fast asleep, so he went to the bathroom, rinsed his face, removed his shoes, and then lay down on the firm mattress and tried to sleep. He couldn't. He thought of Jane. He wished they had arranged a way for her to let him know when she arrived home. He prayed for her. He prayed for Miles. His mind was racing with all he had heard. He lay on his back with his arm folded across his eyes to reduce the glare from the overhead lights. 13-20-10, MTJ, kept running through his mind. Matherton? He wondered if he should write to the lawyers in Nairobi, Matherton & Son, explaining what Miles had told him. He'd check with Miles in the morning. *If he makes it to the morning,* he thought, as he fell asleep.

Driving alone did not bother Jane. After all, she reasoned, she had coped with a lot on her own – for a long time. Really, from Tony's initial diagnosis right up to his death over two years ago. Brett's return from Africa had been an interesting experience. It was exhilarating and unsettling at the same time. Plus a lot of fun. But more: it had a feeling of fulfilment. She had sometimes felt guilty at how easily they had slipped back into their old friendship. Not that there was anything improper about the sequence of events – quite the opposite as they took their time and had been considerate of each other and the public image their close bond presented. But she had been surprised at the level of deep satisfaction she had felt as they rediscovered all their mutual interests, and passion for the Christian faith in action at their church.

Initially, she had been apprehensive about Brett's return to England, especially as he would be living fairly close. She remembered asking herself if she could deal with another complex friendship at that time. She was uncertain how strong his faith was, but she soon realized that Brett had grown in his knowledge and commitment during his years in Kenya. Now she had no qualms on those grounds. She had looked forward to seeing him, but was nervous over their relationship. *I needn't have worried,* she told herself. There had always been a bond of understanding and respect, but it progressed quickly into deep affection. Within five months, it became romance and love.

Brett had been mindful of Louise Emerson's advice just as he left Kenya, when she warned of not assuming anything about the relationship, so he had allowed Jane the time she needed to adjust to her new situation. He explained to Jane that he had a profound admiration for her going back to their teen years. At one level, it was even love, but he had kept at a respectful distance and never allowed it expression. Now she appreciated being taken care of, as Brett was resourceful and thoughtful. He clearly loved her deeply.

However, as she reviewed the visit to Miles, and thought about Brett still with him, she felt some disquiet that she could not define. Of course, it had been a traumatic experience, and it brought alive some of the disturbing things Brett had told her about Miles, but her unease seemed to be focused on something else. Then she blinked and was surprised that a tear fell from her eye. What was troubling her? Surely not the illness of Miles whom she hardly knew, other than as an old scoundrel Brett had encountered in Kenya. Brett seemed fond of Miles, although he had once described him as 'likeably despicable'. Perhaps she was reacting to the time in a hospital again and its associations with Tony's terrible suffering: but she thought she had recovered from all that emotion.

Jane had a gift that she found helpful, but she knew it troubled her friends. She had the uncommon ability to swiftly process situations, accept the outcomes, and quickly adapt to changing circumstances. Over many years she had modified the way she reacted publicly to news – particularly bad news – as she had noticed other people needed more emotional processing time. Her rapid acceptance of disaster, and speedy development of a new plan, often unsettled those around her and caused her to appear callous. She had been keenly aware of this when Tony died. Her natural disposition, and the fact that his medical decline had been slow and obvious, meant she was ready to adapt to her changed circumstances more quickly than others who needed a longer grieving time. Jane followed the conventional grieving stages, but she was not a person to feign lingering remorse. Tony was free from pain, and in God's hands: knowing that was an enormous comfort to her.

She was appreciating the cool September night air on her face, and the light traffic in the darkness. She thought about a relative who had said 'I bet this has tested your faith!' She had thoughtfully responded that she had relied on her belief even more to get her through Tony's illness and death, but her faith had been deepened by all the experiences. Also, the joy she found in writing poems helped her express her deepest feelings. Of course, she had been profoundly hurt and traumatized by Tony's suffering, but she accepted the wonderful times they had shared and felt deep fulfillment at the way they had tackled his final months together. They had worked as a team – as they had always done.

There had been no children. *Not for lack of trying,* she thought, remembering all the medical tests and procedures they went through. She would love to have children, but she trusted the Lord's will in that matter, as with everything else.

Brett was 34. She reflected on their age difference – she being two years older. She joked that she had been sent to take care of him as he had a slightly naive streak which was opposite to her pragmatic nature. Yet, he was a safer driver than she was, she had to admit! Without realizing it, she sometimes compared Brett and Tony. When she caught herself doing it, she reasoned it was natural and not unhealthy. She thought, *Brett is a planner. Tony was spontaneous: he would plan future activities when absolutely necessary but it did not come naturally to him. Brett, on the other hand, is always looking ahead, anticipating arrangements, and organizing in advance.* Living with each character had its stresses for Jane and she was having to make the adjustment to Brett's style.

She smiled as she recalled Brett's preference for going and seeing people in person when there was a matter to discuss.

She had told him, "It's not necessary to go down to visit those offices; we do have phones you know!" He had smiled, and continued to do it! She explained, "Also, you don't need to go around shaking hands with everyone all the time! And it's not necessary to ask their life history before getting to the point of your visit."

Brett had sheepishly explained, "I suppose I've learned to think and behave like an African."

"That's okay, I'm just teasing you," Jane had replied.

Brett admitted, "When I first went to Kenya, I expressed my needs immediately and did not bother to first engage in polite discourse. Once, I was reprimanded at a post-office parcel counter. The lady stopped me when I handed her the form, and said 'First you greet me, and ask me how is my family. Then you state your business!'"

Jane's journey had taken just under two hours. She felt tired, but pleased to be home. As she drove up to their flat, it suddenly dawned on her why she felt uneasy. It was the photograph of Kelsey McNeil.

2

As Brett left Miles that spring evening, those words rang in his ears. "Never trust Moshi." He had not forgotten them.

Hospitals can be noisy places at night. At some point, the nurse switched off the main lights. It felt to Brett that he did not get any sleep: it was a restless night but, in the morning, he was unable to recall many details of the eight hours that had passed. He awoke to see a different nurse standing beside Miles.

"Good morning. How is he?" Brett called over.

"About the same. We are keeping him comfortable. You should get some breakfast."

Later, Tom came back and joined Brett beside the bed. When he heard their voices, Miles opened his eyes. Immediately, he whispered painfully to Brett.

"Go back to my room…take your painting…if you want it."

Tom smiled and said to Brett, "That's fine. We can arrange for you to have that."

A nurse came in and told Brett he had a phone call that he could take at the nursing desk down the hall. He was thrilled to hear Jane's voice and learn that she had arrived home safely. She had to leave for church, so the call was brief. Brett gave her the latest news and said he would stay with Miles, and let her know when he was on his way home.

After about an hour Tom left, but Miles was still awake. He beckoned Brett close.

With difficulty he said, "Thank you for coming. The final curtain is about to fall on…the pathetic charade…that was the life of MTJ."

"I'm sorry. Maybe you're right. So don't leave the important decisions too late."

"You mean faith?"

"Yes. Don't wait any longer. Jesus is very close to you. He loves you."

"I'm beginning to believe, Brett…."

"Listen, Miles: Jesus said 'Come to me, all you who are weary and burdened, and I will give you rest.' That's so true."

"But there are years of barnacles…wasted years. But I know I can trust…in Jesus." He fell asleep.

The long wait continued. Regular checking of pulse and blood pressure showed a gradual decline. Two doctors came by. Brett had many hours to think. He recalled his previous visit to Miles in the late spring of 1988, 17 months earlier. Miles had been back in the UK for seven months and he had kept inviting Brett to visit, implying there was some urgency. Brett had taken a long day to drive across to see him. It had been a rewarding time for both of them. Brett carried his painting of the Zoo scene and surprised Miles with it. Miles told him that Kelsey had written regularly with updates on her life and studies, and expressing sympathy for his condition. They spoke of Louise and her health difficulties, and her decision to delay her move to Australia as she could not cope with the stress of the journey. They shared many memories of Kenya, and recalled some funny times and eccentric individuals.

Miles said, "Remember our camp at Olorgesailie? It seems a lifetime ago. Another world." Brett smiled. There was silence as they both recalled the trip. Suddenly, Miles asked, "How's the scar on your leg?"

"I still have it. But don't worry. You're forgiven." Miles nodded uncomfortably. He did not ask to see it.

Miles said, "Mzee Kamau is ill."

"Oh, I'm sorry. I imagine he's quite old now."

"Yes," said Miles. He looked at Brett but neither of them said anything. They both appreciated the value of silence at certain times.

Brett remembered other things they had discussed at the care home all those months ago.

Miles had told him, "I never lied to you."

"No, but you were often vague or deliberately withheld information."

"That's a different matter. I plead guilty – on both counts!"

Miles' dark eyes were bright as he had said, "I had power at the Zoo. That's why I resented someone like you who challenged the system."

"Sorry about that. I was just curious."

"I know. Now I'm revealing all my aces and cashing in my last chips. You can tell Louise anything you like. Including about Kamau–"

"Doesn't she know?"

"Not the truth. I never told Peter Lancaster either. And then he shot himself."

Brett was astonished. "Why didn't you tell Peter?"

"In Kenya, information is power. Remember that if you return." He was silent, then Miles said, "And you can discuss with her the attack on you."

"She knows about it?"

"I'm not saying that, just you can discuss it with her."

"It's not something to put in correspondence."

"No. Maybe you can visit Kenya again."

"Unlikely. I'm just starting an eighteen-month contract, have plans to marry soon, and I've got no money!"

"I'll give you the money."

"No you won't."

"Yes. Look, I have some funds – and nothing to spend them on. I have no family left. Not even distant relatives. When I depart – and it may not be long now – I'll see you have enough to finance a trip back to Kenya."

"Thank you, but no–"

"Brett, let me handle this my way. Please. It'll be my final gift. This will be the last chance I'll get to compensate you for the leg injury I caused."

"It's not necessary. But thank–" Miles waved Brett into silence.

"By the way, I never told you…Moshi instructed me to arrange the attack on you."

That was another shock to Brett. "No! Really?"

"Yes. Moshi directed the Big Five." Miles added, "Don't trust Smoky Moshi. Never trust Moshi!"

As Brett had left Miles that spring evening, those words rang in his ears: "Never trust Moshi." He had not forgotten them.

Back in the hospital, Miles started to speak, but with tremendous difficulty. Brett sat beside him.

"My stuff at the Zoo...is yours. I have things hidden. Don't let Moshi get his hands...on it. Don't trust him." Brett nodded, but without understanding. Miles grabbed Brett's arm. He was surprised at the strength of the dying man's grasp. He just heard Miles' sibilant voice, "The secret compartment, north of the mosque...."

"Yes. Louise once told me about it."

Miles gave a thin smile, "A decoy."

"What?"

Miles relaxed his grip and lay back. He was still smiling – a pale, painful smile. "It's a decoy."

"A decoy?"

"Yes...it's empty." Miles was fading. "Remember...the code." Silence. Stillness. His eyes were closed; his voice a whisper. Brett just heard a wintery gasp, "I believe Brett. I trust. You were right. I believe...."

A nurse stopped at the door and softly said, "A phone call for you at the desk." She walked over to Miles and checked his pulse. She turned to Brett, "He's very feeble. His breathing is so laboured." She took the chart from the hook as Brett hurried to the phone.

He said, "Yes. Hello."

"Brett?"

"Hello, Jane."

"How's it going?"

"Good. Very good. Good talks. Miles is hanging on, but it can't be long now. I'll get a message to you when I know. Okay?"

"Love you. I'm praying."

"Thanks." He didn't say anything else as he was conscious of the crowded location. He hung up, and wondered if he should go straight back to the room to be with Miles. He decided to take advantage of the break to go to the bathroom.

But, as he returned to Miles' room, the nurse caught his eye and gently shook her head. The door was half closed. He slowly entered and saw the white sheet pulled over the body.

The nurse quietly said, "I'm sorry. The doctor will come soon. Your friend slipped away when you were out. It often happens that way. They seem to need peace for their final exit."

As he left the room, Brett noticed the carnations. They appeared to be radiating a delicate beauty.

Brett left the hospital and found the taxi rank. While waiting for the next car, he took some moments of reflection to say goodbye to his friend. Then he remembered another puzzling thing Miles had told him: Henry Emerson, some months before he was killed, had said, "The centre of the swastika. If I die sometime, look in the centre of the swastika."

Brett directed the driver to the care home and asked him to wait for a few minutes as he then needed to go to the railway station. As he entered the building, Tom met him.

"Tell you what, come to my room. I have your painting there. I thought it'd be simpler. I heard Miles' instructions." As they quickly wrapped the framed canvas in brown paper, they spoke about Miles' faith. "How was he at the end?" asked Tom.

"He told me he believed. I think he was sincere."

"Wonderful. Several of us have been praying for him to find peace. We trust that he's in the hands of our loving and merciful God."

"Thank you for all you did, Tom. It's been good to have met you. Sorry I have to rush. The taxi's waiting. I'm hoping to catch the 9:10 train. Would you be able to phone Jane to update her please, in case I don't get a chance at the station?" He wrote down their phone number.

On the way to the station, he suddenly realized how scruffy and unshaven he must look. In a jolt back to reality, he realized he still had to go to work the next morning. His contract ran until the end of 1989 – just a few months – and then he would need to look for employment. He felt confident he would find it as he had made good contacts during his time working on the university project.

The other passengers on the train closed their eyes. Brett also tried to sleep, but his swirling thoughts prevented it. After rehashing the final conversations with Miles, his memories turned to the time since returning to England. After his visit to Peter Lancaster's daughter, Julie, in March 1988, Brett had begun to look for work. Within days, he was employed by a mechanical engineering firm. He was working on the heating and ventilation installations of a new science block at the Whiteknights campus of the University of Reading. It was a long drive from his parents' home but, when he and Jane were married, it was close to their rented flat in Caversham. They did not have a honeymoon – just a weekend at Southport and a drive past Stonehenge. Brett had not accumulated any holiday entitlement and Jane was very busy with her work in the church at the time.

He had felt God's guidance during the months when their relationship had deepened. He was constantly alert to Jane's situation as a recent widow, and heeded warnings from his friends about moving slowly. Neither of them felt rushed, but simply placed the day-by-day growth of their friendship in the Lord's hands, trusting Him for the outcome. After a few months, there was no doubt what that would be. They were engaged at Christmas – a small affair. Their wedding at the end of March was a large event, with many friends and family in attendance to celebrate with them. Jane continued her work as administrative assistant and 'deputy everything' – as she described it – in a large and thriving church community. Brett deeply respected her experience and knowledge as they grew together in their faith and ministry activities. Jane talked with Brett about Tony and their years of marriage. She wanted to give him a full understanding of their life together.

During the train ride, Brett thought about Jane. She was slightly shorter than he – a perfect height, he told her – with long, light brown hair. Brett, and everyone else, thought she was a very lovely woman. He knew it reflected her inner beauty. She had a gentle spirit and a depth of compassion which was constantly renewed by her daily Bible studies and frequent prayers. Upon first meeting her, people sometimes felt she appeared serious, but suddenly she would give a glint of humour and her light-hearted manner would endear her to everyone she met.

Since leaving Kenya, he had maintained contact with his friends there, in particular Steve Brandon and Louise Emerson. She had postponed her trip to Australia, pending the results of more medical tests. He had also kept in touch with Violet Ridge-Taylor in the UK and they had arranged to visit her in a few weeks.

Several hectic days passed before Brett and Jane had an opportunity to properly discuss the recent events and express, in different ways, their sadness over Miles' death.

Brett explained, "I will miss him, although we had a strained relationship. I wouldn't even describe it as a friendship, but I did have a curious respect for him. You know, he caused a lot of trouble and escaped retribution when he was deported. It's hard to summarize as he was such a complex character. He told me some strange things: something Henry Emerson said, a suggestion to visit Nairobi, and a secret code. One thing was clear, though: he stressed that I shouldn't let Moshi get his hands on his stuff at the Zoo."

"Is that what he said?"

"Yes. I'm not sure if he was cogent some of the time. He even mixed you up with Kelsey."

"He confused us?"

"Yes."

"Maybe you shouldn't trust any of what he said!"

"He repeated himself too. Let's wait and see what happens."

"He was lucid most of the time when I was there."

"That's true. Oh, he said his solicitors had instructions about donations to us and Kelsey."

"Best forget about all that. Look–"

"There was a secret code. He told me to visit Matherton – you know, the lawyers in Nairobi, Matherton & Son."

"A secret code? Was he rational then?"

"I don't know. He may have been hallucinating at the end."

3

"I found some of Thomas' old diaries that I brought with me from Kenya. I was surprised how often he mentioned Miles and what he had done."
Violet Ridge-Taylor

When they planned the visit to Violet Ridge-Taylor, they felt it was too far to drive up and back to Shropshire in one day, so they waited until they could take a long weekend and make arrangements to stay nearby. On the journey, Jane was morose. Brett assumed it was related to their recent visit to Miles. He decided to ask her.

"Are you still upset over Miles? It was a tough visit."

"No."

"Did I stay too long with him?"

"No."

"Was it difficult for you to drive home alone?"

"No."

"Are we spending too much time on matters related to Kenya? Like this trip to see Vi?"

"No."

He tried humour: "Is there a question I could ask that would produce a response other than 'No'?"

"No." He gave up. They didn't speak for nearly half an hour until they reached a motorway service area. He assumed Jane was asleep. It was a Friday in late September; they had taken the day off to add to the weekend to visit Vi.

Ten minutes after the break, as they continued north, Jane said, "Kelsey has nice eyes."

"Oh, you're thinking of that photo in Miles' room. She must have sent it to–"

"She looked very pretty."

"It's probably the way she had her hair…."

"Did you like her?"

"No. Not really. Well, not at first. But I got to appreciate her character–"

"And her intelligence?"

"Er – she is–"

"She must be intelligent, working on a Ph.D. and everything."

"But she has some strange ideas, and doesn't accept Christianity."

"You said she was searching, and respected your views."

"Yes, she did."

"Why did Miles mix her up with me?"

Brett thought, *Okay. Got it! That's what's bothering her.* "He was hallucinating. He was very ill when we visited him. We shouldn't take any notice of what he said. We decided that, didn't we?"

"You and Kelsey went on safari together."

"Miles was with us some of the time. At Olorgesailie."

"And later?"

"It was just us two. I was her guide." Jane was silent as she stared out of the window, so he added, "What's the problem with Kelsey? I never thought of her as anything other than an acquaintance."

"Miles liked her."

"Well, maybe. I think she tried to understand him, and he responded to that."

"I see," said Jane in a voice that communicated the opposite. Another silence followed.

Brett began, "Kelsey is a very complex person–"

"A complex person?" She glared at him.

"Yes. She has many sides to her personality, but she–"

"Endears herself to people?"

"Yes, I suppose so. People at the Zoo came to appreciate her after a while."

"Okay. Now, can we change the subject? Please!"

Brett smiled inwardly as he said, "Certainly. Now that you're reassured."

Jane looked more relaxed and spent the next twenty minutes thinking and watching the vehicles in front, while telling Brett he could move closer to them.

"Why do you drive with so much space between you and the car in front?"

"Also I try to keep ahead of the vehicle behind if I can maintain a gap. It's called 'Separation'. To me, that sounds like a working definition of avoiding an impact!"

"And why do you stare at the road just over the bonnet? You should look farther ahead."

"You're right about that. I'm so used to watching the Kenyan roads just in front in case of potholes or a broken-up surface!"

On the busy motorway, Brett continued to drive carefully.

Jane asked, "Why are we crawling along?"

"I'm obeying the speed limit."

"But everyone's overtaking us."

"I'm only keeping to the speed limit. Slightly faster, actually."

"My friends have voted you the person least likely to get a speeding ticket!"

"Good. I'd prefer to use my limited funds in ways other than paying fines."

It was not long before Jane's preoccupation over Kelsey resurfaced.

"I'm sorry to keep coming back to this, but do you understand my concern? Just the two of you went on safari together….It's just that, from your descriptions of her, I'd formed an impression in my mind. When I saw her photo…well, I hadn't realized she was so pretty."

"We had separate tents. It was all completely proper, don't worry." Silence followed that remark. "As I asked before, has there been too much focus on the people I knew in Kenya?"

"No. I know it was all very important you – your times there – and I am interested to hear about it all."

"Sorry if it all seems rather remote to you." Jane seemed to relax.

"No, I'm fascinated by some of the stories. And you've been wonderful at joining in my life here, with the church friends and the families. Plus helping with moving things, and doing a fair bit of driving for people."

"It's been fun to see how our two lives have blended, and our families. Kenya is still very real to me. I suppose it's still part of my thinking and natural reaction to situations. Perhaps meeting Vi will help bring it alive for you too."

"I expect so. I'm looking forward to it."

"You'll like her, but she must have aged since I last saw her. She's probably in her late eighties, I'd guess."

"Amazing. What a life she's had."

They stayed two nights in a small bed-and-breakfast home close to Sambrook where Vi lived with her daughter. They had insisted that she not try to accommodate them or even prepare a meal. On the Saturday, as they drove along the narrow, winding road into the tiny village, they were amazed at its quaint beauty.

They found Vi's daughter's house along a tiny street and managed to squeeze their car into a narrow gap beside a wall. Vi had a small flat facing the back garden. Geraniums were still flowering along a wall and Jane admired her fuchsias and dahlias. Vi was obviously delighted to see them. To Brett, Vi had aged considerably, but she welcomed them with her usual charm, and Jane immediately felt comfortable with her. She had the tea things and some biscuits prepared on a wheeled trolley. On the side table they saw a small round cake with a number 6 on it.

Vi said, "I calculated this was just about your 6-month anniversary!" A smile lit up her pale, freckled face. "Also, I'm using Kenyan tea leaves," she stated proudly.

After some general chatter and updates, she said, "I heard the sad news about Miles. That little bounder was a good friend to us. He did a lot at the Zoo, although he was a naughty boy sometimes."

"He was very ill at the end," said Brett.

"I suppose so. It was good of you both to visit him. Funnily enough, I was thinking about him just a few weeks before he died. You see, I found some of Thomas' old diaries I brought with me from Kenya. I was surprised how often he mentioned Miles and what he had done."

"He was pretty influential in the Zoo for a number of years," replied Brett vaguely.

Vi clicked her teeth the way old people sometimes do, and said, "Miles and Peter. And Louise too."

"So, you kept his diaries?" prompted Jane.

"Just the last three."

"The five-year diaries that he liked to use? I remember him debating whether to buy a new one!" said Brett.

"Oh, yes. And I told him he wouldn't get the full use out of it, remember? I was right!" she smiled ruefully.

Jane helped Vi glide the trolley into her small kitchen. When they returned, Brett asked, "Did Thomas record a lot of diary entries?"

"No, he just jotted down brief notes each evening. Mainly trivial things that happened. I noticed in later years there were chiefly details of medical stuff – doctor's appointments, blood pressure readings, coughs, how tired he felt that day, how many aspirins, blood in the urine, things like that," she said, smiling towards Jane. Vi turned and lifted the three diaries from the table behind her. "Here they are. See how neat his writing was. Even at the end, he had a fine script."

She sighed and flipped through a few pages. She handed two diaries to Brett.

"Oh, I don't think I should be reading these. They are private–"

Vi waved her hand, "No, go ahead. It doesn't matter now, does it?"

While Jane asked Vi some questions about her time in Kenya, Brett glanced through some of the entries. The notes were brief. Thomas had used capitals and lots of abbreviations with large black dots. Flipping through the pages, Brett saw the occasional references to meetings with him, with his initials B.M.J. clearly noted. He was anxious to read Thomas' recollections of Peter's death, so he found the entries for November 1986. The notes were sparse, with simple references to encounters with Inspector Ponda and Miles. It was an oddly brief account of, what must have been, a dramatic and emotional period.

Going back several years through the detailed notes, Brett suddenly saw a swastika drawn boldly on one page. He stared at it in disbelief. Vi noticed, and interrupted her story to Jane.

"See that swastika? It puzzled me why he would draw that."

Brett looked closely and read the words above the sketch 'Talked with Henry. The Middle'. Still looking at it, his thoughts raced: *Swastika, The Middle. Henry, Heinrick, Nazi? Surely not!*

Seeing his baffled expression, Vi said, "I thought it was a doodle. Or it may have represented a kind of target or something. He was fighting Germans most of his life!" Brett remained silent but wondered if it might mean more. How much did Vi really know? Were she and Thomas as naive about Miles and the others as they pretended? He shut the diaries, snapped closed the clasps, and handed them back to Vi, thanking her. Jane told Vi the diaries were a most interesting insight into her late husband, and how precious they must be to her. Vi smiled in appreciation and then said, "I do miss Kenya and everything there. Louise writes from time to time. She's not well, you know, the poor dear. I hear our cage, N-1, has now been converted to an energy centre – or something like that – along with Peter's cage next door. Oh my, so many changes."

She attempted, unsuccessfully, to stifle a yawn. Jane took this as a signal that their time with her should come to a close. They said a simple prayer together, giving thanks for the blessings in the past and asking guidance on their futures. Vi gave them a pot of homemade strawberry jam, the remainder of the cake, and they left. They both felt happy with the visit.

On the return journey on the Sunday, they chatted about their successful time with Vi.

Brett said, "I'm still puzzled by that swastika Thomas drew."

"What did it mean, do you think?"

"I don't know. He noted that he talked with Henry and then wrote the words 'The Middle'."

"Strange. Anything else about that?"

"No. But Miles also made an odd reference to something Henry said about a swastika."

"Well, I think we've already decided we shouldn't take any notice of what Miles said."

"Most of it, I agree. He was too drugged and ill to be reliable, I know."

Late that evening, they arrived home in the dark. As they opened the front door, they found a package on the mat. The company crest on the envelope displayed the name of a firm of solicitors in Bristol.

4

Brett and Jane spoke about some of the things Julie had told them. The letter she had read created some uncertainty in Jane's mind. There were several unanswered questions.

That night, Brett had a disturbing dream. He was snorkelling alone on the Kenyan reef. In the sand below, he watched a flatfish dart along the pool floor and wriggle to bury itself. Soon, only its two eyes, both on the same side of its head, were visible as they protruded through the sandy bottom. Then there was a gentle movement of the current as it pulled him backwards until his head was below the coral overhang. He held his breath, realizing he was trapped for the moment. But he knew from countless hours in the marine waters that the ebb and flow of the current would soon glide him back in the other direction. Due to the narrow channel, he could not move his arms or legs. He simply hung in the water and held his breath and waited. He knew time was running out.

Then, the water gradually drifted him forwards until he could lift his head above the water, spit out his snorkel, and take a deep, gasping breath. He revelled in the clean air as he stood in the coral pool, his heart pounding. Then, with a terrifying roar, rocks started falling from the cliff above. At first there were a few small stones, followed by rocks, and then larger slabs. It was coming from the place on the headland where the ashes were buried. The urns were exposed, and the torrent of boulders forced him back into the water and began covering him in dust and stones. He flailed his arms to escape the dreadful suffocation.

Suddenly, he awoke, sweating. His heart was racing. Jane was standing beside the bed, staring down at him.

"Brett, you were dreaming. It must have been a nightmare. You were thrashing around and kicking. I was afraid to touch you, so I switched on the light. Are you alright?"

"Yes. What a relief to wake up. Sorry to disturb you."

"What was it about? Can you remember?" Brett briefly described his dream.

"Since my years in Kenya, I have more vivid dreams. They often relate to something that happened but exaggerate the experience, like the rocks falling from the burial site."

"It's probably your brain processing some of the memories. Were there a lot of dramatic events during your time there?"

"A few, but they aren't necessarily what features in my dreams. I haven't fully analysed this, but in Kenya one often thinks an event will be dramatic and it turns out to be fairly tame. Whereas, a calm and controlled situation – like a gentle snorkelling trip – can unexpectedly become threatening or sensational."

The following evening, they had a chance to study the documents from the solicitor. They had been overwhelmed to see a cheque for nearly three and a half thousand pounds. Brett had stared at it for a long time, before finally speaking.

"Unbelievable. Simply unbelievable!"

The covering letter explained that they were representing the late Mr. Miles Tiffin Jolly and attending to all matters pertaining to his estate. The funds were disbursed in accordance with his instructions. A lengthy attachment was full of complicated legal words. In essence, it bestowed upon Brett all of Miles' remaining possessions, assets in England, and property in Kenya.

"Does he still have anything there?" asked Jane.

"No. I don't think so. I know his cage was cleared out and everything donated to worthy recipients. I doubt if there's anything left. It's probably a technical transfer to cover any residual items, that's all."

"But the money! That's so generous of him."

"Well, yes. He told me he wanted to pay for us to have a trip to Kenya."

"That's not very practical, is it? We'd better invest the funds quickly. But they are yours, so you'll have to decide."

"We'll tithe on it. That's what we always do with income and gifts, right?" said Brett.

"Yes, let's wait for guidance on a suitable project."

"Ten percent will mean we have three hundred and fifty pounds to donate. That's wonderful."

"It will be a blessing to some worthwhile cause. Is there any way it can be related to something Miles cared about, I wonder?"

"We'll think about it. Let's sleep on this for a while."

"As long as you don't have another nightmare!"

Since Brett's visit to Peter Lancaster's daughter Julie at her school in Tenterden, they had received two brief notes from her suggesting a further meeting. Jane was cool towards the idea and Brett didn't see much point. They had politely stalled by replying to Julie in a noncommittal way. However, in October, Julie wrote explaining that she would be attending a school administrators' conference at Reading University later that month, and wondered if they might get together. The Jameses invited her to visit them one Saturday afternoon and stay for supper. They both travelled to the university hostel to collect her.

Jane was not impressed at first. Julie came across as austere and uncomfortable. She was an imposing figure, with a large briefcase, and she presented herself as an authoritarian headmistress – even in a social setting. They struggled through the customary niceties of dialogue on the return journey.

However, once they were in their home, Julie became more relaxed and easier to talk with. She admired their decor, paintings, and furnishings.

Conversation was supplemented by the social lubricant of cups of hot tea and cakes. Brett showed Julie the painting he did at the Zoo, explaining how he had received it back from Miles. They spoke of their mutual faith and involvement with the Anglican church. Jane explained that their fellowship was not very formal, as the congregation focused on social justice and interpersonal relationships.

"Perhaps at the expense of ritual," she joked.

Julie smiled and admitted that her church was High Anglican.

"Almost Roman Catholic in our style of worship. But we have room for all forms of liturgy and worshipful expression, don't we?"

"Oh, most certainly," agreed Jane, relieved that she was on familiar ground again.

Brett interjected, "There are many Catholics in Kenya. They do excellent work. Peter – your father – told me he had great respect for their contribution to the lives of the people."

That gave Julie the opening she needed. It yielded a long monologue about her father, and the Zoo, and his life in Kenya. She obviously felt comfortable with Jane and Brett as she unburdened herself of years of pent-up emotion and regrets. At one point, Jane noticed the gold medallion around Julie's neck.

"Is that the shape of Kenya?" she interrupted.

Julie smiled widely and grasped the ornament with her left hand and lifted it up as far as the taut chain permitted.

"Yes. That's what Brett gave me! I wear it a lot. Many people admire it. See, it has CPZ written on the back. Brett said he would explain its meaning."

Jane nodded because she knew some of the story. She was happy to listen as Brett explained the full significance of Cypher-Phoenix-Zephyr. He described how CPZ became a code among the three Zoo founders: Henry, Louise, and Peter. This generated many questions from Julie and explanations by Brett. Henry liked cypher as it signified a secret nothing. Her father, Peter, had chosen the symbol of a phoenix depicting his many escapes from death and a rising from the ashes of war. Louise had been coded as gentle as a zephyr breeze.

After about forty minutes of listening and silent nodding, Jane was feeling bewildered and dizzy, while Brett began to feel overwhelmed by the intricacies of Julie's questions about her father and brother.

Brett said, "Miles Jolly told me your father was a good and generous man." Brett kept trying to make neutral comments in order to bring the discussion to a natural close, but Julie ignored his attempts at empathy, and repeated her ramblings about her father.

Then the monologue stopped as suddenly as it had begun.

Julie said, "Well, enough of that! I'm sure you're not interested in all those details of my family!" Brett smiled in silence as Jane removed the tea tray. Then Julie asked Brett, "Were you with my father at the end?"

"Very close," was his ambiguous reply.

"And you accompanied him to the hospital?"

"No. Just to the Malindi police station. I followed the police Land Rover. But they said I need not go to the hospital."

"I see. I am beginning to understand more of what lay behind his suicide." She adjusted her position, and moved her briefcase closer. "How strong was his faith at the end? Would you say he was committed to Christianity?" Brett thought for a moment and replied honestly.

"I don't think one could say that with certainty. But how would I know? I didn't talk with him during his last few weeks." Julie nodded in understanding.

Jane said, "But, in any case, we cannot judge another person's heart or their relationship with Jesus – at any stage in their life – can we? It's a deeply personal thing."

Brett added, "I know your father was open to those ideas, and he truly wanted to reconcile with you, Julie."

Julie's eyes were moist as she explained to Jane once again that she and Peter had a difficult relationship, adding, "My father and I did write to each other, but very rarely. I appreciated his letters, although I never kept them – apart from the one I showed you, Brett. But, by a curious twist, I still have one that I wrote to him."

Jane looked surprised, so Julie explained, "For some reason, Dad hung on to that one. It was with some of his papers that my brother collected when he went to Kenya. That was after Dad died. I have it in here." She knelt casually on the floor, slid the briefcase towards her and opened it. After a moment, she found an envelope. She scanned the first few lines. "This was written around the time when my father's friend was killed. He must have described that event in his letters because I refer to it in my reply here: 'Dear Dad, How dreadful about your close friend, Henry. I am so sorry. A dreadful car accident. Take time to recover from that shock.' It seems strange, me now reading my letter to him." She demurred and added, "It sort of reflects back what he must have written to me, doesn't it?" She was sitting on the floor and looked up, "I was sympathetic, as it obviously upset him. We kept our correspondence very brief."

Returning to the letter in her hand she said, "Er – where was I? Oh yes, 'That sounds fascinating, Henry's mention of diamonds. Save some for me!' I've no idea what that's all about! 'I am still resentful over Mum's death. I know you were busy with your important work.' I remember, he was away on one of his secret government projects and left Mum to cope with everything on her own. And then that confused driver from the Continent drove…but you know the story." Brett and Jane nodded silently. Julie continued, "I'll just finish this: 'I wonder if your friend's death has revived any feelings about Mum. To be honest, it has for me. Maybe you could contact me when you are in England. Love, Julie.' I don't think he kept any other letters of mine." She sighed, and folded the letter carefully.

During the meal, Brett was walking a conversational tightrope when sharing further insights about Peter. He did his best to describe openly what he knew, whilst being circumspect in areas that were confidential. He felt comfortable explaining a little about CPZ and the way Louise used it as a coded confirmation, in addition to the name of her secret storage area which she referred to as 'CPZ-Store'.

After driving Julie back to the university, Brett and Jane spoke about some of the things Julie had told them.

Thinking of the letter to her father that Julie had read out to them, Jane told Brett, "Peter must have been an amazing man. You know, hearing about his life in Kenya has made me keen to visit there." They spoke about Miles' generous donation for them to have a holiday in Kenya.

"Let's go after all!" she said.

"Now, hold on. There's a lot involved in a trip like that. It needs careful planning.... You don't just hop on a–"

"No, but you'll be finished your work at the end of the year. I can gradually bring others in to cover for me. Why don't we go in January? A new decade, 1990. What better way to celebrate? We don't have to worry about money. We could just do it! Why not?"

Brett started to say something, but his reservations were swamped by the thought, *Yes, why not? January is a good month to go.*

But he said, "It's awfully hot on the coast in January."

"But it's lousy weather here!"

"What about our flat?"

"We'll keep it. We can afford the rent while we're away, with Miles' gift."

"It's a bit sudden."

"We didn't have a proper honeymoon. This can be it!"

"Well, it would be lovely to go back and–"

"Let's look into flights. Hey, this is exciting!" said Jane. "Kenya! Sunshine! Here we come!"

5

"Things in Africa are seldom the way they appear.
Relationships happen in several layers.
In fact, everything takes place at multiple levels."
Brett James

It was not until the plane lifted off that Brett was able to relax. He closed his eyes and said a prayer of thanks as he grasped Jane's hand. Everything had gone well, but the last few months had been extremely busy and stressful. It was Friday 5th of January, 1990, and they were on their way from London on a direct flight to Nairobi. Jane sat in the window seat.

After take-off, she said, "This is a treat for the new decade. I wonder what the 1990s will bring." Brett was phlegmatic.

"It's impossible to predict. Probably a mixture of good and bad, just like the 1980s!"

He was anxious to show Jane the land as they flew over North Africa. He thought about what they were seeing from their position, suspended 33,000 feet above the history that had spanned centuries and civilizations.

They reviewed all that had happened since their spontaneous decision to make the trip. They had both been heavily involved with the practical details related to the holiday: Brett completing his contract commitments, and Jane preparing others to take over her duties for a few months. After a frustrating round of phone calls and long-delayed letters to and from Kenya, Steve Brandon had arranged a room for them at the Zoo guesthouse, and Jim Gossard in Nairobi had kindly negotiated with a colleague on furlough in Britain for them to hire his pickup. It was a vehicle similar to the one Brett had owned previously. Jim had also booked them into the Church of the Province of Kenya, the CPK, guesthouse in Nairobi for a week. Brett had eventually got through on the phone to Allistair Matherton, the Nairobi lawyer. He made an appointment to see him, in accordance with Miles' instructions.

They had had their inoculations, begun their antimalarial regime, and Brett had explained many practical and cultural details. He warned Jane of what lay ahead.

"Things in Africa are seldom the way they appear. Relationships happen in several layers. In fact, everything takes place at multiple levels. I will try to guide you through it all."

"Is Kenya safe?"

"Generally, yes. If we are careful. Of course, it's a developing country, with many challenges."

"So, there are dangers?"

"Yes, a few. I'll warn you of the areas where we need to be careful."

During the long flight, they discussed the plans for their holiday. They would stay about a week in Nairobi before driving down to the coast. Brett knew they would receive three-month visitor visas, but they kept open the option to extend beyond that if all was going well. He was excited to share the Kenyan experience with Jane. She found it fascinating and a bit daunting as she had never flown internationally before, having taken just local flights within the British Isles.

Towards the end of the flight, Jane was fascinated to see the snow-covered peaks of Mount Kenya above the cloud. Brett identified them as Batian and Nelion and explained how the massive mountain, Africa's second highest at 17,057 feet, dominated the scenery and culture of the tribes that had lived on its slopes for centuries. He pointed out several features to Jane. It was all laid out below like a miniature relief map: mountain slopes, forests, ridges, rivers, and channels that formed small gullies.

"What a satisfying time that must have been in Nyeri. Were your years at the coast as fulfilling?" Jane asked.

"Yes, but in a different way. I was teaching at a slightly higher academic level." He added, "But the time at the Zoo was much more stressful."

"I think it all sounds very exciting. I can't wait to land," said Jane, just as the stewardess handed them immigration cards. As he started to fill in his form, Brett mentioned the last time he did that, sitting beside Dr. John Phillips. Jane said, "I'd like to meet Dr. Phillips. He sounds like an interesting person."

"He is, and he's done a lot to support the continuing developments at the Zoo."

"Isn't he involved with satellites in some way?"

"Yes. They use the data for resource exploration."

They each returned to their paperwork. Once they had completed the forms, they chatted happily about the details of their carefree holiday, in the manner of two flies engaged in a delicate dance as they spun playfully towards a cleverly concealed spider's web. What they did not know was, in addition to their friends, others in Nairobi were keenly awaiting their arrival.

A fortnight earlier, in mid December 1989, Inspector Ponda had visited Allistair Matherton. Ponda was in Nairobi from Malindi when he decided to arrange a talk with Matherton & Son. He was reluctant to do it at first. As a senior police officer, he knew every move he made had the potential of conflicting outcomes. On balance, though, he felt it was worth the risk. He had heard that the talkative old man Geoffrey was unavailable, so he reviewed in his mind his earlier encounters with the young son Allistair. By recalling every word of his conversations with the incisive lawyer – particularly at the time of Miles Jolly's escape from what Ponda considered justice – he was able to reconstruct a picture of a casual but competent professional who had respect for authority but a clear understanding that his primary duty was to fight for his clients. As an implacable professional himself, Ponda respected that.

Allistair was troubled when he received the message that Ponda intended to visit him. It was not the lack of payment for his time that concerned him, but the information he knew Ponda would be fishing for. Still, he reasoned, *I can fish also.*

After the half-hour meeting, both men felt uncomfortable. Ponda sensed he had accomplished few of his goals and gained very little information, while Allistair wondered if he had – in his eagerness to appear cooperative – inadvertently revealed too much. Ponda's main areas of concern were Miles Jolly and Brett James. Allistair reasoned that Ponda was probably still smarting over the lawyer's assistance in Miles' release, but Ponda's interest in Brett's pending return was mystifying. He had obviously heard about it from his staff in Mwakindini. He was also puzzled by Ponda's frequent questions about Moshi. He referred to him as 'Smoky' Moshi. Allistair had heard that term before, but he wondered why Ponda persisted in his attempts to extract information. The conflicting thrusts of the inspector's enquiries about Moshi, gave Allistair the impression that Ponda was both antagonistic and possibly sympathetic towards the criminal at the same time.

So they parted with an uneasy politeness. No matter, they both concluded, they had kept their professional relationship, and surely some innocent scraps of shared information might be useful in the future.

At the beginning of the new year, Allistair had another meeting: this time with Moshi, the crime boss from Mombasa. It was a suitable arrangement for Moshi. As he walked the fifty metres from his older sister's shop on the corner to the steps leading up to the office of Matherton & Son, he revelled in the convenience of the location. The general shop and the lawyers' offices were situated within the same block in Nairobi. Struggling up the stairs, he reassured himself that a visit would be worthwhile. His animal instinct told him the financial investment in an informal chat would yield useful information, even though it would be couched in legal cautions and wrapped with obscurity. He well understood such matters.

When he made the appointment with Allistair Matherton, Moshi had reasoned to himself: "I'll pay the ridiculously high fee to that cocky lawyer in his crowded office to pry some information from him. He's sharp enough to know the value of discreetly traded confidential information. He may be able to confirm if Inspector Ponda is still watching me. Ponda knows I snitched on Miles Jolly. He might use that as leverage against me. Ponda probably knows a lot more too. I must be careful of him."

Allistair ushered the portly Moshi into a chair and noticed the sweat trickling among the scattered tufts of stubble on his flabby chin where his patchy beard was struggling to survive. Moshi's bulk seemed to fill the small office.

He said, in his smooth voice, "Honestly, Allistair, I tell you, your stairs are too steep. My breathing is very difficult these days. I've reduced my smoking, if that's what you think. I should lose weight, I know; but it's one battle at a time, isn't it?"

Moshi was oblivious to the cluttered office. In his business, he often encountered squalid environments. But he was obviously appreciating the cooling fan in the corner.

"What brings you here?" asked Allistair, prompting Moshi to get to the point of his visit.

"You will never believe my luck. My brother-in-law owns that corner place – you know, the general store and stationers. He and my sister have a flat above, where I can stay. So, getting here was not too bad...." Allistair felt uncomfortable. He waited and watched as Moshi waffled about the difficulties of travel, and the impossibility of parking, so his driver normally had to drop him and wastefully drive around during his meetings. Moshi was abnormally gregarious which left Allistair wondering where it was all leading. It soon became clear.

"Has Inspector Ponda been here?"

Allistair's masked expression and guarded reply, "Come on, Mr. Moshi, you know I cannot reveal that," told observant Moshi that he had – as clearly as if Allistair had leaped on his desk, shouting, "Yes, yes! Ponda was here and we had a long discussion – mostly about you!"

Allistair mistrusted Moshi, but he was unable to pinpoint exactly why. Upon reflection, he realized that it was his eyes. They were permanently half closed, either due to a visual defect or a habit formed by a lifetime of shielding them from cigarette smoke. But it was more than that: Moshi's eyes never smiled. Over the years, Allistair had learned to watch people's eyes. Sincere people smiled with their eyes slightly before their mouth moved. He had to watch Moshi's mouth to gauge whether some of his outrageous remarks were intended seriously or in jest. Striving for meaningful communication with Moshi was a demanding experience.

Based on the assumption that the lawyer and Ponda had been in discussion, Moshi prodded and probed with general questions and semi-serious comments that left Allistair in awe of his articulate deviation. Moshi lit a cigarette.

"What I really need, Allistair, is your advice."

"On what?" was the cautious response.

"Oh, generally, how I should proceed from here – going ahead, you know...."

Allistair said, "I see," not because he did, but to avoid replying, and to keep Moshi talking.

He did: "You know my late partner, Miles Jolly, in the UK? I sent a friend to..." he took a long drag on his cigarette and inhaled, "...to see how he was getting on." He blew out a cloud of smoke.

"That was thoughtful of you."

"I know Brett James visited him too. I'm curious to see if Miles had any recollections of gold or diamonds. There have been rumours...." He was revealing more than he felt comfortable doing, but he saw it as bait on a line.

Allistair shrugged, "I have no interest in rumours from far-off lands."

Moshi ignored the remark and abruptly said, "Speaking of the UK, I hear that Brett is going to be visiting the Zoo."

"How did you hear that news?"

"A friend at the Zoo told me preparations have been made at the guesthouse for him."

"He and his wife, I believe."

"Ha! A wife. He can hardly take care of himself!"

"Perhaps she's taking care of him," joked the young lawyer, as he casually slid a folder across in front of Moshi to cover the desk calendar which showed Brett and Jane's appointment with him the following week.

After fifteen minutes of further verbal sparing, Moshi said, "I need to tell you, Allistair, I have become interested in religion. The Christian faith, it intrigues me. I know about it." As Allistair attempted to suppress a yawn, Moshi continued, "So, Bwana, I wonder what Inspector Ponda's next move will be."

The sharp lawyer's hackles were immediately raised. Carefully avoiding the precipice that the words offered, Allistair stood, saying, "It will be interesting to see, won't it?" With habitual skill, he indicated that the meeting was over with a casual question: "Does your sister's flat have air conditioning?"

Starting to rise, Moshi replied, "No, but I enjoy the cool breezes up here through the open windows. I like the fresh air in your mile-high city."

"Good," said Allistair, guiding the slow-moving Moshi towards the door, "you will be comfortable when you get back there, I'm sure. Our receptionist will give you a receipt for – er – will it be cash?"

"Of course. And I will not need a receipt. Thank you, Allistair. You have been helpful."

They shook hands. Moshi's limp grip reminded Allistair of a damp sponge.

6

Allistair shifted uneasily. "I have to be careful here–"
"Are you scared of Moshi?" asked Brett.
"No, but I can give you a warning. He's dangerous, Brett; he's dangerous."

At Jomo Kenyatta International Airport, the two travellers followed the crowd to the high immigration counters. Jane was surprised at the number of people and the slowness of the process. They each received a three-month visitor's visa.

After forty minutes, Brett and Jane struggled to wheel their cases to the customs counter. Brett told Jane to let him answer the questions. He greeted the official in Swahili.

"*Hujambo bwana?*" The officer replied politely, looked at his passport, and asked a few questions. He initialed Brett's form and waved him through and then quickly processed Jane without any questions. She was relieved, as she was beginning to feel overwhelmed by the unfamiliarity and excitement.

Once they entered the arrivals hall, they were greeted by Brett's good friend, Jim Gossard.

"*Karibuni.* Welcome. How was the flight?" he said, shaking hands with them.

"Great, thanks Jim. How are you and Mary?"

"Fine, thanks. Welcome to Kenya, Jane. Lovely to meet you."

They wrestled their cases across ruts and ridges to Jim's van, alongside frangipani and hibiscus trees. Brett caught a brief aroma from the smoke of a nearby bonfire where the gardeners were burning dry leaves and seed husks. The familiar fragrance made him grateful to be back. He felt the mild, gentle air and admired once again the lush vegetation: jacaranda trees, cassia trees, and a Nandi flame tree. Once the cases were loaded, Jim drove them to the CPK guesthouse in Nairobi. On the way, Jane was staring around in amazement at all the bustle and beauty.

"Kenya is so lovely!" she said.

"Yes, the temperatures at this time are really comfortable in the highlands," said Jim. "But the short rains were very poor so everyone is concerned about possible drought and crop failures. All the hopes are pinned on the long rains in March."

"I wish we could have brought you some of the rain from England," joked Jane.

On their first Tuesday, Brett had arranged an appointment with Allistair Matherton as seeing him was a high priority.

As they climbed the stairs to his office, Brett told Jane, "You'll like Allistair. He's a bit flippant but their firm really helped Miles and Louise in the past. Plus Peter too, I think. We got on quite well before."

Jane was unimpressed by the office. After brief introductions, Allistair got straight to the point.

"What can I do for you both?" He noticed Jane looking around disparagingly at the clutter in the office. Humorously, he said, "Tourist advice, travel health tips, and fortune-telling. That's what we offer! Ha ha. Don't worry, Mrs. James, we *are* lawyers. But we operate with a low profile." Jane smiled uncomfortably.

Brett said, "Miles told me to give you a code." Silently, Allistair rose and with two steps was standing beside his filing cabinet. He opened the middle drawer and found Jolly's file. Removing it, he rustled through a heap of papers until he located a dirty grey envelope. He opened it and revealed another smaller envelope.

"Miles gave me this while he was in prison. He asked for paper and envelopes. And he borrowed a pen. We had difficulty persuading the guard to let him write this and pass it to me. That was when what we euphemistically call a 'tip' was useful. After some time, he gave me this."

Allistair tapped the small envelope, which had a roughly drawn outline on it. He hesitated in recollection, "Miles was very ill at that time and in great distress. He told me to keep it until someone came, then open it and follow the instructions. I was amused and asked if it was one of his jokes. He stressed 'It's not a joke.' Those were his final words on the matter. He was deadly serious as he entrusted this to me."

Looking at the smaller envelope, Allistair read the words, "It says 'Give this to the person who writes the correct numbers.' Hmm." He flopped the grubby envelope in front of Brett and Jane. On the front, they saw a row of six boxes drawn in pen. Allistair looked at Brett and waited. Brett lifted the scruffy document.

"Yes, I can do that."

In silence, Allistair handed him a pen and Brett wrote the following numbers in the squares: 1 3 2 0 1 0. He passed it across to Allistair who looked at it sceptically. He picked up a letter knife and slit open the envelope. Two tattered sheets of paper were inside.

The lawyer read out the words written on the first page: "Give this map to the person who writes the code 132010." Allistair carefully compared the numbers and said, "This is yours, then." Jane leaned over to see the map as Allistair handed it to Brett. It was a simple diagram with two rectangular boxes connected by a pair of dotted lines running vertically. To the right of the dotted lines were two squares. She saw some writing on the page.

"Did he say what this is all about?" Brett asked.

"No. He could hardly speak at that time. It took all his energy to draw it. That was the day before he was rushed to hospital with that dreadful infection."

Jane asked, "Have you any idea what it means?"

"Absolutely none. Your guess is as good as mine – better, probably."

Brett reasoned, "If he was barely well enough to write it out…the coded letters and everything…."

Jane completed his thought, "Then he'd obviously planned it before."

Brett saw that the sketch matched part of the map of the headland that Peter had given him. Clearly, it was the tunnel connecting the two foundations of the old residential huts. On the top left corner of the page an arrow was placed above the word *Mwakindini*. To the right of the dotted lines, the map showed two Xs. The top X had the measurement 6ft to indicate the distance within the tunnel. Below that was a second X at 6ft from the first one. A set of indistinct words was scrawled along the bottom of the page, but Brett could just make out a reference to the hatch in the upper foundation. He passed the paper back to Allistair who frowned at it.

"On the right here, the writing says *Henry E's*. I remember watching Miles write this. He had trouble doing it, but he was determined to as he sensed that he'd never get out of jail alive. This must be important. Any idea what it refers to?"

"Yes. Partly. I'd need to check." Brett glanced at Jane who was looking confused. "I recognize the layout. It's over in the nature reserve. I suppose the note refers to Henry Emerson's research station. That building was still intact when I last saw it. I've seen the tunnel from both ends, and heard about a hidden chamber. Could this mean there's a *second* chamber, about twelve feet in?" Allistair reacted quickly.

"Don't ask me! And don't tell me any more. I've done my duty. Now it's legitimately yours, my friend. Tell me, how did you know those numbers?"

"Miles told me the code: his initials, MTJ. The number of each letter in the alphabet: 13, 20, 10."

Allistair smiled, "I could have guessed that. But lawyers don't guess. We *know* things!"

"Yeh, yeh, you're omniscient. We all know that!" Brett joked.

Jane added, "And modest too!" All three were smiling. Brett continued to stare at the map.

"There would be very few people who could make sense of this sketch."

Allistair was casual as he said, "Look, I'm not sure he was even being rational. Just take it for what it is and check it down at the Zoo."

Jane asked, "Could it be hidden treasure?"

"It could be, so be careful how you approach it," Allistair warned.

"How would Miles have treasure? He was poor most of his life, wasn't he?" Jane asked. Allistair was silent.

Brett said, "The police emptied the first chamber. They showed Louise some of what they found. Miles hinted that further hidden items were his. At least, he knew about them."

"Knowledge doesn't equal ownership. Be careful with what you do with anything you find."

"Louise has a safe – all the cages do," said Brett. Jane was confused.

"This is too vague...."

"Quite! We can't keep speculating. Let me know what you discover and I'll try to advise you, alright?"

"Thanks, Allistair. A definitive legal opinion on vague speculation is always enlightening," joked Brett. After smiles and a pause, he said, "I was going to ask about Mzee Kamau." Allistair seemed surprised. He looked at Jane.

"Does your wife know the story?"

"Yes. I told her."

"The freedom fighter injured during the Mau-Mau emergency. Does Mrs. Emerson know?"

"Er – I don't know. I don't believe so."

"It's okay. It's just that...soon it may not matter. But I don't want it spread around."

"No. How is he?"

"Not well. He may not have much longer. But we are making sure he's looked after. We'll take care of things properly."

"Thank you," said Brett solemnly.

The mind of the young lawyer had obviously turned to something else as he swung his chair towards the window. He performed his characteristic gesture: placing his hands together with his fingertips touching his lips. Brett and Jane waited. What he eventually said surprised Brett.

"Moshi was here."

"Moshi?"

"Yes. I've had a few visitors recently. This place has been like Piccadilly Circus!" Brett was concerned.

"Moshi! He's still around? I thought he was dead – or in exile."

"So did we. Possibly both!"

"Smoky Moshi. So, he's still around...." Brett repeated, thoughtfully.

"Oh, he's around alright. He's a survivor."

"He must be. He's not popular in some circles."

"No. He has an intrinsic talent for accruing things – mainly trouble and enemies."

"Miles told me Moshi betrayed him."

"No comment."

"Moshi was always pretty rude and abrasive – when one could get him to speak."

Allistair said, "In prison, Miles said the elusive smoker had many contacts but lots of enemies too." He gave a shrug of disdain, "But he claims he's changed. Gone religious, apparently."

"What does that mean?"

"I've no idea. I didn't pursue it. He didn't sound very convincing, but religion's not my speciality. Look, I've said too much already."

"Why did he visit you?"

"I can't say. Client confidentiality and all that. You understand, old chap. But I can tell you a little as he mentioned *your* name."

"Me? Why?"

"He knew you were coming back."

"How did he know that?"

"He must still have contacts at the Zoo."

"What did he say?"

Allistair shifted uneasily. "I have to be careful here–"

"Are you scared of Moshi?" asked Brett.

"No, but I can give *you* a warning. He's dangerous, Brett; he's dangerous. He hinted that you may have knowledge of diamonds or gold."

Jane asked, "Now, where did that idea come from?"

Brett added, "Yes, how did he make that connection?"

"He knows you were in contact with Miles before he died."

"How did he know that?"

"Moshi has agents in England. He sent one of his cronies from London to visit Miles in Bristol. He tried to extract information. Evidently, Miles refused to cooperate."

"Aha, yes, we heard he had a visitor, probably from Africa. I hope he didn't send one of his thugs to pester poor Miles in his ailing condition."

"I've no idea what he did, but it's clear that he thinks you have some inside knowledge from Miles." There was a pause. All three were thinking. Then the lawyer sighed and asked, "Where is all this leading? What do you want to do, Brett?"

"Well, I don't intend to return to the UK with pockets full of Kenyan gold, but I'd like to resolve some of the mystery and follow up on Miles' instructions."

"Which were?"

"Basically, to see you…and give you the code. Then I got this map." He flapped it in the air.

"And now?"

"We'll see if the diagram makes any sense. I think it may. You see, below the–" Allistair quickly held up his hand.

"Don't tell me! I don't want to cope with any more intrigue. The map's yours now."

"Well, I don't want to be walking around with this original. Can't you keep it?"

Jane said, "Maybe we could just have a photocopy?"

Allistair hesitated and then said, "The fewer copies, the better."

"We can risk one. I can't remember all this detail."

"Okay. I'll keep the original in Jolly's file. But our machine is out of toner so I'll send our girl to get a copy for you. They charge by the page there." He took the map from Brett and called out loudly to the secretary. He waved the paper towards her, with instructions to copy it immediately. Sheepishly, Allistair told Jane, "One day we'll get a big office so we'll have to install a fancy intercom system rather than shouting. That will impress clients."

"It certainly will," she agreed, smiling.

They filled in the time discussing what they would do at the Zoo for three months, and their safari plans. Brett asked Allistair about his father, and the rest of their family. Suddenly, the fluorescent ceiling lights flashed and went black. The fan stopped.

"That happens quite often," said Allistair. "Last week I was in the orthodontist's chair when the power went off. He was in the middle of a delicate procedure. He said, under his breath…." He looked at Jane, and said, "No, I won't tell you what he said!"

They then chatted about Miles' will in the UK and his bequest to Brett. He stated, with confidence, "Legally, Miles bequeathed all his property in Kenya to me–"

"It's not that simple," snapped Allistair. "It would not cover illegally obtained assets. Besides, we are dealing with two different legal systems. It's true that Britain's suzerain influences extended to legal procedures and certain classes of financial law, but the interpretation of current case law and local statutes can be problematic. Modalities of inheritance and property transfers–"

"Aren't the UK's and Kenya's systems similar?" interrupted Jane.

"In matters of jurisprudence, to a degree, yes. We have comparable case law, and use of precedence, and Miles could be viewed as a legitimate testator; but I wouldn't fancy arguing your ownership of his treasures in a court here!"

After ten minutes, the secretary arrived with the copy.

"The *stimu*-electricity, it stopped. But it came back. The woman there-down, she helped me. I got it."

As Allistair took the two papers, a wisp of concern – as elusive as marsh-light – drifted across his mind. He handed the copy to Brett and placed the folded original back in its envelope. He stood by his filing cabinet to replace the papers, turned to Brett, and asked him a question with tart humour.

"You're not expecting to gallop off across the high seas with armfuls of Miles' swag are you?"

"No, we plan to *fly* out with it! To be honest, I don't know what will happen. If the stuff exists, we'll have to see if it legitimately belonged to Miles. If it did, you'd better start preparing your court arguments to convince the magistrate that I'm the rightful owner!"

"And if it's illegal bounty, *you'd* better start preparing *your* defence before a hanging judge!" All three laughed, as Brett stood to leave.

"Seriously, I'm not interested in keeping any of it. I'd just like to return it to the rightful hands."

"And not Smoky Moshi's, eh?"

"Exactly."

"Brett, you'd be well advised to be extremely circumspect. Don't tell anyone about the map or what you know about the tunnel."

"I understand. May we keep in touch?"

"Certainly. I find your situation most entertaining. And I still have a reserve of Mr. Jolly's fees in an escrow account. Some of that should cover my precious time that you've wasted today!"

"You have the nicest way of expressing things, Allistair! Thanks for your interest and help." Brett and Allistair clasped hands in the manner of old friends. Jane and Allistair shook hands more formally.

As they walked out into the street, Jane gave her pronouncement.

"I like him!"

"Really, so soon? I found him infuriating at first."

"He has a casual manner, but he's genuine under the bluff."

"Yes, they are good lawyers. His father helped out the Emersons a lot."

"When did you first meet Allistair and his father?"

"I saw them both at Peter Lancaster's memorial. Then I had more to do with Allistair when Miles was arrested and expelled."

"His warning was well put. Be careful with that map."

"Yes, I will. I think Louise is the only person we should discuss it with – if she's well enough to cope with any more excitement."

7

Jane thought about the last few days since they landed: the contrasting sights and variety of emotions. No doubt she would be facing the challenges of extremes that Brett had often described.

During the next two days, Jane and Brett spent time with the Gossards and prepared for the journey to the coast. Brett had immediately felt comfortable driving the double cab Datsun pickup, and they were very grateful to have its use for the next few months. He arranged car insurance and checked that their international driving licences were acceptable. Jim suggested they get a note in English and Kiswahili from the insurance company explaining they were using someone else's vehicle, as the name painted on the side would be different.

Brett wanted to show Jane Nairobi National Park. She was amazed at the variety of animals – including a rare white rhino – so close to a major African city. They saw a lioness with two cubs just inside the gate and watched them in silence for a long time. Jane used the occasion to become comfortable with handling the vehicle.

"At least driving is still on the left here, same as at home," she said.

During their stay at the CPK guesthouse, they met some fascinating people who were doing valuable work in many parts of East Africa.

"It's an education in practical Christian ministry," Jane told Brett. "Humble people doing what they can to share their skills in worthwhile ways."

"And gaining so much themselves from working with the local people," noted Brett.

Once their cases and supplies had been loaded, Brett was grateful to be driving down the Mombasa road again. They travelled southeast, clearing the city, and passing the airport on their left. They both felt relieved to be on their way. However, just before the industrial buildings of Athi River, they saw a long line of vehicles stopped on the road ahead of them.

"A police check. This one looks serious as they are stopping all vehicles in both directions with those awful spikes on the road," Brett said.

"I wonder what they're checking for."

"You never know; it's not the end of the month, so they're not simply hoping for some *chai* from people who have just got paid. Maybe there's been a prison escape, or they could be looking for drugs, or guns, or illegal publications. One thing you can be sure of, they will not tell us," said Brett as he slowly made his way to the front of the line of stopped vehicles.

Two police officers approached them. One looked at the vehicle number plate, then the round tax disc on the inside of the left window. He was in no hurry, as he peered through the passenger window at Jane's bag on the back seat. Meanwhile, the other policeman walked to the rear of the pickup to examine what they were carrying. The men were serious, but not unpleasant. The one on the right asked Brett what he had in the back. He explained, with a mixture of English and Kiswahili, that they were personal belongings which they were taking down to the coast. The officer seemed unconcerned and directed them forward through the narrow gap between the dreaded spikes, and they were on their way again.

Jane was thrilled by the wide vistas, sparse vegetation, and light traffic. The puffy Kenyan clouds that Brett loved displayed their majesty in large banks above them, with ever-diminishing heights as the rows disappeared towards the horizon. The temperature was comfortable, but Brett warned her it would get much hotter as they dropped to lower elevations. They planned to camp overnight in Tsavo West National Park, although sleeping in the cab would be uncomfortable. Jim had given them an old mosquito net to drape over the car to allow for some fresh air with the windows open.

Brett was wondering whether Mount Kilimanjaro would be visible on their right, and he tried to remember the place where, on very rare occasions, one can simultaneously see Mount Kenya to the north.

"Only once have I been able to see both mountains. They are 340 kilometres apart, but sometimes they're both visible," he explained to Jane. That day, there was a slight haze so they could not see Mount Kenya's distinctive peaks, but Kilimanjaro soon loomed dramatically on the southern border. Suddenly, a young wildebeest came running beside them, bounded across the road just in front of their car, and sprung up the shallow ridge on the other side.

Thinking ahead to the situation at the Zoo, Jane asked about Steve and Coreene Brandon's ministry at the small Anglican church in the community.

"The last I heard, things were good. I know that over the years Steve has adjusted his approach, relying more on the local community, and trying to reduce the emphasis on some of the formality and detailed doctrines of the official church."

"That makes sense, I suppose, as it's a simple community chapel in a unique situation."

"Yes, I know Steve has tried to pick up cues from what he sees and hears around them. He stresses elements that he knows are relevant and appropriate for the little congregation." Jane nodded in understanding.

"I'm hoping to spend time with Coreene. She sounds like a wonderful person."

"She is very knowledgeable. Look, we are not far from Hunter's Lodge. Let's stop for lunch." They reached Kiboko, pulled into the petrol station at Hunter's Lodge, filled up, and then parked the vehicle, carefully locking it. They left it under the shade of an acacia tree, in a place where they could keep an eye on it from the snack bar.

Before the meal, Brett said, "Let's hope we get served quickly. I'd really like to push on as we still have a long way to go. By the way, don't eat the salad. You really can't trust it."

"Oh yes, I remember you mentioning that. I was wondering, would you like me to drive for a while?"

"I'd appreciate that, if you feel confident. Thanks."

"At least I can give you a break for an hour or so." After their hurried meal, they carried extra bottles of cold soda to the Datsun. Brett had noticed a group of five children hovering around the car. They started to pester them, asking for shillings and pens, all adding *give-a me-a sweet*. Brett spoke to them gently in Swahili and they moved away respectfully. Jane got into the driver's seat and adjusted it and the rearview mirror.

"You handled that well. Your Swahili is good. I'm impressed."

Brett laughed, "Living at the coast for so long certainly helped my Kiswahili. They speak the purest form there and it's around us the whole time so you'll be able to pick up some too."

As Jane drove onto the main road, she said, "I've noticed you sometimes say Kiswahili and other times Swahili."

"Yes, we use both terms for the language. Swahili is the name of the language and the prefix ki means the language of the Swahili people. I think Kiswahili is strictly correct. Len Moore joked that most of the longterm expats speak Ki-settler!" Brett thought for a while and said, "It certainly helps to be able to use the local language naturally – definitely in government offices and at police checkpoints."

"And even in cases where children mistake us for wealthy tourists!" said Jane.

"It's a shame about those children back at the lodge because they have obviously been spoilt by tourists, and they just hang around begging all day. Drive down south from here to Amboseli National Park and you will see men dressed up as Maasai warriors with spears, and women exposing their breasts to get tourists to stop and take photographs for a fee. The government officially discourages that, but tourists have definitely impacted the local culture. On the other hand, tourism is the third largest income-earner for the country and many people do benefit from that. Look, you can see the Nzaui hills from here. You are driving in Maasailand now."

"Exciting. But it's all looking very dry," she said.

"Yes, it is. Remember to watch the road just in front in case of deep ridges or crevices."

"Oh yes. I told you in England you should look farther ahead."

"I remember," said Brett, smiling. "You can't look far ahead when driving here. You must watch for the next pothole. Also animals can run across the road unexpectedly, as we've already seen. We might see antelopes, possibly elephants towards Tsavo, and definitely baboons along the edge of the road later."

Then there was silence because Brett was asleep. She took it as a compliment to her driving. She was grateful for the strong coffee at lunch that kept her alert on the unfamiliar road. She thought about the last few days since they landed: the contrasting sights and variety of emotions. No doubt she would be facing the challenges of extremes that Brett had often described. She knew he had appreciated not having those in England where life was straightforward and predictable.

They were just north of Kibwezi when Brett woke up and noticed that the lorries coming towards them were operating their windscreen wipers as they roared past, although there was no sign of rain. He told Jane that usually indicated a police check ahead.

"But if they flash their lights, it sometimes means an obstruction or accident or animals on the road." Sure enough, within a couple of minutes, they noticed the familiar sight of two blue-uniformed policemen, with their large, flat, white hats, standing beside the road. One of them stepped into the lane and held up a clipboard. Jane slowed down respectfully, pulled over, and stopped just in front of him. As the policeman walked over to the car, Brett greeted him in Swahili and the officer asked where they were going. After checking Jane's international driving licence, the policeman waved his hand forward.

"*Endelea tu. Safari njema.* Carry on, have a nice trip."

Brett replied, "*Asante,*" and Jane drove off.

"Well, that was easy," said Brett and closed his eyes again.

"No it wasn't! I was terrified!" said Jane.

"You did well," said Brett. "Can you carry on until the Tsavo Gate? Then we'll look around the park and stop for our overnight break." He glanced to his right at the silent Jane and told her he had found interactions with police to be innocuous, except once when he encountered a belligerent and officious female officer.

"I reckon it requires a certain type of woman to survive in that environment."

Outside Kibwezi, he pointed out the fascinating baobab trees on both sides of the road, once again marvelling at their ugly shapes with massive trunks and crooked branches.

"The local people claim the devil ripped out the trees and replanted them upside down."

"They are grotesque-looking," Jane said.

"They provide useful products and supply homes for several animals. They have a bizarre beauty if you view them the right way."

About ten minutes later, Jane was thrilled to see two elephants standing beside a baobab, although they were not yet in the Tsavo West game park. At the gate, they registered in the basic, but pleasant, campsite nearby. As they paid the full tourist fees, Brett missed his previous privileged residential status and the low rates for locals. During a short game drive, they saw a family of giraffes and several elephants, in addition to many zebras and various antelopes. On their return to the campsite, they found some dry sticks and lit a small campfire in the gloaming under the clear sky. Soon, the outline of the mountain lay to the south and distinctive acacia trees arced above it in a dark canopy against the brilliantly clear stars. It was an enchanting experience for them both.

Jane said, "This is a wonderful time. It's such a joy to be able to share this with you."

The mosquitoes were controlled with the sprays Mary Gossard had given them. They heard elephants trumpeting in the distance. Later, they laid the mosquito net across the roof of the vehicle, letting it hang down the sides. It was kept in place with a few strong magnets Jim had given them. They doused the fire and prepared for sleep.

Brett warned, "Don't leave shoes out at night. Also, always shake your shoes upside down before putting them on, in case a scorpion has crawled inside." They climbed into the cab. Jane lay down at the back and Brett squeezed in the front, trying to avoid the steering wheel.

"They should make steering wheels that tilt up," he joked.

"Maybe one day they will," Jane comforted him.

Then their night of discomfort began. They were very hot, but did not want to sleep with the windows wound all the way down for fear of animals.

They left a few inches open at the top, hoping for some cross ventilation. The air was still.

"I can't get comfortable," Jane said.

"Just relax. Enjoy the sounds, and think about where we are."

The crickets were loud, and Jane listened nervously to a couple of strange cries and growls. Then they heard a lion roar.

"Was that a lion?" Jane shrieked.

"Maybe a small one," said Brett.

"How far away is it?"

"A long way."

"How do you know?"

"Its voice was quiet."

They heard the roar again, much louder that time.

"It's getting closer!"

"It could be another lion, closer by. You know, moving away from us. That's how they communicate."

"Are they hungry?"

"No."

"How do you know?"

"Lions who are hunting do not make a noise. They would remain hungry if they did."

"Why?"

"It would alert the prey."

"Prey? Are we prey?"

"Maybe you should pray!"

"Oh, very funny. Brett, I'm scared."

"Don't worry, they are male lions. The females do most of the hunting. The males are defending their territory."

"And we're in their territory! Sorry, I know this is bad timing, but I need to go to the toilet."

"Oh. Didn't you go befo–"

"I need to go again!"

"I'll come with you."

They crawled out under the net and Jane clung to Brett in the dark as they crept across to the unpleasant toilet without a door.

"Use the light," Jane insisted as she stumbled into the rickety enclosure.

"No. Let our eyes adjust."

"Shine the torch! There may be bats in here."

"No, the light will attract them. We'll see more stars this way. I'm looking for–"

"I'm not interested in the stars! We're going to die!"

Brett laughed while he waited for her.

"Let's stand close together and enjoy the wonder of the heavens, with clear skies. We'd never see this at home in Caversham." Jane soon relaxed and they looked up at the clear, dark sky. The Milky Way and the background stars were so bright that it was difficult to make out the familiar constellations. Then the lion roared again and Jane insisted they got back into the vehicle.

Safely inside, she asked, "Do they eat people?"

"No."

"What about the famous man-eaters of Tsavo?"

"Oh yes, but not woman-eaters. You're safe."

"Ha! I read there were man-eating lions here."

"That was long ago. In the early days. When they were building the railway." He started to wonder if they were going to get any sleep that night. He reached over the seat back and held Jane's hand. Then a hyena called out with its distinctive yelping howl.

"What on earth was that?"

"A hyena."

"Are they dangerous?"

"No. They are shy." The cry came again. It was more of a laughing scream that time.

"It doesn't sound shy."

"Just relax and savour the experience. This is the nature that everyone searches for. It's a wild and natural place. We are completely safe in the car. The only creature I fear is man. Oh, and mosquitoes. They kill millions of people every year." Jane was silent. They both lay quietly and listened to the rich sounds of the African night. The crickets had stopped chirping. The lion was quiet, and the hyena's yelping became muted.

Brett reflected, "I imagine the hyena kept away until the lion abandoned the kill. They have strong jaws that can crack the bones that the lions leave.

Animals instinctively understand the behaviour that helps their survival. It's a balance; a give-and-take. Wait your turn, know your limits, follow the rules. We humans have not learned that. We are always trying to get away with breaking the rules."

Jane said nothing. She was already asleep.

8

Half-sitting on his desk – an ungainly habit that he had never been able to resist – the bishop leafed through the papers and thought about his senior position and its responsibilities.

During the week when the Jameses were first exploring Kenya, Bishop Wilfred Onyango was in his Nairobi office. The Christmas season had been very busy for the church community. Now he was preparing for the activities of the new year. A timid knock at his door heralded the respectful entry of his senior associate. The cleric gently placed a folder on his desk. Bishop Onyango looked up.

"Are these your predictions of the new appointments?" He was teasing his colleague.

"Oh no, sir. Just a few notes describing the names that would not surprise me…if they were on the list, Bishop, when you make your final decisions." Onyango knew the man would not even refer to his list as recommendations. But they both understood that was exactly what they were.

"Thank you, my friend. I am always intrigued to see how closely your future 'lack of surprise' matches my reassignment of priests!" The man nodded, and left him, without a hint of a grin.

Bishop Onyango smiled. It happened every year at this time. He was responsible for the promoting and reassigning of staff. He thought, *He knows I dislike the task. Bless him, he tries to ease my discomfort.* But they had a tacit agreement that neither of them referred to the similarity of the new officers and the names on the suggestion list, which was destroyed immediately before the public announcement. For the present, the folder lay unopened on his desk. In truth, the senior priest had his ear closer to the ground than the bishop was ever able to accomplish, and his colleague had a fine appreciation of personnel capabilities and their potential. But, he mused, *I don't always follow his recommendations. I have a few convictions of my own!*

Thoughts of church staff brought to mind Steven Brandon, that committed priest down near Mwakindini, at – where was it? – The Zoo. Steven's open letter and the fruitful discussion it brought in the last two years, indicated to the bishop that Steve merited a wider responsibility and promotion to a higher level of service. But first, he would ask his staff to check the situation of their teenage children. He did not want to disrupt their schooling. *The oldest one might be going to university in England soon,* he thought.

His secretary walked by and reminded him of his 2pm meeting in half an hour. He dreaded the encounter, not because the people were difficult, but the issues were intricate and everyone had their own perspective. He was keenly aware of the interethnic tensions growing in the country, particularly as men from several different tribes would be seated around the table. He knew his colleagues well: they were good men and devoted brothers in Christ, operating with compassion in a harsh world. Naturally, they had cherished ideas which needed to be presented and there would be the usual vested interests to be protected. Onyango accepted that: he had grown through the system.

He stood and stretched his tall form. As he walked over to the window to adjust the blinds to accommodate the sun's westerly movement, he glanced down at the folder on his desk. He placed his hand on it, in an unconscious gesture of endorsement, and picked up a nearby sheaf of notes. Half-sitting on his desk – an ungainly habit that he had never been able to resist – he leafed through the papers and thought about his senior position and its responsibilities. Authority isolates. The pressures of high office can suck one's humanity if they are allowed to. His opinion was sought on many matters and he did his best to dispense wise counsel, based largely on his study of God's Word and his experience. *But how relevant is experience in rapidly shifting circumstances?* he wondered. Sometimes he wilted under the many demands that levered into his time and drained his strength. People, he loved; paperwork, he disliked. He dropped the pile of notes onto his desk and returned to his chair to continue reading letters and signing forms.

A quarter of an hour later, the heap of papers had been dealt with. He pushed them aside and glanced at the clock. He had twelve minutes until the meeting. Bishop Onyango did a rare thing. He leaned back in his chair and closed his eyes. Beyond the practical administrative duties, he was overwhelmed at times by the number and complexity of the issues pressing in upon society and the multitude of errors many people were making. He thought, *So many serious issues are missed by our culture, and even the moral consciousness of our church.*

He recalled a recent discussion with a senior Roman Catholic priest. Their chance encounter at an ecumenical conference many years previously had led to an ongoing, if unconventional, friendship. They both felt comfortable sharing confidential insights with each other. Their points of accord, not their differences, defined the relationship. By tacit agreement, they avoided contentious denominational topics, but they discussed social justice issues at length. Analysing the saying 'Give a man a fish and you feed him for a day; teach a man to fish and you feed him for life', they found it an interesting, if shallow, axiom. They agreed that the person also needed rightful access to the shore, an outlet for his surplus fish, a fair trade price, roads to town that didn't turn into a quagmire twice a year, and security on the way home from the market so he was not robbed of his paltry earnings!

During their wide-ranging dialogue, the Anglican bishop showed Steven Brandon's analysis to the Roman Catholic. Onyango had described the responses to the working paper at their conferences. There had been a diversity of reactions. As an example, at the mention of gender confusion, one group had retorted 'Don't speak of it! It is not an African concern... we have a strong taboo...there are more important needs....' The other extreme reaction, including from the European delegates, could be summed up as 'Let's embrace all forms of human expression. The church needs to modernize. Let us show love and tolerance, so as not to alienate anyone.'

Grateful for the moderate, middle group of opinions, the bishop had privately reinforced his view that the devil is a master deceiver who is extremely active within a lost and searching society. Later discussions at conferences highlighted the fact that sexual infidelity had contributed to the spread of a dreadful new disease which was being described by the acronym, AIDS. The priest had agreed with Onyango that the pernicious effects of sexual promiscuity were obvious, although they both had consistently preached love and understanding.

Onyango had added, "We accept everyone. The church is a place for people who have nowhere else to go. But we must remember that acceptance does not mean approval. The Bible is our only reliable guide." Their concern was the way unbiblical behaviour could block the full blessings of Christ's teaching in people's lives.

Beyond that, the two friends – in their darker moments – each confessed to a deeper fear. This was illustrated to some extent in Steven Brandon's notes and in a few of the closed conference sessions: that was of a foreign ideology or religion taking over Europe, the Americas, and other Christian countries. The threat that terrified them was increasing indifference as the Church's influence declined. Their solace came in looking to the basics: God's word, reliance on the Holy Spirit, earnest intercessory prayer, and their profound relationship with Jesus. Onyango spoke reverently to his friend of the only solution: Jesus Christ, The One whose name he bore and whose cross he carried around his neck. The Catholic described his scars from an attempt to save a younger colleague during a violent attack. The youth had died and the priest received a severe beating, as he put it, "In appreciation for my heroic intervention!"

Onyango had no physical scars, but he had nearly received them during an encounter with security officials. It was at a time of increasing tension in the country. He had spoken at an open-air rally, encouraging the citizens to exercise their constitutional right to vote according to their convictions and not be persuaded by bribery or pressured into voting for a candidate they did not support. He knew that a bag of rice would secure a vote from a poor person.

He was not sure who the men were, but he saw them standing at the back of the outdoor meeting. As he left, two cars slowly followed him out of the town. They kept back while there were people around, but drew up closely behind his car on an isolated section of road. He saw no point in trying to avoid them, so he pulled over, stopped, and got out. He asked the large men what they were doing, following him in that way. There were three of them, in addition to their drivers inside their cars. They aggressively questioned him about what he had been saying and warned him to stay clear of political comments in the future.

He had later told his wife, "I did not expect to walk away from that confrontation alive." Yes, indeed, he carried mental and emotional scars.

As the clock showed five minutes to his meeting, the bishop stood, lifted the papers from his desk, and walked along the corridor to his conference room. His final thought was of Steven Brandon's social analysis. The bishop had set up a small task force of carefully selected clergy to study emerging social trends and current opinions, and advise him on the church's response. He intended to include Steven in the group. These introspections encouraged him to arrange a visit to the Zoo to spend a day with the Brandons and their little community south of Mwakindini.

The dawn offered hope for the stiff couple in their cramped pickup. Jane was excited to see another day while Brett simply felt grateful that they had survived the night. They drove back to Mtito Andei, and filled up with petrol.

Brett told her, "I'd rather not stay long as I'm anxious to get to the Zoo in the light if possible." He went to buy six bottles of cold sodas while Jane parked the car in a patch of shade. He asked her to stay with the car, explaining that Steve's family had previously had articles stolen there. There was a group of young men and a couple of girls hanging around watching their every move. Brett felt the tension, once again, of always being watched. He knew that white people were an entertaining curiosity to the locals.

"Let's drive on and eat our snacks as we go," he suggested.

He thought about their stop at Mtito Andei and told Jane how nice it had been in England to be ignored by everyone and not be the centre of attention all the time. She nodded.

"But don't you get used to being the focus of interest?" Jane asked.

"To some extent, yes. Mostly they don't mean any harm. They are just interested in all the strange things we have, and wear, and do, and say. Sometimes it's simply a reflection of the Africans' wonderful hospitality where they want us to feel welcomed and special. But someone said that living here – especially if you're trying to use the local language – is adjusting to living by somebody else's rules."

As they continued south of the town, they enjoyed the remainder of the food that Mary had given them. The sun was high in the sky – almost directly above them – and they felt the air getting hotter. Soon, tiredness overcame Jane and she drifted off to sleep, grateful for the breeze through the open windows.

She awoke in time to see the baboons near Manyani. A couple of tour buses and several cars had stopped and the baboons were climbing all over the vehicles, much to the delight of the tourists with their cameras. One lady got out of her car to pick up a plastic bag that the baboons had discarded when they had grabbed some bananas. A large male baboon leaped on the vehicle roof as though he was guarding his territory and he would not let her back in her car. Whenever she tried to open the door, he hit her on the head. She eventually climbed back in safely.

Brett said, "That could have been nasty as they can scratch and bite viciously."

"I thought it was quite funny. I didn't realize how dangerous they could be."

"A lot of visitors forget that these are wild animals, and they operate by basic survival rules. It's not like a protected zoo."

"You'd know about living in a zoo, eh? I can drive anytime."

"Thanks, I'd like a nap," said Brett. "Drive to Voi and then it should be a couple of hours to cover the 150 km to Mombasa. We'll go to Biashara Street and buy two double rectangular-framed mosquito nets."

"Why two?"

"I can't remember the configuration of the beds in the guesthouse, and the nets get pretty worn. They are not expensive and–"

"I hope we'll get a double bed!"

"In that heat, you may be grateful to sleep separately," joked Brett. "Seriously, it will be useful to have two."

"I may look for some other things if it's a tourist place."

"We won't have much time. We should allow three hours north from there. It's about 2:30 so we might make it soon after dark."

Stopping only for short breaks and drinks from their water jug, they pushed on. After Voi, they drove across the sparsely populated Taru desert – a dry plateau with low thorn trees and sturdy baobabs.

When Brett was at the wheel again he said, "When I'm heading south, I always think of Voi as being about two-thirds of the way from Nairobi to Mombasa so we're doing well. It does get a bit boring now until we reach the ridge above the coastal strip."

Jane had been thinking for a while and said, "Our experiences here are so totally different from our life in England. It seems like another world and another time. Just think of all the traffic at home."

"Yes, and what do we see here? The occasional dilapidated bus, an overloaded lorry limping along belching out fumes, a few private cars or pickups, and an occasional luxury vehicle," said Brett.

"Quite a contrast. Having just arrived, I feel as though I'm suspended between two conflicting realities. It's all a bit overwhelming at the moment."

"I understand exactly. I've been through those emotions many times. I'm sure you'll feel different once we're settled in the Zoo."

"Tell me about some of the people I'll meet there."

"Speaking of animals," joked Brett, "look on the left, you can see several Thomson's gazelles and some zebras. Well, we'll be staying at the guesthouse, which is fairly close to the church and the Brandons' cage. Also, the clinic is nearby. Louise Emerson used to spend a lot of time assisting there, but I doubt if she's–"

Brett didn't finish. The pickup started to sway from side to side. There was a rumbling noise.

"Oh no! A puncture," shouted Brett. He braked quickly and drove onto the gravel on the left of the road. They both got out and looked at the flat tyre on the front left of the car. "At least there's no traffic around."

"Do we have a spare?"

"Yes. Jim said he checked. The jack and wheel wrench are behind the rear seat so we'll have to move some stuff." As he lowered the spare wheel and bounced it on the gravel, he said, "Can you get a couple of rocks to block the wheels please?" He rolled the wheel along to the flat tyre. Jane saw Brett was on his knees trying to position the jack underneath the front.

She joked, "We're not exactly dressed for this." She pushed a rock against the rear right wheel and shouted, "Does that tyre have enough pressure?"

"It should have. But we also have a foot pump," he said, stepping on the wheel wrench to loosen the bolts.

"Here's another rock. It should be okay to lift the frame now."

After they had changed the wheel and lowered the car, they were both relieved to see that the spare tyre had sufficient pressure. As Jane reloaded the inside tools, Brett hoisted the wheel into the open back beside their cases. They poured a little of their precious drinking water onto their dirty hands and faces to wash them, shook them dry, and climbed back into the car.

"Let's pray that we don't have another puncture before Mombasa. I know a garage there that will fix this," said Brett as they drove off across the barren plain.

9

Beyond the rustling palm trees, she could see the Indian Ocean shimmering a turquoise blue and, beyond that, the white line of the far reef. It was overwhelming in its rich beauty.

The relentless downward slope of the road continued in a southeasterly direction across the arid landscape. Jane marvelled at the large castles of clay scattered about the countryside – amazing termite hills built of red earth. As each kilometre passed, the elevation fell, the humidity increased, and the land became covered in thorn bushes. South from Mariakani, they encountered lush tropical vegetation with many swaying coconut palms and papaya trees until they saw, in the far distance, the first glimpse of the Indian Ocean. Soon, the road wound down in a series of sharp curves until they reached the coastal strip that had for centuries been the scene of many battles, struggles, and atrocities.

A dilapidated rusty sign welcomed them to Mombasa and gave them a sense of relief, knowing that the tyres had held and they were now able to get help. They drove through the industrial area, beside car-assembly plants, and past the road to the international airport. They crossed the channel that revealed the huge Kilindini harbour, and finally arrived in Mombasa. This sprawling ancient town was built on a coral island, raised twenty metres above sea level.

The sun was already dipping behind the Shimba Hills and, in the gaps, the shadows of the tall palm trees lay long across the highway. Brett knew a place where they could have the tyre repaired. But when they arrived, they learned that the electricity had been off all afternoon and the garage was closed until the next morning, as were many of the local businesses. They felt tired and depleted. Brett did not want to risk continuing the journey without a spare, particularly in the fading light.

"Darkness descends rapidly in the tropics, and many vehicles drive without lights, so I avoid night travel unless it's an emergency."

They left the wheel with the *askari,* the guard at the garage, who told them of a cheap hotel nearby which had a locked compound for the vehicle. They entered the hotel and were assigned a small room on the upper floor. Together, they struggled to get their cases up the stairs in the dim light. Brett asked about making a phone call to Mwakindini to tell the Brandons what had happened. The clerk at the front desk explained that, without electricity, that was not possible. Brett spoke to the night-duty *askari* and gave him twenty shillings, a Kenyan pound, as a tip to watch the car. He was delighted. Almost immediately after that, the electricity flickered on and then off again. Soon it came back and stayed on, so Brett tried to make his phone call while Jane looked at the facilities in the hotel and asked about somewhere to eat.

She entered their room and was immediately disappointed. It was tiny, hot, and stuffy, with an odour of stale tobacco smoke. There were two single beds with circular hoops of bamboo suspended from the ceiling above them. Dirty mosquito nets were bunched up and tied below. However, there were clean towels on the beds. Brett joined her in the room, explaining that the phone at the Brandons' cage was not working but he had been able to speak to Len Moore's helper who said he would try to send a message to Steve and Coreene. Brett and Jane were both dripping with sweat. Brett walked across the room and opened the shutters to reveal torn mosquito mesh at the windows. He turned to Jane and grinned.

"Choose which luxurious bed you'd prefer: the one with the blast of icy air from the window or the chilling draft from the door!"

"I'm glad we're not spending a fortnight's holiday here," said Jane, unravelling her mosquito net. She saw several squashed bloody mosquitoes, grubby sticky-plasters over holes, and three places where rips had been repaired by tying a knot in the thin fabric. Brett smiled.

"I'm so tired I don't care what it's like as long as I can get some sleep. But first we need to eat."

They headed down to a nearby cafe and enjoyed delicious fried sea perch and chunky chips, a dollop of *ugali,* a thick maize-meal porridge, with some boiled cabbage and kale. They had locally baked bread, and the small sweet bananas that Brett relished, along with *Sprite baridi,* cold sodas.

It was dark outside when they returned to their room. Brett turned on the tap in the tiny basin and said how grateful he was to have water and electricity. They quickly rinsed and prepared for bed in the clothes they were wearing as neither could be bothered to extricate clean things from their cases piled by the door. Brett sat on one of the chairs and opened his Bible. They always did their devotions in the evening, whatever the circumstances. He found the readings for that day while Jane located the switch for the overhead fan and was pleased to see that it worked, although the blades limped around in slow and wobbly rotations. Brett looked up at it.

"We'd better not stand underneath that thing. It looks as though it's hanging by a thread, and probably that thread is the electric power cable! At that speed, it's probably just pulling down hot air from the ceiling." He read from his Bible where St. Paul describes how transformation in our lives starts with the renewing of our minds.

Jane said, "Yes. Tony often spoke of an intellectual component to transformation – how we need to intentionally use our reasoning powers. He would quote St. Paul who wrote about taking every thought captive to obey Christ. That's a bit esoteric, I know. But I was thinking, in practice, through Christ, we can be a means of transformation in the lives of others."

"That's true. I see a relevance for people in the Zoo, where Christians might become a source of transformation for others – I mean, those who don't yet know the power of Jesus in their lives. That's what Steve Brandon always yearned for." Jane nodded.

"But we must always approach this with humility, gentleness, and great respect, right? I wonder…could we become part of that ministry during our few months there?" Brett thought carefully, wiped the sweat from his face, neck, arms and hands with a damp flannel.

"I learned a lot from Steve and Coreene, but I still need more of the power of God in my life before I feel confident in telling others about it."

Jane assured him, "The Bible tells us that power comes to us through Christ who gives us strength."

After a brief prayer, they both fell asleep despite the confined heat of the nets and the rattle of the fan as it loped around lethargically.

At that moment, in the Zoo, 150 kilometres to the north, Louise Emerson was dreading going to bed. She delayed it as long as possible by remaining in her chair and replaying in her mind an incident earlier in the day. She had experienced an unfortunate encounter with Larry Smythe, the plumbing technician who worked with Len Moore and managed the Energy Conservation Centre. Larry, with his pinched mouth and bright blue eyes, was a difficult man. She smiled at a recollection of when Larry first arrived at the Zoo. One of his neighbours who spent a lot of time fishing near Diani Beach, said he recognized Larry. He asked if he had a girlfriend down there. Larry told him to get lost and mind his own business. The account that Louise heard, contained much stronger expletives.

Len had told her, "Larry has a fine appreciation for biting irony. And bad language. When things go wrong, the air is blue with curses. My vocabulary has doubled since working with him!" On several occasions, intrusive neighbours had been the recipients of Larry's vituperation.

Larry was superficially pleasant and many people liked him, Louise admitted. But to her, he had a vicious side that occasionally revealed itself. During their brief meeting that day, he had made several snide remarks, insinuating Henry's corruption and Louise's ongoing involvement with illegal activities. It had been very subtle, but the pejorative innuendoes were clear. Len had also been there so after Larry left them, Louise had confided in him.

"He's too outspoken and sarcastic for me."

Len replied, "Larry can be offensive but he's very creative. I just have to mention the mere outline of an idea and he'll develop it to build an ingenious device or system enhancement. He may lack decorum, but he knows his pipes and valves. I don't argue with him: he's best left to work on things his way."

"It's his locution – he speaks in half sentences. In conversation, his favourite line seems to be 'So, what's yer point?' I find that irritating."

"It's just his manner. Don't let it bother you, Louise."

"Well, I do love his use of malapropism and mixed metaphors. The other day he said 'To me, it's just water off a cool cucumber'."

Len smiled. "That's Larry! Recently, he referred to ships that go bump in the night! I'm grateful for his help. I let him run the place unhindered. Even his belligerent manner can be an advantage in administering the Energy Centre. It deters too many visitors!"

"It's interesting, sometimes he looks quite young and energetic; other times it appears the years – and alcohol – are taking their toll."

Louise felt guilty about her attitude towards Larry. She recalled a piece of advice Coreene had once offered her: 'Try to find the truth in an insult. Even if it's tiny, there may be a nugget of truth buried within an offence. It's sometimes helpful to identify that and deal with it.' Louise thought, *That's probably why his remarks upset me. Maybe there's some truth in what he said about our recent illegal activities.*

She was tired, but she knew what to expect when she tried to sleep. As a nurse, she understood that Non Hodgkin's Lymphoma is notoriously unpredictable. She felt she might be experiencing the typical early symptoms of a recurrence – night sweats with drenching nightwear, and fatigue. Living on a tropical coast did not help, although she was grateful for the air-conditioning. Louise thought of Brett and Jane who should have arrived that evening. She intended to drive to the guesthouse in the morning to welcome them. She was excited to meet Jane, having exchanged letters with her.

As she finally settled under the mosquito net, Louise knew she could easily outlive her initial medical prognosis which was two years ago. Recently there was nothing wrong with the blood work, or even any abnormality on the CT scan of her chest and abdomen.

In the darkness and gentle cooling from the air-conditioning, Louise relaxed and thanked the God she was increasingly believing in, for each new day of continued life. Her capabilities were diminishing, but she was determined to continue her activities as long as possible. After the disappointment of having to cancel her move to Australia, she had considered other possibilities. She was unenthusiastic about returning to England and wasn't even sure if it was a practical option for her.

She was anxious to remain in Kenya if physically possible, so she had placed several walking sticks in strategic locations to help with balance. She had no carpets and had removed all her rugs. She had trained both her maids – particularly Shafiqah – to take on more of her care and health management. She continued to encourage their training interests in sewing and bookkeeping, but they were both employed full-time supporting her increasing needs. After her decision not to move to Australia, the old man, Mjuhgiuna, had agreed to continue working for her, but in a reduced capacity – more as a security presence than an active worker. Louise hoped the arrangement would continue as long as she was able to remain at the Zoo.

She planned to try staying for a week or so in a Malindi hotel, or even short visits at a care home, to see how viable that would be in the future as her disease advanced. Her son, Alan, was planning to bring his family to Kenya for a visit in 1991. She was excited about meeting the family after so many years. She fell asleep with a simple prayer of gratitude in her heart.

The next morning, Brett awoke suddenly, sweating profusely, and saw it was already light. He lay for a moment, feeling peace about being back in Kenya. It felt right. He was home again. He quietly unraveled himself from the mosquito net and wandered down to the common bathroom at the end of the corridor. When he returned, Jane was up. They dragged the cases down the stairs to the car. Leaving the cases, the car, and another pound with the daytime *askari*, they returned to the cafe for coffee, *mandazis* – local donuts – and delicious mangoes. They were anxious to pick up the spare wheel and begin their journey north. While the mechanic rolled the repaired wheel towards the back of the pickup and wound it up in its place, Jane and Brett looked at the long bent nail he had found in the tyre. As they left, they attempted to shake the hand of the mechanic, but he offered a clenched fist and touched the inside of his wrist to theirs. As they drove away, Brett explained that they often do that when their hands are dirty or greasy.

"That's far more acceptable than not shaking hands."

Driving slowly through the streets of Mombasa, they encountered some traffic because it was still about 9 o'clock. Jane saw an unconscious man lying prone within the median. As they drove on, she asked Brett about him.

"Did you see if he was still alive? In any case, he was in a dreadful condition, lying helplessly in his own filth."

"There are many desperate people, and beggars."

"Why don't the authorities do something?"

"Some are. And the churches and other charities."

"You seem a bit casual about it. Do I sense a lack of compassion?"

"No. It's just that I find it easier to accept things the way they are, after so many years. We are not here to solve all the problems – just those we are invited to help with."

"It strikes me quite hard, seeing it all for the first time."

"I understand. We try to help where we can. But there are so many people in need."

"In Nairobi, you had a way of dealing with beggars, didn't you?"

"Beggars? Most people ignore them. Yes, I had a procedure. I used to carry a pocketful of shillings. I'd look them in the eye, smile, and give them a coin, saying 'God bless you'. I'm not sure what I'd do if I lived there."

They purchased two mosquito nets and then drove north across the channel over the Nyali bridge. Brett felt a surge of excitement at being back in such an invigorating environment. As they travelled up the coast towards Kilifi, he explained that he should phone Steve to give him some idea of what was happening. Although they had not been travelling for long, he suggested stopping at the Seaside Lodge. Jane agreed, adding she wouldn't mind another coffee and something to eat as their early morning snack seemed a long time ago.

The hotel was managed by a German company and many of the guests were there on holiday from Germany. Brett told Jane that Louise liked to visit that hotel and hear German spoken as it reminded her of Henry.

"I can't wait to meet her," said Jane. Brett was unable to make his phone call, but they did not mind as it was a pleasant environment and they thoroughly enjoyed the food and the excellent service.

After the meal, Brett said, "Excuse me, I need to try that phone call again, if the switchboard is operating now."

Jane wandered through the spacious reception court out onto the balcony overlooking the swimming pools. Bright whitewashed walls glared back at her through the arches. Beyond the rustling palm trees, she could see the Indian Ocean shimmering a turquoise blue and, beyond that, the white line of the far reef. It was overwhelming in its rich beauty. Brett found her and related the news that the phone lines were down north of Malindi and the receptionist was unsure about how long it would take to make the connection. They decided to continue their journey immediately.

The ferry crossing at Kilifi Creek was an entertaining cultural experience. As they waited in line, they were diverted by a parade of human activity along both sides of the pickup. A whiff of smoke drifted from the charcoal coals over which maize cobs were being roasted. Although it was stifling hot in the car, they kept the windows up to avoid the diesel fumes from the pick-up running in front of them, and the three men smoking *bhang* beside their vehicle. Nobody troubled them: even the hawkers were fairly casual. A boy offered them cashew nuts in twisted paper cones of old newspapers, and a young man approached the car with a tray of pirated cassette-tapes.

During the brief ferry ride, Jane enjoyed watching the interactions of the local people, some in traditional Giriama dress. She saw three ladies with full grass *hando* skirts, and a few casually dressed tourists who had disembarked from their bus. Brett thought again how good it was to be back, and realized how comfortable he had become with the Kenyan people and their customs over the years, and what a privilege it was to have had that experience.

They continued their journey, passing sisal plantations, cotton fields, and cashew-nut farms, intermingled with large areas of coconut palms. Brett also pointed out many banana and pineapple plants. There was a police roadblock north of Malindi but it did not delay them long.

Jane said, "That is becoming familiar now. I feel I've lived through about two months of varied experiences since we arrived in Kenya just over a week ago."

"I know what you mean. Everything happens at a more dramatic level, doesn't it? What is your overall impression of Kenya so far?"

"It's amazing. I love the intensity of the light and the brilliant colours. But there's a sort of roughness about it. And that's my experience as a protected tourist! Do you remember in England, when you first returned, you said everything appeared so soft?"

"Yes, the rain, towels, pillows, shower sprays–"

"And the toilet paper!"

"Yes, I remember," Brett laughed.

"I formed a certain image of Kenya – rough, and hard, and gritty. Not only physically but in all of life."

"It is tough for the vast majority of people. But you remember last night we spoke of transformation? When you know the country well, you see signs of hope due to the initiative, commitment, and faith of the people."

As they drove into the Zoo on that first Saturday, Jane was disappointed at the scruffy entrance alongside a dilapidated *duka*, a small stall. They passed the signboard at the front, drove along a rutted *murram* track beside some industrial buildings and up to the security gate. Even the uniformed *askari* seemed desultory at first as he unhooked the red-and-white painted pole, balanced by a large cement block attached at the other end beyond a pivoted post. He skillfully controlled its upward swing with a frayed rope. But once he recognized Brett, his eyes brightened. They exchanged brief greetings and he waved them into the compound.

Everything looked lush and green, with people milling around. Some waved at the pickup when they saw who was driving. After a short distance, Brett turned to the right and pulled up in front of a small stone house adjacent to a simple chapel. The Brandon family saw them and greeted them warmly. Their first question was why they were so late. It was obvious that they had not received the message from the previous evening.

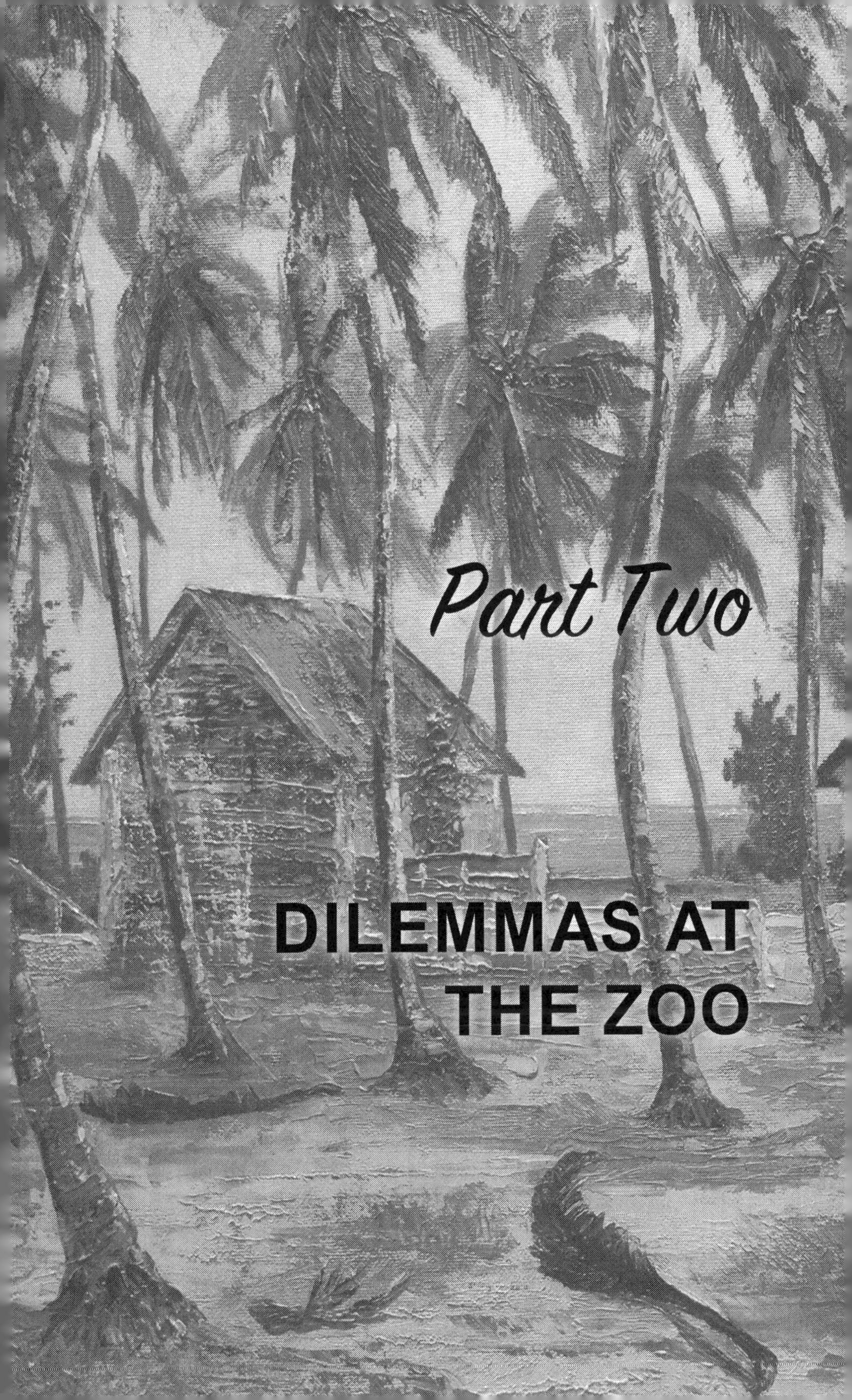

Part Two

DILEMMAS AT THE ZOO

The fictional characters introduced in Part Two

Khadijah: housekeeper in guesthouse at The Zoo
Marie-Anne Moore: Len Moore's wife
Boniface Chengo (deceased): former Executive Officer at The Zoo
Kuvanza: thug in Mwakindini
Fatima: Louise's maid
Karl Bergmann (deceased): Henry's friend in Germany
Ochieng: Malindi police detective
Kinyanjui: Mwakindini police sergeant
Ruth, Andrew, and Graham: Steve and Coreene Brandon's children

10

"Miles was searching all his life, actually.
He described it as security.
Maybe it was something deeper."
Louise Emerson

The two visitors were taken to the guesthouse where they were warmly welcomed by Khadijah, the housekeeper. They shook hands and, using a common Kenyan expression, she greeted Brett.

"How are you for many days?"

Jane was delighted to see how many people knew Brett and their surprise and joy that he had returned to see them. Steve and Brett unloaded the cases. As they unpacked, Brett and Jane were relieved that their cases and cameras had survived the journey. They had already taken three rolls of 35-mm film.

"We'll post those for processing when we go into Mwakindini," he said. Coreene joined them to check if they needed anything, and invite them for supper. "Thank you, we'd love that. Let's have a swim first though," said Brett. "How's the tide, Coreene?"

"It's high tide now," she said and then warned Jane about the intense sun. "Even you, Brett. You look rather white! Come over any time after six, okay?"

As they headed for the beach, they heard a loud thud.

Brett warned, "Did you see that hard green coconut come crashing down? Always walk *between* the palm trees."

Jane said, "I can see the sense in that."

"Also it's best not to stand, sit, or park beneath them. The dead, brown palm fronds also drop without warning. They are surprisingly heavy."

Jane loved her first dip in the warm Indian Ocean. Back at the guesthouse, they inspected their mosquito net hanging with its thin strings twisted around rusty nails banged into the walls. Jane examined everything – including the wobbly double bed – while Brett explained how things worked. They tried the window shutters, the keys, the temperamental toilet, and the lights.

He said, "Some of the electrical wiring dates back to Vasco da Gama's days, I think!"

After supper, the children asked Brett to play a game with them.

"Do you want a number game?"

"Yes, yes, a number game." He knew a game and he was able to outwit the children with his guesses.

He explained, "There's more than numbers at play here. A bit of psychology too."

"I see your time with Kelsey wasn't wasted," joked Steve.

"Time with Kelsey is never wasted," said Brett.

"Meaning what, exactly?" demanded Jane, glaring at him.

"I actually learned a lot from her."

"Oh, did you?" she snapped.

Mildly, he said, "At the very least, a person hones one's arguing skills!"

Sensing tension, Coreene said, "Jane dear, help me with these things in the kitchen, please." She whispered, "You needn't worry about Kelsey. Brett was never attracted to her, other than as an interesting visitor."

"That's what he says, but he seems ambivalent sometimes. He often appears to admire her."

"We all did. She's very bright and alert. But that's all–"

"They went on safari together."

"Yes, but only with Brett as a tour guide. It was all very respectable."

"Hmm. Thanks, Coreene. I'm just being silly, I know."

"I understand. Actually, she's coming back to visit again." Noticing Jane's horrified expression, she added, "But not till April, so you'll be gone by then."

Steve came in, saying, "You can leave those things for the maids. Come and join us. We were having an interesting discussion and we'd like your perspectives." After the ladies joined them, Steve explained, "We were saying how, in Africa, one rarely gets the full picture or all the details; we drift along with half a story most of the time."

"Apparently, that suits everybody," said Coreene.

As Jane sat down next to him, Brett said, "Yes, I learned to appreciate the value of ambiguous statements when people asked me questions. Perhaps they don't want to know all the facts, just enough to keep everybody content and maintaining good relationships. I found out that, to the Kenyans, relationship is paramount."

"That's so true," agreed Coreene. "They say this is a *being* society rather than a *doing* society. Just being together overrides achieving goals. I have to remind myself of that when things aren't getting done according to my timetable, when others seem content with just working together respectfully as a team. Of course, there are exceptions, and some individuals are more tuned in to the western mode of operating."

Jane and Brett enjoyed a day of rest on Sunday, with some exploratory walks around the southern part of the Zoo. Louise sent a message to them, inviting them both for tea the next day. She was not well enough to drive to them herself, as she had intended.

They met Mzee Mjuhgiuna in the doorway when they arrived. He was weaker, but happy to see Brett again. He showed them to the upper suite. Jane was delighted to meet Louise, but Brett was saddened by how frail she appeared. She used her cane to manoeuvre around the furniture. However, she still looked striking with her hair combed back, a smart deep-blue dress, and a glittering brooch. Immediately, Louise thanked Brett for arranging the desert rose in Perth. Her son, Alan, had purchased one and sent her photos of it.

"That was so thoughtful of you. I was terribly sorry I had to cancel my plan to move to Australia, but I have to be realistic now." She turned to Jane and mentioned a practical medical concern. "Are you taking your antimalarial tablets, dear?"

Jane smiled, "Yes, they are the only pills I'm taking!"

Louise caught her look and simply said, "I see." Jane saw the knowing sparkle in Louise's green eyes which said everything. Brett missed the exchange because he was looking at the open CPZ-Store.

After updating one another with details of Miles, Vi, and Julie, they spoke of Brett's final conversations with Miles.

Brett said, "Louise, I have something to tell you."

"Oh?"

"I was not able to tell you before."

"What is it?"

"You remember when I had my serious leg injury?"

"Yes."

"It was not an accident. Miles hired two thugs to beat me up."

"Yes, I know."

"What?" Brett was flabbergasted.

"I know. Er – maybe I should rephrase that. I guessed that's what had happened."

"How did you know?" Brett asked.

"Your injuries did not correspond to your account of the incident, particularly your facial wounds. Then I remembered that Miles felt you were getting too inquisitive and needed to be warned to back off. It was obvious to me what had happened, but it was also clear that Miles did not want me to know. Remember, at that time, Miles was the boss. He controlled everything." She paused. The ripple on her closed lips disclosed a suppressed smile. "I decided to wait until someone revealed the truth, without my probing. Why are you telling me now?"

"Miles said I could if I wished."

Louise thought for a few seconds before saying, "I see you still have a cicatrix." She was pointing to the lower part of the scar visible beneath Brett's shorts.

"Yes. It doesn't tan properly. Still, Miles compensated me well for it."

"He did?" asked Louise.

"Yes, he felt bad about the accident."

"Accident?" Louise said quietly, shaking her head slightly.

Jane had been listening intently to the exchange, while carefully watching Louise. She noticed the sparkling blue and green gems in the brooch she wore. The greens matched her eyes. Jane saw an impressive lady, and sensed in her a depth of – what was it? – experience and wisdom. But more: compassion and shrewdness.

Jane spoke up: "Talking of Miles' compensation, I'm really enjoying this holiday, and the experiences we're having in this remarkable country."

"I'm pleased he was able to arrange that for you," Louise replied flatly.

Brett asked Louise, "So, you know who ordered the attack on me?"

"Miles."

"But who controlled Miles?"

"No one. Miles managed everything in the Zoo."

"But wasn't he manipulated by…Moshi?"

Louise was silent. She gave Brett one of her glances and then looked out of the window. Jane noticed it. She recalled Brett had said a slight look from Louise could convey so much.

"Yes," Louise said, with a sigh. She looked old and tired. "Yes, Moshi was behind everything. We were all his puppets."

"Miles told me that."

"You can believe it." Again, Jane spoke.

"But Miles took the rap for the attack on Brett. Why?"

Louise smiled. "Miles held back information strategically. I think I explained to you once, Brett, that it was a tradable commodity to him."

"He told me he was cashing it all in at the end," said Brett. Louise replied gently.

"Ah yes, the final reckoning. We will all face it."

Jane mused, "So, Miles equated information with power?"

"Yes. He instinctively operated that way."

Brett added, "He described three components…."

Louise responded quickly. "That's right. Miles existed within a triple framework: money, information, and power. With those in balance, he had complete control."

"Even if the information showed him in a bad light? Such as the blame for the attack on me?"

"Of course. We ordinary humans can't understand it, but to Miles the cost of accepting the blame would have been balanced against potential advantages of the secret knowledge. He was a master of obscurity." She offered more scones to Jane, and topped up their teacups. "You see, by remaining silent on Moshi's culpability, Miles held an advantage. Moshi would never know when Miles might leak that information." She laughed. "I can see it so clearly now…a small but vivid illustration which evinces exactly how Miles operated."

After sipping his hot tea, Brett asked Louise about her store.

"Did Miles know about the secret passage and CPZ-Store here?" He nodded towards the back of the room. Louise looked across at Jane quizzically.

"You must have told her."

"Everything."

"That's alright. Yes, he knew we had a clandestine place. So did Moshi, but they never needed access to it. Miles used the northern door in N-1, through the Ridge-Taylors' store. He rarely visited us in S-33. In fact, I don't think he ever came upstairs – no, he didn't." She spoke quietly, and seemed drowsy.

Brett had another question for her. "Do you know Mzee Kamau?"

"I have known many Mz–"

"The one in Nairobi. The old man Miles was supporting?"

"No." Louise was instantly alert. "Which Kamau? What do you mean 'supporting'?"

Brett took a deep breath. He told her about the plane attack, Peter's reckless action which caused Kamau's permanent injury, and the pressure Miles later put on Peter after they arranged a coverup. Brett described Miles' generous continuation of the confidential support for the injured man.

Louise said, "I didn't know that. Well I never! The poor man, Kamau, has lived with a bullet embedded in his leg ever since! So *that's* the hold Miles had over Peter!" She shook her head and it was obvious to Jane that many thoughts were racing through her mind. "That explains a lot. I feel as though I've just completed a difficult crossword puzzle. Thank you for telling me. I assume Miles gave you permission."

"Yes, he did. Allistair Matherton is handling all the financial transactions for Kamau, along with the doctor in Nairobi."

"Yes. Yes, I see. Brett, you knew Miles better than most."

Jane interjected with, "That's surprising as he'd only known him a few years compared to the decades others had lived with him."

Louise nodded. "Yes, but Miles revealed things to Brett–"

"Why?"

Louise confided, "He would have had his own purposes. Maybe he saw a friend who could keep a secret, a sympathetic collaborator, or a non-judgemental outsider."

"Also, I think he was attracted to Christianity, although he didn't reveal that until near the end," said Brett.

"Yes, that makes sense to me. He was searching all his life, actually. He described it as security. Maybe it was something deeper."

"I think it was. Also, he wanted to compensate me for the attack."

"By bringing you into his confidence? If so, it was a gift from him to you."

"He compensated me in many ways." Louise nodded. Her energy was fading.

"It's been lovely seeing you both, but I'm tired now." They left, with assurance of another visit and more talks. "I'd love to have an outing with you both. Let's try to arrange something."

On the way back to the guesthouse, they met several of Brett's friends, and he introduced Jane to Len and Marie-Anne Moore. They spoke for a few minutes before Larry Smythe walked by and Len introduced him to the visitors. Larry was charming, and chattered amiably with the group until he had to return to work.

During her first few days at the Zoo, Jane had noticed several of Brett's paintings around the Zoo – particularly the large canvas in the church, *Transformation,* depicting three palm trees suggesting the crucifixion. It had been moved and was hanging in the hallway.

She admired it, and Brett said, "Yes, you can appreciate my work, spread all over the place. It wasn't too difficult to give the paintings away!"

One lunchtime, Brett and Jane made their way to the restaurant. A rowdy crowd waved them over and Brett introduced several people. Two of them were chiding Len Moore who was positioned in the centre of a laughing group. Brett and Jane sat on the edge, started their meal, and listened. Len was talking about his new scheme with very tall pipes for collecting solar-heated water, and saving on fuel costs. Everyone was teasing him about his notions.

"You can laugh, I don't mind. You can ridicule my ideas if you like. They laughed at Archimedes when the apple fell on his head."

"That was Newton," someone pointed out. Len pretended to be surprised.

"Oh yes. Well, they misunderstood him too, especially when he tried to explain his Theory of General Relativity," joked Len.

One fellow was beside himself with glee. "Get him a cup of tea someone – a lukewarm one. He's going to have to get used to it. So are we all, if his hair-brain ideas are implemented."

A neighbour said, "No, upon reflection, I can see some merit in this idea of the pipes, Len. Where did you first hear about it?"

"I thought it up. I told you, I've thought it through–"

"No, you must have pinched it from someone else."

Len again pretended to look hurt. "The highest accolade around here is to be accused of stealing someone else's ideas. When you are charged with plagiarism, you know you're onto something!"

11

As a trio, they trusted one another and would do anything required to maintain the operation of Moshi's affairs. Legality and morality were immaterial.

Brett was excited to take Jane out on a catamaran. The northeast wind was still stable, so it was a good time. The staff at the boat rental outlet in Mwakindini recognized Brett. They lent them the extra equipment that Len did not have. Brett checked that he had all the usual safety gear. They set out by sailing across to the northern beach of the Zoo. The catamaran was fast, with its large sail area. The winds were light and manageable, so Brett was using the mainsail and the jib. Even though the tide was high, he wanted to get out past the reef quickly, so they came about and made their way out to deeper water. Once past the turbulent line of the reef, they relaxed and took time to look around and savour the experience.

Suddenly, Brett sensed a strange movement in the wind. He noticed that the sails were swinging them downwind, the boat was picking up speed, and the waves rushing past them made an alarming sound. He told Jane to slide back as he also moved his weight to the stern to correct the heeling over. He released the jib and let out as much of the mainsail as he could to slow the rush. He tried steering the Hobie Cat into the wind but the boat did not respond in the usual way. Jane was clinging onto the side rail.

Brett realized that, inexplicably, the wind had swirled around and was driving them back in the opposite direction. He knew he could not fight against it, but simply try to control the erratic swing.

He shouted, "Keep your head down. Be ready for a jibe." After a few more seconds of dreadful rushing and swishing of the water, the sail snapped across with a loud crack and they were tossed about while struggling to keep their balance.

Immediately, all was calm again. The wind was restored to its original course. *Good, we survived that,* he sighed, praising God aloud. He looked at the rigging and everything appeared to have held after the violent jibe.

Jane asked, "What happened? We spun right round."

"I don't know. Maybe the wind's influenced by the promontory. It's happened to me a couple of times before."

After that excitement, they examined the headland which projected a long way out into the cobalt-blue depths. They saw more details of the rocky outcrops, and open patches which were devoid of tall vegetation. He directed Jane's gaze to the part of the protected headland where they could just make out some cave openings. Brett explained that Peter had told him they were used for smuggling. Then they noticed a small sail within the reef, close to shore. It was a dugout canoe. Looking back at the mainland, they were able to appreciate the full panorama of the coastal strip and the spectacular region where the Zoo was located. It was stunning from that angle.

"So few people get to see this," he said.

He knew they were a long way from shore, but he wanted to sail out farther to see if he could show her the end of the peninsula and admire, up close, the white waves roaring against the piles of coral rock along the distant shoreline. *Just five more minutes,* he thought. A brisk headwind had picked up and was challenging him, but it was manageable. The main sail was full and the jib was catching the wind nicely.

"We should loosen that when we run back, as the wind is stronger now," he told her. He turned to see, over his shoulder, the lines of the high plateau above the coastal plain. He was trying to make out the patch of green where the spring was located.

"That's where the Zoo gets its water supp–"

Crack! Instinctively, he threw his weight to the centre of the catamaran while clinging onto the rail with one hand. He felt completely out of control. Jane clung for her life onto the stay and straps on the pitching boat. He saw the mainsail flapping violently in the wind, with no sheets to control it. The jib was pulling them along uncontrollably. Then he thought of what Louise had told him of Henry's response in a crisis. He sat still and evaluated things. He remained calm; he did not panic. *Right. I'll do the same. I'll stay calm and try to figure this out.*

Brett shouted to Jane, "We're not in any immediate danger. I have control as long as we keep the boat heading into the wind." He thought, *I must not let it capsize, with sharks around.*

He grasped the tiller bar and regained control with the jib sheet. Heading into the wind to reduce the bouncing on the waves, and holding the Hobie Cat in irons, he looked at the damaged mainsail. He thought perhaps a shackle had broken during the violent jibe.

They had to get back to shore, but how? *The moment I turn downwind, the boat will pick up speed. Can I control it?* The catamaran was bobbing about like an empty plastic bottle in the choppy water and he feared one of them falling overboard.

He said, "Maybe we can hold the sail loosely and head downwind." Jane had sailed before, but only in controlled conditions and never on a catamaran. She was feeling frightened and was praying silently.

Brett found a short piece of thin, strong line in his lifejacket pouch, so he carefully took that out and made a loop. After several attempts in the bumpy waves, with Jane controlling the tiller and keeping the craft pointing into the wind, he managed to grasp the waving boom and clutch the flapping end of the sail, and thread his temporary loop inside the outhaul ropes. He knew it would be difficult to control the mainsail without the mechanical advantage of the pulleys, but he gave it a try, with Jane steering the Hobie Cat towards the shore. He simply let the jib flap in the wind and concentrated on controlling the mainsail with the loose sheet through the temporary loop.

Everything seemed quiet and calm, but he knew it was deceptive as the impressive wake told him they were travelling very fast. He thought, *Be careful, you're carrying a lot of sail up there, and the waves are rising.* He had always enjoyed running with the waves and seeing them slowly drift past the boat, but this time it was a matter of intense concentration to prevent the sail from jibing again. He did not mind if he reached the inner shore at a different place from the boat club, as they would be safe in calmer waters by then.

After about ten minutes, he felt they were going to make it as they were about halfway home. The wind was still brisk but the push of the waves felt a little less. Jane was silent and tense. He wondered if anyone had seen what happened. Would someone be there to meet them, anxiously waiting to see if they were safe? *I doubt it!* he concluded. *I don't see a fleet of rescue craft heading our way!* As they sailed, he felt peace, and thanked God for their protection so far. He realized how vulnerable they had been and knew he should not have gone out so far.

The wind was calmer near the shore, so they were easily able to sail to the boat rental outlet and beach the craft safely. The boat owner looked at the rigging and concluded that a shackle bolt had broken.

He said, "It must have been rusted or loose. It's broken before and we made a temporary repair while waiting for a replacement part."

Suddenly, Brett felt exhausted. The adventure had been more of a strain than he had realized. As they drove back, Brett confided in Jane.

"It was a bit scary out there. We should praise God for keeping us safe."

"You can say that again!"

"I gave them enough to cover the cost of the repair."

They had survived the sailing crisis, but they would have had no way of knowing that other dangers were aligning to threaten their peaceful holiday.

At the same time, to the south in Mombasa, Moshi had decided what to do. His plan had very few risks but, on the other hand, it promised small chance of success. Still, he was running out of options and his opponents were intensifying the pressure. He instructed his chauffeur to drop him at a public taxi rank. He hailed a random taxi and gave the driver his brief instructions. For five minutes, the poor fellow made several fruitless attempts at conversation, and then gave up. Had he known the identity of his passenger, Moshi reasoned, he may have been more circumspect; but he could not have known who sat behind him, so he was oblivious to the danger he may pose.

At 64, Moshi had become pensive. He used the taxi ride to indulge in some moments of reflection. He considered himself fortunate to still be alive; but, as he pondered his increasingly dangerous situation, his introspections took him back to his childhood. He caught a view down a narrow alleyway and saw the shadows contrasting with the harsh light reflecting off the distempered walls. His mind arced back over the decades to his early years in a similar hovel. Was it the light that wrenched up the memory or perhaps the brief glimpse of an angry man shouting at a ragged boy? The image passed, but his daydreams continued as the taxi drove past the Frere monument to freed slaves, with the bell tower still to be seen, and headed up the coast towards Kilifi.

Moshi was born in 1926 in an impoverished section of Mombasa. His parents were poor and their six children received limited education. But he had been surprised how well they had done in life: he had two brothers with jobs in the government, and his three sisters had married into successful business families. Moshi was the fifth-born. That afforded low status, although he sensed very early that being a male brought enormous advantages. He realized that, if he was going to be taken care of in life, he would be the one to do it. His grandmother lived with them and, in failing health, she allocated as much kindness as possible to each of the children. Moshi's father was rarely home, although he always seemed to appear when discipline was required. During Moshi's disruptive teenage years, a spiteful neighbour told him his mother had an illicit affair when his father had disappeared for many months. Years later, Moshi heard she had a son who was spirited away to be raised by sympathetic friends. The informant hinted that the grown son had joined the security forces, but Moshi was never able to verify that.

Moshi's real name was Ahmed Nasir. Very few people knew that. As a penniless weakling, in his early teens, he chanced upon some cigarettes. Adults sometimes discarded them and the boys snatched them up. Smoking gave the young Ahmed some prestige among the scruffy gang, so he adopted the habit as a badge. It brought some desperately needed recognition among the tough lads. He begged or stole the cigarettes needed to maintain his image. Later, when occasional legitimate income came his way, he used most of that to further impress the impressionable. He was frequently seen beneath a cloud of smoke, so he was taunted with the moniker *moshi*, meaning smoke in Swahili. It was intended as an insult but it appealed to him, so he adopted that as his name in order to neutralize the sting of the offence. That was just one of his tricks, along with some rudimentary human psychology and skillful refining of the art of manipulation.

He despised self-pity – in others and himself. He seldom dwelt on his difficulties. And, heaven knows, there had been many! His disdain for individuals who wallowed in self-pity was frequently interpreted as ruthlessness. So be it! *Let others think what they wish,* he scoffed inwardly.

He wondered whether to engage the driver in some shallow banter, but decided against it. Something might be revealed. Besides, he was enjoying the anonymity that the taxi provided. His car was too well known. He changed vehicles every year as the number plates remained on the vehicles, and his registration number was quickly learned by his enemies. His current car was a silver Citroen. The Mercedes marque tended to attract too much attention. Eighteen months ago, one of his former cars had been discovered mysteriously burned out, south of Mombasa. Still, he usually needed a driver and bodyguard and he valued the convenience of his luxury vehicle – particularly compared to the present stifling discomfort of the taxi.

Thinking about his name, brought to mind his passports. He needed to check the dates in them. The only genuine passport in his collection showed him as Ahmed Nasir, his birth name. He rarely used that. His favourite fake passport had cost him a fortune. A superb forger in Beirut had crafted an authentic-looking document bearing the name Abdul Moshi. He used that for most of his clandestine international travel. His other two passports carried the name Aamir Moshi, but they were nearing their expiry dates. That was troubling him at a time when pressures in Kenya were mounting.

Half of his next cigarette brought Moshi relaxation and further musings. He was not a nice person. He knew that. At various stages in his early life he had tried to be nice but he saw no profit in it. He was acquainted with – and had a grudging respect for – nice people, but pleasantness was not in his nature. Twice married, twice divorced, Moshi described the relationships thus: "One was a disaster, the other a nightmare." 'Devoted husband' would not have appeared on his resume. He realized then that he would live – and probably die – alone. The thought brought scant regret: he accepted that the chance of being dealt an ace was only one in thirteen. *Ha! Lucky thirteen.* But he had a fine appreciation for what a skillful manipulator could accomplish with the other cards in the hand.

An outspoken business associate had once suggested that he could achieve more of his purposes by being pleasant instead of consistently obnoxious. Moshi had responded with a foul expression he had not used since the gutter-days of his childhood in the slums. As he was reflecting on that, he caught sight of a colourful bird. He thought it was a cinnamon-chested bee-eater. They would catch a bee, then hit the insect on a branch. He wondered if it was to stun the bee or knock out the sting before swallowing it. Either way, it was an effective means of avoiding getting stung. He felt he would like to do that with some of his enemies. Then he realized several of them would love to do the same to him.

Several years previously, he had been forced to buy off the piece of scum who had been sent from Mwakindini to kill him. It cost him twice the amount the man claimed he had been promised. Moshi was attempting to pay off all his enemies. Two had yielded to the offers to get them off his back. *All this generosity is depleting my reserves!* he sniffed. He had sold a property in Mombasa and was preparing to let go of his Westlands flat in Nairobi. The pressure was mounting. Hence, it was vital that the Zoo, once again, supply some income for him.

He knew he was moderately intelligent, but he had received limited education. As a left-handed child, he had been beaten at school and forced to write with his right hand. He had honed his English-speaking skills through his multiple international contacts, but his reading and writing abilities in English were barely functional. Fortunately, he was clever enough to conceal this fact. It was sufficient for the business he was in. *Which was what, exactly?* he mused. *Biashara. Buying and selling. Ha! Yes, along with all the subtle deceptive manoeuvres associated with that trade.* But where had it all got him? *Trouble* was the first word in his mind. *But a lot of money too. And possessions.* Indeed, his possessions were a source of pride and comfort. "And risk?" he asked himself quietly. "True. And some of their value will need to be redeemed if the restless hounds keep pursuing me." By a round turn, his thoughts landed back on the current threats to his welfare and survival.

"Next birthday, I'll be 65," he muttered. Then he added the thought, *If I make it that long. Breathing is a constant challenge. I have no energy. I'm scared to have a chest x-ray. I can guess what it will show.* A year ago, an irritating neighbour had asked him how many cigarettes he smoked in a day. He gave forty as a guarded underestimate. The cheeky man had simply asked, "Is that all?" Since then, he developed what he called his 'half and twice' plan. He smoked half a cigarette instead of a whole one, and he spaced them out with twice the time between each one. That way, he reduced his consumption to a quarter. He had many weaknesses, but he was a tough individual when he was determined. Several adversaries had experienced the negative impact of that resolve.

For protection, Moshi relied on his two bodyguards. At least one of them was on duty the whole time; sometimes both accompanied him. As a trio, they trusted one another and would do anything that was required to maintain the operation of Moshi's affairs. Legality and morality were immaterial. The bodyguards worked well as a pair, with a fatalistic acceptance of each other's foibles. Moshi knew they were unconditionally devoted to his causes, and brutally willing to defend them. Moshi had rescued them both from harm and impoverishment in the Likoni backstreets and given them steady employment and rudimentary accommodation in the staff quarters of his north Mombasa mansion. The slow goon was built like a heavyweight boxer. He was mentally dull, openly chatty, and humourless. He had a fondness for small, defenceless animals and – much to Moshi's irritation – regularly carried home tiny kittens to feed. The other hulk was more intelligent, taciturn, and had a cunning capacity to anticipate and avoid threatening situations. When he hired him, Moshi told him, "I don't want a thug who will fight his way out of dangerous circumstances. I need a man who has enough brains to avoid trouble in the first place!" He was a quiet and careful driver, and heavily built enough to intimidate enemies and to protect Moshi against most threats. His only fault was his cache of pornographic magazines that he regularly refreshed with supplies from a friend – a customs agent at the airport who confiscated them from European tourists.

However, staff loyalty was not founded purely on altruism. Base self-interest dominated the relationships. Very early in his criminal career,

Moshi had recognized that his vulnerability extended to his own household. He had provided for that with an elaborate remuneration scheme for his two heavies, and the housekeeper and her slothful husband. The latter pair were a reticent old couple with an obscure past. He met them as devastated victims of a crooked associate's guile, and had built on their loyalty over the years. The man acted as a valet and gardener. He seemed to spend a third of his time raking leaves, a third washing and polishing the car, and the remainder emptying ashtrays. His wife did everything else, including cleaning, shopping, cooking, and laundry. In addition, she cleverly neutralized any irritants that might encroach upon Moshi's management of his nefarious international affairs. Her only flaw was an inability to stop complaining loudly about the smell of cat urine in their garden.

Moshi paid his staff well. They each received a third of their income monthly. That third was a modest sum – which kept at bay sponging relatives – but adequate for their needs, considering that he provided housing and food. A third of their remuneration was given as an annual bonus, accompanied by – frequently unheeded – advice on wise investment options. The remaining third, he accumulated for them in individual inheritance accounts. These were trust funds which increased in value each year, payable upon his natural death. A legal advisor had worked with life-insurance actuaries to include the provision that his premature death by intentional means would void the payout arrangements. Moshi had cleverly ensured that all his staff had a significant pecuniary interest in keeping him alive.

During the remainder of the journey, he half-dozed while continuing his reflections. Realistically, he was not sure if it would be cigarettes or a bullet that would mark his demise. He thought the cigarettes were most likely; but, on reflection, a quick bullet might be preferable. He could list half a dozen individuals who would be delighted to arrange the required projectile. But not yet! He had some things to accomplish first. The main one was to investigate the possibility of hidden treasure at the Zoo. That brought his thoughts to Brett James, the naive expat who had recently returned with his wife. He was one of the last people to see Miles Jolly alive. That fact offered tantalizing possibilities.

Ruefully, Moshi recalled the inconclusive contact with Miles through his agent in London. He had sent the stooge to have a gentle chat with Miles, but Miles had revealed nothing. Moshi concluded that a little interview with Brett could prove beneficial. Hence the trip to the Zoo. But it would need to be approached carefully as Brett was something of a riddle. What might be the most productive approach? In other words, in Moshi's praxis, where was Brett vulnerable? How might he be manipulated?

Careful reasoning had led Moshi to thoughts of religion. He had given no serious thought to religious matters for decades – other than the nominal strictures required by his Muslim faith. His father had been Muslim, and his mother followed the customary obligations of the tradition. But his maternal grandmother was a Christian and she had schooled the young Moshi in the basic tenets of her faith. He dutifully learned the terms and notions of Christianity which, with some fondness, he now recalled. Maybe it was time to dust off the half-forgotten concepts and try them out on Mr. and Mrs. James.

12

Moshi sensed that Brett would be open to further discussions, but a well-honed instrument would be required to pry information from him.

Approaching the Zoo, Moshi directed the driver to the guesthouse. He paid the taxi fare, including a more generous tip than his parsimonious nature normally permitted.

As the delighted driver pulled away, he said, "*Asante sana, Mzee Moshi.* Thank you very much, Mr. Moshi." Moshi watched the retreating taxi and, in spite of the warmth of the air, felt a chill down his spine as he tried to reason how the fellow could have known his name. It was deeply troubling. He asked a passing boy where Mr. Brett was staying and he was directed to the correct door.

Brett and Jane were relaxing after a swim, and enjoying the cooling fan in their tiny room. Brett was reading the newspaper while Jane updated her diary. It was a convenient time to hear a firm knock on the door and "*Hodi*" from outside. Brett was very surprised to see Moshi, but concealed his annoyance with the usual handshake and greetings, follow by a formal introduction to Jane. After cursory pleasantries, Moshi lunged straight to the point.

"When I invited you to join our administration team a few years ago, I knew you were a person of integrity." Brett smiled inwardly at the blatant irony of that statement, but he remained quiet. He shrugged slightly as Moshi continued: "So I was disappointed when you refused." He fumbled with a packet of cigarettes and took out the remaining half of one and lit it.

Brett thought, *Is he so poor now that he's smoking butts?* He said, "I was very busy with my teaching duties at that time and–"

"The offer is still open." Moshi gave a thin smile behind a cloud of smoke. "We could be partners during your time here. You would be my local contact at the Zoo." Brett looked towards Jane. Moshi noticed the glance, and quickly added, "You could both be contacts." Neither Brett nor Jane signalled any enthusiasm for that suggestion. Seeing this, Moshi quickly changed the subject.

"Did you see Miles Jolly in England?"

"Yes."

"How was my old colleague?"

"Okay, but very unwell at the end."

"Did my dear friend say much about me?"

"Very little."

"Did he mention the debt he owes me?"

"No." Brett was astonished by the question, recalling that Moshi had betrayed Miles which lead to his arrest and subsequent expulsion from Kenya.

"But you saw him at the end?"

"Yes."

"How close to – er –?"

"I was with him in his last hour."

"Did he say anything significant?" Jane looked aghast and Brett was uncomfortable.

"He was sedated. The staff warned me he might not make sense." It was Moshi's turn to shrug.

"I have found that deathbed revelations don't mean much. They cannot be trusted."

"Why would a person lie at that stage?" asked Jane.

Moshi pounced on the question: "Miles would lie at any stage! He spent his whole life lying." Brett was surprised at the vehemence of Moshi's response. He silently recalled the saying about the pot calling the kettle black. Moshi interrupted his thought with, "You know, we worked together quite a bit."

"Yes, I know."

"But I felt I could never fully trust him." Brett was silent. "And he probably warned you not to trust me." He studied Brett's expression. He read it accurately. "That would be true…before. But I have changed. I am following Christianity now." Noticing Brett's raised eyebrow, he added, "I have some knowledge because my grandmother taught me. She was a Christian." Brett expressed further surprise. "Yes, she guided me – all us children – in the basic principles. I respect them, although I have never been deeply religious myself."

Brett said, "I assumed you were Muslim."

"Well, yes, of course – in a cultural sense. Through my father. But I was never really…you know, fully committed. But…." He paused, subtle as the serpent, and continued, "But I have seen how you Christians behave, and I like it."

And there it was: the trap was set. Brett was unsure how to respond. Jane was as alert as a gazelle in the presence of a prowling lioness.

She said, "That's nice. We try to get along with everyone."

Unctuous to his script, Moshi said, "Yes, yes, you do. I feel a bond with you for that."

"But we Christians are sinners and have no righteousness of our own," she stressed.

Moshi was ready. "No, no, of course not. I understand that. We all need a saviour, don't we?"

During the next twenty minutes, Moshi elaborated on his respect for Christians, and peppered his sentences with *My Brother, Praise the Lord,* and *Amen.* He called Jane 'Sister' and managed a couple of incomplete scripture quotes. Brett was uncertain how to interpret it all. On the surface, obsequious Moshi appeared genuine; but Brett knew he would have heard Christians use those terms and could simply be mimicking them. Brett was uneasy; Jane wary. The conversation limped along awkwardly for another ten minutes. Near the end, Moshi sought some sympathy.

"You know, I had to spend two – nearly three – years in exile."

"Self-imposed, I believe," said Brett, daringly.

"I tell you honestly, my brother, those police, they were hounding me. I had no choice. I had to get away. There was no otherwise. That man Ponda–"

"Hasn't he stopped hounding you?"

"He has no other way. But now I am clean. I have reformed. He cannot touch me...." Brett had stopped listening to Moshi's ramblings. He had no intention of offering a sympathetic shoulder for any more of his crocodile tears.

One cultural nicety in Kenya that is different from the western style, is the acceptable way of indicating to a guest that it is time to leave. Knowing the custom, Brett gave a signal to Moshi.

"Well, thank you for visiting us, Mr. Moshi. It's been...." It was a relief to Brett and Jane when Moshi immediately stood to leave.

"Let's keep in touch. Nice to see you again, Brett, old chap. A pleasure to meet you, Mrs. James. I will be visiting again soon." Jane hid her disappointment as she shook his limp hand. Brett was noncommittal as Moshi walked out of the guesthouse.

After the encounter, Jane said, "What a smarmy man, with his floppy handshake!"

"Now, now. That's not a nice way to speak of a fellow Christian."

"A Christian! My foot!"

"He had all the right words."

"Huh, anyone can use the right words!"

"You're ruthless, Jane!"

"What narrow, squinting eyes he has. I'm curious, is Moshi his only name?"

"As far as I know, yes."

"Just a single name?"

"Apparently."

"You know, I hate to say it, but he makes me feel very uneasy."

"Welcome to the crowd!"

As he left the guesthouse, Moshi looked at the pickup parked beside the steps. He noticed the name on the side, and his mind registered the fact that it was not Brett James. Briefly, he wondered if that might cause difficulties for them if they were stopped by the police, as the name would not match their driving licences. As he walked slowly into the sunshine,

Moshi thought, *I also have another card to play: Larry Smythe. But not now. I need a rest, and time to think this through.*

He had to get a message to Larry. But discreetly. *Through the church? No. The clinic? Maybe. Let's see who's on duty.* He found a young nurse whom he did not recognize and politely asked for some paper. He instructed her to have the note delivered to the Energy Conservation Project on the other side of the compound. Then he did an extremely rare thing: he climbed into a public *matatu* and travelled into Mwakindini. *Never again!* he told himself later, as he gratefully extricated his crumpled and offended body from the noisy minibus. He found a cheap hotel room where he assumed no one would recognize him and lay down on the uncomfortable, lumpy bed, below an inefficient ceiling fan.

Moshi sensed that Brett would be open to further discussions, but a well-honed instrument would be required to pry information from him. His instinct warned that Jane may obstruct any manipulation he might attempt. Moshi thought, *Integrity. It's a two-way street.* He saw no value in it for himself, but he'd occasionally exploited the childlike integrity of others. Perhaps there would be opportunities with Brett.

Late that afternoon, Brett and Jane walked on the southern beach to watch the sunset. The receding tide left the sand firm, and they met several other people ambling along the same narrow band where it was comfortable to walk. Three old women were gathering *kuni,* scraps of wood, that the tide had deposited in a long twisting row. Brett and Jane stepped carefully around the discarded coconut shells hidden among the seaweed. A person could twist an ankle on those. The sand was warm on their feet. They looked towards the hills silhouetted by the lowering sun's supernal glow as they discussed the encounter with Moshi.

Brett concluded, "He seems genuine, but I'm still not sure if I can trust him." Jane was sceptical.

"Remember, Miles told you not to trust him."

"But Moshi appears to have a good understanding of Christian doctrine."

"Knowledge doesn't equate to faith – or sincerity even."

"So, we have Moshi's word against Miles'."

"If I were a gambler, which – as you know – I'm not, I'd put my money on Miles over Moshi any day of the week!"

"Let's walk over to the dock shall we? I'll see what happens with Moshi. I'll play along with him for a while."

"Be careful. My instinct warns me that involvement with Moshi could spell danger."

"But he was very polite – even uncharacteristically gracious – when he met you."

"That's what I found unsettling! Trust my judgement, Brett. You don't need to get tangled up with him and his shenanigans."

"I'm already involved. I need to follow this path a while longer."

"Why?" They were standing on the dock enjoying the gentle shimmering of the water's surface. In silence, they appreciated the deepening red of the sky behind the coastal hills.

At last, Brett spoke. "Hmm...a difficult question. Partly curiosity, I admit; but I also feel a sense of commitment."

"To whom?"

"Oh, Miles. Peter Lancaster. Even Boniface Chengo in a way. Also Louise."

"You are too attracted to mystery, my dear. But I can understand your loyalty to Louise. I'll support you as you know this society better than I do. But my advice is: be careful."

He waved his arm in an arc. "I think that phrase has many echoes from earlier warnings bouncing off the palm trees in this place!"

As they walked back, Brett asked Jane's impressions of the Zoo. She told him she had found the Kenyans were reserved, but friendly. When she initiated greetings, or brief chats, they responded warmly.

She asked a question. "I keep meaning to ask, what's that word I hear, *mzungus*? Is that us?"

"*Wazungu* is the correct plural of *mzungu* – a white person – but we tend to say *mzungus* among ourselves. We anglicize it."

"So, *wa-* is the prefix for plurals. What is the singular form?"

"*M*, as in *mzungu*, or *mzee* for one old man. What would be the Swahili word for respected old men?"

"*Wa-* something. *Wazee?*"

"Great. You're sharp."

"Thanks. My knowledge of Swahili has just tripled in the last ten seconds!"

They turned and looked along the beach at the timeworn walls and partly ruined structure of the mosque. They savoured the soft glow on the ancient coral blocks and the gentle breeze whispering among the palm branches above them.

13

At the core of their dealings was stealth and disdain, but Larry had earned a modicum of respect in Moshi's hierarchy of distrust.

Moshi awoke from his afternoon doze to a jumble of thoughts, and hunger. A small kiosk next door supplied a drink and a snack. Later that evening, the solitude of his squalid room afforded another opportunity to think. Something reminded him of his childhood again. It may have been a cooking aroma – perhaps a spice ingredient his mother had used. The nostalgia was enhanced by a whiff of bad drains drifting in through the open window. The smells triggered a cascade of memories, as aromas often do.

Having slept in the afternoon, he was unable to drop off at his usual time. That annoyed him. He heard sounds from a nearby bar, but that held no appeal. A fleeting idea about finding a gambling den was rapidly dismissed, but it did prompt some interesting recollections. He used to gamble. He fooled himself into thinking he made money at it. Selective recall of the times when he won obscured what he suspected to be true: overall, he had lost. He had used his experiences to analyse what was happening. This led him to a permanent resolve to gamble only very small amounts, and stop then, whatever the outcome.

The strategy worked for many years, giving him a small measure of satisfaction, some companionship, and a little excitement. He did a lot of research and concluded that the only game that might give a fair chance of breaking even in the long run was blackjack, so that became his game of choice. Then, during an enforced stay in The Seychelles, he met a British statistician on holiday. Moshi was extolling the virtues of 21 when the mathematician confirmed that, with blackjack, there can be bets with unusual positive gains. Hence, some individuals have experienced high winnings. But he went on to explain the numbers and the strategies used by casinos. His conclusion was: you may win a bit but, basically, when you gamble, you lose. The more you play, the more you lose. Moshi countered by accusing the man of missing the point, with his cold numerical analysis. Players enjoy the environment, the action, and the thrill of a chance at winning big against adverse odds.

However, the exchange stuck with Moshi and he eventually realized it was a fool's game, so he quit and never gambled again. In recent weeks, he had been so desperate to obtain funds to appease his persecutors that he contemplated investing a few hundred shillings, trusting that his old luck would return – if it ever really existed. But his firm resolve to stay away from gambling of any kind held strong. He had analysed it too much to go back now. He was amused that the memories of it were swirling in his brain once again, but reprocessing the arguments helped him stave off the longing for another cigarette which was not due for thirty-five more minutes.

Then another train of reverie occupied him. He recalled the conversation with Brett and Jane. Something troubled him, but he could not pinpoint it. They had been polite – even kind – when he had spoken to them. Their innocent response to his unexpected visit seemed to contrast with his conniving strategies. *So what?* he thought. *That's the way things are. I have needs: Brett could provide help.* But there was a lack of conviction in his rationalizations. Recollections of his grandmother's Christian teaching, and his quoting of a few half-remembered phrases, had brought other images. Several Bible verses came to mind, and the unfamiliar theory that he was loved by God and – what was it? – Jesus was knocking at the door of his heart, or some such notion. Curious, the way strange ideas come just as one falls asleep…Jesus is the Son of God – whatever that means. It sounded blasphemous to his ears. But he thought again of Jesus and His will that none should be lost….

When the morning light and the howls of a pye-dog outside his window woke him, Moshi was astonished that he had slept solidly all night. That never happened. Then he was jolted by the realization that he had not needed his essential night-time cigarette.

He asked the half-awake desk clerk where he could get a taxi later. The nearby snack bar provided him with coffee, *mandazis*, and eggs. As he left the cafe, he bumped into a ragged fellow who smiled and shook his hand. It was the crook who three years earlier had been sent to kill him. He had paid him so well to change his mind that the young man greeted him like an old friend. Moshi recalled his name: Kuvanza. He looked surprised to see Moshi alone in that location. Moshi noticed, with distaste, the tufts of uneven stubble on the man's face, until he realized that he too probably looked unkempt. After a brief chat, Moshi – ever the scheming strategist – saw some benefit in having a heartless contact in Mwakindini, so he made a note of where Kuvanza could be located. Then he found a taxi and rode back to the Zoo.

On the short journey, his reflections centred on Larry Smythe, an irascible but functionally useful fellow. Their partnership – he knew neither of them would describe it as a friendship – had begun several decades previously. Moshi did not trust women, with the possible exception of Louise, and he did not particularly like most men. The only people he respected had been Miles and Larry. He trusted them to an extent, as they did him, but warily and according to the rules of the bitter game under which they all operated. At the core of their dealings was stealth and disdain, but Larry had earned a modicum of respect in Moshi's hierarchy of distrust.

It had begun at Lake Martroni. Larry was in middle management at the soda extraction mine which was located on the road between Nairobi and the Tanzanian border. The rail connection to Mombasa was also an asset for Moshi's schemes. Moshi had business contacts who occasionally required a safe holding facility in Kenya for goods – and sometimes people. The mine site could provide that, Moshi reasoned, if he had a reliable and discreet partner there.

He had wangled a tour of the plant and used it as an opportunity to sniff around for a conveniently placed agent. It took several informal and cautious chats with workers before Larry's name had been mentioned three times.

One fellow told Moshi, "Stay clear of him. He thinks all animal and human problems can be resolved with a clout behind the ear or a gunshot."

The muted accounts of Larry's sly belligerence, coupled with his strategic position at the plant, caught the attention of Moshi's sharp ears. He found himself drawn to Larry Smythe.

In the evening, after supper, the relationship was established with two handshakes: one a perfunctory gesture above the table and – more significantly – another below the table. A wad of notes slid across, and the alliance was formed. That bond had lasted through the years, right up to the moment when Moshi stepped out of the taxi and walked across to the Energy Conservation Centre and told the assistant to bring Larry to the front door.

After the meeting with Larry, a taxi took Moshi from the Zoo back into Mwakindini. He intended to catch a bus back to Mombasa, hoping the experience would not be too disagreeable. Len Moore saw Larry returning from the central buildings, having escorted Moshi to find a taxi, but with twenty paces separating them to avoid any obvious connection. Larry was smiling as he walked towards Len. Moshi had promised Larry a generous gift in lieu of interest on a loan he needed.

Len said, "Hello Larry. You look like a dog with two tails!"

Larry warned, "You won't use that expression with Africans, will you? They don't appreciate any comparison…you know, with dogs. Even in jest."

"No, I know that, my friend. I didn't arrive here yesterday! But thanks for the reminder. We can sometimes let things slip in an unguarded moment. But you do look pleased with yourself."

"Do I? Well, I cannot reveal details…but, as I often say 'A stitch in time is worth two in the bush'."

"I'm sure you're right on that," laughed Len.

"Well, I've just demonstrated…you know, how clever I am. An old associate may be very helpful to a penniless waif like me."

They parted, smiling. Len was simply happy to see Larry without his customary scowl.

Moshi, for his part, was also pleased with the discussion. But for a different reason. He had buttered up Larry with fake compliments and implied future lucrative activities. In the interim, he had extracted a short-term loan from Larry to satisfy one of his pursuers for a few weeks. He had also instructed Larry to be on the lookout for any carelessly guarded guns in the Zoo. More importantly, Larry had given his assurance that the Energy Conservation facilities had space for three people to stay overnight if necessary, although no one need know about it. Moshi thought, *Larry has always understood the value of discretion.*

Unfortunately, Moshi failed to realize that his convoluted manner of speaking, pitted against Larry's clipped verbal style, led each to come to vastly different conclusions over what was agreed. Moshi was convinced that Larry had committed to assisting with nefarious plans, while Larry saw the meeting as merely an opportunity to ease Moshi's temporary cashflow difficulty and, later, extract some much-needed cash from the wealthy underworld boss.

Louise Emerson generally avoided speaking with Larry Smythe as she did not appreciate his acerbic tone. Apart from his water installations and plumbing equipment, he seemed ignorant of most other topics.

Coreene Brandon had once admitted to Louise, "Larry appears devious – kind of shifty."

Louise replied, "Yes, he's wily and abrupt. I find him uncouth."

Smiling, Coreene admitted, "I don't mean to sound rude, and I do enjoy some of his mixed-up cliches, oh, and his snappy remarks like 'So, what's yer point?' I love the way he speaks. You know, with short sentences." They both laughed, each feeling guilty joking about Larry.

To her chagrin, on the day following Moshi's visit to the Zoo, Louise found herself sitting with Larry in the cafe. The other customers had left and Louise was waiting for the Financial Officer to bring the letters from Mwakindini before struggling up her stairs again. Larry spoke about the English naturalist working in the Emersons' research station on Monkey Island.

"Seems a capable chap. Got a good setup over there...."

"Yes. We've rebuilt the front hut and the little dwelling at the back. He's picked up some of Henry's earlier work with the monkeys."

"Got a few funds?"

"There's a conservation foundation that covers many of the expenses."

"I was wondering, if he feels.... You know...there could be dangers?"

"Not really. Very few people go there."

"He 'ave a gun?"

"He has a gun for protection when he's–"

"What gun's he got?"

"He'd take his Merkel. I imagine you know about firearms–"

"So, what's yer point?"

"I mean, from your many years in Kenya," she said.

"Oh. Yeh. A bit."

"I happen to know the details. Henry told me a lot about guns."

"He'll have a rifle...no point in–"

"He has a light-weight solution to be able to deal with anything that crops up."

"Bush pigs, I suppose?"

"Mainly. Plus any aggravated male monkeys."

"Need something about three kilos. Lugging it through the undergrowth. So, what gun's he use?"

"A Merkel triple barrel. It's convenient to carry and deploy," said Louise.

"We used to call it the Forester's Gun. A clever invention, with the *Drilling* configuration."

"Oh, yes, I remember. *Drilling*. That's the German word for the three chambers. I speak German, you know," Louise told him. She surprised herself at how friendly she was sounding.

"Me too. Learned it."

"That's interesting."

"In my business...don't want yer international customers...they'd sometimes speak behind yer back."

"When?"

"At the plant."

"Lake Martroni?"

"And before." He stared vacantly into the distance. "But that's a white elephant in the room."

Mystified, Louise said, "You're very knowledgeable, Mr. Smythe."

"I'm not just a pretty face! Call me Larry, by the way."

"Yes, thank you, Larry. Well, it's been nice–"

"He should be okay over there…with that gun."

"That's comforting."

"He got a permit? A local licence, I suppose."

"Of course."

"Lucky him."

"Naturally, he would have a permit." Her tone may have conveyed resentment at the implication that he did not have one.

"Yes, Captain!" said Larry, giving a mock salute.

Louise smiled and said, "Ha, I was a Captain. But I prefer to be thought of as a Nursing Sister." Larry ignored her and continued his thoughts.

"I'd choose two 12g chambers and load them…one with bird shot and the other with buck shot. Allows you to match the threat…even fire them in succession. If the first didn't deter."

"Really?"

"With the rifle barrel chambered 9.3x74RS, you could stop anything. Including a charging bush pig."

Louise laughed, "Oh, I prefer a walking stick when I go over there! That's not very often these days."

"Don't risk it…. Best, you know…not take any chances."

"To be honest, Mr. Smythe – Larry – I often wonder if these weapons are more of a danger in themselves. You know, thieves have been known to rob just to get the gun."

"You don't need to tell me. Had that situation me-self. At the plant."

"Really? I'm sorry." Larry thought, in silence. Then he asked another direct question.

"Where's he keep 'is ammunition? Gun's no use without it."

"It's safe in the underground vault in his small hut. In a metal box." Immediately she said that, Louise regretted it. So she quickly added, "At least, that what I *think* he said a while ago. It's probably changed now."

"Ammo needs to be kept somewhere cool."

"And safe." She was feeling tired and wished the post would arrive. Larry looked at her.

"You okay?"

"Yes, thank you. I'm dealing with lymphoma, that's all."

"Sorry."

"Thanks. I just take one day at a time."

"The only way."

Larry stood and moved towards the corridor.

"Letters should be here by now. Thanks for the chat."

She called after him, "In any case, it's all academic – about the gun and everything – as he's over in Eastern Uganda at the moment, checking for genetic matches in the wild monkey populations there."

As Larry wandered away, Louise was starting to revise her opinion of him. Reflecting on his sapient manner, she thought perhaps she had underestimated him. For his part, Larry was thinking, *A smart lady, that one. I wonder if the conservationist took the gun with him to Uganda. Probably not.*

Len Moore had recovered from his disappointment over the collapse of his experimental tidal energy-generating installation years previously. Recently, his ideas had been vindicated by the overseas funding of the conservation project, and Larry Smythe's assistance had encouraged him enormously. He talked to anyone who would show an interest in his latest proposal to install solar-collecting pipes alongside the main water tower. That day, it was a group in the cafe.

"It could be a double spiral for stability. Like the DNA helix. You see, the temperature gradient in a column of water is such that hot water can be tapped off at various levels. The water at the top of the column gets very hot. That's useful."

One customer voiced his opinion. "I fail to understand how this new project is going to be any more successful than your first attempt."

Undeterred, Len responded, "Well thanks for your universal and enthusiastic support! Anyone else got any encouragement?" Nobody raised any specific objection to his proposal, which Len interpreted as an overwhelming endorsement. Such was his positive nature. The group started to disperse but Brett and Jane remained and continued chatting with Len.

"So what's the main idea behind all this, Len?" asked Jane.

"Independent, self-sustaining mechanisms are my aim," replied Len. "I appreciate the simplicity of unsophisticated machines. I like the idea of a natural process which we can harness for our benefit. I know we can accomplish a lot with technology and power, but there's deep satisfaction in utilizing ordinary mechanisms in a self-sustaining manner – especially if they operate with no external inputs of energy, fuel, or money – like my tide-power installation and wind-generating station."

Jane was impressed by Len's reasoning, and Brett later told her he had always respected the logic and commitment Len brought to his conservation projects.

14

In fact, you could stay over there if you feel like a break from the Zoo. It's very peaceful and secure, with access to a lovely private beach."
Louise Emerson

Brett and Jane drove Louise to Malindi as they all wanted to visit the Safari Club hotel. On the journey, Louise described the developments with Henry's research.

"I'm pleased that a naturalist from a British university is working in the old facility."

"All on his own?" asked Brett.

"Yes. You know how conservationists like to be in the wild with their animals. Henry's original research station is still there with all of his materials. That's the building to the east of the compound that we searched, Brett, remember? Since then, we have rebuilt the two residential huts."

"With the connecting tunnel?" asked Brett. He was waiting for an opportunity to mention the map to Louise. She described the rebuilding of the huts.

"Yes. We made them very strong. They are well constructed of stone for security. They have small windows and heavy bars, with strong doors and locks. The whole area is becoming more open than previously, with a greater number of people having access there."

"Where does the naturalist live?"

"He stays in the upper hut, and the one closer to the sea is used for guests. Sometimes a professor joins him, or Dr. Phillips occasionally spends a couple of nights in the front cottage."

"John Phillips?"

"Yes. He's on the Board at the Zoo and likes the solitude over there during his visits. He knows the naturalist from long ago."

"What are they researching?" asked Jane.

"The naturalist stealthily spies on the monkeys from his sylvan hideaway. Mostly, he investigates monkey scat I think, while Dr. Phillips quietly examines the rocks."

"It must make for some exciting after-dinner conversations!" said Brett.

Jane said, "Like: I found an interesting rock today..."

"...but that's nothing compared to what I discovered – a semi-digested seed pod," added Brett.

Jane said, "You can just imagine it, eh?" Louise was laughing so hard that she started to cough. "Are you alright?" asked Jane. Louise waved her hand, smiled, and continued coughing.

When she had recovered, she said, "The stars are incredibly clear over there, with no artificial light. Henry and I used to see Scorpius overhead with the red giant Antares. Jupiter was sometimes brilliant: 'Jove's planet rising yonder' or however Shakespeare expressed it. Also distinctive Orion was on display and occasionally the Southern Cross above the low horizon."

"Sounds stunning. What exactly is the naturalist studying?" Jane asked.

"He's picked up Henry's earlier work with the groups of resident monkeys. I am so pleased. There appears to be a chromosomal similarity with several troops on the Kenya-Uganda border. He'll be away, out west, quite a bit in the next few months so you may not meet him. In fact, you could stay over there if you feel like a break from the Zoo. It's very peaceful and secure, with access to a lovely private beach."

Brett was enthusiastic. "That would be amazing. You know, Jane, we can observe many southern constellations that we'd never see in England. Also, the planets along the ecliptic are well defined."

"What would we do?" asked Jane. "Just relax?" The idea was sounding appealing.

"Yes. Just take a break in a unique environment."

"But what about cooking...you know, supplies and–"

"One of my girls, Fatima, could come over during the day to help. She would welcome the change from dealing with all my problems! She's a resourceful woman. She'll do all the organizing you need. There's cooking propane and kerosene lamps. Anyway, think about it."

"It would be wonderful, thanks," said Brett.

"I wish I could join you. Maybe, one day I could go over with you. I haven't been along there for ages."

Brett asked, "What about access? The main door is locked."

Louise told them the naturalist had his own key, and then reminded Brett about the large key hanging on a hook by her front door.

"That's the key to the door below Kismet Kantara, our 'arch of destiny' built into the ancient wall. Mjuhgiuna knows about it. Fatima will use that key and she'll explain how to find the key to the hut. She's very practical and communicates well. I'm using her more nowadays to run errands for me, like picking up my medications from the clinic when I don't feel like driving."

At the hotel, Louise made enquiries about renting a suite with an adjacent room for her other maid, Shafiqah. She explained that she wanted to test the arrangement for the future. Shafiqah was working on dressmaking, but Louise had also trained her in medical support services as she was thoughtful and gentle. After making the enquiries at the hotel, Louise suggested they go to the Frangipani Terrace for lunch. Brett and Louise were excited to see Jane's awed reaction to the beauty there. During the meal, Louise answered Jane's questions about Henry and their early years in Kenya. Louise enjoyed reliving some of her recollections.

"I have many happy memories. Did I tell you, Brett, that Heinrick used to call me *Vogel*, his little bird."

"Not Zephyr?"

"No, that came later. I was Vogel. I never particularly liked being called a bird but he meant it well – and affectionately," she laughed.

"And you would accompany him as part of his disguise – a typical married couple in Europe?" asked Jane, recalling what Brett had told her.

"Yes, but completely innocently as I had little idea of what was going on."

"Really? Were you kept totally in the dark?"

"Yes. And I knew better than to ask for details. The stage props like coats and shoes don't ask the actor to explain the character or the plot of the play, do they?" They laughed. Louise smiled, and then became serious. "Thinking of myself as Vogel, reminds me that a bird can sometimes be held in a cage."

"Like the cages in the Zoo?"

"No. One can be caged in other ways."

While waiting for coffee and dessert, they stood by the low wall on the cliff, overlooking the coast. Pointing beyond the reef to the Indian Ocean, Louise described some of the history of the region.

"Dating back to the late nineteenth century, there were German influences in Tanzania to the south by the Una River and north of the Tana River in Kenya. Later treaties redistributed the control." As they returned to their table, Jane's question interested Louise.

"How would you describe Henry – physically?"

"Medium height, medium build. Grey hair – medium grey! Average in everything except intelligence. In a group he'd be almost invisible. He'd blend in the background like a piece of furniture. He'd simply look, listen, and remember. If he couldn't overhear what was being said, he'd watch how people stood and interacted." Louise was relaxed, and the memories flowed back. Brett and Jane were happy to enjoy that splendid place and listen to her reminisce. "During the 1950s, Henry and I had wonderful times in Europe."

Jane was anxious to hear more about Louise and Henry's espionage activities. Louise explained that Henry did not refer to it as espionage, but simply careful observation. She described several trips in the 1950s and 1960s. Later, they had revisited some places after retirement. She recounted one memorable holiday in Germany.

"It was in the early seventies in Ulm on the Danube. The cathedral, Ulm Münster, has the highest church steeple in the world, you know. We attended a wonderful concert in the cathedral – an orchestral programme...." She suddenly stopped speaking and frowned. "I've just remembered something. For some reason we left during the first intermission. We found our way across town while Heinrick kept checking his watch. We met an old man. What was his name? Oh yes, Bergmann. Man from the mountains. Karl Bergmann. Ha! He wasn't much of a mountain man when I saw him. He was barely alive as far as I could tell. He was there with his daughter. He referred to me as *Vogel*. Only Heinrick called me that so I assumed those two had an extremely close relationship. I disliked the name, so I pretended not to have heard. However, it added to the mystery and tension of that encounter." Louise's tone was serious and her recollections bemused as they came to her at random. "It was a weird visit – that dark evening in Ulm. Heinrick had the address. From the cathedral, we walked over to Bergmann's home. It was one of those tall tenement style, sombre buildings. The lift was a grill cage with scissor gates. You know, where you press a buzzer and the person lets you in and you operate the two sets of metal sliding gates. We arrived on a dark landing and rang their apartment bell. A dour housekeeper ushered us into a cold reception room. We waited for about ten minutes until a sick man was wheeled in, wrapped in a thick blanket. Heinrick introduced him as Herr Bergmann. I felt uneasy with him. He had strange eyes – the way he looked at me. Not unkindly but.... He was very frail. After formal introductions in German, the two men began speaking in a local dialect, with his daughter too. I thought it was deliberately to exclude me."

"Why?" asked Brett.

"I didn't know at the time; but I recognized that they were using colloquialisms and slang that I was not familiar with. Still, I caught the gist of their discussion. When the old man realized I was listening, he motioned to his daughter and she pretended to want to show me something in the kitchen. We fiddled around with English bone china and some antique cutlery, just to divert me I thought. When we returned, the two men were finishing their discussion. I heard snatches of Bergmann's final words: '... swastika I scratched on the wall...a meaningful symbol for us both...never return to East Africa. The diamonds are yours...I owe you so much, my friend...I will never need them. We have all we....'

"After the meeting, Heinrick was perturbed and remote. Later, he told me that, as a young man, Bergmann had worked with his father in the German steel-fabricating factory. He respected Heinrick's father and was devastated by his accidental death. After the war, Heinrick had helped Bergmann escape from Tanzania through Kenya. He made it across the Zoo headland to a ship heading for Egypt."

"Through CPZ-Store?" asked Brett.

Louise nodded. "I never saw him, but I learned later that he was one of the people who stayed for several days, hidden in there."

"Was Henry sympathetic to the Nazis?"

"No, but he probably gave Bergmann that impression. I once told you, Brett, Heinrick was a chameleon, adapting to match the people he dealt with."

"Wow! What a story," exclaimed Jane.

Louise smiled. "He told me to forget the whole evening and anything I had heard. It was all in the past and settled."

While the trio continued their after-lunch discussion, a few kilometres away Inspector Ponda and Detective Ochieng were meeting in Ponda's Malindi office.

"But how are we able to trace Moshi's movements so accurately?" Ochieng asked as he sat timidly in front of the inspector's huge desk. Then he thought, *And why are we bothering to this extent?* The big man smiled and then responded seriously.

"We have helpful agents at the ports."

"But he's so secretive–"

"So are we!"

"Yes, sir. But it's been a long time since–"

"Good police work needs time," Ponda interrupted, thinking, *Why does this little fellow start every sentence with But?* "We have set in place groundwork to follow Moshi's travels. We know some of the names he uses on his false passports." He paused. He studied Ochieng, hunched before him, and recalled the effective work they had done together over the years. "Your promotion to Western Kenya has been approved, Bwana Ochieng. You will be leaving us soon, so I wanted to give you an update on the investigations in the Mwakindini Zoo and over on *Kisiwa Wa Kima,* Monkey Island." Ochieng leaned forward slightly. He blinked and thought, *I could give you an update. That is my area of investigation.*

Ponda continued speaking. "I am in communication with a man in the government here in Malindi. He deals with immigration and transport matters. We share information."

"Share information? With some risks, perhaps."

"Of course! I understand the risks. Information he gives me helps us... in our investigations." He stopped and watched Ochieng process his remark and continued, "At the airports, we have cooperative staff in important positions. There-down in Mombasa, an officer in Customs supplies Moshi's streetwise driver with dirty books. That gives him regular contact with the other bodyguard – the brainless oaf – who carelessly reveals a lot, hardly knowing what he's saying–"

Ochieng nodded, "I know both men."

Ponda hated to be interrupted. He glared at Ochieng, but then his mood eased. The two policemen had a tense but professional relationship, so Ponda felt comfortable sharing more.

"I do not want to lose track of Moshi as we did two years ago when he outwitted us. We have covered all the transport sectors. His picture has been circulated discreetly among selected bus and car-hire companies. Oh, travel agents and taxis too. We have a good idea of his location at most times. But very quietly. He does not suspect."

"I have heard the *wazungu* say 'Give him enough rope and–"

"...and he will hang himself'," Ponda completed the saying. For a brief moment of mutual confidence, the two officers shared a smile. The fleeting warmth encouraged Ochieng.

"But, if there is anything more I can do...."

"There will be. Before you leave, I need your sharp eyes in and around the Zoo. Moshi has interests there. Our officer on Biashara Street in Mombasa overheard a whisper about gold coins, and he thinks he heard 'gems'. I recall a rumour from years ago about diamonds."

"You remember well, sir,"

"I remember everything, detective!" Ochieng nodded admiringly.

"Yes sir, you do."

"Stay in touch with the people who trust you. Follow the James couple while they are there. Also, I am uncomfortable with that technician from Lake Martroni, Smythe."

"Larry Smythe?"

"Yes. He's deceitful and insulting when he deals with Sergeant Kinyanjui from our Mwakindini detachment. There's nothing definite, but we are uneasy about him. Keep a close watch for guns."

"Ahh, that is your area of speciality, sir."

"You're right. My early training taught me about many types of handguns. Your skills are in careful observation, detective. See what you can find out. Put on your swimming trunks and wander along the beach beside that energy set up they have there." He suppressed a snicker at the image that his suggestion presented in his mind. Ochieng noticed the twitch of Ponda's lips and laughed too.

"But that is not my familiar style of investigation, sir."

"Broaden your repertoire, Bwana! You will need many tricks when you return to the Western Province and have to deal with your own people again. They will not be as tolerant of you as we have been here at the coast!"

And so the meeting ended on a high note. But neither man felt the ease and confidence they displayed superficially. Moshi was still at large, and was probably getting desperate. That could be dangerous.

As Ponda watched Ochieng leave his office, he suddenly resolved to do something. Although he respected Ochieng as a capable investigator, he was not sure how committed he still was to this case, given his pending relocation. He decided to pay a visit to the Zoo himself within the next few days.

15

"I seem to be getting hardened to the reality of all the disasters and suffering here. I wonder if I'm becoming callous. That's what's bothering me now."
Coreene Brandon

After returning from Malindi, that evening Brett took Jane for a walk through the central gardens to show her his former cage, N-12, and the northern beach in front. They had previously driven around briefly, but walking gave them more opportunities to meet people. Looking out across the Northern Bay, they saw the white waves breaking across the fringing reef.

As they walked, Jane said, "I noticed Louise uses two names for Henry."

"Yes, she'll switch between them without realizing. Henry and Heinrick." Suddenly a bird swooped and rolled past them.

"What's that?" said Jane.

"A lilac-breasted roller. They have a rolling motion in flight. Once, an ornithologist on a bird walk told me he had seen one roll over completely and continue flying."

"I was thinking...did you pick up Louise's brief mention of diamonds when they were in Germany?"

"Yes. Interesting, but I doubt if it's significant."

"But someone else referred to diamonds too. Miles?"

"No. He never said anything about diamonds, just to see Mathert–"

"Julie!"

"That's right! Julie Lancaster. In her letter to her father that she read to us." He was excited.

"She wrote something about 'save some for her'...."

"Jane, you're brilliant! What did she write, and why?"

"I think it was linked to...it must have been referring back to something Peter had written. I wish she had kept his letters to her!" she said.

"She showed me one, but it's none of our business. But I agree–"

"How are you my friends?" called out a lady working in her garden.

"Fine. And you?"

"Just fine. *Asante*. Thank you." They both smiled and waved. They resumed their conversation.

"Didn't Miles say something significant that Henry spoke about before he died?" asked Jane.

"Yes. Just before he was suddenly killed near the ranch."

"Someone else said that."

"Vi? No, hang on, it was written in Thomas' dairy. I remember, he noted that he'd talked with Henry." They had strolled past Brett's old cage and were on the beach. "Let's walk up to the fence. We can see the new Conservation Project up against the wall. They are using the Ridge-Taylors' former place for equipment and the cage at the back, N-3 near the street, as an office. Larry Smythe lives in N-2 by the shore. He's a crusty old fellow, but pretty good at his job, according to Len."

"So, where were we? Oh yes, Thomas' diary."

"Did you see the entry there?" Brett asked.

"Sorry, I don't remember. But there was a drawing of a swastika."

"Yes. A clear swastika. Vi said it was because he'd fought the Germans. But he'd written 'The middle'."

"So, what's it all mean?"

"Search me, I've got no idea."

They walked beside the wall. Brett pointed out the fake security cameras and the place where he had climbed over in his first year, and the trouble his escapade had caused.

"Let's go over to the cafe for a drink."

Jane was still puzzled. "What did Miles say about a swastika?"

"He said Henry told him to look in the centre of the swastika if he died."

"Look in the centre? Why two references to that? What swastika? A flag–"

Brett gasped, "No! I've got it! I told you I had to disguise an impression of a swastika scratched on the wall in the hiding place? CPK-Store. Henry drew it, much to Louise's embarrassment."

"So, he could have been referring to that?"

"But Louise told us she heard the old man – 'mountain man' in Ulm – say *he* scratched the swastika."

"Yes, Bergmann."

In unison they said, "The middle of the swastika!"

"Do you remember seeing anything in the centre?" she asked.

"I didn't notice anything."

"Do you think Louise would mind if we had a look?"

"No point, it's all covered over now."

"Might be worth a try."

"Okay, I'll ask her. But not tonight. Let her recover from today's excitement for a while."

Two of the mathematics teachers at the polytechnic were grateful for Brett's offer to help some students who needed remedial instruction. On Friday afternoon he met to review with them how he might volunteer during February and March. After the meeting, Brett called in to see Steve. He found him at home, writing letters. They were just settling down with a cup of tea when Coreene came in with their daughter, Ruth. They both looked very upset. The boys had stayed outside to play. Ruth went straight to her room.

Coreene said, "We saw a terrible accident."

"Sit down, dear," said Steve. "I'll get you some tea. What happened?" Coreene was extremely distressed as she described her experience.

As she had left the Zoo, she was annoyed that the mock Englishman *duka*-owner had delayed her at the Zoo entrance, with his waving and asking where she was going. She was late and resented the diversion, although she admitted it took less than a minute. As she was driving to Malindi to pick up Ruth, Andrew, and Graham from an after-school event, a *matatu* kept overtaking her dangerously, suddenly stopping in front of her to collect passengers while she passed, and then roaring up behind to overtake again.

Steve and Brett nodded as they had also experienced the same reckless *matatu* drivers.

"Unfortunately, many of them are high on bhang or *miraa,*" said Steve.

She continued, "You know that quiet section through the forest – where there's the rock face on the right? The road was deserted, and suddenly I saw two *matatu* minivans side-by-side both smashed into the rocks. Everything was completely silent, with no other vehicles around, so obviously it had just happened – a few seconds before. I didn't stop because…well, because my instinct kicked in and I knew I had to pick up the children. I felt bad driving past but I knew there would be nothing I could do to help…you know, not having plastic gloves or much idea of dealing with serious injuries, especially with my weak back. I recalled the horrors of my car accident. I just prayed that no one was seriously hurt. I hoped the vans were empty of passengers."

"That's pretty unlikely. *Matatus* are always overloaded with people."

"Yes, I realized that. Also, there's always the fear of being vulnerable to theft or attack if I stopped…I don't know what I felt!"

"What happened then?" asked Steve, gently.

"I explained to Ruth and the boys what I'd seen, but I had no idea what we'd encounter on the way back. It was about half an hour later when we had to stop because the line of cars heading north had slowed down where the accident was. Two policemen were directing the traffic around a chaotic scene. Many vehicles were pulled over but we were waved on and not allowed to stop. I saw the back and side doors of the wrecked vans open with people still inside. I have no idea how the vans got into that position. Maybe they each swerved in the same direction to avoid a head-on collision and both rammed into the cliff face in parallel. There were several bodies lying in the grass and people sitting on rocks, bleeding. Fortunately, an ambulance was there too. There appeared to be enough people helping."

"How did Ruth react?" asked Brett.

"She hasn't said much, but she's pretty upset. When I collected them, I explained to her and the boys what I'd seen and why I hadn't stopped then. They were a bit prepared, I think."

Steve said, "All our children have seen accidents and violence here. I think they're getting used to it."

"That's what's really troubling me. Not so much that I didn't stop to help – because I can reason through that – but the fact that I seem to be getting hardened to the reality of all the disasters and suffering here. I wonder if I'm becoming callous. That's what's bothering me now."

They continued to console Coreene and prayed together for the recovery of the survivors and the families of the victims. They gave thanks that Coreene had not been involved in the crash, although she was seconds away from it. She felt sorry that she had been irritated by the shop owner because that brief delay probably saved her from being part of the accident. They all looked up as their maid came to the door, looking shocked.

"Khadijah says there has been a bad accident. Some of our neighbours are…." She broke off, crying, and returned to the kitchen. Coreene went to speak with her, and Brett saw it would best for him to leave.

"We'll keep in touch when we know more. Thanks for your support," said Steve, as he headed towards Ruth's room.

Jane was working that afternoon with several ladies at the church, giving sewing lessons. She had set up a similar programme at their church in England, and was looking forward to passing along some tips. Brett did not need to get involved, so he walked over to collect the post. Near the building, he slowed his pace and fell into step with Marie-Anne and Len Moore. They were discussing the accident and had already heard of two families in the Zoo who had lost a relative.

"Three others are injured and are in hospital," said Marie-Anne.

"It seems we have a crisis at the Zoo every month," said Brett.

"Be grateful," said Len ruefully. "We are protected in here. Most people outside are facing a crisis a week in their lives, with young people dying of this new disease called AIDS, and all the violence, oppression, and unrest. I miss the old days in Kenya."

Marie-Anne replied, "I do too, but we shouldn't glamourize them, Len. We had many disasters then too, remember?"

Larry Smythe met them as they reached the central building. The Moores were able to avoid him as they stopped to offer comfort to a distraught lady. Brett thought Larry seemed drunk. He recalled what

Louise had told him of the rumours from earlier years at the soda-lake plant, about Larry's intemperate ways and dissipation. He and Brett spoke about the accident and the violence and injustice in many people's lives.

"So, what's yer point?" demanded Larry, swaying slightly.

"I wonder if the accident isn't partly related to poverty and lack of regulation–"

"Bribery!" Larry snapped.

"How long do you think it will be before the Kenyan people are relieved of it all?" asked Brett, "Fifty to a hundred years?" Larry's blue eyes focussed uncertainly in the distance.

"I think you're being very optimistic. Some people around here will cut your throat – with a smile on their face." Brett felt Larry was in no condition to drive home, so he steered him into the cafe and insisted he bought him a coffee. Brett was hoping someone from the northeast area would come to help Larry home. He saw that Larry was content to sit and chat.

Larry said, in his curious way, "That reminds me of a contractor.... Worked for a bloke once. Bob was 'is name. His favourite expression...he'd say 'In this business, you've got to learn to cut a man's throat, with a smile on your face.'" Brett responded politely while sipping coffee and scanning the cafe for help.

He remembered Louise telling him Larry was a former builder and still knew many in the trade. He had made a substantial amount of cash during his time as a contractor – by less than totally honest means, according to some. Then he worked in the soda plant. He was able to semi-retire, keep his expenses low, and enjoy life at the coast. Since moving to the Zoo, he had worked effectively, supervising the construction of the new water tanks in N-1 beside the wall. He turned towards Brett and spoke defensively.

"I knows me trade. I ain't intellectual. Not like you lot with education and degrees and all. But I can follow Len's ideas. I sees merit in what he's about."

"Great, Larry."

"Like I say, I knows me trade. I've done more successful plumbing jobs... than you've 'ad hot dinners."

"Yes, I'm sure you have. You've done great work at the Energy Centre over the last–"

"Two years."

"That's right. You came down just after I left in early 1988."

"So, what's–"

"...my point? I'm wondering...are you enjoying it here?"

"Now, you've got me there. Eh?" He was silent, took a sip of coffee and said, "Yep. I'm happy as the night is long. Len's a good boss. Leaves me alone, see?"

"That's great, Larry."

"Me other boss – Moshi – he's different. 'e don't say much but he's loaded. Tons of cash, see? I should be alright wiv' 'im." Brett was confused so opted for a neutral response.

"You've certainly achieved a lot over–"

"I respects the hier...hier–arch...Pecking order. See? The order of labour. Yer don't ask a driver to unload stuff, right? He drives. He don't unload. What I always says is...don't expect an office clerk...to wash the car. Recognize the order of ranks."

"That is respectful of you, Larry. It's good to understand your workers and–"

"I'm tough on me staff, I knows...." He lost his train of thought, but remembered and continued, "I often say 'Let's knock the T out of can't'. I tells 'em, I don't want to hear what *can't* be done. You find a way...and come and tell me how you're going to–" Brett was getting frustrated by Larry's slurred belligerence.

"But, wouldn't you get better cooperation if you–"

"I'll do things my way! You just judge by the results, okay?" Brett was relieved when he spotted Len in the corridor.

"No quarrel with the results, Larry. No quarrel there. Here's a man who's happy with your work." He gratefully waved Len over to get his assistance. Len knew the strategy. He directed his remark to both of them.

"Marie-Anne told me I should come back to see you." He sat down next to Larry and asked, "Telling Brett about the great projects we work on together, eh?" Larry's mind cleared slightly.

"Yeh. I was explainin' me management methods. I remember the best manager I ever had...if we slowed down and started nattering too much, like, slacking off, he'd say 'Let's have a bit more and less of it. A bit more talk and a bit less work!' See? Ha ha. We all knew what he meant. Best manager I ever–"

"Ready to go Larry?" said Len, taking his arm. Larry rose slowly and waved to Brett as Len guided him towards the door.

"Thanks mate. Best manager I ever had. A bit more and less of it...." They all chuckled.

16

Brett was surprised, as Louise wasn't usually so cranky. She looked very tired, and drained of energy and enthusiasm.

Brett heard of Inspector Ponda's arrival at the Zoo while he was at a staff meeting. He was in a followup discussion with the principal and mathematics teachers about the students he might help. The office messenger entered the room and spoke to the principal. He took Brett outside and told him to use his office to meet with the Inspector.

Once they were seated, the tall, well-built policeman referred back to their earlier meeting at the time of Peter Lancaster's death. His appearance was intimidating but he was obviously making an effort to be polite. Brett reciprocated, and expressed his thanks for the assistance from the police on that terrible evening. Ponda's expression then indicated: Enough of the sociable rituals. Let's get to the point.

He said, "I understand you met with Mr. Miles Jolly in England."

"Yes."

"How often?"

"Twice."

"Why?"

"He was an old neighbour from the Zoo and he wanted to see me during his last few years."

"You visited him in Wales, I understand." That was a test, although Brett was unaware of it.

"No, in England, just north of Bristol." Ponda nodded.

"What did you talk about?"

"His health. My marriage to Jane. Mutual friends."

"What did he say about Kenya?"

"He missed it, the warmth, and the people."

"Hmm. The people. Did he mention my name?"

"No, he didn't–"

"Detective Ochieng?"

"No."

"Officer Kinyanjui?"

"No."

"No one in the police force or law enforcement?"

"Not that I recall."

"Did he talk about his prison stay?"

"I think he was anxious to forget that."

"Answer my question! Did he talk about it?"

"No." Brett thought, *This man is tough. No wonder everyone respects him.*

"You said he referred to people in Kenya. Who did he mention, specifically?"

"Steve Brandon and family, Len Moore, Louise Emerson, and a few–"

"Did he mention Moshi?"

"Yes."

"What did he say about him?"

"He told me I should not trust him." Brett was surprised to see a rare smile. Ponda's voice softened.

"He said that?"

"Yes, he warned me to be careful of Moshi."

"Mr. James, that may be the best advice Miles Jolly ever gave you." Brett thought, *He's almost human.* Then Ponda's face returned to stone and the formal facade was re-established.

"Did he speak of hidden treasure or valuables?"

"No. Not specifically." Ponda looked up. He appeared to savour the word 'specifically'.

"Gold? Cash?"

"No. He made no reference to those."

"What about diamonds?"

"No." Brett wondered if he was being tested. It certainly felt like it. But he had nothing to hide and was answering truthfully. In an abrupt tone, Ponda asked another direct question.

"What did you two talk about at the end?"

"His health. He was very weak." Brett wondered if that might elicit some sympathy from Ponda. It did not.

"Did he give you anything – a gift?"

"We spoke of a gift I gave him – a painting that he valued. It was a scene–"

Ponda interrupted him. "That was not what I asked you! Did *he* give *you* a gift?"

"Not then."

"Not then?"

"No."

"Later?"

"Yes, in his will. He left me some cash and other items. He wanted to fund this return trip to Kenya with my wife. We are thinking of it as our honeymoon. We were not able–"

"Why was that necessary – for him to provide the money?"

"It was in his will. It's all official–"

"You are an electrical engineer, working in London?"

"A mechanical engineer. Working in Reading."

"Aha, yes. My mistake. As a professional engineer, you must receive a substantial salary?" *What's he getting at now?* Brett wondered. He wanted to tell Ponda it was none of his business, but he was not the sort person you said that to.

"My contract is over. I am at present unemployed. Between jobs." He hoped Ponda might smile but he was disappointed.

"What did he reveal near the end?"

"Nothing. He was dying."

Ponda gave a tilt of his head and a tolerant grin. "Er – yes. But I have found that what is said in the final moments is often most interesting. A person has, we might say, nothing to lose." It looked as though he expected Brett to smile. Instead, he offered Ponda an explanation.

"Miles was receiving sedation. I was warned by the nurse that he may not be coherent."

"Mr. James, I have a suspicion that you are not telling me some things."

"I have answered all your questions honestly, Inspector."

"I believe you have," said Ponda. He gave Brett a penetrating glance that conveyed a myriad of possible thoughts. To ameliorate his discomfort Brett added a different thought.

"His last words were to tell me that he believed and trusted. He told me I was right." Ponda was alert.

"Right about what?"

"I assume about the Christian faith. But he was almost inaudible in his final moments."

Ponda looked out the window of the principal's office, thinking in silence. Brett also was silent. He was becoming weary of the interview. He must have unintentionally communicated that, because Ponda suddenly stood and drew himself to his full height.

"You realize you are dealing with a senior police officer?" Brett also stood.

"Yes, and I respect you, Inspector Ponda, and the fine work you and Detective Ochieng are doing to keep this community safe. I have also developed an appreciation for your fellow officer, Kinyanjui."

"Oh? Senior Sergeant Kinyanjui?"

"I know the Kikuyu well. I lived with them for five years. I understand a little of their culture." Brett did not intend it as a gibe against the coastal tribes, but he wondered if Ponda may have interpreted it that way as he responded curtly.

"Detective Ochieng has been promoted and will be sent back to Kisumu. Let him do his fishing among the famous Luo fishermen!"

Brett smiled. "They are excellent fishermen – wherever they go. Is that not true?"

"Indeed. So, Bwana James, you will soon have just me to deal with while you are at the coast."

Brett replied as warmly as he could. "That will be a pleasure, Mr. Ponda." Ponda moved towards the door.

"Please pass my greetings to your wife, Mr. James."

They parted amicably, each with several matters troubling them. Ponda sensed he had learned little – other than Brett was honest. Brett felt as though he had just passed a difficult exam, but he was not sure in what subject and certainly without full marks. He left the college and met Steve.

"I saw the police car. Who was that?"

"Inspector Ponda. He questioned me about my meetings with Miles. He's still suspicious about something."

On Friday, Brett and Jane had just finished a late breakfast in the cafe when they saw Louise in the hallway beside the post boxes. They joined her, and Brett described Ponda's visit. They spent some time discussing the *matatu* accident and people they knew who had been affected. Then Brett swallowed.

"Er – Louise, do you think it might be convenient…you know, Jane and I…would like to look inside your CPK-Store."

"Heavens, no!"

"Please."

"What on earth for?"

"Just to follow up on an idea. Something Miles mentioned."

"If Miles mentioned it, then it's probably not a good idea! No, it's a real mess in there."

Jane pleaded, "Oh, please. I'd be fascinated to have a look. You know, having heard so much about it. It would complete the picture for me."

"Next thing, you'll be asking to climb up on the roof!"

"That's an idea! I could show Jane the view and the rope ladder down into the secret passageway–"

"No! Someone is bound see you two up there and it'll become known…." Her voice trailed off into silence. Brett was surprised, as Louise wasn't usually so cranky. She looked tired, and drained of energy and enthusiasm. She noticed his look of disappointment and let out a long sigh.

"Oh, alright. You may look, if you like. You can tidy up and dust while you're in there! But not today. Come on Monday. Mjuhgiuna will have tea ready. About four. It's the traditional time for tea. It was in Victorian England in the late nineteen century, so it has to be here in Kenya in 1990!

Part Three

DISCOVERIES

The fictional characters introduced in Part Three

Faiz: assistant Imam at The Zoo
Simion Katana: The Zoo director, former principal of polytechnic
Hamud Sita: The Zoo accountant
Mzee: fearful and resentful old man in Muslim sector
Iha: Mzee's dishonest younger son

17

Brett spoke under his breath.
"A prank? A fuss over nothing?
I don't think that's how Louise would describe it."

The Jameses were anxious to visit Louise on the first Monday afternoon in February. They sat through the tea ceremony before glancing overtly towards the store at the back. Louise noticed the looks.

"Oh, you wanted to see in there, didn't you? I'm not sure it's–"

"It won't take long. Do you have a torch we can borrow, please?" Louise pointed to one on the shelf.

"What's all the interest about?"

"We want to see if there's anything still visible of the swastika."

"Oh yes, that. I hope it's still well-and-truly covered up. You did a good job disguising it as four squares, or a window shape."

Brett and Jane went inside, sideways, through the narrow opening. He shone the light around. They saw some furniture, old cloths, fans, tools, and boxes.

"Do you see anything on the wall, Jane? I think it was up there."

"No."

"Let's try a different angle." He held the torch flat against the wall. "How's that?"

"I see something. Just an outline of a box around four smaller squares." He stood on a stool.

"That's it! It was originally a swastika that I plastered over." Louise joined them in the narrow space.

"What are you two up to?"

"A couple of people in England referred to the middle of the swastika."

"Really? Who?"

"Miles. And it was written in one of Thomas' diaries."

"Well I never!"

Brett looked closely where Jane was pointing and prodded around.

"It's softer here. There's some packing or.... Do you have a screwdriver or an old knife, please?" Louise squeezed out while Jane held the light. Standing on the wobbly stool, he scratched at the surface. "Why didn't I notice this before?" Taking a knife from Louise, he dug out a small twist of cloth. They saw a hole bored in the wall between the blocks of coral-rag masonry. The knife made a metallic sound. "There's something here. A cap or bolt or something." He dug and scraped around the edges.

"Be careful," warned Jane, "It might explode!"

"That's all I need," joked Louise who was watching excitedly.

"I'll prise this out." Brett widened the hole with the point of the knife and tried to lever out the metal object. Eventually, he said, "It's an aluminium container of some kind." After much digging he wiggled it free. Louise examined it in the torch light.

"It looks like an old cigar canister. You may not remember the tubes the men used years ago. With screw tops." They took it out into the light of the open room and shook off the coral dust. They saw a thin cylinder, just over four inches long. "Be careful with that," Louise warned. "It could be explosive, but it looks like a simple cigar case." Brett tried to unscrew the top but it would not budge. "Use a rubber band. Here," Louise said as she handed Brett an elastic band. He wound it around the top and, after several attempts, managed to unscrew it. None of them expected what they saw.

Suddenly, a cascade of bright glass-like stones spilled out and rattled onto the table and over the floor.

"Diamonds!" gasped Jane as she examined one closely. Brett got on the floor and picked up several. Louise took the tube and looked inside. She shook out a few into the palm of her hand.

"They feel cold! I read that diamonds do feel cold."

"There are lots more. Yes, they are cold," Jane said.

"So, there *were* diamonds, hidden in the–"

"We don't know they're genuine. They could be ersatz diamonds. Fakes. Probably are," cautioned Louise. "Don't let's get too excited."

"Would Henry have been so serious if he knew they were fake?" asked Jane. Louise shrugged.

"Maybe he thought they were real." She paused, and whispered, "Karl Bergmann's diamonds."

"*Your* diamonds," said Brett. Louise shook her head.

"They were given to Henry, so now they're yours," Jane said.

Louise was silent. She simply stared at the heap on the table and those still in the tube and then spoke, almost to herself.

"Bergmann. A miner or man of the mountains. Bergmann's diamonds."

"We'd better keep this a secret for now. You have a safe, don't you?" said Brett.

"Yes, yes," Louise replied absentmindedly. "Herr Bergmann's diamonds. He must have hidden them there before he escaped to the sea." Jane frowned.

"How would he have got so far with them? Where were they from?"

"I don't know. A lot of precious items, including jewellery, found its way into Tanzania during the war. Mostly from Europe or the Middle East. Lives were lost fighting over the stuff. Debts were paid, old scores settled. These could have been traded for food."

"Food?"

"If you were starving, and at the point of death, would these pieces of carbon mean more to you than half a loaf?"

"I wonder if Bergmann held them legitimately."

"For all we know, they could be Third Reich spoils. We may never discover the story now."

"How could he have transported them across the border and travelled here with them?" Jane asked. Louise smiled.

"This tube could have been concealed in – in a body cavity. Sorry to be crude, but I am a nurse!"

"That would be pretty uncomfortable," said Jane, frowning.

"Yes, but essential if they were to be concealed. At least for a short time – at critical moments." Jane lifted up a few diamonds.

"They are different colours, some of them. Quite a variety of sizes too," she commented. Louise held one up to the light.

"This has a purple tinge. It's cold but sparkles like a flame. Ice on fire!"

"How much are they worth, if they are genuine diamonds?" asked Brett.

"I have no idea. I can't think about that. I just hope we can keep them secure until we know more. I'll find a little bag for them." Then Louise was silent for a while until she said softly, "Maybe Heinrick didn't carve out that swastika. Perhaps it was Bergmann – as he said – and it was left there to mark the location."

"Would Henry have known about them?"

"He must have known. But I only overheard that single mention, and he never spoke of the stones himself."

"He hinted about them to at least two others," noted Brett. Louise didn't appear to hear the remark.

She said, "Perhaps that's what Henry meant when he spoke of our nest-egg as security." Brett sat down and ran his fingers over the gems.

"What will you do?" Jane asked Louise, sitting next to Brett.

"Keep them in the safe and think about it. I may need legal advice. I'm sure I will."

"Should we hand them over to the police?"

"Maybe. But first we must keep them away from Moshi. I'll make sure they're secure until we find out what we have here."

The following week, on Valentine's Day, Brett and Jane were sitting in bed, drinking their early morning cup of tea. Brett had arranged an electric kettle and basic supplies in their room. He tuned into the BBC World Service to hear the 7am news on the shortwave radio that the Moores had lent them. Suddenly, there was a loud banging at the door and they heard Steve Brandon's voice. Brett opened the door.

Steve gasped, "There's been an attack of some kind north of the mosque! Can you come with me? I hope Louise is alright." Brett scrambled to get ready. As they left, Steve asked, "Can we use your pickup? Coreene will drive our car over with Jane in a few minutes."

When they arrived in the square, there was a crowd of distraught onlookers staring at a demolished clothing stall. Steve and Brett saw clothes, *kangas*, scarves, and shoes scattered in the dust. The small kiosk had been pushed over to expose a stone slab which was laying to the side. It revealed an open crypt. Looking closer, they saw several steps leading into the vault below the north face of the mosque wall.

A man spoke to them. "Imam Faiz, he is very angry."

After several minutes of utter confusion, Louise appeared. She looked bedraggled and anxious.

"I thought I heard some noise early this morning. It's hard to tell with the fans on. Mjuhgiuna says they toppled over the stall to get to the hidden crypt leading through to the mosque. He knew about it, but very few people realized it was there." The stall owner was in tears and the mood of the crowd was becoming hostile. The three of them moved away just as Coreene drove up with Jane. They noticed how upset Louise was, so they offered to help her back to her cage. "Thank you. I'm going back to bed," she said. "This is very worrying. Are we safe here anymore?" Brett took Steve aside.

"Louise once explained to me about that hidden vault. But Miles told me it was empty. He described it as a decoy."

"A decoy? For what?"

"I've no idea."

"How was Miles involved with it?"

"I don't know. You remember Miles – good at dispensing partial truths."

Louise came back to them. "I hate to accuse anyone, but this has Moshi's fingerprints all over it, I'd say."

"More than likely," said Steve.

"I think we'd better be careful. I hope Kinyanjui or Ochieng are onto this quickly." She turned to Brett and whispered, "I'm worried about… those…stones. I don't like having them in my place."

"What can we do?"

"I'm going to phone Matherton & Son. They may be able to help. Perhaps they can get them identified. So we know what we're dealing with." Steve was listening, mystified.

"Is there somewhere else that's more secure? Definitely not the guesthouse," Brett whispered to Louise.

Steve said, "We have a strong safe in the church office. Is there something we can store for you?" They arranged for Brett to take them over to Steve later that day. Steve said, "If it was Moshi or his gang, it will be safe with us. Muslims would not attack a church."

"Someone broke through into the mosque," Brett pointed out. As she left, Louise gave them both a look which clearly signified sympathy at their naivety.

"Let's have breakfast in the cafe while we're here," Steve suggested.

Coreene said, "You three go ahead, I'd better get back to the children."

During breakfast, between numerous interruptions from people anxious to talk about the attack, Steve told them that Bishop Onyango was planning to visit the Zoo.

"It will be an honour to host him for a day. You two may meet him." Steve spoke about his analysis of current social trends and his concerns, "There's much confusion and selfishness. I foresee unrest as there's a darkness in the land. I wake every day under a dark cloud. But I have Jesus. Everyone needs Jesus. He understands and He longs to help us." Brett and Jane were taken aback by Steve's despair. He then brightened as he described the response to his working paper at several church conferences. "Generally, it was well received, but it put the cat among the pigeons in some quarters, I can tell you!" Jane looked surprised so Brett explained to Jane about Steve's analysis.

"I had the privilege of reading it in its initial stages."

"What was so controversial?" Jane asked. The crowd had left the cafe by then.

"The main concern at the discussions was increasing sexual immorality. But some participants focused on gender confusion. To me, that is not the most serious issue, but it may become more of–"

"Why?"

"It is not the African way. Those groups are thrusting it into public view. It is their choice to do that."

"Why? What do they want?"

"Acceptance for who they are. And love, I believe. Just what we all want. Plus equal respect and protection. The churches provide that."

"So, where's the problem?"

"Well, the church's biblical position is being attacked. There are also *ad hominem* attacks on individuals who speak out."

"Where do you stand, Steve?"

"I love those who choose any lifestyle. The One I serve loves them and died for them. I cannot do differently. We welcome everyone. You see–" An *mzungu* came over and interrupted him.

"Imam Faiz is furious. Apparently the vault is connected to an opening at the side of a dais inside the mosque." A second man joined them.

"There's a hardwood panel that no one noticed. But the Imam knew about it." The two stood by the table and gave more details.

"The kiosk operator says nothing was stolen."

"So, no harm done."

"Probably a youthful prank."

"A bit of a fuss over nothing, if you ask me."

"No doubt that's what happened," said Steve, glancing at Brett. As the pair left them, Brett spoke under his breath.

"A prank? A fuss over nothing? I don't think that's how Louise would describe it."

That afternoon Brett drove over to S-33, Louise's cage. She called him upstairs and handed him two small cloth bags.

"I found these velvet pouches. I separated them into two sets to reduce the risk – maybe. Let's refer to them as 'stones' from now, shall we? We don't know that they're genuine diamonds."

"That's true. How are you feeling?"

"Better, thanks, but still a bit unsettled."

"Any luck contacting the lawyer?"

"I phoned Allistair Matherton. The difficulty is we can't speak openly on the phone. I described the goods in general terms. He said I should get them to him safely and he'll take care of them until we know more. His dad, Geoffrey, may know a jeweller in Nairobi who can advise them."

"Well, sure, but how do we get them up to Nairobi? It's sensitive stuff," said Brett.

"And possibly valuable. I'll think of something. You put your thinking-cap on too." Brett had brought Miles' map of the tunnel. He showed it to Louise, and explained how he got it. Her reaction was a blend of surprise and fascination. "I wonder if that's where he kept his stash of belongings?

I always knew he was up to something in the foundations in the restricted zone. I had no idea there was a second chamber. We should investigate before anyone else gets wind of this."

Brett left. As he reached the bottom of the stairs, Louise called after him.

"I hear Kelsey is coming back."

"Oh, when?"

"April sometime, I think. Thanks for your help, Brett. Be careful. Look innocent!"

As he drove away, he smiled to himself. Was she referring to the diamonds, the map of the tunnel, or Kelsey's return?

Coreene Brandon and Jane James were developing a close friendship. As ministers' wives, they had similar backgrounds in church work, although their lives had followed very different paths. During one visit to several outreach projects, Coreene told Jane about her chronic back pain from the injury caused by a car accident many years previously. Jane was sympathetic and admired her fortitude in carrying on with her demanding activities. Jane was deeply impressed by the impact the church work was having, and the excellent relationships which had been built up over the years.

Coreene told Jane, "We encourage the local people to take the initiative. Our role, as we see it, is to be supportive and come alongside their efforts. Sometimes we are able to provide funds, but we operate on a very limited budget."

"Are you working mostly with Christians?"

"No. The coast is largely Muslim, as you know. Most of the Giriama are Christian, although some still have their animistic beliefs. We just help people – as people! If they see Christ in us, then God can work through that."

"So, it's social outreach rather than evangelism?"

"I suppose so, but one cannot separate them: they are two sides of the same coin. It's a dual mandate: working for social justice and sharing the good news about Jesus. I see both as love-in-action. Healing can flow from that."

"Oh definitely. What about physical healings?"

"We have seen some miraculous healings which encouraged and inspired people. It's often through miracles that families come to know Jesus' love." Coreene continued, "The other area of assistance has been the loans for women's micro-financing schemes. These provide individuals with a small loan to start their own business."

"What are they using the funds for? What sort of businesses do they have?" asked Jane.

"Small enterprises like selling fruit, vegetables, or fish. There are clothing-repair businesses too. Each day, they make a small profit. They are very industrious and hard-working ladies!" Coreene added, "They encourage their children to take responsibility early too. I heard a cute expression the other day: a mother proudly described her young son, saying 'He is now old enough to send to the *duka* to buy a bag of sugar.' That's how they measure growth – in practical ways." Jane laughed and confided in Coreene.

"People ask me if I have children. When I say 'No', invariably they ask how long I've been married. To keep it simple, I tell them less than a year. They look at me sympathetically and assure me 'God will provide'. One lady asked if I want a child. I told her I do, but I have Brett to take care of in the meantime!"

Later, when Jane described her visits to Brett, they discussed the programmes and decided to donate the tithe from Miles' gift to support the work that the Brandons were helping with.

On the Friday after Valentine's Day, Brett and Jane met the Zoo director, Simion Katana, in the entrance to the central building. Brett invited him to the cafe for coffee. Simion gave them fresh insights into several current events in the country. He also explained the improved accounting system at the Zoo and the strict financial controls in place.

"This has enabled our new Board of Governors to encourage donors. They have funded several excellent projects already. There are more to come, including developing our tourist potential." As they sipped their drinks, Simion added, "Hamud Sita has made a wonderful contribution here." Brett reminded Jane that he was the accounts clerk falsely accused of embezzlement, and then cleared of the charge. "He is an honest man," said Simion.

"I suppose much of the corruption and dishonesty we hear about is due to poverty," Jane mused.

Simion immediately responded: "Not completely true! I know many people who are poor but they are still honest. To me, poverty is not the whole explanation. Poverty doesn't lead to dishonesty. There are wealthy crooks."

Brett added, "In Nyeri, I saw the dilemma of many honest youth who enter the working world and find it is saturated with corruption. Do they resist or comply? If they don't cooperate, they are fired. There's always another unemployed worker eager to take their place."

Simion nodded. "It is a real problem. For example, with Sita who was pressured by Boniface Chengo and Moshi. The bookkeeping training is a lot of work and he invested much effort to get that qualification. But now he is rewarded with the senior position as our accountant working under the Financial Officer." Brett asked if Sita was still resentful towards Moshi for having him framed. Simion said, "I think he has mostly got over that, but he does keep watch over Moshi's actions at the Zoo. You know, Sita has friends in Mombasa who were unjustly jailed with him who still trace criminal activity. He keeps me informed. We are aware."

Later, Jane told Brett how impressed she was with Simion's insights during the honest discussion.

"Yes, isn't he marvellous? I was privileged to have an excellent working relationship with him when he was principal at the polytechnic."

Jane said, "Now I'm beginning to understand some of the cultural revelations you told me about."

18

Louise appeared to be slightly defensive.
"In any case, it gives me another means of escape if necessary.
Heinrick always allowed himself several of those."

A week after the demolition of the stall, police sergeant Kinyanjui visited the Zoo. He had requested an interview with Louise to clarify some details of what happened at the mosque. She suggested that Brett be present. Brett asked if Jane could join them, as he thought she would be interested to meet Kinyanjui. Louise arranged for coffee in her lower suite.

"So, Bwana Kinyanjui, you have come to discuss the details of the stall attack," was her opening remark.

The three of them told him what they saw of the aftermath of the event. Sergeant Kinyanjui revealed nothing of his investigations, but he did warn of increasing troubles, both locally and nationally.

"One house just outside the Zoo has been attacked. Two strong men held a heavy rock in a sack and swung it back and forth against the front door to break it down." He added that a new trick was being used: the thieves would return after about two hours. By then, the sympathetic neighbours would have left, and the family would not be suspecting that the crooks would come back. Brett saw the point.

"Clever. Then the robbers could steal whatever remaining items they wanted. Very sneaky." Jane sat listening in disbelief. Kinyanjui made a confession.

"Honestly, I tell you, it is getting so bad. We police are at the end of our wits." Louise raised her eyebrows.

"You mean at your wit's end?"

"Yes, like that."

Louise related the story of a recent robbery at the Catholic Sisters' clinic in Mwakindini. As she spoke, Kinyanjui nodded in agreement. A gang had demanded cash and equipment.

"One nun challenged them 'If you take these supplies, how will we treat you and your relatives when you are sick?' A thug replied 'You just shut up and give us the money'." Louise added, "The nuns were fortunate that they were not attacked physically. Sometimes dreadful things are done to women in these situations. Mr. Kinyanjui, I'm glad Major Peter Lancaster had the foresight to provide some cages in the Zoo so that police families can be resident here."

Louise tried to guide the conversation to the recent news of the death of a senior government Minister. Kinyanjui was reluctant to discuss that matter and, as he had collected the information he needed, he stood to leave. As they shook hands, Brett spoke a few words to him in Kikuyu.

Before Brett and Jane left, Louise again mentioned that if they still wanted a break they could stay in one of the huts on the headland. They arranged to be there for three nights, starting the following day.

Louise's maid, Fatima, carried the food and water that Brett and Jane would need for their sojourn. She had the key to the main door in the wall and, after they had passed through, the three of them walked carefully along the path. Brett warned Jane to be alert for snakes. She was fascinated to see the area that Brett had spoken about, particularly the path along the beautiful shore, the old witchdoctor's ruined hut, and Henry's compound on the isolated beach. Coming into the clearing, Brett immediately noticed the improvements. The old research station was still at the far end, but two new buildings stood over the vaults at either end of the tunnel, and the whole compound had been cleaned up. Fatima showed them where the key was hidden in the rear rafters of the lower hut, and let them in. She told them she would come back and cook their supper.

The beach was wonderful at low tide and they explored the compound and up some trails. As they settled into their little hut, they loved the isolation and peace. The other buildings were locked. Louise had explained that all of Henry's research materials were in the research station and the naturalist's belongings were secured in the upper hut. Jane asked why the monkeys remained isolated on *Kisiwa Wa Kima*.

"What stops them clambering through the trees to the mainland?"

"Nothing. They're content here as they have sufficient food and there are no predators. I suppose they've learned that it's dangerous to approach humans. Also, Larry told me they hung several imitation leopard-skin cloths along the wall. They droop down over this side to deter the monkeys from crossing that barrier. It's effective as the monkeys are terrified by images of their feared enemy."

As they sat in the shade above the beach, Jane was overjoyed to be in such a unique place, while watching the trees wave in the breeze and the gentle movement of the glistening sea. She laid her head on Brett's shoulder as he stroked her hair.

"So, this is the elusive place you schemed to visit by climbing over the forbidden wall. You could never have imagined you'd be back here with me! You know, for the first time, this feels as though we're alone on our honeymoon."

In that peaceful location, sitting close to each other, he talked about why nature was so relaxing.

"I've concluded that our eyes are naturally drawn to movement, possibly as a primeval defence or hunting instinct, but the movements in nature are non-threatening."

"So, we enjoy watching them because we can do so in a relaxed manner."

"I've given myself many opportunities to test my theory!"

"You must have explored a lot of the reef too."

"Yes, quite a bit. There's something to do at any level of the tide. See, it's coming in now and you can watch the birds as they follow the edge of the advancing waves. The water movement activates many creatures." She saw through the binoculars that the birds fed for a while, and then flew up and over the small wave as it drifted across the hot exposed coral bed. "Constantly changing, but according to fixed and predictable cycles," he said. They were silent for a long time, absorbing the gentle mood of the place.

Fatima returned, carrying fresh bedding. She prepared a meal using the small propane stove in the hut. Jane worked with her while Brett checked to see if there was any access to the tunnel through the upper hut. It was locked but he saw it had been built directly on top of the original foundations, as the access hatch was enclosed within the building. He remembered that the tunnel was very narrow and rough as it angled towards the sea from there, but the police dogs had located the first hidden chamber back in 1987.

They had enough food for the rest of their stay, so they walked back with Fatima and let her through the main door. Brett kept the key.

That night the stars were spectacular with virtually no light pollution to disturb their enjoyment. They stood arm in arm, revelling in the sights and sounds. Jane's senses were heightened as she listened to the rustling palm branches and the whispering of the waves. She felt a pleasant tightness on her shoulders from the dried saltwater and the sunburn of the day.

Suddenly, as they looked out over the sea, they both saw a meteor streaking across the sky. They turned to each other, excited at sharing that unique experience. Brett gently moved from her face a stray wisp of her long brown hair that the soft wind had caught. He kissed her while she clung passionately to him.

If they had looked up through the palms arching overhead, they might have noticed the stars moving steadily on their course through the heavens. But their attention was focussed on each other in their exclusive location and precious solitude.

The next day, they explored an ill-defined trail to the north. It was very dense so Brett felt certain there was no easy access to the northern shore that way. They followed the pathway southeast over to the site where the ashes of Henry and Peter were buried. Brett found the route easily, but it took him some time to locate the slab above the two interment urns. Much debris had fallen and some patchy grass had grown over the site. They sat for a while in silence and each pondered the significance of the place. The view across the southern bay was – as always – stunning from that high point. They watched several boats of different sizes drifting across the coruscating waters.

Brett recalled his vivid dream when the rocks and slabs of stone tumbled down the cliff onto him in the bay far below. When he shared the thought with Jane, she offered a comforting word.

"Helping Louise bury the urns was obviously an emotional experience. No doubt your dream reflects that. Perhaps coming back here will bring closure for you."

That evening, they made a small fire from driftwood on the beach, just above the water's edge. They mellowed into the gentle atmosphere.

"I feel totally at home in Africa," she said. "These are the Golden Joys one dreams of."

"Many westerners express that feeling when they visit."

"Why is that? Is it the primordial forces on display? We have elemental fire, life-giving water, vital air...."

"One is close to the earth, soil, dramatic mountains, and spectacular skies." Their conversation turned to the balance of nature.

"We see such harmony in all aspects of creation," Jane said.

"Yes, there's an overall unity. None of the diverse elements could have evolved separately. There is so much interdependence and–"

"Interrelation – in the way everything works. The harmony of creation."

"We should not be surprised. One would expect synthesis and synergy as it's all the product of the same great mind."

"God's creative intelligence. So obvious. Everywhere," said Jane.

"And, at the same time, the world is such a mess!"

"As one would expect. Creation was designed to function according to God's plan. As we have largely rejected that, it's not surprising that there's wrong-doing and chaos." She was animated. "It would be astonishing if things *did* work in harmony with God's purposes, considering we are excluding Him and trying to operate most things in our own way – in the opposite direction!"

"Pastor Steve has often spoken about that. He feels the evolutionary processes we are expected to believe in don't make sense to him."

"Me neither. I do question it all," said Jane. "For example, a dinosaur couldn't have watched a whale swimming about, and thought 'That looks fun, I think I'll evolve into one of those'. There are no directed processes in random variation."

"Or, think of a specialized organ, or an apparatus like echolocation. A fish can't say to itself 'Look at that dolphin. Echolocation seems an effective way of finding food, I'll develop that mechanism'."

"Of course not. Evolution, by definition, has no foresight or plan."

"I'm glad we agree," said Brett as he hugged Jane, kissed her, and then stood to douse the fire.

She stood also and said, "This is so wonderful here. We are completely alone, with all this beauty and peace to ourselves. It's like another world." They stood looking out across the inky water, listening to the gentle waves breaking on the beach, with arms around each other. It was a long time before they slowly made their way up the beach to their private hut in the isolated compound.

After the break on their own, on the return journey to the wall, they suddenly saw two bush pigs on the path staring at them. The animals gave loud grunts and dashed into the bushes.

"Do they attack people?" asked Jane, clutching his arm.

"I hear the males will if they are agitated."

"Are they herbivores?"

"Louise told me they are omnivorous so they do eat meat. And they will attack if provoked or feel the need to defend their territory."

"Are there many here?"

"I've seen a few on my occasional visits. Peter Lancaster thought bush pigs made most of the footpaths through the forest."

Brett was itching to explore the tunnel shown on Miles' map. Jane knew that, but felt they should not push Louise for access until she was ready.

"She may not have recovered from the diamond discovery or the stall demolition."

An opportunity came naturally on Shrove Tuesday; as Jane was passing the clinic, she saw Louise outside.

"I'm making one of my rare cameo appearances here," joked Louise. She seemed strong and positive so Jane chanced asking her if she and Brett could borrow the key and explore the tunnel. She was taken aback by Louise's positive reaction.

"Yes. I want to come too. Let's go soon. I'm dying to know what that map means. How about tomorrow?"

When Jane told Brett, he was thrilled. He had not seen Louise but he began to plan the logistics.

"We should wear old clothes–"

"I don't have any!" Jane said.

"Well you can't come then!"

"Ha ha. You don't have anything old either."

"We'll be careful. I remember that tunnel is pretty dirty and rough. Let's carry some cardboard or old matting to crawl on."

"There must be something suitable over there as a base to kneel on."

"Let's talk with Louise about it. Where did she go?"

"I assume she drove home."

"Let's follow her. We need to be well prepared for this. I can't see us traipsing over there too often."

Half an hour later, they drove to cage S-33 and asked Mjuhgiuna if they could speak to Mama Louise. He pointed upstairs with his chin. They slowly climbed the stairs and knocked. Louise appeared at the door and welcomed them in.

"I'm glad to see you. I'm struggling with a clue in my crossword. See if you know it." They entered and she showed them the paper.

"Treelike branching. 9 letters. I have DE**RIT**."

"Dendritic," said Jane.

"That's it! You're a genius," said Louise as she filled in the missing letters. Brett was impressed.

"How did you know that?"

"I remember it from my Science classes, I think. Crystalline structures."

"Sounds like fractals in mathematics," stated Brett.

"That's another good word: fractal. I'll capture that one," said Louise as she wrote it down on the large notepad on her table. She had an assortment of pens and pencils and an eraser. "If I keep learning one new word or fact every day for the rest of my life, when I die I will be…just about as ignorant as I am now!"

"We need to plan our trip tomorrow," Brett said.

They sat down and discussed all the details. Louise had most of the items they would need, including a torch and an old rug.

"We'll take a second torch. There are other basic tools over there for scraping the ground. You are familiar with the front hut and what's in that."

"This is exciting. I wonder what we'll find," said Jane.

"I'm getting excited too. You have the map, Brett?" asked Louise.

"Not with me. I'll bring it tomorrow."

"Good. Everyone loves a treasure hunt."

Jane said, "Ha. That reminds me of one of Jesus' parables where He likened the Kingdom of Heaven to treasure hidden in a field."

"Why? Do we have to dig hard to find it?" asked Louise.

"Not that so much, but the man was willing to sacrifice everything he owned in order to secure that treasure by buying the field," Jane clarified.

"Tales of buried treasure have engaged people's imagination throughout history, I suppose," Louise said.

Jane added, "St. Paul wrote of incomparable riches that are ours if we believe."

Louise laughed. "Well, that puts our planned scramble in the vault tomorrow into perspective, doesn't it?"

"In that, we are just following Miles' guidance," said Brett. Louise suddenly had a melancholy expression.

"Thinking of Miles…they are all dead: Miles, Peter, Chengo, Henry. My original cabal of crooks!"

"The Big Five," said Brett.

"Only me left."

"The Big One."

"More like half a one, I'd say!" Louise stressed, "I want us to be careful. And stay legal."

"We will. Do you have all the keys?" asked Brett.

Louise waved towards the key on the hook by the door. Then she pointed to a large dish on the shelf.

"I have a huge pile of keys. Some from Miles. Most of them are duds."

Jane raised her eyebrows. "Duds?"

"Yes. Decoys. The useful ones have a tiny spot of red nail polish on the ends."

As Brett looked back at the heavy shelving, he asked Louise if the CPZ-Store was secure.

"Of course. Nobody uses that now."

"But is it locked through to the boardroom?"

"No. Just piles of junk in the way and the really heavy bookcase across the end." Jane look worried.

"Couldn't someone come through that way?"

"Why on earth would they? No one knows about it." She appeared to be slightly defensive. "In any case, it gives me another means of escape if necessary. Heinrick always allowed himself several of those."

"What about a weapon? How do you protect yourself?" asked Jane.

"No need. I sold all our guns. You remember that, Brett?" He nodded.

19

Taking back the list from Brett, Louise was worried. "Oh my, in the wrong hands this is dynamite!"

The next day was the start of Lent, a Wednesday. Louise took her cane for support while Brett and Jane carried two *kikapus* loaded with supplies. Brett placed a small roll of carpet under his arm while Jane held another walking stick. Louise collected the key and led the way through the main door in the wall.

"People will see us," said Brett.

"No problem. A few people come through here these days. It's just that I want to protect the research area from too many visitors." Louise took them to the upper hut, farther inland than the one where they had stayed. "This hut's foundation is drawn at the top of Miles' map." She directed Brett to climb on a wobbly bench outside at the rear and reach under the eaves to find a key. A second bench was placed in the shade, with some old sacks piled to the side. The small windows were high and it looked very secure. Unlocking the door, she showed them inside.

"Isn't someone staying here?" asked Jane, reluctant to enter.

"Yes, but while the naturalist is away, no one else comes in here." It was similar to the hut they had stayed in: sparsely furnished, with a small cooking stove and water jugs beside the sink. Everything was neatly in order. Brett saw that the lid to the vault was covered with a woven matting. Louise noticed his glance.

"If you lift that mat we can look down," she said.

"Is it locked?"

"No, we removed the locks." She pointed to an open padlock lying on the floor behind the hasp.

"No one would want to go down there. It's filthy. And it's mostly empty." Louise sat on the bed while Brett and Jane slid the matting aside. Brett lifted the metal hatch. The vault looked gloomy and uninviting as he stepped down inside. Jane handed him a torch and they noticed a metal trunk on the floor.

She asked, "What's that for?"

Louise stood and peered down. "Oh, yes. Ammunition. The naturalist told me he keeps his ammunition in that. How does it look down there?"

"About the same. The tunnel's pretty grubby," said Brett.

"Could you kneel on some sacks with the carpet on top?"

Brett's voice sounded from the gloom. "Yes, I'll try that."

"Before you go digging, let's have a drink," suggested Louise.

After a sip of water, they collected several dirty sacks. Using those on the rough floor, with Louise's carpet on top, Brett crawled along the tunnel and located the first recessed chamber on the left. It was empty. The rocks, which had obscured it before, lay on the floor in front of him. The tunnel was so narrow that there was no room to turn around and he marvelled that Miles had managed to force himself in there. Emerging backwards, he dragged the rocks out.

"Oh," said Jane, "You look sweaty and dirty!"

"And you look wonderful, my dear. Being covered in dust is appropriate as it's Ash Wednesday today!" Louise sat on the floor near the edge of the opening and watched admiringly.

"This is fun," she said. "It reminds me of the old times. I don't get much adventure these days."

Brett, whose elbows were getting scraped and head kept bumping the low roof, was less enthusiastic. He grasped the torch and crawled back along the rough floor. About twelve feet in, he was thrilled to see the second chamber with the opening sealed by three small rocks. They were wedged tightly.

He called back to Jane. "I need a lever or rod of some kind to shift the rocks." His voice was muffled, so he wasn't sure if she heard. In the silence, he suddenly felt uneasy. It was not fear, just a sudden realization of where he was, and how horrible the environment felt. His mind flashed back to his earlier thoughts of witchcraft and the dreadful smell he had experienced before. As he waited in a crouched position, twelve feet into the narrow tunnel, he felt grateful that he was not claustrophobic.

After several minutes, he was relieved to hear Jane's voice.

"Are these any use?"

He felt some things hit his foot. With enormous difficulty, he hooked his toe around one of the tools. It was a large screwdriver. Dragging it along the floor with his knee, he brought it within reach. The tool allowed him to force one stone to the right. After a couple of minutes of wiggling, it fell out and dropped with a thud on the floor in front of him. The second and third stones came out easily, with two more thumps.

"What was that?" called out Jane, shining the second torch. He did not reply as his hand was groping cautiously inside the opening. In amazement, he felt a bulky bag which he pulled out. He shone the light around to see if there was anything else. The chamber was empty. With the screwdriver, he tapped and prodded all around the edges to reassure himself that there was nothing else hidden in there. He pulled the package between his legs and replaced the three stones. With some difficulty and enormous relief, he wriggled his way backwards and out of the disgusting grotto. Jane looked very relieved in spite of Brett's obvious discomfort from kneeling on two other tools that she had thrown behind him.

"What did you find?" called down Louise.

Without replying, Brett handed the dusty pouch to Jane.

"Here. A gift from Miles."

Jane smiled and passed it up to Louise.

"Here. A gift from Miles."

As Brett climbed up the five steps and out of the hole, Louise gave it back to him.

"A gift from Miles. It's not mine. It's yours. Didn't you say he bequeathed all his possessions in Kenya to you?"

He took the tightly wrapped bundle and stared at it. It was heavy. In an instant, Miles' words came back to him: 'My stuff at the Zoo is yours. I have things hidden.' Then, with a chill, in spite of the heat, he recalled Miles' next sentence: 'Don't let Moshi get his hands on it.' He stood in the centre of the hut, filthy and uncertain.

He looked at the bundle. "What's in here, I wonder?"

"Let's open it," said Jane, in an excited voice.

"What do you think, Louise?" he said, crouching on the floor in his dusty state. He clutched the dirty green canvas bundle. It had a dank smell. Jane perched on a chair. Louise sat on the bed again and stared for a long time at the package that Brett was holding. A dozen thoughts flashed through her mind: *It cannot be good...there are so many possibilities...too much history...where will this lead? We should chuck it in the sea!*

She looked Brett in the eye. "Open it!"

"It's so hot and stuffy in here. Let's go outside," suggested Jane, standing.

They found a place in the shade at the rear of the hut and sat down on the rickety benches. Brett started to unwrap the canvas bundle. Inside, they saw three smaller cloth-wrapped packets. They each held one. Louise opened hers to reveal a sheaf of papers. She gasped as she leafed through the pages.

"Names, addresses, telephone numbers, dates...." She passed it to Brett.

"Some of this is in Arabic or something." He read, "Ankara, Doha, Beirut, London, Tabriz, Goa...." He clicked his tongue, as his eyes scanned the columns, "Passport numbers, phone numbers, aliases...." Louise looked again inside her envelope and brought out three passports. She handed them to Jane who turned them over.

She read, "Kenya, Lebanon, United Kingdom." Taking back the list from Brett, Louise was worried.

"Oh my, in the wrong hands this is dynamite!"

"Open yours, Jane," said Brett. "It looks pretty fat." She carefully undid the wrapping to reveal a huge wad of bank notes. She flipped through them.

"British pounds, fifties, hundreds. American dollars – all green – loads of Kenyan shillings, many colours, dirty notes. Lots of clean ones too. And here, Swiss francs, Deutsche marks, and I don't know what else. There's a fortune here!" She passed the pile of notes across to Brett.

"Singapore dollars! What are they doing here? And all these Indian rupees. What are we going to do with this lot?" He stood and gave them to Louise, who placed them on the bench next to her and stared silently at the piles of currency.

"Oh my goodness," she said. Brett sat down and lifted his small package. He shook it.

"It's really heavy. It rattles. I hope it's not what I think it is." He gingerly unwrapped the layers of cloth. In his mind flashed images of the game Pass the Parcel, but he said nothing. He almost dropped two cloth bags. As he caught one they heard chinking. Inside, he saw a heap of bright coins. "Is this gold?" he asked, handing the bag to Jane. He opened the other bag and more coins and medallions slid out. Then he saw two gold bars. He brought them out, "Wow, these feel heavy!"

Louise said, "Gold is heavy – about nineteen times more dense than lead." She looked at the heap of coins in Jane's lap. "Those definitely look like gold. Where, in heaven's name, did Miles get all this?" They were stunned. "I bet some of this belongs to Moshi. You know those two worked together as agents for a huge international smuggling scheme."

"How long has this been here?" Jane asked. Louise was shaking her head.

"Impossible to say. Miles has had access over here for many years, through the secret door in the store at N-1. He provided the connections for Moshi's smuggling activities over here and in the caves and out to the boats– in both directions."

Brett was puzzled. "Didn't you know about those two hidden chambers, Louise? You must have seen the tunnel during construction."

Louise looked uncertain. "You know, I really can't remember. I don't think I paid much attention to it all while it was being built. Henry cordoned off the site and wouldn't allow anyone through here apart from the foreign workers. I must have respected that order and kept away too. I simply can't recall. I do admit I was surprised when Ochieng told us about the first wall chamber. If I'd remembered the layout, I'm sure I would've sent you farther down the tunnel the first time we were here, Brett."

While they were talking, Jane was kneeling in front of Brett, feeling a bit overwhelmed. She fingered the exotic coins.

"Some have strange writing. Is this Arabic? These are British sovereigns, I think." She passed them over to Louise who was looking pale in spite of her suntan. She turned over several coins in wonder. A rush of thoughts came: *What shall we do? We can't bury them again, but it's dangerous to walk about with all this.*

"We'll need legal advice. I don't want them in my safe. Suppose someone finds out about it all. Perhaps Steve will–"

"We must pray for guidance about this," Brett said.

"Yes, we will. This is all yours Brett. What do you want to do?" asked Jane seriously.

"It's not mine! I only found it–"

"Well, that takes care of your next birthday present!"

Louise admonished her: "Jane, dear, this is nothing to joke about. I'm worried. This could lead to trouble."

"Sorry. I just think it's funny – we three sitting here, riffling through all this stuff! Unbelievable really."

"I'm glad there's no one else around," said Brett as he placed all the coins back in the bag, gathered the papers and cash, and wrapped everything together in its original covering. He stood and stretched.

"Now I feel very weary. All this excitement," gasped Louise. "Please pass my stick, and we'll tidy up here and return the key to its position. Then we'll see if I can make it back home for a cup of tea!" As she stood up, Louise turned to Jane and said, "We must keep this to ourselves. Just we three."

"One for all, and all for one," quipped Brett.

Louise muttered, "*Un pour tous, tous pour un*. I learned French from the troops in North Africa."

"But who will be d'Artagnan?" asked Jane.

"It will have to be Steve," stated Louise.

As they left the compound, a crow gripped the swaying frond of a palm tree above them, watching intently. It was puzzled by the presence of the unfamiliar trio and the strange noises they were emitting. It did not make a sound.

20

Out in the bay, they watched the fishermen's dugout canoes in the shallow water, poled along by two standing men, with a third fisherman crouched inside.

Brett and Jane took Louise home and immediately drove to the church with a bulky *kikapu* set firmly between them on the front seat.

"Should we tell Steve what's in here?" asked Jane.

"No. It wouldn't be fair to burden him with the information. He'll be okay with us just adding a package to the other one. Louise has taught me how knowledge can present a danger. 'Entrapment' is how she describes it."

Steve was meeting with someone in his office, so they waited nervously outside with the precious package wedged between them on the bench. Brett pointed to his painting on the wall and described some of the symbolism to her. Eventually, Steve emerged and invited them into his office. They showed him the wrapped bundle.

"Can we add this to your safe please? Will you have room? Louise knows about it. We thought it should be kept secure until she has spoken to her lawyer." Steve nodded and opened the combination lock.

"Coreene is the only other person who has this code. I don't need to know what you're up to, but we will be praying for you both." As they left, he said, "Bishop Onyango will be visiting us in a couple of weeks. I've arranged for a tour of the Zoo and some informal discussions. I hope Dr. Phillips can join us as a Board representative. It would be great if you two could meet him too."

"As international ecclesiastical representatives?" said Brett.

"Or maybe just waifs off the beach?" said Jane.

"In whatever capacity you care to present yourselves! I suggest: recalcitrant tourists up to no good!" said Steve.

Jane said, "That would be me. Brett could be there as a former Zoo resident who can't stay out of trouble!"

Louise visited the clinic at the beginning of March to advise on the purchase of pharmaceutical supplies. Afterwards, as she got in her car, she saw Brett and Jane walking to the beach for a swim as high tide was approaching.

"Get in. I'll drop you down there," she said. As she drove, she told them, "I phoned Allistair Matherton again. I gave very few details, but I told him enough that he was worried. He said we should get it all to him as soon as possible and he'll ask his dad to look at it and advise. He stressed how careful we must be. Can you phone him, please? Better use the Brandons' phone if possible. I keep hearing strange clicks on mine. It could be nothing, but I'm suspicious."

"I'll phone Allistair as soon as I can. I wonder if Jane and I can take the goods up to him. I'll see what he suggests," said Brett.

"Thank you. Be very careful how you express things. He'll be able to read between the lines. We need to plan how to get you two up to Nairobi."

"We'd like to apply to stay three more months. So we'll have to renew our visitor permits in any case."

"When?"

"Before the end of March."

"Perhaps you can take the items to Nairobi at the same time," Louise said. "I will work on a plan and let you know."

They saw Coreene with two other ladies sitting on a bench above the beach. Louise sat with them while Brett and Jane swam. Later, they joined Coreene and Louise who were then alone and deep in conversation under the shaded overhang of the flimsy roof above the seat. Coreene and Louise were obviously having a serious discussion, so the pair sat quietly drying off. Out in the bay, they watched the fishermen's dugout canoes in the shallow water, poled along by two standing men, with a third fisherman crouched inside. Many of the canoes had outriggers, and several hoisted small cotton sails. Dories and dinghies scurried around in the shallows, but Brett knew that the traditional wooden canoes were better at withstanding the buffeting of the waves and the scraping along the coral rocks at low tide.

Coreene was speaking. "It's going to require greater forces than the power I have."

"To improve our world?" asked Louise.

"Yes. It has to be God's work."

"But why is he allowing everything to deteriorate?"

"He gives *us* strength to work for change."

"Can't God work for change in society?"

"He can and He does, but He chooses to work through human beings."

"Frail humans?"

"Yes, but strong in His strength."

Louise asked another serious question. "Why doesn't he deal more severely with the wicked and perverse?"

"He will. But for now, the reality of evil intertwined with good allows all to grow together. The cleansing will come at the final harvest – the ultimate separation."

"Meanwhile, there's so much injustice and suffering," sighed Louise.

"True, but we have the mandate to help to alleviate those and lead people to the truth."

Louise nodded. "As you have been doing, I recognize that. But, if God is as powerful as you say he is – omnipotent, omniscient, and everything – then surely he can intervene in a person's life and make his instructions clear to them."

"Of course. We get direction when we pray and read His word. But, as I said, He uses us as His agents. It's actually a dilemma for Christians."

"A dilemma? In what way?" asked Louise, glancing across to Jane. Coreene hesitated before replying.

"We are required to witness, but we know it can be a challenge for some to hear the gospel – the good news. I don't want to offend people."

Jane felt comfortable joining in: "Jesus said His message would be an offence to some."

"Yes, but *we* should not be offensive. A wise man said we are seldom persuasive when we're abrasive!"

They laughed, which encouraged two dusty boys to shyly approach them. Coreene questioned one of them.

"You are not in school?"

"*Ndiyo*. Yes."

"Why not? No school?"

"*Hapana*. No."

"Are you sick?"

"*Hapana*."

"Why?"

"No pen."

"You don't have a pen, is that it?"

"*Hapana*. Me, I had a pen. The big boys, they took it."

"You go to our house. You ask our *ayah*, our maid. You tell her I said you should come. She will give you a pen. Then you go to school. *Sawasawa*, okay?" He smiled. Coreene asked the other boy, "And you, what?"

"No shoes."

"You were sent home because you have no shoes?"

"*Ndiyo*."

"You do this. You go to the church. You speak to Mister Brandon. He will see if we have shoes for you in our box there. *Sawasawa?*"

"*Ndiyo. Bila shaka. Asante mama*. Yes, without doubt. Thank you mama." The pair wandered away happily. Jane had watched the exchange with fascination.

"Their education depends on having pens and shoes?" she asked.

"Yes. They are requirements in many schools," Coreene replied. "Without them, they are sent away."

"Everything seems so complicated," said Jane. "What's behind the economic mess in the world?"

Coreene had an answer: "As far as Kenya is concerned, the unjust international economic order. The foreign debt burden is overwhelming for this country. Kenya can hardly pay the *interest* on its international loans. Many developing countries face the same challenges."

Brett said, "Several years ago, I remember the Norwegian Prime Minister stating that foreign aid mostly benefits the donors."

"That's what I've been saying for years," said Coreene. "A lot of aid is tied to trade deals."

Louise became animated. "That's true! Much of the so-called foreign aid never even leaves the donor country. More than half is tied to contracts for goods and services from the donors."

Jane smiled and added, "I heard someone say international aid is a system where the poor in the developed world donate money to the rich in developing countries!" As she spoke, she viciously kicked a coconut shell which rolled down the slope of the beach.

Brett said, "You don't need to take it out on a coconut! There's a fair bit of cynicism too about what happens to the funds that do get here!"

"It must be very complicated, with many factors at play." said Jane.

"Steve feels it goes back into history – colonialism, exploitation, wars, and so on," added Coreene.

Louise responded. "The second war devastated the world economy. We're still paying the price."

"The war had a huge impact on people's lives, didn't it?" Brett asked.

Louise's reply was serious. "Enormous. It's dominated the lives of our generation and those following us – along with the crippling economic situation here in Kenya. It's been a terrible burden on everyone."

A gust of wind lifted a panel of *makuti* matting from the roof above them. It dropped back in place but continued flapping as Brett stood and stretched. Jane stood beside him as they looked at an excited group of children splashing in the rushing waves.

"They wake up each morning to warmth and endless sunshine," said Louise.

Jane laughed. "They probably have no idea of what life is like in a cold climate. I expect they think the whole world is warm and sunny like the Kenyan coast."

Reluctantly, Coreene said, "I hate to break up this fascinating conversation in such an idyllic setting, but soon I have to get going. I need to make plans for the bishop's visit next week."

"The bishop?" asked Louise.

"Yes, Bishop Onyango from Nairobi. He's spending a day with us after a conference in Malindi. You may get a chance to see him."

Louise said, "I don't recall ever meeting a bishop before. It could be intimidating."

"For you or him?" asked Brett.

"Ha ha. I meant I would find it intimidating."

"That's what worries me, too!" joked Coreene. "But, no, Steve says he's a kind and gentle man."

"I wonder what insights he'll have on some of the social issues we've been discussing," Jane said.

"I'm sure his perspective will be refreshing and enlightening," averred Coreene.

Brett said, "I've appreciated frank discussions with Simion Katana on some religious and cultural topics over the years."

Louise told him, "Treasure such a close relationship. It's precious. But now I'm getting tired. Can I drop you back?"

They all piled in her car. On the short journey, Jane asked a thoughtful question.

"Your points of view are so interesting. I understand the concept of the separation of the three main groups in the Zoo, but what about the Africans who live in the White sector?"

"You mean the domestic staff?" Louise asked.

"Yes, the workers who are housed in the cages of their employers."

"I suppose that would include Mjuhgiuna and my two maids, Fatima and Shafiqah," said Louise. "I imagine Kelsey McNeil would be fascinated to hear their perspectives as inter-cultural relationships are part of her research."

Coreene said, "Our two maids would have some interesting insights to share with her. They have unique experiences of two very different communities."

"Can we ask them? You know, what it's like living in a different cultural setting," asked Jane. Louise smiled.

"You can ask. But they may be too courteous to give you a completely honest answer!"

21

Brett said, "Moshi offered us a trip to Lamu."
"No! I don't want anything else to do with him," Jane replied emphatically. "You'd do well to avoid him too."

March was halfway over so Brett and Jane finalized their plans to visit Nairobi at the end of the month to renew their three-month visas. They were both enjoying the holiday, so Brett decided to extend their stay. He was very keen but Jane appeared to be less enthusiastic.

On Wednesday the 14th, Jane was visiting a nutrition education project with Coreene near the Tana River delta, when Khadijah told Brett a nice car was waiting for him at the end of the building. He went out and saw a sleek Citroen. The rear window was wound down and Moshi thrust out his head.

"Come and enjoy the air-conditioned comfort of my luxury car, Mr. James."

Somewhat apprehensively, Brett got in and sat next to Moshi. The driver ignored Brett's attempt at a greeting. The second bodyguard in the front seat said nothing and just glared out the front window. He was protectively holding a tiny cat. The car drove slowly around the compound and over to the Muslim sector. It stopped directly beneath the Kismet Kantara arch, in front of the heavy door leading over to the restricted area. Moshi chatted about Brett and Jane's holiday, and asked if they had visited the inaccessible region beyond the wall. Brett replied noncommittally which confirmed to Moshi that they had.

"I'd love to go over there," Moshi said.

"It's still out of bounds, due to the protected anim–"

"I wondered if you would give me a quick tour. You have been there, I know."

"Sorry, you'll have to ask Louise–"

"Well, I thought that, as a fellow believer in the faith, you would be able to just come with me for a short walk to appreciate god's beautiful creation, and – you know – fellowship quietly. I'd value your company, brother Brett." Brett was spellbound by Moshi's eloquence. It was very impressive for a non-native English speaker. He thought, *What a contrast to the first few years when he hardly bothered to speak a word to me!* There were times when Brett caught himself almost liking Moshi – or was it an inexplicable sympathy? Then he recalled Louise's pronouncement 'He's a nasty piece work, that Moshi!' He wondered if he was being manipulated. His thoughts were interrupted.

"My friend, have you and your lovely wife visited Lamu? I have a business associate who owns one of the best hotels on the island. It would be my pleasure to host you both for a few days. It's a fascinating place and a good example of an original ancient Islamic community." Brett was feeling uneasy. *Where is this leading?*

"Yes, I know Lamu. I've been there. Unfortunately, I don't think we'll have time. Thank you." He was wondering how Moshi intended to get through the door in the wall, so he nodded towards it, "That's locked, anyway."

Moshi ignored him, as he thought, *So! The bait didn't work. I'll try a threat.*

"Oh, by the way, I noticed you are driving another person's pickup."

"Yes, we borrowed–"

"Does it cause problems for you when the traffic police see a different name on your driving licence?"

"No. Not so far. We have a letter from the insurance company."

"I see. You know, Mr. James, I have a brother who works in the transport department. I should not want him to feel it was necessary to follow up on any irregularities–"

"There are no irregularities."

"Er – possibly not. But, it can be – you know – somewhat inconvenient to have to explain these simple documentary matters to awkward officials who–"

"Excuse me, Mr. Moshi, why are we sitting here? The door is locked and–"

"I was just wondering…you say you do not have much time left here. How long are your visitor permits? The usual three months?"

"Yes."

"And you arrived in early January, so you will be leaving soon?" Brett noticed that Moshi was sweating in spite of the cool air-conditioning in the enclosed car interior.

"Well, actually, we are planning to apply for an extension next week."

"Oh? Where?"

"In Nairobi." Brett was looking for a polite way out of the situation. Moshi lit a cigarette, much to Brett's annoyance.

"That's interesting, Mr. James. Most interesting. I believe that renewals are not automatic. That is, sometimes they are refused."

"I see no reason–"

"Quite." Moshi sensed the surge of excitement he used to feel when he held a high trump card at the gambling table. "No reason, as such. It's simply that I have another brother who works in the Immigration Office in the capital. I doubt if he'd see your application. But, I suppose, I might mention to him that there could be possible–"

"Irregularities?"

"Yes. Irregularities. But, no, not really irregularities, as such…." A crowd was starting to gather around the attractive car as its engine had been running for so long, and they saw an *mzungu* inside.

"There are no irregularities regarding our stay here."

"No, but even a suggestion–"

"Of irregularities?"

Moshi stared out the side window at the group of interested faces. He knew the trap was ready to snap shut. His servile voice was distinct from where Brett sat.

"You see, brother James, it's not worth the authorities taking a chance with two insignificant tourists…."

As Moshi's voice trailed away and he nipped the end off his cigarette to save for later, Brett's mind swung back several years to the time Louise told him how Peter had been sent to kill Henry. She explained that Henry's cardinal rule was to never reveal he was aware when he was being followed or lured into a trap. Brett sensed that it might be a helpful strategy for him at that moment. He knew he was ensnared, so he calmly followed along with the script.

"How would we get through the wall? I don't have a key. And why are we going over there anyway?"

Moshi guessed he was close to agreement but he did not know that his next move was tantamount to playing the ace of trumps. He reached into his pocket and pulled out a crumpled paper. He showed it to Brett who gasped in astonishment. It was the top half of Miles' map. Moshi did not fail to notice Brett's reaction, although he had no way of knowing its significance.

"Where did you get this?" Brett asked, before he could stop himself.

Moshi hesitated: normally he would not disclose information like that, but he was maneuvering into a position to gain Brett's cooperation. Quietly, he slipped his half cigarette into the packet. He decided to tell Brett how he happened to have the paper. A week after a meeting with Allistair Matherton in Nairobi at the beginning of the year, he had phoned his sister. She told him about an office girl who worked in one of the lawyer's offices near her shop. She would occasionally come in to buy supplies or get photocopies. That week, the power had gone off while the girl was copying a page.

"The copier had jammed and, when the electricity was restored, my sister helped her remove the half-printed page and threw it away. Later, she noticed the wrinkled page in the waste basket and saw the word *Mwakindini*. She kept the discarded paper in case I might be interested in it." Brett remembered Allistair's reluctance to have the map copied, and now understood why. Moshi motioned to the page. "See, the top part points towards Mwakindini. I see a reference to Henry so I imagine that was his research laboratory. But, what is this box and those dotted lines?" Brett was unsure how to reply. Moshi continued his reasoning: "I wonder if this is a duct or a channel, with that X at the six foot point inside. My old colleague, Miles Jolly, once referred to a tunnel and a hidden chamber, but I never knew where it was." Brett remained silent, as Moshi pressed his enquiry, "I wondered if you may recognize any of this?"

"Yes, I have been there." Snap! Brett was caught. Certainly, he recognized the map, but he also knew a lot more. He was thankful that only the top recess was indicated on the incomplete map. Now, if he feigned ignorance, Moshi was bound to disbelieve him. Better to play along, knowing the goods were no longer there. What harm could there be? The threats to block their visa renewals still smarted, but Brett felt safe pretending to cooperate – at least for a while. It was probably better than outright resistance to a ruthless man and his two intimidating companions. "Okay, I can show you. At least the places I know. But how can we get over there? I don't think we should trouble Mrs. Emerson for her key."

Moshi sprang into action. He directed Brett to leave the car, and climbed out and beckoned to a scruffy fellow who had been loafing against the wall. Brett did not know him. He heard Moshi direct the driver in Swahili.

"Take Kuvanza over to Larry Smythe and wait there." As Kuvanza climbed in the car, he handed Moshi a large key. Then the car swooped around the plaza, leaving a trail of dust.

Standing next to Moshi beside the heavy door, Brett thought rapidly. Moshi was open and pliable at that moment, but his threats were fresh in Brett's mind. He decided to be friendly. He knew he was playing a risky game with a dangerous person.

"If you really want to explore the beauty along there, we could see if your map makes sense." Moshi was delighted. He paused to ensure that the crowd had dispersed and no one was taking any notice of them. Unlocking the sturdy door quickly, Moshi guided Brett through and banged it closed. He locked it.

"Who's that person you sent over to Larry?"

"He's one of two men in Mwakindini who help me occasionally – Kuvanza and another man who used to work for Miles. I bought him off." Moshi had perfected the art of innocently dropping confidential tidbits to maintain cordial relationships. As Moshi walked with difficulty along the uneven path, he said, "The other man is the one who attacked you. I recommended him to Miles."

"You did *what?*"

"I recommended him. For the warning Miles gave you."

"Oh brilliant! Thanks!"

"We did what we had to do. At that time, things in the Zoo were very delicate, sensitive and–"

"Fragile and vulnerable! I know, I've heard all the excuses. Thanks for trotting them out for me once again!"

"Listen, Brett, I wanted to tell you honestly about the attackers. I feel there should not be any secrets between us. We are Christian brothers–"

"I don't think that term has the same meaning for us."

"I told you, I know the teachings of the Christian faith that my grandmother explained to me." Immediately, Brett recalled Jane's words 'Knowledge doesn't equate to faith' and he remained sceptical. Moshi added, "She told me she prayed for us children. Anyway, Kuvanza works for me now." The oddly matched pair continued their slow walk along the shoreline.

Brett gave a warning. "Be careful of snakes."

Moshi sneered, "I am aware. I was born on this coast, you know!"

Brett walked ahead while Moshi struggled, with laboured breathing, some way behind him. Brett stopped in the shade next to the witchdoctor's hut and waited for Moshi to catch up. He observed Moshi's baggy shorts and loose shirt. He wore his usual round white hat, known as a *kofia*. He was wearing an expensive-looking watch and clutching a bag. They looked at the wrecked witchdoctor's hut in silence as they passed it. Continuing, Brett wondered how little he would be able to disclose and still satisfy Moshi. Also, he was trying to think how he could retrieve the key to the upper hut without Moshi seeing.

As they entered the compound, Moshi looked around intently. Brett pointed over to Henry's locked research station.

"You can look at the outside of that if you wish. Also, there's a pit toilet at the back that we can use." Brett was pleased when Moshi followed his suggestion as it enabled him to look for the key in the rear rafters of the upper hut. Moshi glanced over a couple of times, so Brett made an elaborate fuss over lifting stones and tapping walls, during which he stepped up and surreptitiously grasped the key from under the eaves of the upper hut. Brett unlocked the door while explaining to Moshi how awkward he felt about entering the naturalist's hut and how angry Mrs. Emerson would be.

"Don't tell her," snapped Moshi, looking at the simple furnishings. Brett removed the matting from the floor to reveal the hatch. As he opened it, Moshi accidentally kicked the open padlock across the room. "So, Miles' secret compartment! Go down and look. Tell me what you see," said Moshi. Brett climbed down the familiar steps while Moshi stood at the top. Immediately, Moshi noticed the metal trunk.

"What's in there?"

"Ammunition, I think."

"Open it." As Brett started to lift the lid, he had an overwhelming fear. Was it the smell of the place or the same trace of ancient evil he had sensed before? Suddenly, a terrible thought came to him: *Moshi could flip back that hatch, snap the padlock closed, and lock me in! My friends don't know I'm here!* Quickly, he looked up at Moshi's bulk silhouetted against the light. "Well, what's in there?" Brett rapidly climbed back up the steps and, with considerable relief, stood to the side and directed Moshi down.

"You look. I don't know anything about guns or ammunition."

Moshi struggled down the steps, knelt, and lifted the lid to reveal several boxes wrapped in grey cloth, lined up in neat rows.

"Strange the naturalist leaves this unlocked," he mused.

"No reason to lock it, I suppose. No one comes here. We'd better not touch anything else."

Moshi slowly lowered the lid and swivelled around to look inside the tunnel entrance. Brett heard his muffled voice.

"The chamber must be in there on the left. That's what the map shows. It's so dark."

"Too dark to see, and I know it's empty."

"How do you know?"

"I looked recently. Also, the police removed the items years ago."

"Oh yes. I heard about that. Some of it was linked to Miles which led to his deportation," he mumbled.

Brett thought, *You dolt! Your betrayal of him played a significant part too.* Moshi fumbled in his short's pocket and pulled out a box of matches. He lit one and eased around the stones at the entrance. *Surely he's not going squeeze himself in there!* thought Brett. He did, and he seemed determined to find the recess which he knew was six feet in. The match went out so he lit another. *That's going to stink in that confined space,* Brett thought as he watched Moshi's large rump and sandalled feet disappear in the tunnel. *He looks like a giant mole,* he thought disrespectfully. In a flash, Brett thought, *I could lock him down there! I know where the padlock slid to.* Immediately, he felt ashamed of himself. And then a strange thing happened: he suddenly felt sorry for Moshi. He looked so soft and vulnerable, worming his lonely way along the filthy and rough tunnel. Brett thought, *Maybe he's not such a bad bloke. How much do I know about him or his background? What sort of life has he had that led him to criminal activities? Is it true that I shouldn't trust him?* His introspections were interrupted by Moshi slithering back.

"It's so smelly in there. And the recess is empty." Brett resisted the obvious response.

Moshi climbed out and Brett quickly lowered the hatch and replaced the mat. They both stepped outside. Brett's next suggestion was strategic.

"I expect you'd like to sit in the shade and have the other half of your cigarette after all that excitement." Moshi looked at his watch.

"I'm allowed one now. I have timed myself to space them out."

In order to prevent Moshi from seeing where the key was kept, Brett waited until he lit his cigarette and was looking out to sea. He called over to Moshi.

"I'll lock up here." He rattled the door and patted a window frame and then went to the rear and took the opportunity to slip the key back in its place, unnoticed.

Standing in the shade, Brett felt thirsty. He wished he had checked to see if there was any water left inside the hut. Moshi stood up and walked back to look at the ground where he guessed the tunnel ran. He turned to follow the line of the tunnel.

"Do you know where this goes?"

"Over to that other hut."

"So, they are connected?"

"Apparently."

"Any secret chambers below that hut?"

"No. Just an empty vault."

"Can we look?"

"We'd better not. In any case, your map shows just one chamber." Moshi appeared to make a decision. Much to Brett's relief, he gave his instruction.

"Let's go."

Back at the wall, Moshi unlocked the door and they returned to the public plaza. He slipped the large key in his pocket.

"Where did you get that key?" asked Brett. He was beginning to lose his reticence towards Moshi, and felt emboldened to ask questions.

"From an *mzee* down there."

"The crazy old man?"

"He's not crazy. Just fearful."

"Of witches?"

"Yes. And other things. He carries hatred."

"He shouted at me in a wild way."

"He hates all *wazungu.*"

"Why?"

"His younger son told me he had some bad experiences with white people – a long time ago."

"Did his son get the key?"

"Yes. Then I borrowed it." Moshi called over a teenage boy and spoke to him so rapidly that Brett could not follow. But he heard 'Bwana Smythe… Energy Centre.'

Brett said, "I need a drink. Would you like one?"

"Yes. Bring me four cold sodas, outside."

"You can come into the cafe."

"No. Kuvanza will be joining me with the car. We will stay outside." He waved his chin to the east. "Thank you for showing me there-over, brother Brett. The offer to visit Lamu is still open."

"Thank you. Maybe on another holiday. Goodbye, Mr. Moshi."

As they parted, with the briefest of handshakes, Moshi said to himself, *That's all the information you'll get from me! You are holding something back, Mr. James. Maybe you have removed the goods. Where are you storing them? You would not keep them in the guesthouse. So, where? Mrs. Emerson has a safe. That's it!* He waited in the shade for his car. Reluctantly, he sent Kuvanza back to the old man's son with the key as he had promised he would. He wanted to keep his convenient relationship with the cantankerous old man.

Moshi smiled at the thought of what he had not told Brett – information he had extracted from Iha, the cooperative younger son. Decades earlier, the *mzee* had worked for Henry Emerson on the initial construction of the Zoo.

But he had disobeyed the instruction to stay out of the protected area. One evening, he had wandered through to where the foreign craftsmen worked and saw what they were building. He got a close look at the half-built tunnel. He was immediately fired and had been resentful ever since. He had become mentally unbalanced, but he was smart enough to hang onto his precious key to the main door. *What else had he seen? What did he know?* Moshi decided to try to extract the information from his son, although he knew it would cost him a substantial bribe.

Brett added the four drinks to his tab and sent the waiter out with them. He was not sure when Jane would be back, so he relaxed in the cafe for a while. He began to feel guilty about caving in to Moshi's pressure, so he decided to tell Louise right away. She was bound to hear about it, although Khadijah had only watched them drive away from the guesthouse. Someone must have seen him with Moshi and know they went across to the other side. He walked along to S-33 and asked Mjuhgiuna if Mrs. Emerson was in. He directed Brett upstairs where Louise was struggling with her crossword puzzle. *Oh no, not more crossword questions,* he thought. He got straight to the point and told her he had shown Moshi the hut and the tunnel.

"No! You idiot! You didn't take him over there!" Louise was furious. "I can't believe it. The less he knows the better." She threw her newspaper on the floor, slapped the pencil on the table, and grasped her stick to stand up. "I don't want him to know his way around that section. Who knows where this will lead? I told you, we can't trust him!" At each of the last four words, she banged her heavy walking stick on the floor in frustration.

"I'm sorry. I had little choice."

"Rubbish! Of course you had a choice! He's the last person I want snooping around Henry's place."

"I thought I'd string him along. Appear to cooperate."

"You don't *cooperate* with a person like Moshi. He's poison," she expostulated.

"He put pressure on me."

"Pressure? Huh! What pressure? How?"

"He threatened to make it difficult with my name not matching what's written on the side of the pickup."

"That's nothing!"

"Also, he had the top section of Miles' map, from a discarded copy his sister found in–"

"Oh, brilliant! Stray copies lying around all–" Mjuhgiuna appeared at the door, wondering why Memsaab had knocked for him. All three of them laughed about that, which cheered up Louise. Once Mjuhgiuna had left, Brett used a mollifying tone.

"It's not a problem, there's nothing over there."

"No, but Moshi doesn't know that. He thinks Miles' loot is still hidden. He'll keep on looking."

"Oh, I see what you mean. But maybe he'll be satisfied now."

"I doubt it."

"He seemed okay with what I showed him."

"I still can't understand why you were so stupid as to show him around."

"He applied more pressure. He said he'd block our visa extensions."

"How?"

"He has a brother–"

"Oh yes, I know all about his brothers! He claims he has important brothers in the government. I've worked with Moshi for years. He'll inveigle his way to get what he wants."

"Transport and Immigration, evidently." Louise thought for a moment.

"I suppose he could have made that awkward. He was always going on about his brothers, and how influential they are. What he called his 'tall relatives' – in high places." She breathed in and out deeply. "Another thing I can't understand: how did he get the door key? I have one there." She nodded towards the large key hanging beside her upper suite front door.

"He got it from the *mzee* beside the eastern wall near the southern fence."

"Aha, that old fool! He's always been a troublemaker. He supplied the key to let the police over there, ages ago." She looked glum again.

"As I said, I'm sorry," said Brett.

"I imagine you are."

"He saw only the first chamber. He doesn't know about the second one farther in."

"Hmm. Well, maybe no harm's done. I'm sorry I got angry. Did he see where we hide the hut key?"

"No, I was careful to stop him seeing where it's kept."

"Well, at least he knows there's nothing over there, so maybe he'll leave us alone now."

Brett paused. "Actually, I felt sympathy for him."

"You *what?*"

"I felt a bit sorry for him."

"You needn't. He's a scoundrel."

"I suppose so. But he appeared so frail and desperate. We parted on amicable terms."

"Well, maybe it's not too serious. More people are going over there these days and the layout of Henry's research station is becoming known. I realize *Kisiwa Wa Kima* isn't my private headland." She paused and picked the newspaper up from the floor. "Oh, I've thought of a crossword clue to send to my friend. Let me try it on you before you go. Argumentative straight alignment."

As he left, Brett replied, "I've no idea. If you write it down, I'll ask Jane."

Brett told Jane all that had happened when she returned tired after her long outing. After he had heard about her day, he described his meetings with Moshi and Louise.

"Louise gave us a clue for a crossword." He showed Jane the paper. Immediately, she knew the answer.

"Row. A homograph."

"You're clever. By the way, Moshi offered us a trip to Lamu."

"No! I don't want anything else to do with him," she replied emphatically. "You'd do well to avoid any further contact with him too."

Part Four

ATTACKS

The fictional character introduced in Part Four

Shane Carson: marine biologist from Galveston, Texas, USA

22

"But we have hope. The churches – and other fine organizations – offer a message of peace and love. In a small way, our lives can bring healing and joy."
Bishop Onyango

He often recalled the incident. It had taught him much. Bishop Wilfred Onyango had been waiting at a busy bus stop in central Nairobi. Suddenly, he saw a pickpocket in the crowd. A small boy put his hand into the pocket of a man in front of him. Instinctively, Onyango had grabbed the boy's arm and clutched it firmly. Then he saw the look of fear in the boy's eyes. It was a silent and terrified plea for mercy. They both knew he would be dealt with severely by the group around him if Onyango had shouted out.

Years before, Onyango had witnessed a thief being beaten to death by an angry mob. There was nothing the bishop could do except watch in horror. He understood the group's hostility towards a captured thief, but he was astonished to then see an elderly woman continue to beat the lifeless form with her umbrella. Such was the vengeance of poor and frustrated people who so rarely had a chance to experience or enact justice in their oppressed lives.

Onyango's strongest memory of the lad at the bus stop, though, was the surge of remorse he felt when he saw *himself* reflected in the terror of the young boy's eyes, as he was confronted by God for *his* sin. When he suddenly realized how he must appear to God, and how his Lord was merciful to him, he silently waved a finger at the boy, mouthed, '*Basi! Hapana!* Enough! No!'

and released him to disappear unharmed into the crowd. He wondered why the vivid image had come to mind at that moment. It was so powerful that its unexpected recollection surprised him.

The bishop was in Malindi for a conference. The next day, after the event had finished, he planned to visit the Zoo. He was unsure what to expect, and he felt a little apprehensive. He knew it was a diverse community and he had an outline of what Steven Brandon had arranged, but he wondered how he would be received. He thought about what to wear and rehearsed some things he might say at the more formal meetings.

Then his thoughts returned to the boy at the bus stop. The memory always forced him to confront his flaws. He knew them: impatience at the demands placed on him, and a tendency to judge people by their outward appearance. Even after all his years as a pastor, he still had a propensity to look at individuals as they *are*, rather than through Christ's eyes to what they could become by accepting His love in their lives. He also had a fear of the future when he viewed modern society and the church's role in it. If unchecked, he knew that dread could become debilitating for him. He strengthened himself by recalling how many times Jesus had said 'Fear not.'

He had another covert sin: his delight at wearing clerical regalia and the prestige and authority it afforded him. He knew it enabled him to hide behind a protective cloak of approbation. He had resolved to relate to his flock in a less formal way. Those were Bishop Onyango's thoughts as he prepared to interact with the unique group at the Zoo and observe Steven Brandon's relationships there.

Steve was also thinking about the following day as he sat in his office, reviewing the simple arrangements for the bishop's visit. He respected Bishop Onyango and had developed a good relationship with him over the last few years, but still he felt nervous. They would have just a few hours together – including lunch and a church meeting – and Steve knew several people wanted to meet the bishop.

He stepped outside into the small enclosed garden at the rear of the church. In the stillness of the evening, a vivid thought came to him. He felt an inner voice from God saying, 'It's not your job. Worrying is not your job. Let go. Trust me for the rest.' A further flash of inspiration suddenly infused him with an accepting peace. Jesus revealed to him, 'It is not about *you*, it's about Me. Tomorrow is about Me.'

A driver from Malindi delivered Bishop Onyango to the front of the church at 9am. Steve was there to welcome him. He was astonished at the bishop's casual clothes. On the way to the office, the bishop commented on Brett's dramatic painting in the hallway. After half an hour of discussion, they went into the church sanctuary for a prayer together. The bishop suggested they move the large table at the front closer to the congregation.

"I'd like this to be quite informal," he said.

Then they went over to Steve's cage for coffee. Coreene introduced the bishop to their Muslim and Christian maids. He shook their hands warmly and greeted each one with equal respect, making them both feel they were the one person he had been looking forward to meeting all week. When Brett and Jane joined them later, she could not help looking in surprise at the bishop's sandals, shorts, and gaudy shirt. He was also wearing a baseball hat. He noticed her stare.

"What did you expect me to be wearing, sister Jane? A mitred hat and a cardinal-red cape?" Jane looked embarrassed so he comforted her with, "I don't often get a chance to visit our coast and dress like a tourist. So, I thought, why not today?"

Quickly, the conversation turned to serious matters. Jane mentioned that her late husband had been a minister in England and described more of Tony's international ministry. This produced sympathetic and encouraging remarks from Onyango who then mentioned the names of several mutual acquaintances who had worked in African aid programmes. After a moment, his mood became grave.

"You know, in many ways, Africa is still a brutal and violent place. Our people are sick and suffering."

Steve responded, "Many individuals in society are lost and searching too."

"Yes, unfortunately, it is so. But we have hope. The churches – and other fine organizations – offer a message of peace and love. In a small way, our lives can bring healing and joy."

Coreene said, "You must feel a sense of urgency, though, bishop."

"Oh indeed I do! The good news of the gospel is only effective in the lives of individuals if it reaches them in time...and for those who receive it and accept its message of salvation from sin – I struggle to express this idea, sometimes. You see, I deeply desire that the church should be a safe place for those searching for fellowship and wholeness...those who perhaps have no other means of support and encouragement."

Steve said, "I feel that too. But we cannot compromise essential doctrine in order to accommodate people's preferences."

Jane added, "One of our new church members in England had been challenged by a friend over his dangerous lifestyle. The friend hated to confront him, but he cared enough to tell him the *truth* about the source of his sin. The friend's words touched the man. That led to a radical change in his life and it yielded a deep faith."

Bishop Onyango smiled at her. "That is an encouraging story. Thank you, sister. You see, there is no shame in the gospel. Share the truth courageously in love, even if it may be uncomfortable to some of those we know."

As they got ready to leave, Coreene said, "Thank you for your insights, Mzee Onyango."

"I tell people that all that is required of them is to believe. God wants us so badly that He has made the condition as simple as possible: only believe."

Three church elders and Dr. John Phillips were waiting by their cars as the group emerged. They drove the bishop along the shore and across to the central buildings. They stopped at various points so Onyango could see the beauty of the area and meet some of the residents. Several children attached themselves to the group as they walked through the narrow lanes between the Muslim buildings.

"Just like Lamu," remarked Onyango.

Entering the dining hall, he was greeted politely by a few people, including Louise Emerson.

Steve suggested, "Let's have lunch and then we'll go over to see the northern bay before our formal gathering at two o'clock."

Louise sat opposite the bishop at the dining table, with Coreene beside her. The conversation turned to the topic of truth as a foundation for our beliefs. Louise picked up on the point with a question.

"Don't we *all* believe that our actions are founded on truth? I mean, individually we operate based on our convictions, don't we?"

Onyango gave a mild acknowledgement and gratefully deferred to Coreene who touched Louise's wrist and explained that some religions do not encourage their adherents to examine the truth, but simply force them to obey unquestioningly.

She ended, "Christianity offers full opportunity for the enquirer to examine the faith openly, at whatever level of complexity they wish."

Louise said, "But we each have measures we take to process the information we receive. We feel confident with those...those filters and the pegs we trust to hang things on."

The bishop responded with a gentle smile. "Using your metaphors, Mrs. Emerson, our 'filter' must be the Cross and Jesus must be the 'peg' on which hang our beliefs. Only through those can we have true insight and conviction. Those are the sources of the strength and grace to transform hearts, to renew the culture, and heal our land." Then he smiled again. "We Kenyans love to remind ourselves that Christianity is close to our hearts. After all, Moses was an African, and Jesus visited Africa!"

Louise's expression changed from a frown to understanding.

"Oh, yes. As a baby in Egypt. That's right, bishop."

As the meal was drawing to a close, Onyango said, "All that we do is centred upon the saving work of our Lord Jesus Christ. We are in Lent now. That is exactly what we will celebrate at Easter! We can confidently speak His truth into a confused and hurting world!"

Steve reminded everyone about the meeting in the church that afternoon.

"You are all welcome, and please invite your friends. Bishop Onyango will be addressing us."

The bishop stood and clarified, "Yes, but just briefly. Mainly I would like to hear from you. Please come with enquiries. And bring along your questioning friends. I have learned much today and I want to hear more from you! Please join us."

The afternoon gathering in the small church overflowed outside, with faces peering in the back and through the open windows. John Phillips sat with the Katanas in the front row. Steve had arranged the heavy table with two chairs behind, but the bishop preferred to stand in front of the table, closer to the congregation. He spoke to the assembly.

"My friends, we are often overwhelmed by the needs of our society which are enormous. Today's conditions are so perplexing, and many wonder why God allows it all to happen. But we must remember that the one great driver of all Christian endeavour is Jesus' words 'You will be my witnesses'." His experienced eyes took in some glances of scepticism, so he added, "Of course, we should also address people's immediate physical needs. We must trust God's wisdom and guidance as we respond to each opportunity that is presented to us."

Steve stood and shared from his revelation the previous evening.

"It's not about us or our plans to do good things. It's about Jesus and following what He has already accomplished. What He needs from us is obedience to His instructions."

The bishop nodded and leaned back on the table.

"Yes, brother Steven, you are right. It is not what we do for God, but the work that He can do through us. That is what counts. Now, please, I would like to hear some questions."

Coreene had invited Larry Smythe and she was pleased to see him there. He stood and boldly stated his question.

"I hear Christians talk a lot about sin. Are all nonbelievers condemned?"

"We are all sinners in a practical sense; but when we believe, God sees us as perfect in Christ." Larry and several others looked puzzled, so the bishop continued, "We simply need to commit our lives to Jesus." By that time Onyango was sitting on the table.

Dr. Phillips said, "I think what's behind Larry's question is the topic of hell and the obvious sin we see all around us."

Simion Katana added, "Yes, it is there. At all levels. Even in our politics!" Several people smiled, knowingly. Onyango caught their smiles.

"I view this on two levels. The Kingdom of God *will* come: those who live by faith know that God will, at the end of time, be both seen and acknowledged by everyone. This will be at the final separation between those who accept Jesus and those who refuse Him. But, practically, the *present* is of immediate concern to us. And politics? In addition to our role in the lives of individuals, the church has a mandate to proclaim the message of the Kingdom in the political arena."

Two of the church elders looked uncomfortable at that comment. Brett noticed it, while Jane was anxiously waiting for the bishop's next statement. His casual manner gave him an affinity with the group as he expanded his point.

"It is a delicate matter in our country; but in my view, the church and state should work in harmony and mutual respect. I feel strongly that politics, economics, commerce, and trade need to come under God's authority as much as spiritual matters."

Another man got up the courage to express what had been troubling him.

"Excuse me, Bishop, I hope you don't mind me asking, but I have often wondered why Christians pick on certain issues to oppose, like drugs, alcohol, sex, or abortion? Why not speak out against corruption, theft, wife-beating, or child abuse? What about all the injustices we experience?"

Onyango was serious. "I understand, and we are deeply concerned about all those things you mentioned. But we should not look on this simply as Christians opposing isolated issues. You see, sir – how can I express this? – we try to get into the mind of Christ – on all issues – to bring His love to all people so they shall be saved, not lost."

One of the elders asked, "Do you see it as a battle between good and evil?"

"In essence, yes. It could be viewed that way. But the two forces are not equal! God is victorious. It is not a matter of God's domain and Satan's domain. This is God's world. His throne has been established for eternity and He has already defeated our adversary."

Louise quietly said, "But God must be allowing the devil and his agents to continue practising their deception."

"Yes madam. That is why we are seeing the evils of society and the confusion spreading all around us, but only for a little while."

After almost an hour of lively discussion, Steve attempted to bring the meeting to a close.

"If it were not for Christ, we could never do what we do – as individuals and as a society at large. He alone is the key to every success we achieve. It is Jesus who energizes the change we all want to see." The group seemed reluctant to leave.

One man called out, "But, to me, many people don't know or care about God."

Bishop Onyango nodded. "But God loves them anyway, and He allows us to be the channels through whom His good news is explained. We have all been chosen for this noble task. May God bless you as you share the message with your friends, relatives, and neighbours."

Steve drove Bishop Onyango to Malindi. He had timed it to collect the children from school afterwards. On the journey, the bishop picked up on Larry's question about sin.

"We can present sin in any form we like, and call it choice, or personal preference, or our right, or freedom, but it's still sin. I expect you've heard the African saying: Paint stripes on a donkey and call it a zebra, but it's still a donkey!" Steve laughed. "As I see it, words are symbols which point to a reality but their meanings can be changed. That's starting to happen with marriage."

Steve agreed. "It seems to me that Christianity is becoming the last defence against the destruction of the family as a holy institution. That's just one example of a society searching for the wrong things."

"Exactly. I feel that a redefinition of marriage would be the undoing of our civilization as we know it. It could open the floodgates to – well – anything!" said Onyango.

As they entered Malindi, the bishop suggested that Steve make a concerted effort to deepen his working relationships with the clergy in Malindi.

"I'd like to broaden your outreach into this community, brother Steven. I will endeavour to initiate some closer contacts with your fellow priests here." Steve nodded his appreciation. Onyango concluded with, "You will recall St. Peter's description of our high calling to devote our lives to God's praise: 'But you are a chosen people, a royal priesthood, a holy nation, God's special possession, that you may declare the praises of Him who called you out of darkness into His wonderful light'."

23

Allistair said, "I'll give you directions using an indirect route. That way, you should be able to avoid any trouble in the street. But be very careful."

They had planned it well. Louise helped with logistics. She also insisted on paying all the expenses.

"I would like to think of it as a holiday for you two," she said.

"*You* might think of it that way, but to me it all sounds extremely stressful and dangerous!" Jane told her.

Afterwards, Jane asked Brett, "But what about the deception of what we are planning to do?"

His reply was terse: "It's in the very fabric of the Zoo!"

"It doesn't bother you – the lying?"

"No. It's essential in this case. Besides, Louise and Steve have approved it."

"Steve? Hardly approval! Mere innocent acquiescence, I'd say."

"He had to know our plans. No one else does. On the surface, we are flying to Nairobi to visit the immigration office and extend our visas."

"And watch a pantomime!"

Brett laughed. "Yes, that's probably more unbelievable than what we are *actually* intending to do!"

Steve had agreed to drive them south from the Zoo. Careful organisation enabled them to be outside the church office with their cases loaded at a time when relatively few people were around. Getting the lumpy packages out of Steve's safe was the easy part. Distributing them inconspicuously about their bodies took Jane and Brett considerable time. They both gained weight in minutes and Jane boasted that her figure had improved instantly. Brett laughed, while Steve hovered discreetly in the corridor to keep others away. Steve's only challenge that evening was explaining why the journey to Malindi airport and back had taken him all day. He spoke vaguely to avoid revealing that he had driven straight through Malindi and continued directly south. By mid afternoon, he had dropped the padded travellers at Mombasa train station in good time to catch the overnight express. As far as everyone else knew – including Moshi's contacts in the Zoo – they were on the plane to Nairobi that afternoon.

They sat in the railway waiting room, nervously hanging around for the 7pm train. They blended in with the mixed crowd but felt uneasy with the long wait. They took breaks for drinks and a snack, lugging their small suitcases along with them the whole time.

Jane said, "I feel like a stuffed hamster."

"I feel like an overfed walrus."

"*That's* what you remind me of!"

"So do you, but I was too polite to mention it," Brett said. They looked like two innocent tourists, joking as they waited for their train. He added, "Try to look poor and unencumbered by possessions!"

"My natural pose, eh?"

"This is no more dangerous than normal."

"Whatever 'normal' means, travelling with you," joked Jane.

He whispered, "One is always at risk of robbery."

"But the consequences of theft now would be much greater," she added in a low voice.

"Catastrophic!"

"But it's nothing to us," she said.

"Oh really?"

Brett had reserved a double-bunk carriage in First Class. Jane was relieved that they had the luxurious compartment to themselves. They relaxed once the journey began, as the old-world charm of the experience diverted them from the stress of their mission. It was dark when the train slowly climbed up the escarpment. Later, they enjoyed supper in the luxury Pullman dining carriage, with two lively German tourists at their table. They returned to their compartment immediately after the meal as they had left their cases inside.

The clandestine articles were sticking uncomfortably to them in various places. Louise had insisted they wear them the whole time. She had supplied several strips of folded cloth which they wore like inner cummerbunds. They had divided the items equally to spread the risk. They each had two money belts. They had pouches tied with straps and taped together. Their underwear was stuffed as evenly as possible.

Louise had told them the preparations reminded her of some of the tricks she and Henry had employed years before.

"This is like Heinrick and me in Europe, disguised as a blithe-spirited and carefree married couple."

"We *are* a carefree married couple!" insisted Brett.

"I'm not sure. Maybe we'll be carefree when this is all over," admitted Jane.

They both wore undershirts with pockets to carry their documents. Their personal papers and cash were in plastic pouches hung from cords strung around their necks. They had loosely flowing outer shirts and baggy trousers. They were very hot and uncomfortable. Through the open carriage window, they savoured the cooler air, and saw a few vehicle lights when the train track ran alongside the road. They prepared for bed in their own tiered bunks.

Brett said, "I'm afraid we'll have to keep all this stuff on tonight. It won't be comfortable."

"I hope we can get some sleep. I'll be glad when the journey's over. Then we can relax at the hotel."

The arrangements on their arrival in Nairobi the next morning had been thoughtfully planned. It was early, but Allistair Matherton had promised Louise that he and his father would be in their office to receive the goods. After considering several methods to get from the railway station across to

Matherton & Son, they had reluctantly involved Jim Gossard. He agreed to meet them in his VW van, drive them to the office, and then take their cases to his house. When they saw Jim, he described the latest situation on the streets after the rioting in recent weeks. Halfway to Matherton's office, all the traffic was stalled by a disturbance on the road ahead.

Jim said, "There were demonstrations along the Uhuru Highway yesterday, but this is unexpected. It's very early for rioting to have started. Can't you postpone your meeting? The lawyer will understand with all that's been happening in town."

"No, we need to get there," was all Brett said. Jim did not know what they were carrying.

"Sorry to trouble you, Jim," added Jane.

After twenty minutes they had not moved an inch.

"It's no use, you'll have to walk the rest of the way," Jim said. "We're a bit vulnerable, stuck here. I'll turn around and get home with your bags, okay? I'll be praying for your safety. I wish you would come with me."

Brett told him he was anxious to get to the office.

"Thanks Jim. Everyone's looking up the road so they won't pay attention to us."

Jim rattled off instructions as he looked for a gap in the traffic to turn around.

"Go single file. Let Brett walk in front. He knows the route. Jane, you stay close behind. If there's trouble, don't run. Step slowly into a shop or side street. Stay together. Blend in. Watch for pickpockets if you get in a crowd. Be careful if anyone starts pushing you. It could be a diversion. Put your hands in your pockets."

They stepped out of the van and walked purposefully through the unsettled crowd. No one looked at them. Everyone was straining to see the source of the trouble. There were shouts and horns blasting but no sounds of gunfire. With enormous gratitude, they reached the corner shop near Allistair's office. They climbed the stairs just as a siren began blaring in the street below.

Allistair Matherton met them. "Come into my father's office. We've cleared out his safe. Just place the items on his desk. No one else will come in." When Brett explained how well concealed the valuables were, Allistair left them alone. They gradually removed the items and peeled off the sticky wraps and bindings. They placed all the bundles on the desk and dressed again.

They heard voices outside. Brett opened the door to see Geoffrey Matherton in the small reception area. They shook hands and recalled when they had met previously. Geoffrey was introduced to Jane.

"Lovely to meet you, my dear. You're visiting us at an interesting time. You've not come empty-handed, I hear." As he stepped towards his office he said, "Sorry I'm late. It's chaos out there. It must be about six weeks since the Foreign Minister was murdered and still no news from the investigation. People are getting pretty upset." He looked at his desk and exclaimed, "Well I'm blowed! You've hit a six with this lot."

Allistair stood beside him. "Louise warned me it was quite a haul. We need to list these items. Then we'll decide how to proceed." Geoffrey turned to Brett.

"I was a bit stumped when Allistair called me in early this morning. This bowls me over: you two marching across town, bold as brass, carrying all this stuff. Louise mentioned diamonds."

Brett handed him the two bags. Geoffrey peeked inside and raised an eyebrow.

"I know who'll be interested to see these. I'll check with him and then we should phone Mrs. Emerson to advise her."

"We have to be careful how we speak on the phone," warned Allistair.

They arranged the packages, itemized the passports and lists, and examined the gold bars and coins. Then they started counting the cash, listing it by country. Allistair made detailed notes as Geoffrey described the items. Brett and Jane assisted. They were grateful that the responsibility was no longer theirs.

Jane said, "Sorry to dump all this on you."

Brett added, "Louise didn't feel comfortable entrusting it to the local police. And we just want to get it to the rightful owners, if possible."

Geoffrey smiled. "Your rectitude is commendable. But you took a bit of a chance lugging this lot around. Wouldn't want to be caught out off this spin ball. Still, it'll be safe now. Ha ha. Safe." He pointed to his safe. Polite grins acknowledged his attempt at humour. Brett remembered Louise's assessment of Geoffrey as a long-winded social buffoon with a fondness for cricket terms, but a superb lawyer.

As they checked the varied goods on the list, Allistair again flipped through the Kenyan notes.

"Enough here to buy three brand new vehicles."

"Yes, Range Rovers, probably," added Geoffrey. "How did Miles get his hands on all this loot? Not all of it looks above board. I know he was something of a bounder." He looked at Jane, "Sorry, it's a bit *infra dig* to speak that way. I hear he died."

"Yes," said Brett.

"Still, he had a good innings."

"He did. I was named in his will. He left his things in Kenya to me."

Geoffrey looked at his desk and glanced at his son.

"I'm happy to let Allistair be the first batsman in this match. I'm perfectly content to be twelfth man unless I'm needed. Alright, old chap?"

Once everything had been listed, all four of them signed the bottom of the sheet and Allistair dated it 27th March, 1990. They lifted everything into the safe and locked it. Jane gathered up the pieces of damp cloth and sticky tapes and dumped them in the waste basket, brushing her hands in a gesture of relinquishment.

"Now what?" Brett asked.

Allistair said, "I'll notify the police and invite Inspector Ponda here when he's next in Nairobi."

"Champion! Splendid!" said Geoffrey. "We don't want to be caught off side on this one. I wouldn't like to be on the back foot when Ponda's the bowler. He gets a bit stroppy if he thinks we're doing things behind his back."

"I want to maintain our good relationship with him," Allistair said, moving towards the door while clutching the papers. "Where are you going next?

"The immigration office," Brett replied.

Allistair said, "I'll give you directions using an indirect route. That way, you should be able to avoid any trouble in the street. But be very careful."

"Thanks. We will. Once we've submitted our passports, we'll walk over to the Livingstone Hotel."

Geoffrey said, "I'm not sure about the process for visitor renewals these days. It's the start of Ramadan which sometimes slows things. You may have to return to collect the passports later."

"We'll see what happens. We'll register at the hotel and then I hope we can get a taxi to the airport," Brett said.

"The airport? You're leaving?" asked Allistair.

"No, we'll rent a car from there for a few days."

Geoffrey stood next to Jane. "Well, excuse me, must run-out." He nudged Jane, "Ha! Run out. That's a cricket term. Ha ha."

"Yes, I know. My father used to play cricket," she said in a polite voice.

"Did he? Well I'm blowed. Jolly good. A fellow cricketer. Champion!" As he moved to the front door, he said, "I told the team I'd be over when the traffic clears. It's still noisy out there. I haven't seen this much fuss since a dog ran out on the pitch at Old Trafford. They couldn't catch the blighter. Had to stop early for tea. Never seen such a thing!"

After leaving the lawyers, Brett and Jane had a tense but uneventful walk through normal-looking streets to the government office and left their passports. Then they reached the hotel safely. They confirmed the reservation that Louise had made and took a taxi to the domestic air terminal. They rented a small car and drove to Hurlingham to collect their bags from Jim. He updated them on the situation in the country.

"There's much unrest. Student riots in Nairobi and other parts of the country are making travel difficult. We had to drive through Nairobi last week to collect a couple of doctors who were speaking to our group about AIDS, and we saw smoke in the direction of the university. We realized afterwards it was tear gas. There was fighting, and traffic was being rerouted."

To switch to a lighter mood, Mary gave them two tickets for the Friday evening pantomime performed by an amateur theatre group. A friend of theirs was in the production but they were not attending as Jim preferred not to drive in Nairobi at night.

During the next two days, Brett and Jane did some cautious sightseeing and changed their return flights to England to the end of June. They extended the insurance on the pickup. During the long waits in various offices, Jane was intrigued to see framed photographs of two presidents, and an ingenious use of old electric light bulbs as vases. They were suspended by thin sisal strings and filled with cloudy water. A sprig of green vine dangled down. They were able to collect their passports with the extended three-month visitors' permits. Brett was elated.

"Great! We got them – Moshi's relatives, notwithstanding. We'll now have time to take a safari through some more of the game parks I've wanted to show you." Things appeared quiet in the streets, with only occasional hints of unrest.

On the Friday evening, Brett drove them to the theatre in the northwest of the city. The pantomime was raucous fun, with members of the audience yelling out unrestrained comments and taunts. There was much hilarious ad-libbing and some inane humour. The traditional brawny man dressed up as an old dame was the usual hit. They stayed to chat with the Gossards' friend, so it was late when they left. As Brett drove home, Jane was still laughing.

"That was just what I needed after the stress of the train journey up here and all the uncertainty this week."

Driving down State House Road, they noticed that the cars coming towards them were flashing their lights in warning. Rounding a bend, they were suddenly confronted by a large mob of young people shouting and advancing towards them. Brett immediately double-checked that the doors were locked – which they always were when he drove in Nairobi. He stopped and switched off the headlights. As the rabble approached, two students started to hit the headlights and others began kicking the car. Heavy boots hit the side panels with loud thumps. Brett remained calm and did not blast the horn, flash his lights, or rev the engine. They just waited while the crowd surrounded them.

"Don't do anything to upset them," Brett muttered, while Jane looked terrified.

Three rocks hit the side window and two more crashed into the back glass. If they had broken, Brett would have driven on through the crowd. They simply sat and waited. They were praying under their breath, feeling very tense and helpless in the dreadful situation. Some students at the sides began rocking their car in a coordinated manner, trying to turn it over. As the rocking became worse, Brett knew he had to prevent the car being rolled on its side. He drove forward very slowly towards the students standing in front. He and Jane were waving and smiling in a friendly way. Fortunately, as they advanced, the youths in front parted and allowed them to pass through. Slowly, the bulk of the mob flowed around them and started to attack the car behind. Brett and Jane gradually eased their way through to the back of the crowd, receiving a few more thumps on the way. Later, Jane estimated that there were at least a hundred students in the crowd. They remembered there had been riots and attacks in previous days as the students demonstrated against poor food, high fees, and the unresolved murder. Brett had read about vehicles being rolled over, set ablaze, and the passengers beaten.

They drove back to the hotel, feeling stunned.

"The Lord protected us there," said Brett.

"You did well to stay calm. If they had broken the glass they could have opened the doors easily. Or if they had rolled it over…we could be dead."

"I wonder how much damage there is to the car."

"Never mind about that. We're safe," said Jane.

"I used to have some sympathy for the students as they will often raise important issues relating to injustices in the country."

"But why take it out on us?" demanded Jane.

"They probably think we represent the oppressors."

"Because we look wealthy? Because we're white?"

"I don't know. They appeared to be attacking *all* the cars in the dark," said Brett.

"That's true."

"It's strange because – if anything – our sympathies would probably lie with them, rather than some of the authorities!"

"What will happen?" she asked.

"The government will probably close the university again. The students will be sent back to their home areas and told to report to their chiefs. Only those with a good recommendation will be allowed to return."

"But those university students must represent the favoured ones whose parents can afford the fees," mused Jane. When they were safely in the hotel car park, they examined the damage. The car had several dents and footprints along the sides and Brett had noticed the headlights were pointing in strange directions. The windows were not cracked but there were several nasty chips in the glass. Jane said, "This is probably going to cost us extra on the insurance."

The next day, they visited the Gossards. They hoped Jim could help them clean up the car before they had to return it. He was able to remove most of the shoe marks with a paint restorer and he sucked out some of the dents with a 'plumber's friend'.

"I've done this a few times," he said, waving the toilet plunger around. "The ones where there's a crease or the metal is split...sorry, I can't do much about those. Still, it looks a bit better. Let's have a go at realigning those headlights. At least they're not broken." When they returned the car the following day, the harried rental-company representative was blasé about the damage, as though he was used to their vehicles being returned as wrecks. But they had to pay the excess insurance charge.

The airport was busy as they waited for their flight back to the coast; but they were relieved to be at that stage of the stressful visit to Nairobi.

24

He was interrupted by a firm knock on the door. Brett walked over and opened it but to his surprise no one was there.

It was the first Thursday in April. The daylight was fading as a sleek car dropped two men in front of cage S-33. It then drove around and parked outside Larry Smythe's cage. Kuvanza, holding a stout stick and carrying two coils of rope, hid while Moshi knocked on Louise's lower door. Mjuhgiuna appeared and Moshi asked to see Mrs. Emerson. As the two men climbed the stairs, Mjuhgiuna did not see Kuvanza following them. Mjuhgiuna knocked and called out.

"*Memsaab, hodi.*" He tried to open the door. It was locked. Louise struggled to walk over to unlock it. She was using her cane to steady herself. As Moshi quickly stepped in, he instructed Kuvanza to take the old man downstairs and tie him up. He pushed Louise inside and told her to sit down. Her cane slipped and clattered across the floor.

"What on earth are you up to, Moshi? Pushing in here–"

"Where's the safe!"

"What?"

"Where is it?"

"Get out of here," Louise shouted. He ignored her and began to look around while Louise sat helplessly in astonishment. After several minutes, Kuvanza came in and placed his stick in the corner beside the door. "And who might you be?" demanded Louise.

"Tie her up," snapped Moshi. He strode over to the telephone and lifted the receiver. He placed the phone on the table and grabbed a thick cushion to cover it. Kuvanza stood over Louise and held her while he looked at Moshi. "In the bedroom," he snarled. Kuvanza grabbed Louise's shoulders, pulled her to her feet, and thrust her towards the bedroom. She struggled but she was too weak to resist. She called out for help and slapped Kuvanza's face. He lunged towards her and they fell on the bed. Louise became tangled in the mosquito net and pulled it down from the ceiling attachment. Moshi was there in an instant. He picked up the rope that Kuvanza had dropped, "Get up you fool! Just tie her up." He lashed Kuvanza across his shoulders and flopped the rope on the bed.

As Kuvanza stood, he sneered at Louise, "Eiye, you are so old and ugly!"

Moshi cuffed him around the head and shouted at him.

"Do as I say! We need to search this place and get out quick." Louise looked at the rope and saw that further struggle would be useless, and may result in injury. She decided to pretend to cooperate, thinking that Mjuhgiuna would soon get help. Neither Fatima nor Shafiqah were around, so banging on the floor or trying to get to the buzzers wouldn't help.

She said, "The safe is in that corner, behind the curtain." Moshi exposed it while Kuvanza tightened Louise's bonds.

"It's locked. Tell me the combination."

"739. You have to spin the outer knob–"

"I know how to open a safe!" he shouted over his shoulder, as he set the dial and easily opened the door. All he saw was papers and envelopes which he roughly pulled out and flipped through. He grabbed an envelope of cash and stuffed it in his pocket. "Where's the treasure?"

"What?"

"Jolly's treasure. All the gold. The cash. Where?" He stepped towards the bed and stood over her. Kuvanza raised his hand. Moshi nodded. Kuvanza hit her hard across the mouth. "Tell us!" he yelled.

Louise was defiant. "Listen, you two louts. You might as well stop this nonsense right now and release me. Help is on the way. You'll both be in big trouble."

"Shut up!"

"The money you've taken is my staff's wages for the next two months."

"Where's the loot? The secret chamber was empty."

"It's not here. You'd both better leave...."

Moshi walked away. He almost slipped on the papers scattered across the bedroom floor. Kuvanza followed him. They sat in the front room while Moshi thought. It was almost dark outside. He hoped no one would notice his car by the Energy Centre, or at least not suspect he was at the Emersons' cage.

In the lower unit, Mjuhgiuna was angry, but helpless. Kuvanza had forced him down the stairs and into his room. He had hit him twice on the head with his stick, gagged him, and tied him up on the floor behind a large chair. Kuvanza had locked the door from the outside and held onto the key. Mjuhgiuna knew he was bleeding and he kept losing consciousness. The gag had slipped so he tried to call out but his voice was very weak. He attempted to slither across the floor but Kuvanza had roped him to the stout legs of the heavy chair. He felt miserable, in pain, and sorry he could not help *memsaab*.

Upstairs, Moshi stood by Louise's bedroom door and looked at his watch. It was fifteen minutes before he was allowed a cigarette but he felt in his pockets for them. Louise noticed.

"I'd rather you didn't smoke in here."

"I have to."

"I thought you weren't supposed to smoke during Ramadan, anyway."

"It's dark now. Smoking is permitted. What do *you* know!"

"Can't you step outside?"

"No."

"Go along to the patio if you have to smoke. You two have had the run of my place already!"

"I'll smoke where I want!"

"You are so rude," she told him.

Kuvanza interjected, "You shut up, woman!"

Moshi snapped at him. "Don't speak to her like that, Kuvanza. You just sit there and do your job."

Louise added, "And have some respect young man!"

"I told you to shut up," Kuvanza shouted.

Louise simply glared at him, partly to send a message of arid scorn but also to study his face in case she had to identify him later. She made a mental note of his name. Moshi was still thinking: Louise's safe was empty.

"I heard you have a secret hiding place. Where is it?"

"I don't have one. It's now an open store. Forget this foolish endeavour of yours."

Moshi reasoned: *If Louise does not have the goods, where are they?* He instructed Kuvanza to search all over the unit, but he felt convinced that the treasure was still buried somewhere in Henry Emerson's research compound. Iha, the compliant younger son of the *mzee* who lent him the key had hinted at another hiding place. Moshi desperately needed more cash. His tormentor had told him he would hold off for one more week. Then? Moshi was aware of the sum being demanded. He was worried. He knew what he had to do.

He snatched a writing pad which lay beside the newspaper on Louise's table. It was beside the crossword puzzle. *What a waste of time those are!* That trivial thought crossed his mind as he grabbed a pen.

"Where's your chequebook?" She nodded to a box on top of the safe. "Here, write a letter," he said, thrusting the pad and pen at Louise.

"Huh? Using my teeth?" she retorted.

"Kuvanza! Untie her hands," he called out.

"What shall I write? And to whom?" She spoke with a sarcastic inflection, wondering what he was up to.

"Write to Brett James. Tell him to cash a cheque. It will be for a quarter of a million shillings. 250,000/-." He dictated the words she should write, giving Brett precise instructions. Louise suppressed a smile.

"Think this will work, Moshi?" she asked with mock seriousness.

Ignoring her, he found the chequebook and held it while Louise took a long time to write the letter.

"What have you written? What does it say?" he asked without looking at it. She read out exactly what she had written. He nodded and handed over her cheque book. "Write a cheque."

"Payable to Cash?" Again she was inwardly amused by her sarcastic inflexion.

"Yes."

"250,000/-?"

"Yes. You have that much in your account?"

"Naturally." She forced herself not to smile, and wrote the cheque. She handed it to Moshi, along with the letter. "You'll need an envelope. There are some where I keep the chequebook." She was relaxed, in spite of the pain in her face.

Moshi threw the chequebook on the bed and grasped an envelope. He snatched the letter and skimmed the lines, pretending to read it. A few words made sense to him and she appeared to have followed his directions. He handed the letter to Kuvanza. He looked at it briefly, gave a shrug, shook his head, and returned it. Moshi stuffed the letter and the cheque in the envelope and gave it back to Louise.

"Address it to Brett James." She did as she was told, licked it and tried to seal it. Moshi grabbed the envelope and told Kuvanza, "Tie her again." He did as he was told. Moshi handed him the envelope. "Now deliver this to Brett James at the guesthouse." As the pair moved to the front door, Louise heard Moshi say, "Don't let him see you. Leave it outside the door, then knock. Move away and watch to be sure he gets it. Then get back here immediately." Kuvanza left them.

Louise was confident that if Brett received her note, help would soon be coming. Although her two maids were visiting their families that evening, she knew Mjuhgiuna had seen the intruders and would be alerting someone. She simply needed to remain calm and placate Moshi to avoid antagonizing him. Moshi repositioned a chair in Louise's bedroom, sat down, and stared at her in silence. He admired her. She had all the qualities he lacked. Also, during the years they had worked together, she never appeared sorry for herself. She simply accepted the circumstances she was in. Today, he saw her stoical response to his violent intrusion and inwardly he was impressed. Her next words challenged him.

"What are you up to now? Surely you don't expect to get away with this outrage."

"I need money. Fast."

"Sell your fancy car. Get rid of your luxurious assets."

"I am. It takes time." Moshi stood to leave. "I don't need to listen to your advice. But thank you, Captain Louise, for your unhelpful opinion!" He waited for Kuvanza in the front room.

Brett and Jane had just returned from watching the sunset. The incarnadine sky with bands of clouds radiating from the setting orb had almost overwhelmed Jane. She wondered if she could find written words to describe it. On their slow walk back, Brett told her he planned to set up the radio, explaining that the shortwave reception would improve once darkness came. As Jane settled to write her poem, Brett adjusted the radio dial.

"The quality of the reception also changes according to the sunspot activity. I read that it occurs on an 11-year cycle. We are coming into a period of–" He was interrupted by a firm knock on the door. Brett walked over and opened it but to his surprise no one was there. He looked out into the darkness and then noticed something on the floor. He had almost stepped on it. He picked up a small crumpled envelope. Checking outside again, he shut the door. "It's addressed to me," he said, opening it. "From…looks like Louise." He read it in silence. Jane watched his expression transition from amusement to concern. In silence he read it again.

> Dear Brett,
>
> All is well with me – as fine as a Calm Pacific Zephyr wind. Its all for a good clause. I'am sure your aware of that. I have a simple request. I'm shore you will insure that its done rite.
>
> Please meat Mr. Moshi's driver at the front of the Mwakindini bank when they open at 10am tomorrow. Go with him to the manager and arrange to cash the enclosed cheque for 250,000/-.
>
> The manager nose you, and our relationship, so their will be no difficulty.
>
> Love from Louize

Brett handed the letter to Jane. She read it.

"This is strange...."

"We should reverse what she says. This message is false," Brett insisted.

"How do you know?"

"The letter is full of errors that she would never make. Also she's built in her Zephyr code name – see? And the disguised CPZ. It's a warning."

"Let me see," said Jane, taking the note and studying it again. "Is this written by an educated woman?"

"Yes. It's a signal that she's in trouble."

"What's going on do you think?"

"I don't know, but Moshi's obviously behind this." He started to put on his shoes. "Let's find Steve and get over to Louise's cage immediately."

As they dashed over to the Brandons' cage, Jane asked, "Would Louise have that much money in her account?"

"Possibly," said Brett, "but the bank may not have that amount of cash! But it's academic. We're not going to try cashing it." They banged on the door. Coreene opened it. They showed her the letter and Brett quickly explained his concern. Coreene tried to phone Louise.

"It's engaged," she said. Coreene's tone was urgent: "Steve's at the church. No point in phoning. He's in a meeting. Brett, go and find him. Jane, we'll see if one of our police neighbours is home. Can we use your pickup?"

Brett had to interrupt the meeting to tell Steve. Once he read the note, he was worried.

"That's absurd. We should find Katana."

Brett said, "We'd better not delay. We must see what's happening over there."

Steve and Brett rushed to get Steve's car. They were both panting. The children were waiting outside.

"You three stay here. Tell Mum we've gone to Mrs. Emerson's cage." He grasped two torches and they both climbed into Steve's vehicle. As Steve drove, he said, "If Moshi's involved, it could be dangerous. I hope the others have found a policeman."

Jane drove Coreene to try the cages where she knew police lived. No officers were home but they left messages with their families. At each cage they asked them to inform Sergeant Kinyanjui in Mwakindini that there was an urgent incident at the Zoo and someone was possibly in danger.

25

Louise thought briefly, and added, "As a young person, I saw things on the battlefields of North Africa that you could never imagine."

Twenty-five minutes passed slowly, during which Louise schemed silently and occasionally called out gentle warnings to Moshi who was sitting outside her bedroom. She heard Kuvanza's voice as he returned. Moshi told him to make sure the front door was locked. He asked if Brett had got the letter. Louise did not hear Kuvanza's response. She called out from the bedroom.

"Forget this wild scheme, Moshi. Sell your assets. That's my advice. You'd be a fool to continue on your present path."

Kuvanza jumped over and stood in the doorway. He shouted at her.

"Don't you speak to my boss that way. He is not a fool. He is a powerful man. You should learn some respect."

From her defenceless position, Louise responded boldly.

"And you, Kuvanza, should learn some manners! Be careful who you associate with! Put your life straight and get a proper job."

Before Moshi could intervene, Kuvanza leaped across the room and slapped Louise hard across the mouth. In an instant, Moshi was on his feet. He was livid. He grabbed one of Louise's heavy walking sticks, stumbled over to the bed, and clouted Kuvanza across the ear with it. Then he hit him hard three times across his cheek. Kuvanza let out a cry of pain and flopped on the bed, holding his bleeding face.

"That's enough from you!" bellowed Moshi and then spat a torrent of words that Louise did not follow. Kuvanza slumped on the floor sullenly, with Moshi towering over him, stick in hand.

Louise spoke up. "Alright. This is getting out of hand. Untie me, and I'll try to treat that wound, and deal with my bruises too."

As Moshi undid her bindings, he offered a mild apology.

"This is a bad situation. Two black men attacking a white woman."

Louise rubbed her wrists and headed towards the bathroom.

"It's got nothing to do with black and white. Or male and female. It's simply a rich person, a poor man, and a defenceless individual. Get your analysis straight, Moshi! It's exploitation of the poor and vulnerable by the rich and powerful. Simple!" She called over her shoulder, "The same elements occur everywhere in various combinations." She thought briefly and added, "As a young person, I saw things on the battlefields of North Africa that you could never imagine."

Moshi scoffed, "And I've experienced things that *you* have no concept of. I wasn't born rich. You get *your* analysis straight, Captain!"

Louise looked at Moshi and closed the bathroom door. She turned to wash while pondering his words. She knew they were true. She felt pity for him. She could not imagine how his early life had been. She remembered that Brett had felt sympathy for him too, but her irritation returned when she saw her reflection and the injuries to her face. She opened the door and called out to Moshi.

"You don't have to take out your anger on me and force me to give you cash."

Moshi snapped back, "Miles Jolly owed me something. You two were always close. You sided with him."

"Yes, in order to keep the Zoo functioning. We did what we had to – chiefly in response to *your* demands."

"But you always favoured him," said Moshi.

"Not in the slightest."

"You were in league with Miles all along."

"I don't think that's true."

"You bailed him out when Ponda put him in jail at the end."

"I arranged for Brett to contact Matherton, yes."

"That enabled him to slip out of the country."

"I'd hardly describe his being deported in those terms! You have a strange perspective on–"

"Enough!" Moshi glanced at Kuvanza, standing outside the bathroom waiting to be treated. "It's better we do not talk of these things now." Moshi sat down and lit a cigarette. He appeared to be smoking casually, but he was thinking. He felt confused. He had the power, but felt he was losing control of the situation. It promised to be a long wait.

As tempers cooled, Louise washed and applied ointment to Kuvanza's wounds and wrapped a long bandage around his head. He was pleased with her careful treatment and how impressive the white dressing looked. She gave him a glass of water and some painkillers. He began to chew them.

"Don't bite them, just swallow," she instructed as she shooed him out into the main room. She stood over Moshi. "I hope you're not intending to continue this nonsense all night, expecting that you'll get money tomorrow."

"Of course I am. I have to. Now, let's get some rest." He sat back farther in her chair. Louise returned to the bathroom to deal with her face injury.

Moshi thought about what she had said. Exploitation of the weak by the strong is the core issue, he admitted. He had been mistreated by dominant people of all colours and races in his early years. White and Asian bosses had been rough. Also, he knew of tough Kenyan women who were as ruthless as any man. But intelligent and tenacious as she was, Louise was now in his power and offered a means of funding. The riches he sought were not in her safe, but he was convinced she was hiding them over the wall somewhere. He felt confident and strong; in charge again. His years of gambling had taught him the folly of overplaying his hand, but he could afford to be conciliatory with Louise. He would act kindly towards her from now on.

But Moshi misjudged the situation. He failed to recognize that, from that moment, Louise was in control. Decades before, she had learned how to deal with men behaving badly. After she had dressed her wounds, she spoke to them both.

"Look, this is getting us nowhere. Why don't you two just leave? I won't discuss this with anyone, and I'll tell Brett my note was a joke. Kuvanza, you should go to the clinic to have your injuries checked properly. There's not much more I can do here."

"I cannot afford it," Kuvanza mumbled.

"Tell the Sisters I'll pay."

"They will not believe me."

"They will. Tell them I said it." Kuvanza looked surprised. He sat silently. She spoke to him like a child: "You have suffered enough for your foolishness. Don't make it worse. Get seen at the clinic. Alright? I know it's Ramadan, but you will find the clinic open." He simply nodded uncertainly while sneaking a glance at Moshi. Then he walked to a chair and flopped down. He tried to adjust a cushion into a position that was comfortable for his bandaged head. Moshi motioned Louise to sit back on the bed. He retied her bonds. She saw no point in resisting.

After five minutes, Kuvanza was almost dozing. Louise looked at him through her door and, for a fleeting moment, wondered if she should have given him a tranquilizer along with the painkillers. Immediately, she regretted the unprofessional thought. Moshi had dragged the chair across to the bedroom door so he could watch Louise. He knew she was wily, and he did not trust her.

"You know, Moshi, we've worked together for many years. You, me and Henry. We've been through many challenges here at the Zoo. Why are you turning nasty now?"

Moshi stared at her. Then his face relaxed and he decided to be honest. What did he have to lose?

"I'm desperate. I need funds. My enemies are getting dangerous. I want the loot that Miles stole from me."

"Really? I thought you owed him a debt when you ratted on him to Ponda."

Moshi glowered at her. "I had to get Miles off the scene. I assumed it would be jail. Not freedom!"

Louise hesitated and then spoke in a low voice.

"You know, Moshi, I'm very ill. In fact, I'm dying."

"We all are! I'm ill too."

"I'll probably die before you do," said Louise in a combative tone.

Kuvanza opened his eyes and shouted at her, "You will die now if you don't stop talking!"

Moshi snapped at him, "You shut your mouth, Kuvanza! Haven't you learned your lesson? You are just here to do a job." Sullenly, Kuvanza slumped back in his chair. Moshi spoke to Louise, "We all need to sleep. When I get that cash tomorrow, I'll leave you alone. You won't be hurt."

"I'm already hurt! So, what do you plan to do? Leave me tied up all night? I may need to use the bathroom. This is my home you know!" Moshi reluctantly untied her bindings. As he did, she said, "If you two are planning to stay here all night, you'd better make yourselves comfortable in the front room. Keep your foul tobacco smoke out there." She sounded bolder than she felt but she was confident that help would soon be coming. Her belligerence rattled Moshi.

"Kuvanza was right: you should show some respect. I tell you, I am a powerful man and I have access to weapons."

"Your threats don't impress me, Moshi. Remember, I did my six-year 'nursing practicum' surrounded by guns, bullets, and bombs!"

Steve drove quickly to the south side of the central buildings. He parked in front of the scullery, sensing they should not drive up to the front of Louise's cage. He and Brett crept along and knocked on the front entrance door but it was open. Surprisingly, Mjuhgiuna was not there in the hallway to greet them. They knocked on his door in the downstairs suite. It was locked and there was nothing but silence. Brett led the way up the stairs. They knocked loudly on the upper door but there was no answer. That door also was locked so they continued banging and calling out to Louise. There was no sound from inside.

"Something's wrong," said Steve. "Let's try Mjuhgiuna again. He's always there."

Moshi had heard the voices first. Kuvanza was startled by the loud banging. Louise heard it too. She was laying on her bed, hardly breathing. Moshi picked Louise's heavy stick off the floor and quietly closed her bedroom door. He waited in silence with Kuvanza, behind the front door.

Downstairs, Steve was frustrated when they could not locate Mjuhgiuna.

"We shouldn't break in. What can we do?" They climbed the stairs and tried Louise's door again. "Still locked! Is there another entrance to her upper flat?" asked Steve.

"Yes. There's another way," whispered Brett, turning to the other side of the landing and opening the door. They crept into the dark conference room. To Steve's amazement, Brett attempted to pull the bookshelf away from the alcove where it appeared to be firmly fixed.

"What are you doing?"

"Hold the light a minute. There's a lever which should help us slide this unit out." After a few seconds of wiggling, the shelving cabinet slid towards them and they glided it out into the room. "Let's be very quiet," he whispered to Steve. "Mind your head on the low lintels in here."

Brett was able to edge his way through the cluttered room which he knew as CPZ-Store. Steve followed him. Shielding the torches with their hands, they eased their way through the dark space. A heavy curtain blocked their view. Brett's heart was racing. Steve was mystified over what was happening.

Louise had got off the bed, picked up another heavy cane, and silently opened her door. She stood behind Moshi and Kuvanza, watching them. Suddenly, Brett and Steve ripped back the curtain and appeared in the corner of the front room. Immediately, Moshi unlocked the front door and dashed out onto the landing. Brett looked over at Louise and was horrified by the red marks on her face. He was about to ask if she was alright, when Kuvanza pushed past him and rushed out the front door.

"Let them go!" commanded Louise. "Don't try to stop them!" Steve stepped over to Louise to help her.

Brett shouted out, "Kuvanza! Why are you here?"

The young man was at the top of the stairs while Moshi was halfway down the flight. Hearing Brett's shout, Kuvanza spun around to look at him. The bandage on his head slipped and covered his eye. He lost his balance and fell backwards, crashing into Moshi who toppled down the remaining stairs, letting out a loud yelp of pain. Kuvanza grasped the handrail and leaped over him and dashed out into the night. Brett saw Moshi struggle to his feet and limp outside, clutching his right shoulder.

Steve helped Louise back to bed as he noticed the collapsed mosquito net, with blood splattered on the bed. Papers were scattered all over the floor, and the safe door was wide open. Steve was horrified at the mess.

"What ever happened here tonight?" Louise did not reply.

"Did you see Mjuhgiuna?" she asked. "We should check if he's alright."

"We didn't see him. The door's locked down there."

With Steve's help, she hobbled over to the shelf and picked through some keys.

"Here, try this."

Brett got downstairs just as his pickup arrived. Coreene and Jane climbed out.

"Are you okay?" asked Jane. "We've just seen two men rushing out. One was limping. They went north."

Steve was at the lower door trying the key. It opened and they quickly found Mjuhgiuna. In the darkness Brett thought he had been doused with water, but soon realized that he was seeing blood glistening on the old man's black skin. He was horrified. Steve and Brett untied him but he was barely conscious. Steve turned to Coreene.

"See if Louise is able to come down. Jane, help us here please."

Louise struggled down the stairs and examined Mjuhgiuna. She was very concerned when he started vomiting.

"He should go to the Mwakindini clinic. They often stay open until nine."

"I'll drive him," said Steve.

"Shall I come too?" asked Brett.

"No, it's okay, thanks."

They gently eased Mjuhgiuna into the back seat.

"Does he need pain killers?" asked Steve.

Louise said, "Better not. He'll only bring them up. Just comfort him as you drive." She patted him on his shoulder and spoke some soft words in Swahili.

Coreene asked Louise, "Can I phone the children, please? They'll be wondering what's happening."

"Use my phone upstairs. It's hidden under a cushion."

Jane and Brett stayed down with Louise. They had just started to clean up the mess downstairs when they heard car doors slamming. Sergeant Kinyanjui and two other policemen walked in. Louise and Brett gave the officers their statements. The police informed them that the watchman had let Moshi's car out through the entrance gate just before they drove in. After a brief inspection and a promise to follow up the next day, the police left.

Brett found the envelope in his pocket. He handed it to Louise.

"You may want this cheque back. Interesting information in the letter."

"But atrocious spelling!" said Jane.

As Louise tore up the cheque, she said, "You got the coded message. Thanks. Henry would have been proud of you."

Jane helped Brett slide the boardroom shelving unit back in place. He asked Louise if they should secure it somehow. She told him to leave it as it was. Coreene insisted on staying with Louise until she felt ready to sleep.

Brett said, "Jane and I will walk home and leave our car here for you. We need to clear our heads anyway."

Coreene asked, "Would you be able to pop in to see the children, please? Tell them I'll be home later."

Jane assured her, "We'll stay with them until you return."

Coreene said, "Thank you."

26

Coreene said, "You see, this is not just a religious conviction that we have against abortion. It's based on human rights and justice. Values you hold dearly, Kelsey, I know."

At times, Jane had seemed reluctant to extend their stay. Brett assumed it was because she was missing her family. He also probed to see if it might be related to the violent attacks they had witnessed. Jane was sullen for several days which Brett could not understand.

Coreene discreetly mentioned to Brett the possibility of Jane's apprehension over Kelsey's return. He was forearmed with that insight when he later spoke to Jane.

"I expect you'll be interested to meet Kelsey; but, don't worry, we won't have much to do with her." Jane was silent, so he added, "You may even like her!" Immediately, he saw it was not a beneficial comment. Jane remained uncommunicative for the next quarter of an hour.

Eventually, she asked, "Do we *have* to collect her from the airport?"

"Why not? We're the obvious people."

"Can't the Brandons go?"

"They're both so busy and we're here on holiday."

"I see."

"We don't need to let anyone know it's a sensitive issue with you," Brett said, still trying to be helpful.

"It's not a sensitive issue!" There was another silence. Brett looked out of the window. Two minutes later, Jane said, "Okay, we'll go."

A week after Easter, on the way to collect Kelsey, Jane could not clear her mind of the photo of Kelsey that Miles had in his room.

She told Brett, "We don't need to hug each other or anything, do we?"

At Malindi airport, Kelsey came bounding out of the arrivals section, smiling and waving.

Brett said, "Kelsey, I'd like to introduce Jane. Jane, this is Kelsey."

Brett and Jane started to shake Kelsey's hand but she said, "Hey guys, why so formal?" She reached up and hugged them both warmly. "It's real good to see y'all. Nice of you to meet me. It's so cool, seeing you Jane. I love your hair. Wow, I can see why Brett fell in love with you. You're so tanned and pretty!"

In spite of herself, Jane smiled. "Well thank you. It's lovely to meet you, after all Brett has told me–"

"Oh no! I sure hope he wasn't too honest about me!"

"Oh, surely you–"

"Hey, I love your accent, Jane. So refined. But you know, I still tend to say the wrong things – you know – in social situations and all."

"Not so far, you haven't!" Jane said. They laughed together like old friends.

"But man, I must look a wreck after that journey. Give me some sun and salty air. Oh, and a few of those amazing mangos too." Brett was relieved to see Jane laughing at Kelsey's commentary. As he loaded Kelsey's cases, the two ladies continued chatting. "This is so cool, us all being here. It's thanks to Miles, you know. He paid my way."

"Ours too," said Jane.

Kelsey asked, "Really? Where did that guy get all his dough? I thought he was, like, poor."

"He worked hard and didn't have a lot of expenses, I suppose," interjected Brett.

"I guess so, being a reclusive bachelor. He didn't have many interests...." Kelsey said, "But, know what, he told me he did have some contracts on the side." She giggled, "What a character!"

As Brett drove, Jane and Kelsey spoke about the plane journey and what the Zoo was like at that time. They were completely at ease with each other. Kelsey again mentioned the gifts from Miles.

"I was amazed when I got the letter from his attorney. That's so cool, him sending me that cash. My own money went on school fees."

"School?"

"University. My Ph.D. is costing me a few bucks I can tell you. Well, my dad helped some."

After they had taken Kelsey to her room at the guesthouse, several of the neighbours came to see her, so Jane and Brett left.

Jane said, "She's so nice."

"I told you she was fun."

"Then why was I nervous about meeting her?"

"I thought you…well, I don't know what you thought!" said Brett in despair.

Jane admitted, "On the journey home, I listened to Kelsey and I thought: this girl is sharp. She notices things and analyses them before I've even seen them! She's so relaxed and natural."

"And fun?" asked Brett.

"Certainly. Fun. You know we've been thinking about a safari to the highlands? Do you think Kelsey would like to join us? She's had some experience of it all before. And I'd like another girl along with us." This time, Brett could not smother his smile.

He said, "That's a sudden change."

"Not really. I was a bit uneasy about Kelsey before, but now I've met her, I like her. You know how I can quickly adapt to new circumstances."

The Brandons had invited the three visitors for supper. After a delightful meal, the children dispersed and the adults caught up on the changes since Kelsey's last visit. Kelsey was completely comfortable with Steve and Coreene, so after talking about the plans in the community for Eid-ul-Fitr at the end of Ramadan in a few days, they quickly found themselves discussing deep topics. Coreene updated Kelsey on some of her projects and explained how some local women were still treated poorly. That riled Kelsey.

"So, submission to the group means following customs like wife beating, arranged or forced marriages, female circumcision and all," she challenged.

Jane pointed out, "It's not just local traditions that oppress. Well-funded international agencies promote abortion services under the euphemistic term 'family planning'."

"Aren't they also providing free contraceptive devices? That must help the women with birth control when they're not ready to get pregnant," said Kelsey.

"Yes, that's true," Coreene acknowledged. "Let's give credit where it's due, but they also aggressively push western notions of abortion. African women are against abortion. They want help to deliver and raise healthy babies!" Kelsey said she understood but avowed that she strongly believed in individual rights. "Such as the right to chose? Including abortion?" asked Coreene.

"Yes, a woman has the right to decide what she does with her own body."

"And the right to choose for someone else?"

"No."

"What about the right of her unborn child to choose?"

"That's a fetus. It has no rights."

"Up until it's born…then it is a child?"

"Yes. Obviously before birth it's not fully human as it cannot survive outside of the mother."

Steve spoke: "Really? So, you decide on the basis of dependance?"

"Sure."

"Have you ever looked after a baby?" Coreene asked her.

"Yes, my nephews and nieces. They're cute."

"Were they independent – able to survive on their own?"

"No, of course not. They were young."

"So, dependance isn't the issue. Would you say that location or level of development were factors? What about convenience? Can we kill *babies* because they are a nuisance, or an embarrassment, or an economic hardship to us?"

"Babies? No, that's crazy. What are you getting at?"

"I'm just trying to find out on what basis you justify abortion. Is it simply based on the mother's right to choose?"

"I'm a feminist, so I believe in that."

"As a feminist, do you believe in the rights of all females?"

"I sure do."

"Even those in the womb? About half of unborn babies are female you know! Don't they have the same rights?"

"Look, are you guys trying to trap me?" Kelsey laughed.

Coreene smiled and replied, "No, of course not. Just offering another point of view. Science is increasingly showing how babies have full personhood even at conception. And many can survive outside the womb much earlier than previously thought."

Jane had been listening silently. She made a serious statement: "To me, the key question is: What is it?"

Kelsey frowned. "What do you mean?"

"Imagine this situation: Coreene's two boys are playing outside. She hears Graham call through the window 'Mum, is it okay to kill this?' What you do you think her first question would be?"

"What is it? Obviously she'd want to know what it was before answering," said Kelsey.

"Exactly. If it was a mosquito, or a badly injured chameleon, or, say, a captured rat, she may well say 'Yes, it's best to kill it'. But if it's practically any other living thing, she'd probably say it should not be killed."

"And if it was an unborn baby?" asked Steve, pointedly. A hush fell on the group.

Jane continued, "So, it depends on how we define what's in the mother's womb. The abortionists will never describe it as a baby – although that's exactly what it is. They refer to it as a fetus, or a mass of tissue, or a problem. Never a baby. They don't want the mother to think of it that way, as she would never consider killing her baby."

Coreene said, "You see, this is not just a religious conviction that we have against abortion. It's based on human rights and justice. Values you hold dearly, Kelsey, I know."

"And it's clear that unborn children feel pain during the abortion process," added Steve. "Here, the methods are simpler. Girls will sometimes carry to full term, then 'flush-out' as they say. A dreadful expression. They deliver their babies in pit latrines and abandon them to die."

"That's awful," said Kelsey.

"Yes. But some live. Occasionally, baby-cries are heard from a pit toilet and people recover the child."

Kelsey was appalled. "Terrible. How can the girls do that?"

"They are compelled by circumstances. But is it really worse than painfully killing the baby in an abortion clinic?" said Coreene gently.

Steve added, "That's why I made abortion the second of my major concerns in my thesis. It followed the lie of evolution in the degradation of our society."

Kelsey stared at the floor for a long time. Knowing they had a good relationship and had discussed controversial topics before, Coreene felt comfortable sharing more with Kelsey.

"I simply cannot understand why western feminists are not trying to do more to address the terrible ways women are treated all over the world. I don't hear many voices raised against female circumcision – some call it 'mutilation' – and other dreadful practices. Or are you just concerned about your own personal agendas and so-called rights?" Immediately, Coreene realized she had spoken harshly and added, "Sorry, that wasn't aimed at you Kelsey. But I see so much pain, suffering, and injustice. I'm in almost constant pain myself. I'm just weary. So weary of it all." She looked down at her hands. She was almost in tears. Jane touched her arm.

"I understand," said Kelsey. "I sure appreciate you sharing. I like that you are being so open about your beliefs. I know y'all have deep convictions. I respect those and will sure think about it all."

"You're very gracious, Kelsey," said Steve. "We understand and respect your point of view too."

Brett added, "We're all searching and questioning, right?"

Jane added, "I know I am. We have to base our opinions on truth."

After a morning swim the next day, Jane and Brett invited Kelsey for lunch in the cafe. The Moores were there, so they sat with them. Len had news for Kelsey.

"I received a letter from a chap in the United States. He's planning to visit us next week. One of your countrymen."

"A yankee invasion! Will we survive?" joked Brett.

"You'll even thrive. I'll see to that!" was Kelsey's cheerful rejoinder.

"Who is he?" asked Brett.

"He's from Galveston, wherever that is. I think his last name is Olsen or something–"

"Carson," said Marie-Anne. "I have his letter," she said, opening her handbag. "Yes, Shane Carson. He's an environmentalist who attends the Unified Stewardship Church. Galveston is in Texas, you know." Kelsey smiled and gave a slight nod. Marie-Anne continued, "The church read some information on Len's project and is thinking of supporting it. They are environmentally minded they say. Let's see '...support appropriate technology and small-scale projects in developing countries' is what he wrote."

"But didn't you have to demolish your first installation along the shore?" asked Brett as Marie-Anne folded the letter and returned it to her handbag.

Len replied, "Yes, but I kept some of the equipment and applied to build a proper jetty. That's partly what Larry Smythe is working on at the Energy Centre by the fence."

"I'm a bit surprised you got away with that for so long. Isn't it illegal to construct permanent structures out into the water?" Brett asked.

"There are jetties everywhere! People like them for fishing, mooring boats, and walking on," said Len defensively.

One afternoon, at the end of April, Len drove past Brett and Jane and called out of the car window.

"I'm off to collect our next visitor from the United States of America."

"Oh yes, the chap you told us about. He wants to see your energy projects."

"Yes. His flight arrives in a couple of hours."

"Where will he stay?"

"In the guest wing, next to Kelsey. I've arranged it all. He'll pay his own way."

"She can welcome him in his mother tongue!"

Jane and Brett discussed what they knew about Shane. He was arranging funding for Len's project so he could continue constructing the ducts and tanks. Details of generators, solar panels, and batteries were still being investigated. The expanding Energy Conservation Centre would be partially supported by Shane's church. Also, Len was optimistic that the European agencies would soon be finalizing their donations to his energy scheme. Len was always optimistic.

27

As Larry moved along the balcony, he said, "Be careful. Things are getting a bit rough...in parts of this 'beautiful country'."
"Thanks for the warning. I'll tell Brett."
"He knows," Larry smiled.

When Len brought Shane Carson to the guesthouse, Kelsey was visiting one of the villages to the north. Brett and Jane were outside, so they were the first to meet Shane. He was over six feet tall, and well built. He had short-cropped, slightly greying hair. Brett judged him to be about forty. At first impression, he was shy and withdrawn but he watched and listened carefully. He asked few questions but when called upon to respond, his replies were thoughtful and thorough. As Len commented to Marie-Anne later, Shane was the complete opposite of Kelsey.

During supper in the restaurant, Shane answered Marie-Anne's enquiry about his home church.

"It's the Unified Stewardship Church. We are evangelical charismatic Christians with a strong concern for the environment. I guess it's an unusual group in some ways, but we take seriously the Genesis commandment to be stewards of God's creation. Too often, humans have interpreted that to allow exploitation of nature's resources. True stewardship means more."

Marie-Anne said, "That's so interesting. How did you get involved in that work? It must be fascinating."

"Yes ma'am, it is. My background is in marine biology but I've become interested in energy conservation technologies." Len felt encouraged at

Shane's comments, but said they would need to confirm what type of structure would be permitted out in the water. Shane concurred, "Once we're on a legal footing, with a solid proposal, I've found three things are necessary for success: funding, the right personnel to operate it, and a demand for the product or service. Funds, we can handle. There's a Houston group that also provides great support. Staff, you'd have to identify and train. The product – electricity – I assume there's a market for that!"

Marie-Anne asked, "But how can you get your electricity to the market, the customers?"

"Well ma'am–"

"Please call me Marie-Anne."

"Thank you. Yes. Marie-Anne, ma'am. There are two ways to use the power – immediate or stored. With variable power sources such as tidal, wind, and solar, the electricity is available for use as long as the supply is there – for hot-water heating, lights, radios, some small appliances, and so on. But we need backup storage to cover times of low wind or no sun."

"We get sun and wind most days here."

"Yes, you do. I looked at the weather data. And at night, the reserve power from the potential energy of the stored seawater kicks in."

After a long discussion of technical details, Shane looked tired and jet-lagged but he livened up when Kelsey joined them. She presented an animated review of her day in the community. Taciturn Shane simply sat and listened, absorbing it all in fascination, until Kelsey asked him a question.

"How long are you here for, Shane?"

"Six weeks. It's partly holiday, partly working visit."

"So, you're both from the USA?" Marie-Anne asked the two visitors.

"Yes."

"Did you know each other before?"

"No. We're from different States," said Kelsey.

"But we're quite close. Galveston is only about 1,000 miles from Savannah," added Shane.

A neighbour looked surprised and said, "Close? I wouldn't call that close! I sometimes think Larry Smythe in cage N-2 isn't very close to me in my cage."

"That's because you can't walk in a straight line, you devious fellow," teased Len. That produced a sharp retort and much frivolous banter within the group.

Shane whispered to Kelsey, "They're very rude to each other, aren't they?"

She smiled and said, "That's the British way. It's a bonding thing."

"What do you mean?"

"If you're being teased, it shows you're accepted in the group."

"Teased, yes; but rudeness?"

"It's all in fun. They mean it kindly. You'll get used to it."

"I'm not sure I will!"

The next morning, Shane explored the reef in the southern bay with Brett, Jane, Steve, and the children. He was intrigued by the variety of marine life, and pointed out some interesting features that the children had not seen before. Shane explained that, by keeping very still in the shallow waters and waiting patiently, one could watch many small creatures.

"They won't appear at first, but there is a miniature world below the surface." On the way back from the beach, they met a man returning from fishing. He greeted Brett warmly. Shane was impressed that Brett knew so well a fisherman who just happened to be passing by.

When Shane returned to his room to shower, he saw Kelsey walking towards the guesthouse. She shouted over to him.

"Hey Shane, we're planning an upcountry safari soon. Wanna come with us?"

"I can't just invite myself along."

"You didn't. I invited you! It would be great to have someone who understands my accent! I'll talk to Brett."

"No. Let me ask him and Jane, okay?" said Shane.

"Sure. I don't wanna get ahead of the curve and push the wrong buttons."

"I'll see if he thinks it's feasible."

Kelsey replied, "Hey, that's cool. I don't have a problem with that."

The next day, Kelsey noticed Larry Smythe working in the hallway at the guesthouse. She called along to him.

"Hi Larry. What ya doing?"

"Good morning, Miss. I was asked to look at the water distribution set up…we have here. Low pressure they say."

"It all seems copacetic to me."

"Oh. Okay is it?"

"Sure."

"They're looking into expanding this guesthouse. Want to have extra accommodation. For more visitors. I hope they're not clutching at red herrings. They say there's going to be an ecotourism boom. Whatever that means."

"Can't be bad. Brett said there are lots of natural and unspoilt environments nearby."

As Larry tightened a gate valve, he asked, "Staying healthy?"

"What?"

"Yer stayed healthy here?"

"Sure have. But it's so hot and humid."

"May's wettest month. Heaviest rainfall. But it's always humid. All year. Tropical coast, see?"

"Yeah, it's hard to get things dry."

"Not much variation in temperatures. Wind's consistent strength but changes direction. From southeast now."

"Oh yeah. Today I'm going with Coreene to a village."

"A bit of advice, Miss. When you're out visiting…not sure if yer cup's clean, trickle a bit of hot tea over the rim. Where your lips will touch. Also, to wash hands, carry a paper towel. Dribble some coffee or tea on it. You can do that without anyone seeing."

"Good idea. Thanks."

"So much to learn, eh?"

"I'm an anthropologist. I'm fascinated by cultural conventions."

"So you've probably heard that we should never indicate something with our foot, or show the soles of our shoes – that's mainly with the Asian community, I think."

"I read that."

Larry paused. "Not married?"

"No."

"I wonder why."

"So do I!"

"Ha. You're spunky."

Two young children were leaning on the rail watching Kelsey and Larry chatting on the verandah. The girl had a baby strapped to her back using a *kanga*. They were staring wide-eyed at the two strange creatures snapping words at each other in an incomprehensible tongue. They laughed when the adults did. Kelsey smiled at the kids. Larry ignored them.

She told Larry, "I'm too busy to find a husband."

"Busy? Doing what?"

"Studying."

"Studying what?"

"My post-grad work."

"What's that?"

"For my doctorate. My Ph.D."

"You gonna be a doctor?"

"Kind of. Not medical."

"You wealthy?"

"Not yet!"

"Will you be?"

"Hope so." She was beginning to like crisp sentences.

"Never count your blessings before they hatch."

"Ha. I plan to get rich."

"That'll attract a husband."

"Ha! You're real practical, Larry."

"That's what they tell me. Practical."

"So, what's it like, living in the Zoo?"

"Okay." He glanced over at her. "You religious?"

"No."

"I'm with you on that one. Don't see the point of it," confessed Larry. "But a lot of people around here are...into religion."

"Know what? – I'm a bit interested."

Larry sneered, "Huh! Good for you!"

"Sometimes I wonder about it all. But I don't think anyone's got all the answers, do you?"

"No. I've heard it all many times, though."

"But I'm interested in relationships," Kelsey said.

"Oh, there's a few of those here!"

"Cross-cultural relationships."

"It's a good place for those."

"I've been using the community as a case study."

"Cultural stuff?"

"Yeah."

"On that, in Kenya, never point at or count people. Even animals. It's against their custom. I've known cases of child shepherds or goat-minders who knew exactly how many animals they had in their flock. But they never count them."

"Interesting. I'm learning loads of new stuff."

"Otherwise, all okay?"

"Sure. The only hassle is a bat indoors, flapping and squeaking around my head in the evenings."

"Yer get that."

"I know I get it. I don't want it!"

"Hit it with a fly swat."

"No! That's cruel. And it might bite."

"Just ignore it then."

"Great! Thanks!"

"Don't you get bats in America?"

"Sure we do. But not in my bedroom."

"Be grateful. But you must like it here. Your third trip?"

"Right. I love it. Kenya's such a beautiful country. I'm sure looking forward to our next safari."

"Upcountry?"

"Yeah."

As Larry moved along the balcony, he said, "Be careful. Things are becoming a bit rough…in parts of this 'beautiful country'." His blue eyes conveyed concern.

"Thanks for the warning. I'll tell Brett."

"He knows," Larry smiled. "Cheerio."

"'Bye."

For some reason, Kelsey felt uneasy as Larry walked away to continue his investigation of the water pressure.

28

Brett said, "I learned that community-based projects have the greatest impact – especially when they are initiated by the local people to meet the needs as they see them."

In early May, Len and Shane had been visiting some energy projects along the coast, when they arrived to join the others in the cafe for supper. During the meal, Shane spoke more about his interests.

"I guess our preference is for small-scale individual projects as they are sustainable and effective. I was intrigued when I read about Len's original dream of independent, self-sustaining energy installations suitable for individual dwellings or small business enterprises."

Brett added, "In Nyeri, I learned that community-based projects like a well or water collection and storage facilities have the greatest impact – especially when they are initiated by local people to meet the needs as they see them. Supporting those small start-up projects is actually the philosophy of the National Christian Council of Kenya, the organisation that I worked with. I really admired their approach."

Jane asked Shane, "Would small-scale electricity generation fit that description, I wonder?"

"I think so, as it saves money and supplies a viable energy source locally," said Shane.

Brett recalled their experience on the catamaran when the wind swung around wildly.

"How do the wind generators cope with varying wind directions?"

"I understood that your winds here are pretty consistent from the two main directions."

"Yes, but during the transition seasons, sometimes the wind swirls right around," said Brett.

Len spoke: "The voice of experience there! He nearly capsized a catamaran when the wind did a 360 on them."

Shane was unfazed. "Good quality installations can cope with changing winds. No problem."

Kelsey spoke up, "I'm from Missouri on that one."

Brett look puzzled so Shane explained, "That means she's skeptical."

"I sure am. I can't see windmills reacting well in variable winds. Isn't that what brought down your previous set-up, Len?"

"Partly, yes. Along with the storm surges and corrosion."

Marie-Anne had a question. "How is the power stored? Len has tried batteries but they tend to grow legs!"

Shane smiled. "For low-demand DC uses, batteries are fine. You just have to secure the bank of batteries. You've built tanks for water to give the potential energy to run generators to cover the downtime when the active sources are unavailable."

"What about staffing?" asked Jane. From her discussions with Coreene, she knew good personnel were a vital aspect of any project.

Shane replied, "I hope Len's colleagues will be able to recommend some trained staff. I won't be here long...."

"And I can't be too heavily involved much longer," admitted Len. "But Larry Smythe is a good man."

"Larry Smythe? Is he honest?" asked Shane.

Len grinned. "I doubt it, but he does his work, fulfills his obligations, and produces results."

Shane responded, "I get your point, but I'd like to feel we're relying on a person of integrity. You know, someone we can trust."

"We can trust him as far as the conservation project is concerned."

Shane simply said, "Got it. The project sounds like a go."

Marie-Anne said, "It's kind of you to be so encouraging, Mr. Carson."

"You bet. Please call me Shane. I feel it's worth taking this to the next stage."

Len said, "So do the two agencies in Switzerland and Norway. They feel strongly that we have to get off conventional fuel sources – particularly hydrocarbons – so any innovative approach is worth investigating."

"Also, increasing your solar panels is something that we would be prepared to support. If you build the right structures in convenient places, they can provide shade underneath for, say, carports, or small vendors' stalls, or social activities."

Len was pleased. "Wonderful, thank you."

"What about clean water? We're blessed with the spring up on the hill, but as the community grows, we should be collecting rainwater, don't you think?" asked Marie-Anne.

Shane nodded, "Certainly. I understand that sufficient rain falls in Kenya, but it's not often collected, stored, or distributed efficiently. It's not part of my mandate on this trip, but I agree that any integrated system should incorporate clean water-collection surfaces and storage tanks."

"Maybe we could install channels at the base of the solar panels to capture the runoff," suggested Brett.

"Right. Talking about potable water, there are some interesting sea-water desalination technologies coming out of Israel. Worth looking into. But they require a lot of money and they take up space."

"Unfortunately, we have neither!" joked Len.

Marie-Anne saw that Kelsey was getting tired of the technical discussions, so she asked her about her visits to the villages.

Kelsey explained, "Everyone likes to shake my hand. Then they invariably ask for something. Sometimes it's like shaking hands with an octopus! They must think I'm a rich American."

"That's how you appear to them," said Marie-Anne.

"I guess so. Know what, I admire their moxie."

Len explained, "Asking costs them nothing, and it occasionally produces results."

Kelsey added, "But, y'know, some of the kids are terrified of me. They're not used to my white skin, I guess."

Len laughed and described an experience:

"I once saw village children running away in terror from an elderly British lady who had white flowing hair. They had been told what a lion looked like and had been instructed to run away immediately they saw one. To them she looked like a fierce lion!"

"It shows how misunderstandings can happen," said Marie-Anne.

"But aren't most people here used to seeing white people?" asked Shane.

"Yes, but out in the remoter villages, we *wazungu* are rarely seen. You'd be surprised how things vary in different regions. Many of the elderly folk don't know any English, or even Swahili, as they only learned their local tribal language. It's fascinating to visit those people if you ever get an opportunity."

"I'd love to, actually," said Shane.

"Would you have time while you're here? We'd like you to join us on safari to make up a foursome," said Jane.

"Thanks for the invitation. That's real kind of you. I have to see the technical aid guys at the US Embassy in Nairobi, then I'll have a couple of weeks to myself."

"Let's do it!" said Kelsey. Brett was uneasy, but said nothing. He was still thinking about transport and other logistics.

The plans for the safari were coming along well. Jane was enthusiastic about having Shane and Kelsey join them. Brett outlined the proposed route to Kelsey.

"Would you like to revisit some of the places we saw before?"

"I sure would," she replied.

Jane smiled, "It'll be great to have you come along with us."

That night, Brett and Jane had supper with Len and Marie-Anne and the topic of the proposed safari came up. The Americans were not there so Len shared a thought.

"Kelsey's quite a character; a lively young lady. Shane seems a bit more low key. I wonder how you four are going to get on under stressful travelling conditions?"

"I don't know. I haven't given it much thought," said Brett. That was not entirely true because he had been wondering how it would work with two very different personalities joining him and Jane on a trip.

"May I make a suggestion?" said Len. "Before committing yourself to an extended safari, maybe try a day trip somewhere, just to see if you all get along."

Brett brightened. "Good idea. I want to visit the Shimba Hills National Reserve while we're here. Maybe we could all go there together on Saturday. I'll suggest it to the others."

The experimental day was successful. Brett drove, and the others alternated sitting at the front. The four got along well, and enjoyed their adventure in the game park, which was inland from Mombasa. They saw a family of giraffes, a buffalo, and two elephants. Brett was thrilled when they located a herd of large sable antelopes – the only place in Kenya they can be seen. The visitors were impressed by the drier atmosphere, which was a relief from the humidity, and admired the dramatic panoramic views of the coast from the height of the plateau. Brett pointed out Diani Beach, the tourist-saturated resort area, which was just visible to the south along the coast.

On the way home, they stopped for supper at one of the fancy hotels north of Mombasa.

Just before they began their meal, Kelsey said, "I'm surrounded by Christians. I feel I should say grace or something."

"It probably wouldn't do you any harm," quipped Brett.

"I remember something my grandmother used to say." They closed their eyes and Kelsey prayed, "For what we are about to receive, may the Lord make us truly grateful."

Jane said, "Amen."

"There," said Shane. "That wasn't too painful, was it? We might make a Christian out of you yet!"

Kelsey laughed and said, "Well, you've really come out of your shell! The shy Shane Carson isn't as shy as we thought."

"Let's give credit to the vivacious company I've been keeping today."

Kelsey said, "I was thinking, we make an interesting foursome. Remember our little game with Miles, Brett? There are several possible combinations."

"Oh really?" Jane said, cautiously.

"Yes, I've analysed our quartet: two Yanks and two Limeys. That's two Americans and two Englishmen."

"Oh, so I'm an Englishman now, am I?" laughed Jane.

Shane added, "Two guys, two gals."

Brett was enjoying the exchange. "Two experienced Kenya hands – me and Kelsey – and two naive tourists!"

"Y'all think my few weeks in Kenya qualify me as *experienced*? Wow!" Kelsey responded.

Over coffee, Kelsey joked, "You Christians sure know how to order good coffee."

Brett replied, "It's all part of the package: flavoursome coffee, stimulating discussion, and guidance on the promise of eternal life."

Shane spoke up. "Many churches stateside offer that combination – some with their own coffee bars! Not a bad deal, eh?"

"Well, I'll accept the tasty coffee!" was Kelsey's snappy rejoinder. Then she said, "I've been thinking, you could match us up in other ways. For example, three youths and an old man!" she laughed, patting Shane's arm.

Shane said, "Oh, very funny. I'm not forty yet."

They were all laughing, so Brett risked offering, "Two intelligent men…." and deliberately let the words hang in the air.

Immediately, Kelsey jumped in with, "And two *brilliant* women! No remarks from the cheap seats, please."

Shane was impressed. "We're going to need her sharp wit on this trip. What do you feel, Brett?"

"Indispensable, I'd say."

"Know what? I think this safari idea will fly," said Kelsey.

Jane responded, "I agree. It'll fly. Shane?"

"Sure!"

They raised their hands in a four-way handshake and shouted in unison, "Let's do it!"

In the four weeks since his unsuccessful attempt to extract money from Louise, Moshi had received treatment for his injured arm and shoulder. Nothing had been broken in the fall down the stairs, but it was extremely painful and it limited his movements. He had been warned of a long recovery time. However, it did not stop him from scheming. After he and Kuvanza had rushed over to Larry's Energy Centre that evening, they had immediately driven out of the compound. Moshi and his driver had dropped Kuvanza at the clinic in Mwakindini and then driven back to Mombasa in the dark. Moshi used the pitiful sum from Louise's safe to temporarily appease one of his pursuers. The loan from Larry enabled him to make a small downpayment of good faith to postpone the threats from his other main opponent. He knew he had a few weeks of grace.

He had managed to dodge an interview with Inspector Ponda, but knew Kuvanza had been questioned. Larry Smythe told him Ponda and Sergeant Kinyanjui had been seen in the Zoo on two separate occasions. Louise had opted not to pursue a complaint against the two attackers, hoping that the injuries they sustained would deter them from future nonsense. She also wanted to avoid drawing attention to why Moshi had entered her cage. Mjuhgiuna had recovered well and he was not inclined to push for punishment. He knew the wisdom of not making enemies in such a confined community. Brett and Steve would have preferred that the police charge the two intruders to forestall any further attacks, but they kept their views to themselves.

Moshi knew what his next move would be. The chamber north of the mosque was empty, as was Louise's safe, so the treasure had to be over on the headland. He needed to question the unbalanced *mzee* who held the key and reportedly knew what Henry had built underground in the early years. But would he be willing to talk, and could Moshi trust what he said? Iha had been cooperative, but the older son wanted nothing to do with Moshi or his schemes. Which son would the senile old man listen to?

Once he had a clear picture of other hiding places in Henry Emerson's research base, he would pay Iha to get the key from the old man again. Then he would take Kuvanza and Iha to help him locate the treasure that he was convinced lay hidden somewhere in the underground vaults or within the tunnel.

He reasoned, "But I need a backup plan." He had learned from Henry Emerson, many years previously, the importance of an escape hatch. "I must have a second exit route in case I need to work my way out of the confined headland." He already knew how he would dispose of his car, meaning it would not be available, so transport would be difficult. Then an idea struck him: a hostage! "With a valuable hostage, I can negotiate anything." His strategic mind was occupied for the next three days refining the details of that scheme.

Part Five

SAFARI

29

Jane said, "I wondered how we are going to wash on this trip?
Will there be showers or running water? What about washing clothes?"
Brett joked, "It's a basic camping safari. We don't wash."

The journey up to Nairobi was an entirely new experience for Shane. Brett explained some of the interesting sights on the way. At several places along the road, they saw the train tracks which reminded Brett and Jane of their tense train journey.

She said, "That train was an interesting experience, wasn't it, Brett?"

He replied, "It's an amazing project when you think of how they pushed the rail line across the plains, over the mountains, into the Rift Valley, and over to Uganda. It was named the Uganda Railway after its final destination although all of the tracks were within Kenya's borders, 660 miles in length, Miles told me."

"You have a good memory," said Kelsey.

Brett laughed. "I found it useful to remember facts that Miles told me – in case I could use them against him later!"

Kelsey said, "Look at that old truck staggering towards us. It's coming sideways like an inebriated crab."

"Yes, some lorries seem to have the cab pointing one way and the chassis going in a different direction."

Shane noted, "I think they have serious mechanical troubles."

"It's a credit to the drivers and mechanics that they continue moving at all. But I'm always relieved when they've gone past us!"

They stopped at a lonely place on the roadside for a bathroom break. Brett gave shouted instructions.

"Boys to the west, girls to the east. Watch for thorns and snakes!"

"No! Where?" shrieked Kelsey.

"Snakes? Only on the boy's side of the road."

Shane called out, "Brett, you son of a gun, don't tease the gals. There'll be enough to frighten them on this safari, I expect."

After a rinse and a drink, they climbed back in the pickup. Jane took over the driving. Kelsey turned to Shane and asked him a direct question.

"So, Shane, are you, like, single or what?"

"I'm widowed. My wife died eight years ago."

"Oh, I'm sorry," Kelsey said quietly.

Shane said, "Thanks." Then his silence did not seem to invite further discussion, so there was an awkward pause. Finally, he asked, "What about you, Kelsey?"

"What about me?"

"Have you ever been married?"

"No, not yet. Interesting men keep spotting me before I can pounce. But I will catch one soon!"

Shane said, "Be patient. Live to pounce another day!"

Everyone enjoyed that. Jane added her encouragement.

"There are lots of good fish in the sea."

"Yeah, but I'm not interested in a fish!" stated Kelsey.

Jane said, "As we were rinsing our hands back there, I wondered how we are going to wash on this trip? Will there be showers or running water? What about washing clothes?"

Brett joked, "It's a basic camping safari. We don't wash. I find one shirt can last about two weeks."

"I hope you're listening to this practical conversation, Kelsey," said Shane.

Kelsey responded, "Oh, we get into all kinds of topics on these long safaris, I can tell you. Last time, with Miles, we spent ages anaylsing fear and death, as I recall."

Shane spoke, "It's a deep and troubling topic. But one that–"

"Oh brilliant! Let's have a cheerful chat about *death* on this glorious sunny day shall we?" said Brett. The gentle ribbing and repartee helped to pass the time on the long drive.

They were each processing the experience of the journey: Brett was focussing on time, distance, and fuel level; Jane concentrated on the road and traffic while she was driving; Kelsey and Shane shared details of their work and people back home.

Kelsey commented to Brett, "Your pickup seems to go faster when Jane's driving!" Then she turned to Shane and said, "You mentioned something about death earlier. It sounded like you had something you wanted to say." Shane was silent for a moment while the others tactfully pretended to concentrate on the telegraph poles flashing past them.

"Yes. I experienced it real close when my wife was killed." A respectful silence ensued. "My wife and son actually. She and our small boy were killed in a car accident eight years ago. It was on a highway north of Galveston. A drunk driver…it was a head-on collision. He survived. They were both killed. I was in Houston at the time."

"That's awful…." Kelsey started to say. Shane turned and spoke earnestly to her.

"I wrote him. He was jailed for only a few months. He'd had his license suspended before for being intoxicated at the wheel. Unbelievably irresponsible. But I forgave him. And I wanted him to know I forgave him."

"You forgave him?"

"I forgave him."

"How? How could–"

"Yes, I forgave him. It took a while but I had no peace. Don't you see? I had nothing. No wife. No child. No peace. But I had my Christian faith. Vengeance yields nothing. Unforgiveness yields nothing. No peace. I had to forgive him."

"But–"

"Jesus forgave me far worse sins. Far worse. I'm a total sinner forgiven by a perfect God."

"Did you hear back from that guy in jail?" asked Kelsey.

"No. But I received a message that he appreciated my letter. He was truly sorry."

"You never saw him?"

"No. It was not necessary for us to meet – not from my point of view, anyway. I had forgiven him and that freed me. We never know true freedom – however much license we claim for ourselves – until we receive forgiveness from God and experience the release to forgive another person."

There was a solemn silence. Kelsey studied the distant hazy plains as they swept across to Mount Kilimanjaro. A quietness had settled over the foursome, as the pickup sped northwest towards Nairobi.

The two days they spent in the capital, staying at the Silver Waters hotel, allowed them to connect with the Gossards, finalize their plans, and purchase supplies. They bought a new tent for Kelsey. Once again, Jim lent them some camping equipment, which included a well-used tent for Shane. This supplemented what they had borrowed from the Brandons, including a double tent for Brett and Jane.

Brett had planned a similar tour to the one he and Kelsey had taken three years before, including a visit to the impressive Chania Falls at Thika. While they viewed those, Brett explained how significant they were to Louise because she was there when she heard that her husband Henry had been killed. As they drove north to Nyeri, the sky became slightly overcast but the road was clear. They had booked three adjacent rooms at the Outspan Hotel and, after checking in, they went for a swim in the tiny pool.

Jane commented, "The light here is special."

"Late afternoon in the highlands has a unique feel. I love this time of day," Brett said.

Afterwards he showed them the small house within the hotel compound where he had stayed for his first three months in Kenya while waiting for his accommodation at the school to be ready. He explained that many of his neighbours in the hotel grounds at that time were the families of the senior hotel staff. While they were walking back through the reception area, Brett met the hotel manager who remembered him. Brett expressed his concern about leaving all their belongings in the back of the pickup, but the manager assured him that an *askari* would be guarding all the parked vehicles overnight.

They enjoyed the classic colonial style of the high-ceilinged dining hall with trophies, tapestries, and decorations reminiscent of stately

British country houses. During the evening meal, the wine waiter sent a complimentary bottle of wine to their table.

"Do you get VIP treatment everywhere?" asked Shane. "How do you manage it?" Brett explained that he remembered the names of the trainee managers during his earlier years and often asked about their families and sent greetings when he saw them in various hotels across the country.

He told them, "Tomorrow morning, we'll drive back into Nyeri town to look around and return here for lunch. After that, we'll watch the Kikuyu dancers and then we'll be driven by bus up to Treetops."

In Nyeri the next day, they visited St. Peter's Anglican Church and saw the graves of the Baden-Powells, the founders of the Scouting and Guides movements. Brett took them around the school where they met some of his former colleagues. It was poignant for Brett as he drove down the familiar track beside large fields of coffee. The visitors were interested in looking closely at coffee bushes and picking one of the deep red berries. The two pale grey squishy beans inside had a familiar shape but they tasted nothing like coffee.

Brett told them, "They need to go through a three-stage drying process and then roasting before they resemble the coffee beans we know and love."

Back at the hotel, as they were entering the dining hall, the manager took Brett aside and whispered that he had heard a rumour. There were reports of vicious attacks on travellers in the Rift Valley over the mountain range where they were planning to drive.

Brett said, "Thank you for the warning. I'll be careful – as always." He decided not to mention it to the others.

After the meal, when the manager came over to ask if everything was to their liking, Shane complimented him on the impressive spread at the dessert table. He replied seriously.

"Thank you, sir. We always have seventeen different desserts. You see, some visitors may not like custard." Shane smiled and confided to him that it would be his fortieth birthday the following week. "Congratulations, sir. You look very fit."

After the manager left, Shane said, "He might have added that I looked young too. But he didn't."

"No," explained Brett. "Age is respected, not youth. He may also have told you that forty is the age when they traditionally take a second wife." Immediately the words left his lips, he realized it was a tactless comment; but Shane showed no reaction.

Jane saved Brett with, "But, yes, he should have said you look young! And what's this about a fortieth birthday? You never told us."

To cover his residual embarrassment, Brett added, "Forty is when you might be appointed a Kikuyu elder. But you have to be married, your first-born son has to be circumcised, and your oldest daughter has to be married." Then he realized that had just made things worse.

"Well, I guess I miss out on being an elder on all counts," laughed Shane.

"We will have to do something special for your birthday," insisted Kelsey.

"I think this amazing trip with you three is enough of a special celebration, thank you all."

After lunch, they watched the traditionally dressed dancers present authentic Kikuyu singing and dancing. Each song told a story or enacted a legend. Many had an instructional component relating something of historical, cultural, or moral significance. With their overnight bags, they clambered on the bus which drove the foursome along a special access track leading to Treetops. The hunter-guide provided a running commentary.

As the bus neared their destination, he explained, "The lodge, on the Treetops salient, is built in the branches of a giant *mgumu* fig tree beside a watering hole. It became world famous in 1952 when Queen Elizabeth's father, King George VI, died during the night she was staying there, and she became Queen."

While sipping four-o'clock tea on the balcony, and again after dinner, they watched the herds of animals up close at the salt lick. During the night, they had signed up to be woken if the elusive bongo appeared. The buzzers woke them just after 2am, so they stumbled out of their rooms and joined several other bleary-eyed tourists to catch a glimpse of the rare brown-striped antelope. Soon the thin mist closed in and at the sound of a camera shutter from the lodge, the evasive creature disappeared back into the bush. The cheery wood fire in the comfortable lounge, along with all-night servings of tea and coffee, looked inviting; but their warm beds had more appeal.

A short stroll across open woodland after breakfast, accompanied by an armed guard to protect them from nearby elephants and buffaloes, brought them to the large green bus. They were soon back in the bustling reality of the town and the hotel. The night's adventure felt like a dream.

To cheer them up Brett said, "Now we'll spend two nights at the Aberdare Country Club – which is another old-world experience." Indeed, the grounds and atmosphere of the Club were delightful. It was a peaceful and relaxing time, including a night at another game lodge, The Ark, before their challenging independent journey through the high Aberdare Forest.

30

Nothing could measure the effects of the unexpected downpour that night on the four adventurers camped high in the Aberdare mountain range.

Before they set out on the next stage of their journey, they picked up fresh supplies in Nyeri and then drove west on a narrow track that gradually wound up into the Aberdare National Park. Entering the mountain forest again took them back into a secluded world, but this time the four travellers were on their own. After a leisurely picnic among lumpy tussock grasses, they continued to climb the high wooded route. They found a pleasant camping area before dark and set up their tents. Brett and Shane dug a small pit as a toilet. After they had finished, they noticed that an old buffalo had been watching them. He was sitting very still on the other side of the bush that formed a barrier for the pit.

"He looks old and sick. He doesn't seem bothered by us. Let's just be careful," said Brett.

"Should we tell the girls?"

"We'd better warn them."

"That's all I need!" Kelsey said when Brett mentioned the buffalo. "Will he charge?"

"He looked pretty docile. If he was going to, I think he would have reacted when we were digging right next to him."

"But aren't buffaloes dangerous?"

Shane said, "I read that they are the most dangerous animal in Africa."

"Apart from hippos which kill more people," said Brett with an unconvincing positive tone.

"That's supposed to make me feel, like, comforted?" said Kelsey glancing towards the bushes.

Shane told Brett, "You seem kinda blasé about wild animals."

"No. Not at all. I respect them and give them their space. But I do enjoy watching them and learning their habits. If we abide by their rules, they will allow us to get close and we can appreciate them."

Jane tried to console Kelsey. "Actually, man is the most dangerous creature."

"Apart from mosquitoes," quipped Brett. "Let's get some food." After supper, they put all their supplies in the rear seat of the pickup cab to avoid attracting animals. At the onset of darkness they looked at the threatening clouds and decided against a campfire. They retreated to their flimsy canvas shelters and prepared for sleep.

Weather chronicles tell only part of the climate story. Nothing could measure the effects of the downpour that night on the four adventurers camped high in the forests of the Aberdare mountain range. Mere rainfall data would not have captured the extent of the misery they endured in their rain-soaked tents.

They had placed the three tents as close together as the guy ropes would allow, and strung Jim's large tarpaulin between some trees above them as a canopy. This afforded a minimal measure of protection against the driving rain. The shouted dialogue in the dark reflected their discomfort, with Kelsey in the centre complaining half-jokingly:

"I don't wanna be a tourist any more!"

Shane called out, "Where's that burning-hot equatorial sun we hear about? This rain was not expected."

"Right. I thought there was a dry season!" added Kelsey.

Brett spoke up: "Rainfall can vary. There's always some precipitation in May. It's usually a mountain mist."

"Some mist!" This came from Kelsey's tent.

"Are you mystified?" joked Brett.

Amid groans, Shane called out, "Brett, we're not paying you to be a comedian!"

"You're not paying me at all! As your under-remunerated tour guide, I can assure you this is a typical mountain drizzle."

"Hey, water's getting in," shouted Kelsey.

"Don't touch the inside of the canvas."

"There's water trickling along the floor."

"It can happen."

"It *is* happening!"

"Move to a dry place."

"There isn't a dry place!"

Shane comforted her. "We're all suffering the same conditions. Just go to sleep."

After a pause, a tentative voice called from Kelsey's tent, "Do you get leopards up here?"

"Yes. But they are hard to see as they hunt only at night," Brett replied.

"This *is* night!"

"Oh yeh. Right," said Brett.

Then Jane asked, "Are there lions here?"

"A few, but it's not their natural habitat. They won't be prowling around tonight as they prefer the open, dry, savanna plains."

"So do I!" exclaimed Shane.

"Savanna. Ah, I miss Savannah, Georgia," Kelsey sighed.

The good-natured banter continued with Shane, Brett and Jane exchanging humorous platitudes and Kelsey positioned between them listening. At one point, she called out, with mock pathos.

"I'm an American citizen. This shouldn't be happening to me!"

Finally Brett said, "Listen you softies, be grateful there are no mosquitoes here."

Kelsey's last words were, "Oh yeah, sure I'm grateful. Real grateful. Goodnight guys."

Brett said, "Tomorrow, the sun may shine. Goodnight." The silence from Shane's tent indicated that he was already asleep. There was no sound from Jane next to him.

Brett was worried. His uneasy feeling was not due to the nearby buffalo or the dampness of their bedding. He was thinking about the effect the heavy rain would have on the sticky laterite road surface, and the steep hill that they needed to climb the next day in order to reach the west gate of the park.

By morning, the rain had stopped and they saw a brightening sky. As they dumped the wet tents and equipment in the back of the pickup, they all felt more optimistic.

"At least our supplies in the cab were safe, and we can enjoy breakfast now," said Kelsey, setting up the propane burner. As if to match her mood, a shaft of sunlight broke through the heavy clouds above them. The lone buffalo was in the same place when Brett went to cover their hole. His doleful expression indicated that he had not enjoyed the stormy night either.

As Brett had feared, the road surface was muddy and slippery. They made good progress for over an hour, including stops to watch buffaloes, monkeys, several bushbucks, and three elephants. Brett explained that the elephants cause trouble when they cross the park boundary and devastate gardens and crops, so ditches and a fence were being constructed to contain them within the forest.

"Ditches are effective as elephants can't jump."

They continued their challenging drive across the lush moorlands and through forested areas, seeing beautiful waterfalls swollen from the rain. When they climbed a hill, Brett had to concentrate on keeping the vehicle in the centre of the narrow track to avoid slipping into the side ditches. Using a combination of moderate speed and low gear at a crawl, they kept moving forward and upwards. As he had done countless times, Brett wished he had a four-wheel-drive pickup. But he felt the limited-slip differential engaging, and continued with a prayer in his mind. He comforted himself with the knowledge that friends with four-wheel drive got stuck more frequently, simply because they went to rougher places and were sometimes less cautious.

Then they met their most daunting challenge: the long, steep hill. The pickup stopped and the wheels spun.

"Are we stuck?" asked Kelsey.

"No," said Brett as he rolled back down the hill. "See, we're moving."

"Yeah, in the wrong direction," she joked.

He stopped at a flat area and took another run at the slippery hill. He held it in second gear and drove so the engine was just at the point of stalling when maximum traction occurred. Steadily, they climbed higher and reached a spot farther up this time, when the rear wheels began to spin uncontrollably. He rolled back a few metres to a wider point in the road and switched off.

"We'll have to wait. Maybe another vehicle will come by and tow us."

"We've seen no one since we entered the park yesterday," Shane pointed out.

"Let's gather some branches and put them on the road for traction. It may help – we almost made it." For the next half an hour they slithered around in the mud, collecting wood and leafy branches.

Brett told Jane, "This is typical of the sticky mud in the highlands that forms an extra layer on your shoes at each step. You appear to get taller and taller as you walk, with a thick layer of compacted mud forming an extra sole."

The physical activity in the pure air and increasing warmth was good for them.

"That sunshine is powerful at this height. It may dry off the surface," said Brett.

After an hour a thin, dry crust of mud had formed on the muddy road. They tried again, and the combination of the branches and slightly drier surface allowed the tyres to grip. Slowly, they made progress up the hill and eventually reached the flat section at the top.

"Well done!" said Jane. "We'll enter you in the Safari Rally next year!"

From that point, the journey to the west gate across montane moorland and forest glades was delightful. They enjoyed spectacularly clear air which revealed stunning vistas. When they reached the forest guard-post at the gate, the warden beamed.

"Not many vehicles are making it through there." Brett asked him about the road ahead. "It is dry and then some good surface. You are safe now." He added, with delight, "You can unlock your four-wheel drive." Brett smiled, thanked him, and said nothing else. He offered a brief silent prayer of gratitude as they climbed back in the pickup.

"I was praying during that tense time," said Shane.

"So was I," added Jane.

"So was I!" exclaimed Kelsey. "That experience turned me from an atheist to an agnostic."

Shane was pleased. "Great. With your ability for intelligent reasoning, perhaps you'll move along towards an honest-to-goodness sceptic by the end of this holiday!"

They descended the steep and winding slope down the escarpment onto the floor of the Rift Valley, and then drove north. Two nights in a sheltered site at Lake Nakuru gave them a chance to fully dry their equipment.

31

The remaining embers of the low fire cast their final flickering glow across the faces of the four friends. The mood changed: the evening was coming to a close.

While camping on the shores of spectacular Lake Baringo, farther to the north, they appreciated the beauty of countless birds but kept a safe distance from a lone hippo along the shore. They took a boat on the lake for an enchanting day trip. After their evening meal, they lit a fire and sat talking as darkness fell rapidly. Kelsey began to speak openly about some of her challenges in life. Taking control of her fitness had helped enormously but she confessed there were dissatisfactions in her studies, career options, and friendships back home.

Shane was sympathetic; Jane watched the flames; and Brett remained silent. He sensed she wanted some frank advice. He remembered how she had dished it out to Miles around a similar campfire at Olorgesailie, so he was pleased to see that Shane felt comfortable responding to her directly.

Shane told her, "You have a fine mind, but you need to get to the root of the matter. The problem is not your background, your circumstances, your limitations, or your friends. The main issue is your lack of faith. To be fair, I need to tell you that, Kelsey, not because I *want* to but because you need to know."

"I have faith."

"In what?"

Brett got up and walked away to look at the dark sky. They didn't need him. Jane joined him at the edge of the clearing.

The last words they heard were Kelsey saying, "...in my abilities, my skills, and my training." They heard the start of Shane's response:

"Plus your intellect. All gifts from God. But you don't acknowledge...."

Brett and Jane stood arm in arm, looking across the mysterious lake. They heard the snort of several hippos nearby.

Jane said, "Shane has the right insight and experience to help Kelsey."

"Yes, if she'll listen."

"She listens."

"We can't prescribe decisions or behaviour for others," he said.

"No, all we can do is be ready to say a helpful word when the person is ready. Shane's doing that."

After fifteen minutes, they returned to the glow of the campfire. They heard Kelsey ask a pointed question.

"Why are you trying to convert me, Shane?"

"I'm not trying to convert you."

"You're not?"

"No. Simply because I can't. It's not my job. It's the work of the Holy Spirit. I don't want to confront you either. But I would like to save you years of fruitless searching. That is, if you will allow me to share from my experience and understanding of the truth."

"I know the truth. I deal with facts all the time. There's plenty of evidence to support the facts I accept."

Shane said, "Let's do a little test. Just for fun. Think of South America: the whole continent lies to the east or west of the line below Miami? Or is it positioned directly to the south?"

Kelsey said, "Probably due south but you're obviously making a point, so I'd say all of it lies to the west of Miami."

"In fact it is all *east* of Miami. Another example: the Panama Canal. Is the Atlantic entrance to the east or west of the Pacific entrance?" Brett and Jane looked at each other.

Brett said, "The Atlantic Ocean is east of the Pacific, so the Atlantic end of the canal would be to the east."

"Wrong again. The Isthmus of Panama is angled, so the Atlantic port is to the west of the Pacific one."

Kelsey smiled. "Well, I won't argue with a marine biologist on those facts!"

"And you'd trust a geophysicist or a map maker?"

"Of course."

"A cartographer who slowly evolved from the primordial slime?" Shane joked. "Yet, you ignore the Word of God, life's ultimate authority on all matters of truth?"

Kelsey laughed. "Shane, you're merciless!"

"You do drive a hard bargain, Shane," said Jane. Shane waved a hand in acknowledgement.

"Okay, okay. I know I won't persuade anyone with my *opinion,* but I might be able to convince Kelsey with facts. The problem is not a lack of evidence for God as the creator. Everyone has sufficient evidence."

"You know what, Shane–"

"You can't reject the signs you have and then demand more!"

Kelsey spoke up. "Okay, guys, I'll come clean. I'll give you the Evolution thing." They all stared at her. "What I mean is, I'm no longer convinced by the theory of evolution." The others were attentive. "I've researched and studied this since Coreene first challenged me on it, and I haven't found one credible example to illustrate that evolution is true!"

"What?" gasped Shane.

"I've been thinking about what you said, Brett, after our meal with Coreene and Steve, about basing our opinions on evidence and truth. I've used the intelligence that you all so graciously credit me with, and I see no convincing proof that evolutionary mechanisms can explain our world."

Shane gasped. "Kelsey, that's wonderful!"

"Hang on a minute. In my mind it's unsustainable, so there must be another explanation of how everything got here. I can't accept your religious reason, so we'll just have wait for a more plausible idea to emerge."

Shane was conciliatory. "I agree that all sides of the debate should acknowledge that, in the future, some other grand explanation may be revealed to us, but until–"

"I see there's adaptation within a species over time due to environmental changes. But I no longer accept the evolution of one animal into a completely different one."

Brett said, "But we have to recognize that evolutionary theory is buttressed very effectively by the fact that most scientists *believe* it's true."

"But that doesn't *make* it true," said Shane.

Kelsey clarified, "I'm not saying I believe in a creator god, just that evolution ain't the explanation! See?"

Jane asked, "So, why does the notion have such wide acceptance?"

Kelsey explained: "I've thought about that too. It's because most people look at the evidence with a pro-evolutionary bias. Many scientists do. That's what we've been conditioned to believe. And you don't get far in academia these days if you challenge those fundamental presuppositions. You have to frame your conclusions in that widely accepted context. There! I've shown you my Achilles' heel!"

After that revelation, Kelsey and Shane stood, stretched, and turned their backs towards the fire. Then they settled again around the welcoming glow. Brett reminded Kelsey of the time they had spent in that same campsite, three years previously, discussing similar ideas of faith and theology.

"Coreene feels that our desire for happiness, meaning – even love – is often a veiled search for God." He concluded, "In our yearnings we need to be, as the Bible says, 'transformed by the renewing of our minds'."

Jane added, "You have the gift of reasoning, Kelsey. You just need to process all of the valid data you're receiving, with an open mind."

Kelsey replied, "Sure. I am willing to listen to your ideas. They are persuasive, I guess." Brett put more logs on the fire as Kelsey sighed and turned to Shane, "But why do you bother to try to convince me?"

"Because I care."

"Really?" Kelsey was curious. "Why?"

Shane hesitated. "My wife was about your age...when she was killed. Also, you – all individuals – are worth every bit of attention and persuasion I can muster!"

A silence followed. Then Jane expanded the thought.

"My first husband, Tony, was 43 when he died. It's all too young, isn't it?"

Brett felt awkward as he added, "It forces me to realize that we never know...I mean, no one can assume anything about when we'll die, can we?"

The logs collapsed. The fire became dull and smoky. After a few seconds it burned up again, even more brightly.

Kelsey said, "You're right, I guess, Brett. We never know...."

Jane said, "But there's always hope. Look at the fire now. It seemed dead a moment ago."

No one wanted to move. The honest sharing of deep ideas captivated all four campers. Shane posed another question to Kelsey.

"Why are you unwilling to accept a free gift?"

She thought for a while. "Pride, I guess. Independence. I don't know!"

On the holiday, away from the regular routine, Jane had been thinking deeply about the purpose of her life. She shared something with Kelsey:

"We're not a cosmic accident, you know. You were created for a reason." Kelsey was listening.

Brett added, "And Jesus loves each one of us, equally."

Kelsey said, "Okay, let me sum up your points: I'm not an accident; I was created with a purpose for my life. I am loved by your God who created the universe that he rules. Christianity defines all there is about our behaviour, though I might challenge that. When I look around I see many societies suffering under the burdens of greed, selfishness…revenge…fear, superstitions, even witchcraft…."

"You're describing the effects of sin–"

"Yeah. The sins of two people. Adam and Eve. I know the reasoning. I've heard it all before! It's not fair for your God to punish us *now* for the sin of a disobedient couple at the beginning of the human race!"

Shane displayed the calm patience of conviction.

"We are all capable of sinning. And we are guilty, not because of our inclination to sin, but our *refusal to believe* that Jesus Christ came to deliver us from it."

There was silence. Brett and Jane changed places around the fire.

Kelsey said, "That's interesting, Shane. From what I've read, sin is the big issue. I admit I do see a difference in Christianity compared with other religions. I read that all religions require their adherents to *do something* to please their god. But in Christianity, it has all been done, right?"

Jane said, "Yes! The punishment for our wrongdoing has been taken by Jesus. There's nothing we can contribute. We just have to believe and accept."

Brett said, "Kelsey, I'm impressed. You have good understanding of the essentials of our faith."

Kelsey nodded, "As a discipline, I've memorized the basic teachings of all the major religions."

"That's amazing," said Shane.

"I feel it shows respect if we can articulate what others believe, even those we disagree with." The others were listening to her in awe. "For example, I can probably tell you more about Christianity than most Christians can!"

"You're no doubt right," admitted Shane. "You *know* about it, but what about your heart? Do you know Jesus as your friend?"

"Maybe not. But I remember all of Steve Brandon's points in his much-discussed thesis." She recited, with considerable detail, the structure and his four main points: the fallacy of evolution, the error of abortion, disastrous redefinitions of marriage, and the threats from a false ideology."

Brett exclaimed, "My, you're bright! You've caught the essence of Steve's concerns, and described some things I'd forgotten!"

Kelsey was pleased, and a little taken aback. But not for long.

"Sure, I get all the main things, but what bugs me is Christians are always touting their own ideas about how everyone else in society should behave."

Shane jumped in. "And secular liberals aren't? In the States, we hear nothing but materialistic, secular values being pushed on us from every quarter these days! Immorality is being splashed all over us like a tidal wave of–"

"Stop arguing, you two!" Jane laughed.

Kelsey said, "We're not arguing. We're discussing important topics."

"When you intellectuals discuss important ideas, it always sounds like arguing to me!" joked Brett.

Everyone laughed. Then Kelsey became serious.

"I've said this before: we value our individual freedoms–"

"Yes, the freedom to drink alcohol. And the right to get drunk! And drive a car!" Shane surprised everyone by the force with which he made that statement. "And the right to kill innocent...." He placed his head in his hands. "I'm sorry."

Jane reached across and placed her hand on Shane's arm.

"I won't pretend I fully understand your loss, but I do feel your pain."

After a few moments of respectful silence, Brett stood up and spoke gently.

"You know, Kelsey, you're sounding less convinced every time you challenge Christianity."

"No! Well, maybe yes. Okay, your arguments do have a certain merit, I agree. But not enough to change my mind." The other three looked at her silently. "It's just that you are making me think about it. That's all."

The remaining embers of the low fire cast their final flickering glow across the faces of the four friends. The mood changed; the evening was coming to a close. They packed up the chairs.

Brett asked, "You two live some way from each other in America. Do you think you'll meet up when you get home?"

"It's possible," said Shane. "I often have to go to Houston and it's only a two-hour flight to Savannah."

Kelsey said, "We could exchange photos and reminisce, eh? That would be cool."

"Yeah. Sure. I'll have to see how the photos turn out. I'll send them for processing as soon as I get back."

Brett carried the water bucket to the lakeshore, filled it, and brought it over to douse the fire.

"Well, time for bed. Tomorrow, we'll head down to Lake Naivasha. There's a lovely campground on the southern shore – several actually."

Jane said, "I'm not sure if I'm up to any more wild adventures just yet."

"Lake Naivasha and Maasai Mara are safe."

They all prepared for bed. Brett was feeling good about the way the safari was going. They were having fun, getting great experiences, and enjoying good discussions.

As he fell asleep in that idyllic location, the one phrase that would never have entered his mind was: 'The best-laid plans of mice and men…'.

32

The scene was swept by subtle hues from an artist's pallet, bathed in constantly changing dappled sunlight.

The four explorers rose early on the shores of Lake Baringo. They went to the nearby lodge for a substantial breakfast. Kelsey and Jane had also taken over their toiletries to shower and wash their hair. The guys complained that Kelsey in particular needed to wash her hair almost daily which seemed to them indulgent on a camping trip. Shane and Brett walked back to the camp ahead of the ladies to start packing up. They were not expecting the sight that confronted them.

Shane's tent was covered in excrement. Some had also splashed on Kelsey's, but Shane's was an unbelievable mess.

Brett cried out, "Oh no! Hippo!" In horror, they dashed over and inspected the damage. Quickly glancing around to confirm that the animal was not still nearby, Brett explained, "That's what they do. They're probably marking their territory but some experts believe it's also to show they like another hippo. The greatest compliment is to cover them with poo. They back up and spin their tails wildly as they squirt out the excrement which sprays everywhere. They sometimes do it to other objects such as rocks or bushes if they fancy them. Tents too!"

Shane was appalled, but then he laughed. "So, it was a compliment?"

"Yes. You should feel flattered!"

"Oh, I am! Deeply honoured."

"I'm just grateful it wasn't Kelsey's new tent or Steve's that was selected for this special treatment."

"This is dreadful. What can we do? Will it come off?"

"I doubt it, as it's everywhere."

"But what about poor Jim's tent?"

"I think we'll have to replace it, but let's try to wash it before the ladies get back. They'll go spare!"

They gingerly approached the ruined tent, carefully pulled out Shane's bags, sleeping bag, and sponge mat, and heaved the stinking fabric down to the shore. After several minutes of splashing and wiping with branches, it was obvious that the tent could not be cleaned.

"It's useless now," said Brett. "We'll just dump it in the rubbish bin. Jim's had good use of it over the years, I'm sure."

"Kelsey's going to freak out when she sees this and the splashes on her tent too," said Shane.

Kelsey and Jane ambled along the path through the bushes, chatting happily, when they saw the men standing in the lake with the soiled brown canvas floating in the water.

"What's going on, guys?" Kelsey shouted. Once they explained what had happened, they were shocked and Kelsey was displeased when she noticed the filthy splattering on her new tent. "Oh my gosh! That's so gross!" she said.

"We can clean that off, I think, if we do it quickly before it dries," said Brett.

Jane hugged her, "I'm so sorry, Kelsey. I'll help you clean it." Then she asked where Shane would sleep. Brett had been thinking about that.

"We only have a few more nights in the tents. We'll find you a *banda* – a basic cottage – or we can go in a lodge sometimes. At least the hippo didn't come by when we were here, or attack us. That would have been far worse – possibly fatal."

They hauled the dripping, foul fabric over to the office. The manager smiled knowingly. He was phlegmatic as he unhelpfully gave them an explanation.

"It's happened before. 'Dung showering', it's termed. There's not much we can do. They are wild animals and this is their territory. We are guests here. It could have been worse. Think of it as a compliment! Ha ha! Leave it by the rubbish bins there and we'll deal with it. Sorry about that."

"It means there's less to pack up and drag around, I suppose," mused Brett as they returned to their campsite, finished cleaning Kelsey's tent, packed up the equipment, and loaded the pickup.

There is a unique smell that rises from the dead ashes of an old campfire when the sun has been burning down on it for hours. Brett smelt that familiar aroma as they drove into the camp at Lake Naivasha, the highest of the Rift Valley lakes. It felt good to be on safari again. He looked around to decide where to place the tents and selected a spot next to a *banda*. The campground was situated on grassy lawns sweeping down to the shore. Papyrus plants grew along the shoreline in front of the camping area. Brett pointed out the view across the bay to Crescent Island. An African Fish Eagle gave its eerie high-pitched cry from the top of a tall shoreline tree.

"Any hippos here?" asked Kelsey.

"There could be. This is their night-time feeding ground."

"Oh. And they're the most dangerous animal in Kenya?"

"Just the worst behaved," said Shane.

Kelsey smiled. "Know what, I don't have a problem with that. I'm not fazed any more. I've seen the reality of Africa and I can face the terrors of the wild now!" She giggled, "Yeah, right!"

As they started to set up camp, Shane offered to let Kelsey have the cabin and he use her tent. After looking inside the small *banda,* she thanked him.

"It's kind of dark and dusty, and see all those spiderwebs? Also I noticed a huge lizard. I think I'd prefer my dirty tent. Thanks anyway."

"Okay, I'll stay in here," said Shane.

Brett told him, "I'll ask at the office if we can borrow a mosquito net." Kelsey was looking on the ground at a line of large ants forming a trail beside their tents. Brett explained, "Those are safari ants. The soldier ants give a nasty bite. We'll sprinkle a circle of ash from the fireplace around each tent. They won't cross that barrier."

Their two-day stay at the lake refreshed them all. As they sat around the campfire on their last evening, Brett spoke about the next stage.

"Ready for the drive to Maasai Mara tomorrow?"

"Sure. That's exciting. But it's our last park, eh?" said Kelsey.

"Yes."

"How long will it take to get there?" asked Shane.

Immediately, Kelsey cried, "Wrong question!"

Brett smiled. "It's impossible to say. It depends on what happens on the way! But we should get to the lodge before dark."

They headed west across the floor of the Rift Valley on the undulating road towards Narok, then turned southwest into the park. As they got deeper into the Maasai Mara, Brett remembered the story Louise had told him of Henry and Peter's encounters in that area.

He said, "Just down south is the Tanzanian border. Louise related some stories about her husband's wartime exploits in that area beside the Sand River." He could have told them a lot more.

"Do the game-parks continue into Tanzania?" Shane asked Brett.

"That's the massive Serengeti National Park. Of course, the boundary does not affect the wildlife crossing up and back down again to follow the fresh growth of grasses that come with the seasonal rains."

"What animals will we see?"

"Well, there are Thompson's gazelles and some zebras right over there. Later, we should see topi and wildebeests. They travel in massive herds as they follow the grassland rains."

They did see many animals as they drove through the park, including several lions and two cheetahs. They were heading for the Maasai Tourist Lodge deep within the western section of the park which meant they had to cross the mighty Mara River. Just before they reached the bridge it was obvious that there had been a recent shower which had turned the road to mud. When they stopped on the banks of the river, they looked down at the red doughnuts of mud on their wheels which made the tyres seem twice their normal size.

Laughing, Brett said, "No wonder the steering was a bit heavy on that last section." He drove onto the bridge and stopped in the centre so they could appreciate the river in both directions. There were no other vehicles. "This should give us a good view if there are any animals or birds to be seen. I'll get the binoculars."

Kelsey looked down river and saw baby hippos sliding down a muddy channel in the bank and splashing into the brown water.

"Looks like they're just having fun!" she said.

"Yes, hippos do enjoy the water. They spend most of the day in water and then come out to graze at night."

"And do other things!" said Jane, patting Shane's shoulder to comfort him as he leaned on the bridge rail.

Kelsey joked, "Life for the wild animals isn't just about survival, I guess."

As they left the river, the rich glow of the late afternoon light gave them an opportunity to photograph more animals against spectacular backdrops. Maasai Mara game park presented magnificent views to the visitors, including open vistas across grassy plains, small hilly ridges, and a variety of sienna brown and deep-green vegetation. They were awed by the sight of animals set dramatically against the pale-purple mountains in the hazy distance. The scene was swept by subtle hues from an artist's pallet, bathed in constantly changing dappled sunlight. Turning north after the river crossing, they encountered some muddy sections which Brett was just able to get through. This brought them to the luxurious lodge. Brett had explained that public camping was not permitted in the park, so they would stay in the hotel.

As they entered, they were greeted enthusiastically by a smartly dressed Kenyan staff member who recognized Brett. After a moment's discussion, Brett remembered that he had been one of the maintenance staff at the school in Nyeri. They exchanged news while Shane and Kelsey walked through the lobby to locate the pool and enjoy the spectacular vista. Brett and Jane booked in while the other two savoured the captivating scene across the distant plains. When they returned to the reception desk, Brett announced that he and Jane would have a luxury suite, while Kelsey and Shane were placed in adjacent rooms normally reserved for VIPs. Shane was amazed.

"How *do* you do it? Do you have friends *everywhere* in this country?"

Brett said, "It's not me. Thank my friend here. He's now head of operations and wants us to feel comfortable and welcomed – all at the basic room price. That's Kenyan hospitality. They like to encourage tourism." The rooms were splendid and they were all treated like special guests. The manager also greeted them and he swapped news with Brett of mutual friends in the hotel industry.

They had originally planned to stay just two nights, but they felt so relaxed and comfortable that they decided to extend another night. This gave them extra opportunities to explore the remote and unique surroundings of the lodge environs, even though it cut the timing tight for Shane's return to Nairobi for his flight home.

33

*"Certainly, there are risks. Adventure is risk with a purpose.
Without a purpose, taking risks is just for thrills.
That's pointless, and possibly foolhardy."*

During their stay at the lodge, the visitors appreciated the stark beauty around them. The views were enhanced by the occasional charcoal-grey clouds and the gentle angles of rain showers falling beneath them. However, one of those imposing clouds passed over the intrepid travellers three days later as they stood in the hotel lobby waiting to load their vehicle and leave.

As they travelled, Jane noticed that Kelsey continued to ask perceptive questions about culture and indigenous communities.

She told her, "I can tell you're still working, Kelsey, and not here for a holiday!"

Kelsey laughed, "I'm on holiday, sure, but an anthropologist is always working, observing, and analyzing. The world is our laboratory. It's never a vacation for me when there are people around."

Shane said, "Maybe you should have a holiday where there are just animals."

"Like at the Zoo!" said Jane.

"Ha! This is a working holiday, I guess. I've been making notes on the different tribes, regions, and religions. Maybe I could check some details with you later, Brett?"

"Sure, if I can remember. There's a wide variety of tribal groups and customs. It's very regionally based. You may have detected some slight intertribal tensions."

"No. They must be too subtle for me to pick up as a visitor."

"They are there, below the surface," Brett confided.

"You say different regions, but is it related to tribalism?" asked Jane.

"Tribalism is very real. There's fierce loyalty to one's tribe, and tensions can develop. I've heard general comments about how unsettled things are in some areas. The peace we see around us can be shattered unexpectedly."

Kelsey asked, "Too many people, not enough resources?"

"Yes, fundamentally it's about economics, land, food, and opportunity. Also, small disputes are often presented as political divisions. One never knows where the next unrest will originate or what the source of the trouble might be." He told them briefly of his tense experiences during the attempted air-force coup in 1982. "Sunday, the first of August. Everything seemed to change then," he concluded, with a reflective tone.

A heavy rain had been falling but the road surface was *murram* and the traction felt good. Then, ahead of them, Brett was dismayed to see a wide puddle of shining mud that stretched across the whole road, into the edges of the track and as far ahead as he could see. He stopped to examine the situation. Sometimes he would take a run and drive straight through the middle, just keeping the wheels gripping while hurling wide arcs of muddy water to each side. Other techniques included a very slow and cautious approach, feeling his way across and keeping the rear drive wheels on firm ground, ready to back out at anytime. The difficulty was not knowing if there was a deep crater submerged in the centre, or dangerous rocks in the path. Even the recent tracks of other vehicles gave no indication of the best way through.

They all got out and stared in bewilderment at the coffee-coloured wash of muddy goo before them. It yielded no indication of what was below the surface. Brett was hoping that another vehicle might come by to give some guidance, but they were alone.

"Send Kelsey ahead with a long stick," suggested Shane.

"Send Shane ahead with an even longer stick," she snapped back. "Then I'll hit him with it when we get safely to the other side!"

"*If* we get safely to the other side," added Jane, looking a bit desperate.

"Well," said Brett, "unless we intend to stand here helplessly for the rest of our lives – and I admit there are worse places to die – then we'd better have a go at it." After laughter, he explained, "I've found that puddles tend to be deep in the centre and shallow at the sides."

Brett's reasonings were not helping them, so they climbed back into the vehicle and Brett started the engine. He felt that pushing along the edge would be better than driving down the centre. He was wrong. After a promising run at the brown water, the vehicle slid to the side and the wheels began to spin. He tried the old trick of rocking back and forward – a fairly easy technique with the manual gear lever – but the wheels kept spinning.

"No point in digging deeper," Shane said.

"No," said Brett, switching off, and stepping out into the deep mud.

"Looks like we're in trouble, big-time," said Kelsey.

"Are we stuck?" asked Jane.

"No, just temporarily immobilized," joked Brett as he dug around under the driver's seat to remove the tow cable. "I'll attach this at the front and we'll just have to wait for help. There must be a vehicle soon. Ow! This mud is cold! Operations such as this are best performed in warm coastal waters."

It was about half an hour before they saw a green Toyota Land Cruiser driving up behind them. It was one of the lodge trucks and it moved effortlessly along the centre of the road and stopped beside the helpless pickup. As Brett called over to the two men, he got out to lift the dripping tow cable. The Toyota drove ahead and then backed up towards them. One man climbed out and waded back.

"Get four blue twenty-shilling notes," Brett called over to Jane. Shane passed some forward to her.

Soon the cable from the stranded pickup was attached to the rear hitch of the rescue vehicle. It was clear that the men had done it many times before. Brett climbed in and started the engine. The Toyota driver did the same and moved forward slowly. As the cable lifted out of the mud, Brett waited for the snap of the tension, followed by a moment of hesitation and then the satisfying pull on the front. His Datsun pickup plowed along in the ditch and then easily glided sideways up onto the firm road surface. The

Toyota continued pulling them until they were past the sticky section and the road was solid.

As they unhooked the chain, Brett gave the men their small gifts. They were very happy.

"Asante sana," said Brett.

"Ndiyo asante. Asante. Safari njema, rafiki. You are welcome. Thank you. Have a good journey, my friend." The driver added, "It is more better that you stay in the middle here. The road, it is more firmer in that place."

Brett thought, *I think I know that now.* As he coiled the filthy cable and pushed it under the tarpaulins in the back of the pickup, he pondered, *I wonder if I can dig out some clean shoes or just let these boots dry out as we go.* He decided on the latter. A little discomfort was a small price to pay for the exhilaration of being on the move again.

Shane said, "The vehicle sure is muddy now."

"But we're no longer stranded," said Jane.

"And facing the threat of a slow, isolated demise," added Kelsey.

The Toyota drove ahead and pulled over to let Brett pass. The lodge vehicle stayed behind them until they were well clear of the muddy patch and then overtook with a friendly blast from the horn. Obviously, Brett was driving too slowly for their liking.

Brett told Shane, "I owe you four pounds."

"Forget it. That's okay, whatever it is you're referring to."

"The twenty-shilling notes. Their tips."

They loved the peaceful return journey eastwards through the park, and made frequent stops to photograph animals and birds. Everything was going smoothly as they headed north to the park exit gate when Brett felt a familiar wobble in the steering. Immediately, he stopped, got out, and saw a flat tyre.

"Oh no! That's never convenient, but this isn't a bad place for it to happen." They were at a junction where a small road joined them from the right side, giving plenty of space for other vehicles to drive around them. They removed the jack and crank handle from behind the rear passenger seat.

Jane said, "This is going to be messy with all that mud."

Shane watched Brett as he began cranking down the spare wheel.

"I hope it's got enough pressure," he said.

"It should have. I checked it before we left," Brett told him.

"Let me help. I'm pretty strong," said Kelsey. "I'll loosen the wheel nuts."

"Are you sure?" asked Jane.

"Yep. Remember Brett? Like you found out last time, we Georgia girls sure know how to change wheels," she said, standing on the wheel-nut wrench as each nut yielded to her skillful attention. Kelsey was in charge then. "Just wedge the opposite wheels with rocks, Brett. I don't want a Texas wimp like Shane doing any heavy lifting!"

Jane looked around and noticed three buffaloes watching them from a grassy mound on the other side of the Y-junction. Immediately, Brett thought of Louise's account of the buffalo which attacked Peter's camp.

He said to Shane, "If they approach, look as tall and threatening as you can."

"Sure. I'm from Galveston. I know how to handle mountain buffaloes!"

Smeared in mud, Kelsey looked up from below the vehicle and called out to Shane.

"And tell them Ms. McNeil is the boss, and to stay clear."

Brett added, "Keep them occupied by explaining the concepts behind yours and Len's integrated energy projects. That should send them away."

From the ditch, Kelsey shouted, "Or send them to sleep!"

Jane and Shane watched the buffaloes warily. Brett bent down to help Kelsey and called over his shoulder to Shane.

"They'll understand the notions of independence and self-sustainability. Stress those. Seriously, please tell us if they move any closer. We'll need to get back in the pickup immediately."

Poor Kelsey was in the mud under the vehicle to position the jack when a tour bus pulled up, asking if they needed help. They gratefully said they were able to manage. In fact the exchange of the large filthy wheels went smoothly. They did not bother to look for the source of the puncture, but simply raised the damaged wheel up on its chain into the rear storage compartment. Without troubling to store the tools properly, they dumped them in the back of the pickup as they admired each other's messy appearance. Brett sacrificed an old towel and they splashed water and wiped themselves clean as best they could.

"You were great Kelsey. Thanks for all your help," said Shane.

"Yes, thanks Kelsey. You look fantastic. Mud and slime suit you," added Jane as she wiped her mouth with the back of her hand. Shane pretended to look seriously at Kelsey.

"Have you changed your hair? It looks different."

"Yeah. I added a few streaks," she quipped as she tugged on a muddy strand.

Brett told Jane, "She's an amazing young lady. An asset on any safari adventure. Thanks Kelsey."

"Yes, terrific job, Kelsey," said Jane as she clambered into the driver's seat. "I vote we keep you – at least until the next disaster!" As Jane drove, she called across to Brett. "You love these adventures don't you?"

"Yes, I do. I think we can live life on a higher plane, somehow."

"What about the risks?" asked Kelsey.

Jane said, "Brett's not intimidated by risk."

He responded, "Certainly, there are risks. Adventure is risk with a purpose. Without a purpose, taking risks is just for thrills. That's pointless, and possibly foolhardy."

Jane was grateful for the uneventful drive from Narok to the eastern edge of the Rift Valley floor. As Brett took over the wheel again, he noticed some roadworks to the south and decided to try a diversion along a gravel road that looked promising. It was mid afternoon so they still had several hours of daylight before reaching Nairobi. Construction equipment and vehicles were dotted along the roadway but there was little sign of activity. The main signpost pointed to Bonde. A confusing array of temporary notices mentioned a detour and gave warnings to drive slowly. The potholes were more effective at slowing them down than the warning signs. They also kept Brett alert as he wrested the pickup across steep ridges and over gaping holes. Dust and grit were everywhere. They saw two other vehicles coming the other way, but there was surprisingly little traffic. As they bumped along, Shane sat beside Brett while Kelsey and Jane hung onto the handles to stabilize themselves in the rear seats.

Brett remembered a thought that had occurred to him occasionally in the past. Every journey, each safari, every trip, has a natural end. It's a feeling of satisfaction when one's thoughts turn towards future events, which does not always coincide with the physical arrival home. He often felt that the trip was over, or the experience complete, although a few hours remained and more kilometres were still to be covered. Thinking back on their adventurous safari, he wondered if the others felt the same way. He was about to ask how they felt about returning to Nairobi, when without warning he noticed something strange ahead of them. He slowed down, which caused Kelsey to lean forward and ask what was wrong. They saw someone stretched out in the middle of the road with a man bending over him. As they slowly approached, Shane spoke with concern.

"Looks like there's been an accident."

Brett was cautious as he saw the upright person glance towards them and wave them to stop.

"Someone's hurt," said Jane, staring ahead. Brett stopped about twenty metres from the scene and watched carefully. The man on the ground was still, but the other man started to beckon them forward. He was a young man, but Brett could not see the condition of the person on the ground. Something looked odd to him. As he drove slowly towards the pair, the young man was glaring at Brett and trying to look into the pickup.

Brett's instinct suddenly kicked in. He glanced in the driving mirror and then immediately roared the engine and thrust the pickup forward. The rear wheels spun wildly as he sprayed gravel behind him. He drove straight towards the man and then abruptly swerved to the right, skidding around him in a shower of stones and dust. Once past the pair, he managed to keep control of the vehicle as it slid in a rasping arc across the road surface. The noise was deafening. Jerking the wheel around, he forced the tyres along the gravel ruts in a barrage of stones. He drove as fast as he could. Gravel and stones rattled against the underside of the pickup. The bumping and lurching were unbearable to the passengers as the vehicle streaked along the corrugated surface. Brett glanced back in the rear-view mirror several times. It had all happened in a few seconds.

"What *are* you doing?" shouted Kelsey, trying to look back at the couple through the clouds of dust.

"We should have stopped. That man was hurt," snapped Jane. Brett ignored her and concentrated on the road ahead.

"We may have been able to help. You nearly hit him!" Kelsey cried.

"Shut up! And keep your head down!" shouted Brett. He looked again in the rear-view mirror. Jane opened her mouth and Brett yelled, "You both keep quiet and lay down. Don't move!"

"Don't you speak to her like that!" shouted Shane. "She's–"

"You shut up too! And keep your eyes open. Look ahead all the time. If you see anyone standing at the side of the road, duck down. They may hurl a rock through the window!"

Shane was stunned. The curve of the road now hid the pair from Brett's sight but during his rapid glances back he had spotted the supine man stand up and the couple began running after them, shaking their fists. Through the dust, he thought he saw another figure emerge from the bushes behind them. The older man picked up a rock and threw it at the retreating vehicle. Brett felt vindicated in his drastic action, but he was still alert and watchful as he drove as fast as he could on the rough road. The other three were angry and silent.

After about three kilometres, Brett slowed and breathed deeply.

"Sorry about that," he said.

"What happened?" asked Kelsey in an unsteady voice.

"You couldn't see it, but the supposedly injured man leaped up and threw a rock towards us. They were both running and jumping about, waving angrily. There was a third man. I'm sure I saw him waving a club in the air."

"So…it was…all faked?" intoned Shane.

"Yes, staged to get us to stop. I'd been warned in Nyeri that there've been attacks in this area, so I was half-prepared. I said nothing as I didn't want to worry any of you."

"What would they have done to us – if we'd stopped?" asked Jane.

"I don't know. Stolen things I suppose. Maybe taken the pickup." He didn't mention the physical attacks he'd heard about.

"Are we safe now?"

"I think so, but let's still be careful." During the next five kilometres, two cars drove towards them. Brett flashed his headlights as a warning, not sure if it would be helpful. Nothing overtook them.

"Should we report it to someone?" asked Shane.

"I'll stop if we can find a place soon. Let's not get upset. It's over now. We're safe."

"Thanks to you," said Kelsey.

"Thanks to the Lord," said Brett. As he drove, he was very conscious that they were carrying a heavy load, without an inflated spare wheel. He was praying all the time.

Shane mused, "It looks to me like one lives at a higher intensity here."

"Right on! That's true," affirmed Kelsey. They were all subdued for the next twenty minutes.

Soon, they rejoined the main road and continued their journey south.

"That was a confusing diversion. I wonder how official it all was," said Shane.

"They've been doing road work here for ages, so lots of informal side routes have evolved," Brett told him.

Kelsey spoke. "Oh, so you *do* believe in evolution!" They felt relief at being able to laugh together again.

When they arrived safely back in Nairobi, Jim Gossard was horrified at what he saw.

"My goodness! What a mess – you four and the pickup! What *have* you been up to?"

Mary joined them. "You must have encountered some bad roads."

"No. Nothing out of the ordinary," said Kelsey, covered in dried mud.

Jane added, "All routine stuff for Brett on safari, apparently!"

Kelsey said, "Now I need to wash my hair."

Shane and Brett looked at each other and grinned. In unison they said, "Not again!"

The next morning was a time of relaxation and recovery in the hotel. In the afternoon, Brett and Shane returned to the Gossards and unloaded all the messy camping equipment to clean and dry. Jim's guard washed the pickup.

"He enjoys doing that. But my van is not usually as interesting for him to clean!" said Jim. "By the way, what happened to my tent? I didn't see it."

Shane said, "Right. We were waiting to tell you about that. We're really sorry, but a hippo–"

"A hippo befriended it," said Brett, as Mary arrived.

"Oh. I see." Jim knew about hippos. "A write-off I suppose?"

"No doubt about it!" exclaimed Shane. "We felt really bad about that. We'll replace it with the new one Kelsey used. It's about the same size. Is that okay?"

"That's kind of you. It's a nicer tent, I think," Jim said.

"What did you do without the tent?" asked Mary.

"I slept under the stars. And watched for hippos! Just kidding," said Shane.

"Well, the new tent is a generous replacement, thank you."

Brett said to Jim, "It's the least we can do. Thanks for lending us all the other equipment. Can you check that no damage was done to the pickup, please?"

"I'll cover any costs to repair it," said Shane. "Also, let us know our shares of the safari expenses, Brett. I'm real grateful for the experience. Thank you for a memorable birthday trip. I'm sorry to be leaving y'all so soon."

Mary invited them to supper that evening. They described their safari adventures in dramatic detail and acknowledged the protection they had experienced. Kelsey joined in with a brief prayer of thanksgiving. She was invited to stay with the Gossards after the others left Nairobi. During the rest of her time in Kenya, she wanted to visit more projects with Mary in some remoter communities. Jim gave them an update on some of the disturbances in various parts of the country.

"There's still considerable unrest – particularly over the unresolved murder of our Foreign Minister in February."

Shane and Kelsey continued to talk about the wonderful experiences they'd had and their plan to meet up in Savannah sometime in the Fall to catch up and share their photos.

The following day, Kelsey and Jane worked with Mary to wash the clothes from their trip and plan the next few days of activities. Jim took the vehicle to be inspected and have the tyre repaired. Allistair Matherton had left a message with Jim asking Brett and Jane to see him while they were in Nairobi. Brett phoned to arrange a meeting. Unfortunately, the first available appointment was on the 4th of June at the exact time when Shane needed to be at the airport. Also, Mary and Kelsey had planned to visit a post-natal care project in Mathare Valley that day. Jim offered to take them after dropping Brett and Jane at the lawyer's office. Then he would take Shane to the airport.

The next day, all six of them met for lunch at the hotel. Jim was carrying a newspaper and looking sombre.

"There's an article about a terrible incident, up near Bonde," he explained, pointing to the headline 'White couple attacked in Rift Valley'. The piece outlined what was known. Jim clutched the newspaper and read out loud.

"Here's what it says: 'Two local residents (believed to be missionaries) stopped to help an injured man, when suddenly they were both hit on the head. According to the man, the lady had bent down to help the person on the ground when they were attacked from behind. He believes it was with a metal bar. A third person emerged from the bushes and climbed in their car. Police confirmed that the woman was killed, while her husband remains in critical condition in hospital. It is not known if he will recover, although he is occasionally conscious and can talk with difficulty.' How awful."

Jim looked up, with a deep frown. He continued reading. "Sorry this is hard to hear. 'A motorist saw the woman's body beside the road and then heard cries from the bushes. The man had hidden there for several hours, pretending to be dead in case other bandits came. He explained that the attackers drove away in their car and his wife died in his arms. He told our reporter 'Those men need Jesus' were her last words.' That's so sad," said Jim, folding the newspaper. The group sitting around the table was speechless. At last, Jim said, "It sounds like the men you saw."

They were all thankful that they had been spared. Brett said very little, but he silently gave thanks for the warning he had received in Nyeri because his first instinct had been, like Jane's, to stop and offer assistance.

34

As the couple left, Allistair waved a dismissive hand. "Don't worry, I'm not working pro bono on this one!"

Allistair Matherton swung around in his chair and stared at Brett.

"Let me get this straight: you're suggesting that Miles Jolly used his illegal income for everyday expenses and squirrelled away his legitimate government pension payments in an underground vault?"

Brett was trying to reason with the lawyer.

"I'm just sounding out the legal position." Allistair had insisted they discuss what he called the 'treasure trove', before talking about the diamonds. Brett continued, "I'm trying to clarify my thinking on this–"

"I'll clarify your thinking for you! You can't keep any of it!"

"I don't want it for myself, but I wondered if part of it could go to benefit projects at the Zoo. Some of the wealth might have originated there."

Jane was feeling frustrated by Allistair's attitude.

She said, "Surely, a shilling is a shilling. Miles could have converted some of his lawful income into gold or international funds." As she said it, she realized she was not sounding very convincing. Allistair showed his frustration.

"Yeh, gold with Sanskrit inscriptions – or whatever. Since when has the UK government paid its retired colonial administrators in exotic gold coins? What about the sham passports? And the mystifying lists of names and goodness knows what other explosive details are on those sheets. You're on shaky ground if you think you–"

Jane interrupted him. "We have Miles' will. He left all his Kenyan possessions to Brett–"

"I'd hate to argue *that* before a judge!"

Brett was emphatic. "To me, it's pretty straightforward: if the goods were held by Miles, then he bequeathed them to me."

Allistair's wry smile matched his next words.

"Ownership is not necessarily proven by mere possession, Brett." There was a hush in the cluttered office. Allistair sighed and looked out the window. He paced his next words. "You can't go digging around in caverns and underground vaults like a badger or a–"

"A mole?" offered Brett, smiling.

"A badger," countered the lawyer firmly, "and expect to keep what you unearth." He sat surrounded by dishevelled piles of files, folders, and heaps of papers.

Brett admitted, "Of course, if the goods were illegally obtained, that's a different matter."

"All of Miles' Kenyan possessions are of dubious provenance," stated Allistair pointedly.

"But if one could isolate the items with an authentic ownership...."

"Then a shilling is a shilling!" Jane chirped brightly.

"I think we've already established that, my dear!" Allistair snapped and then he spoke slowly to Brett, "So, you claim to be the legitimate legatee from Miles' estate?"

"He promised me a gift to compensate for an injury he caused–"

"Hold on. Surely you don't expect an objective adjudicator to view Miles Jolly as a latter-day philanthropist, with you as the beneficiary of his votive gestures of compassion! Come on Brett, we have to live in *this* world!"

Inwardly, Brett was relieved. He did not want to lay claim to the loot for himself or appear greedy. He turned to Jane.

"I suppose we sensed all along that the stuff was illegal?"

"Yes. It had that appearance. But we were hoping that folks at the Zoo could benefit, somehow."

"At least we kept it out of Moshi's hands. That was my mandate from Miles."

Allistair shifted in his chair and leaned forward.

"Now, don't let's give up on this. I have carefully catalogued and photographed everything and turned the information over to the police."

"That's probably best. Did you give them everything?"

"No. I gave them the raft of papers – a keg of gunpowder that is – and the passports. They were delighted with the list of names. Their initial reaction to the passports was that two of them were stolen and other one was counterfeit. I further informed them that I have the other items safely stored. Not here, but they are exceedingly secure."

"Thanks. You are obviously doing what is right and following proper proce–"

Allistair interrupted with a conciliatory proclamation.

"Look, you two risked a lot to keep it all secure. I suppose one might argue that the Kenyan currency is different from the other items."

"You mean we can have the Kenyan funds? There was a lot. I've never seen some of those higher-denomination bills. We didn't add it up. We'd donate it all to the Zoo–"

"Hang on a moment! I'm just thinking out loud. I'd need to consult with my father and a couple of specialist colleagues on this. You're right, there was a small fortune in those crisp new bills. You'll be leaving Kenya soon. I'll draft a note for you to sign, donating the cash to the Zoo. I know the exact amount. It's a simple format and we'll get a witness. I'd like to have that document on hand in case we can swing something. No promises. How's that?"

"That's probably the best we can do for now. Thanks," Brett said.

"I'd like to see some of it used for a worthy cause," Allistair acknowledged.

"So would we," said Jane.

Allistair appeared to relax. "Let's hope for a glorious denouement to this story! If you go for a coffee and come back in an hour, I should have the release paper for you to sign. I have another appointment, but our secretary will deal with it. Now, the diamonds...."

"Oh yes, what did you find out about those?"

"A lot." He smiled. To Jane it seemed that he became less combative and slightly smug as he recounted their firm's activities over the last couple of months. "My father has a good friend who's a jeweller. He specializes in custom crafting of brooches and pendants using unique gems. Dad showed him the two bags of stones you brought to us."

"Are they genuine diamonds?"

"Oh yes. Definitely! Worth a princely sum, apparently. Father learned a lot about diamonds from his friend," Allistair said, as he adopted a didactic tone. He was enjoying himself. *No doubt at his usual rate,* Brett thought. "Diamonds are much rarer than silver or gold."

"Really? Where do they come from?" asked Jane.

Allistair explained, "For most of history, no one knew *where* diamonds came from. People just found them lying around – chance discoveries in the beds of rivers or in gravel. Diamonds are very durable so they can get transported over enormous distances."

"We know!" joked Brett. "We did some transporting ourselves!"

He was rewarded with a sympathetic nod from Allistair.

"They say you don't actually look directly for diamonds, but you trace their footprints in suitable prospective conditions. You search for surrogate indicators in likely locations, hoping to find a few diamonds." Allistair picked up a file and checked his notes. "Locating them nowadays is a professional enterprise. Sadly, there's no opportunity for the old-time dilettante prospector."

"You mean, no amateurs digging for them?" asked Jane.

"For the most part, yes."

"That's what we did!"

Everyone laughed, then Allistair said, "Yes, during your labyrinthian burrowings!" He looked at his watch and again glanced down at his notes, "This is interesting: a diamond is the world's hardest substance but it can be shattered along crystalline planes by a blow at the right angle."

"Or the wrong angle," quipped Jane.

Allistair smiled. "There are different colours – hues from various regions of the globe."

"We noticed some of ours had a different tinge."

"Yours?"

"Louise's."

"I wouldn't regard her ownership as axiomatic." Continuing to read, he said, "The colouration is actually due to impurities. Some people find them attractive, but pure, white diamonds are the most prized. Hence, the most valuable."

Suddenly, Jane said, "I wonder...would the different colours help identify their source or even possible ownership?"

"Source, yes. Ownership, no."

"So, how can Louise establish her rightful–"

"One step at a time. My father's jeweller friend put him in touch with a Dutch lapidary."

"What's that?"

"A gemstone engraver or polisher."

"Can he put a price on them?"

"Very approximately. Diamonds are a luxury item. Useless carbon in one sense. They are not a good investment, I understand. The market varies according to the demand. Hence their price fluctuates."

Jane said, "So, could the colours identify the source? I saw hints of orange, blue, and almost black in them."

"Aha!" said Allistair. "I noted where the muted colours come from." He proudly announced, "Orange from South Africa; blue, South Asia; black out of Russia."

"Where are the diamonds now?"

"The lapidary is taking them to Antwerp."

"Antwerp? Why Antwerp?"

"That's where most diamond buyers are, so that's where they should be if you want them sold. Or even appraised accurately. Louise Emerson approved of this while you were on safari."

Brett asked, "Will they be safe?"

"Safer than they were hidden in a hole at the Zoo! Yes, the gems will be safe. These are professionals we're dealing with."

"When the diamonds are sold, will Louise get the money? They are rightfully hers," Jane stated flatly.

Allistair sniffed, "Some might challenge that last statement, but that's what we are hoping. In the absence of any other information, we are proceeding on the basis that she inherited them from her late husband who was given them after a valuable service rendered – albeit of questionable legality. But it's so long ago that I doubt it could be challenged."

Brett saw the potential difficulty. "Unless the original owners or their descendants can be located."

"We trust that the lapidary and his lawyer will be investigating all those aspects before offering them for sale."

"So they should yield a lot?" That question came from Jane.

Allistair nodded, "That's my impression." Again, he looked at his watch.

"Louise wants to donate the proceeds to the development of the research facility at the Zoo."

"And maybe fund a water treatment project. There's a severe short–"

"Good for her!" said Allistair as he snapped his folder closed, indicating that the discussion was over.

"Thank you for all you're doing, Allistair," said Brett as he shook Allistair's hand. Jane and Allistair shook hands and she also thanked him.

As the couple left, Allistair waved a dismissive hand. "Don't worry, I'm not working *pro bono* on this one! Miles Jolly's funds are still financing my invaluable efforts. We have to cover the rent on these luxurious premises, don't we?"

Brett and Jane found a small cafe and ordered a snack.

"Well, do you still like him?" asked Brett.

"Allistair? He's amazing. I trust him."

"So do I, but what an irritating fellow."

"No, he's loquacious and confident. A rich personality."

"He didn't tell us what we wanted to hear."

"Really? What did you expect? He told us the truth – which is what we needed to know. What more do you want from a professional?"

"I see what you mean. He also gave us a promise to follow up. I actually like him too. One just has to take him on his terms."

"Oh, totally on his terms!"

After an hour at the cafe, they climbed the steep stairs to the grubby office and Brett signed the paper the secretary handed him. He was surprised at the total value of the Kenyan cash. He skimmed the words and saw it simply gave authorization for the cash to be donated to the Zoo in order to assist the community.

After completing that step, they were both feeling relieved as they made their way back to the Gossards. They were completely unprepared for what awaited them.

35

Brett said, "Allistair is on our side. Doing what he can."
"How does he see it? Be careful–" replied Louise.

As they walked into the Gossards' home, hoping to get some sympathy after their stressful meeting with the lawyer, they were astounded by what they saw. Both Mary and Kelsey were sitting with white bandages on their left hands. Jim was fussing around, looking overwhelmed by the situation.

He said, "We phoned the lawyer's office but you had just left. After I dropped Shane – that all went well – I drove back to the charity's office to collect the two ladies, but they weren't there. They were both in Emergency at the hospital."

"What on earth happened?" asked Jane, looking at the women resting forlornly in the living room, nursing their hands. Between them, with interjections from Jim, they explained. They had been walking near the Mathare Valley shanty town to visit a health centre. To reach it, they had to cross over a ditch that looked like an open sewer. Their guide from the charity directed them across a wobbly paving slab and their attention was focused on that. Suddenly, a young man jumped out at Mary and tried to pull the wedding ring from her finger.

Jim said, "It wouldn't budge so he then tried to bite off her finger!"

"He did *what?*" Brett gasped.

"He tried to bite off my finger to get the ring," said Mary, waving her left hand in the air.

"That's unbelievable."

"I had no idea what he was doing. But I was in agony so I tried to fight him off. He just continued to force his teeth into my finger, and started twisting and shaking his head. He broke my finger and there was blood all down my arm. I could hear myself screaming." They described what happened next. Kelsey was standing beside Mary and instinctively swung out her left arm to hit the man.

Kelsey said, "I hit that jerk real hard with the back of my hand. I had to get him away from Mary. I was ready to punch him too."

Jim continued the account. "Evidently, she swiped his head with such force that he was knocked over. He got up and stumbled around the corner, clutching his eye. He disappeared into the slum. Kelsey was amazing and definitely saved Mary."

Mary said, "Yes, by her quick action. We were in shock and the pain in my finger was terrible. Poor Kelsey hurt her wrist really badly. Our guide quickly took us back to the driver who was waiting with the car and he rushed us to the hospital. On the way, I held my arm up and Kelsey wrapped her wrist in a damp scarf."

Jim said, "By the time I found them, they had seen a doctor and were being bandaged up. It was awful, but we felt thankful it wasn't worse."

"I was given a tetanus shot as a precaution," said Mary. They wondered if the man was deranged, or just desperate to get something precious to sell. They both had taken painkillers and were resting as best they could.

"May I phone Louise, please?" Brett asked.

"I'll try for you," said Jim, looking relieved to tackle a familiar task. While he tried several times, Brett waited with the three ladies. After half an hour, Jim called out and waved the phone receiver in the air. Brett took it.

"Hello."

"Hello Brett. Zephyr here."

Brett smiled. "We saw Allistair."

"How was he?"

"About the same."

"Sorry to hear that!"

"Ha. He was his usual chirpy self. Jane likes him."

"She's a tolerant person. What did Allistair say? Be cautious how you express it. I know what he plans for the stones."

"Before I tell you about that, there's other news. Mary and Kelsey were attacked and are seriously injured." He briefly outlined the story. "You can talk with Kelsey, if you like."

"Yes, alright. But first tell me about the meeting."

"The small things we pulled out of CPZ-store are going overseas to be evaluated – as you know. The stuff we dug out of the ground is safe. Some still with lawyers, others given to the rozzers."

"So, out of our hands. That's a relief."

"Ownership is up in the air. But Allistair is on our side. Doing what he can."

"How does he see it? Be careful–"

"He's confident–"

"He's always confident! How was the safari?"

"It all depends on who you ask! I think it was an adventure. Kelsey will tell you her version. Shane has left, so we can't get his opinion!"

"What are your plans now?"

"Not sure. We'd better see that the two patients are okay here before we drive back to the Zoo."

"Be careful. Things are getting dangerous in the country."

"Jim and Mary have their fingers on the pulse. That's a medical expression for you! We'll get their advice before leaving. How are things at the Zoo?"

"In a word: tense."

"Sorry about that. I'll get Kelsey." He called out to let Kelsey know Louise wanted to speak with her. As she came in, he said, "Here's Kelsey. 'Bye. CPZ."

The next day Jim drove Mary and Kelsey to their doctor at Hurlingham. The doctor sent them both for x-rays and insisted that Mary should have an AIDS test too as the man had broken her skin. The doctor prescribed stronger analgesics. They contained codeine so they were advised to use them sparingly.

"No way," said Kelsey. "I'll use them as I need them!"

"We'll make sure you eat lots of prunes, then," joked Mary, "as they can make you constipated."

Kelsey said, "Not like hippos, I guess." Her wrist was very uncomfortable and she was worried about it, so she decided to leave for the States as soon as Jim could help her change her flight. "It's a good thing it's my left hand. I have a thesis to write when I get home!" she told them.

Jim and Kelsey managed to change her flights to the following day. The whole group went to the airport to see her off.

"Thanks so much for another great trip. I really appreciate y'all and your kindness. It was great – right up to this injury." She waved her arm in the air. "Ow! Shouldn't do that! But – know what? – I've already forgiven the guy who attacked you, Mary."

"Really?" said Jane.

"It was real hard at first, but every time he came to mind and I felt angry, I told myself that I had forgiven him," Kelsey told her.

"That's wonderful," added Mary. "I have too."

"That's great. See, I remembered what Shane told us about how he was able to forgive…and how it helped him."

Brett said, "Yes. It was the only way he could find peace, right?"

"I didn't want to leave while holding a grudge against that guy. And I did injure him too!"

Mary said, "We've been praying that he has recovered and will find employment."

Jane turned to Kelsey. "It's been really nice to have met you and got to know you. We had fun, didn't we?"

"We sure did. You guys make a real neat couple. It's great the adventures we had together. And, hey, I'll think about all the things you told me. You know, the Christian faith and all."

As they left her, with hugs all around, Brett said, "We'll be praying for good treatment and healing for you. Best wishes with your final dissertation."

"Thanks."

"We'll keep in touch, okay?" Jane told her.

"Yes, I'll write. Say goodbye to Louise for me. And the Brandons. And everyone. 'Bye."

Mary returned to the doctor to get the x-ray results. She was told the finger would heal but possibly with a permanent distortion. It still needed to be immobilized with strapping to the adjacent fingers. They were delighted to learn that the AIDS test was negative. As Jim paid the fee, Brett told him Shane and Kelsey had given him all their Kenyan cash towards the safari and to cover any additional expenses. He would reimburse them for their costs, for which Jim and Mary were very grateful.

Brett and Jane returned to their hotel and collapsed in exhaustion. They had experienced many stressful events and the next day they had to make the long drive back to the Zoo. Just before they fell asleep, Jane had a thought.

"What was it Shane said? Something about living life at a higher level of intensity here?"

"That's true. England is so boring. Goodnight, my love."

Brett did not realize it, but he might soon be yearning for some boredom.

While the Jameses had been away, life at the Zoo continued with its usual intrigues and tensions. Coreene Brandon felt uneasy with Larry Smythe, which troubled her. She got on well with most people, but Larry was a difficult man to understand. For his part, Larry was decidedly uncomfortable with Coreene and he knew why. She unwittingly challenged him with her Christian values. He decided to speak directly to her about it when he had a chance.

The opportunity came after Moshi had visited him to arrange to borrow some tools in the future, although the reason remained obscure. Moshi had hinted at other requests in the days to come. Larry felt apprehensive about Moshi – as he often had – but decided to go along with him for a while, sensing profit in keeping the powerful man happy. Nonetheless, Larry suspected it was a game with no promise of real satisfaction. He had a much deeper need – unrelated to money – which drove him to question what life was all about and where it was leading. After completing a small repair job at the guesthouse, the thought of companionship in the restaurant bar gave him the comfort he sought.

Just as he started to drive to the restaurant, he saw Coreene limping from a neighbour's cage. Normally, he would have simply waved or tried to avoid eye contact as he drove past. He surprised himself when he offered her a lift home, although it was in the opposite direction. On the short journey she said something about Jesus sending him at that time as a blessing, so he decided to be bold.

"Coreene, you bring everything around to…to Christianity!"

She turned to him and smiled. "Oh, I think you're probably right, Larry!"

"But it gets a bit wearing – you always talking about…your precious Jesus!"

"Yes, you see, that's what He told us to do. When He returns I want Him to find me doing exactly that."

"What?"

"Telling people about Him and what He taught us. Those were His instructions."

They reached the front of the Brandons' cage. Larry stopped and saw Steve outside as he waved over to Larry. Coreene started to open the door, but turned back to Larry.

"I'm sorry if it upsets you. I don't mean to–"

"No, no, it's okay." He blurted out, "You know, I used to pray…in the past. They were not very good prayers. There was no answer."

"Sometimes, when we pray, it seems there's no answer. Often God says 'wait'. Then He always has something better for us. There's never no answer."

"Well, it's all very complicated. And confusing."

"Not if you're familiar with the Bible. Do you read it?"

Larry shook his head. "Don't get much opportunity. As I say, it's all too complicated."

"Not really," Coreene said as she got out.

As Steve approached the car to help Coreene, Larry leaned over and spoke to her.

"Okay, I'm a man of few words. And I don't read much. Give me a simple summary of what it all means. You know, this Christian gospel. I need it in one sentence!"

Coreene smiled. "Oh, you're an interesting man, Larry. I've never had to do that before. I'll try." She thought for a moment and then took a deep breath. She said, "No, I'll need to think about it. But I *will* give you an answer, I promise. Thank you for the lift. That was very kind you. We'll chat again, alright?"

"Sure. Thanks." They both waved goodbye as the car left.

Coreene told Steve, "I sense a deep need in Larry. Perhaps, when I next do some baking, I'll take it over to him. Maybe with an encouraging note."

As Larry drove away, he began to think. He felt pleased he had been direct with her. Of course, he'd been a bit abrupt, but that was his nature and she didn't seem to mind. But maybe he was a bit rude. Perhaps even disrespectful. Umm...he needed a drink.

Part Six

RESOLUTION

The fictional character introduced in Part Six

Hamisi: Kenyan fisherman on north shore of The Zoo

36

Larry had guests coming, he thought. Kuvanza had been vague about the dates, but obviously Moshi was planning something.

Nursing a slight headache, the next morning Larry Smythe drove to the guesthouse to take some measurements for the extension on the facility. Brett was still half dozing after the long journey from Nairobi the previous day, but Larry's distinctive voice roused him. He decided to go out to speak with him to get the latest news from the Zoo. As he squinted against the sun, Brett didn't see Larry but was surprised to notice Kuvanza sitting in Larry's car. Curiosity overcame his anger at Kuvanza concerning the attack on Louise, so he walked across to speak with him. After some initial reticence, Kuvanza answered Brett's questions with monosyllables. He saw the two-month-old scar on Kuvanza's head.

"How is the injury?"

He mumbled, "Fine."

Brett was reluctant to say sorry, so he asked, "Did you go to the Sisters at the clinic?"

"Yes."

"They treated me when I was injured," Brett told him. Kuvanza's indifference was clear in his sullen silence. Brett asked what he was doing in Larry's car. He revealed that he sometimes needed to speak with Mr. Smythe and do small things *huko na huku,* here and there. Kuvanza was a strong fellow. Brett did not trust him, but he felt safe speaking to him while he was sitting in the car. Kuvanza was clearly uncomfortable and began to slowly wind up the window, just as Larry returned. He had seen the pair talking, and snapped at Brett.

"You'd better...mind your own business. Remember, you're a visitor here." Brett looked surprised at his abrupt words. Larry called across the roof of the car, "Don't think you're not at risk. Just because nothing bad has happened to you yet. You are dealing with...it's out of your league. Stay away from it all!"

After Brett watched them drive away he went back inside. He was puzzled by Larry's hauteur and the connection between him and Kuvanza. He sensed that Moshi was still involved somehow. He decided to mention to Len Moore that Kuvanza was connected to Larry, in case Len was unaware of Kuvanza's criminal tendencies.

"We must inform Inspector Ponda." Simion Katana was speaking to Hamud Sita, who had come to his office with surprising information. What Sita had just told him was almost unbelievable but he could take no chances. Katana picked up the phone and dialled the Malindi police station. It took a long time to get through to Ponda. Sita sat patiently. He had heard from his friend in a Mombasa shipping company a few scraps of information about a plan Moshi was putting together. Sita was not sure if it was true – or even if Moshi's intentions were illegal – but his instinct told him to inform the Zoo director and let him decide. When Ponda was on the line and heard Katana's news, it was clear that he also was concerned and appreciated being told. Katana replaced the receiver, telling Sita, "We did well to give him that information. He'll follow up. He has been hearing similar things from their officer at the port."

As Sita left, Katana said, "I heard a strange report last week that Hamisi and his brother have been seen a couple of times in deep conversation with a rough-looking stranger. They meet up behind the maintenance workshops."

Moshi was angry. He thought, *That moron of a mzee refused to cooperate! I think his awkward older son has persuaded him to pretend he's lost the key. I wish*

I'd kept it. He's either lost it, or he hid it and stupidly forgot where, or he's lying. Either way, I have a problem. The other son, Iha, had agreed to cooperate with Moshi. Iha revealed that, years previously, his father had spoken of two chambers set to the east of the tunnel, several metres in from the north end. That was all he saw – or remembered seeing – from his quick, illegal visit during the construction all those years ago. Moshi was furious with himself for not looking deeper into the tunnel when he was down there.

Iha agreed to keep looking for the key to the door in the wall and later work with Kuvanza to dig out the treasure that Moshi was convinced lay hidden there. Moshi knew he did not have the strength himself to use the tools he had arranged to borrow from Larry Smythe.

The other parts of his plan had fallen into place. He knew what he intended to do. Secrecy was vital. And timing. He would draw the two unsuspecting young men, Iha and Kuvanza, into his confidence, but only to a limited degree. He trusted that his other contacts would be sufficiently remote from the Zoo to keep his plans secret. He was delighted when he heard that Louise Emerson had gone to a hotel in Malindi for three weeks with her maid, Shafiqah. He felt sure the other girl, Fatima, could be pressured into compliance and Louise's old manservant, Mjuhgiuna, could likewise be persuaded to cooperate if necessary. He had experienced enough of Kuvanza's brutality that Moshi knew he would not resist.

It was the next Saturday when Steve Brandon drove their car up to the Energy Conservation Centre. Coreene got out, balancing a plate. As Steve stayed in the car, she knocked on the cage door. After a moment, Larry opened it.

"Hello Larry. I did some cooking and thought you'd like these."

He was surprised but took the plate, wondering what to say. He nodded over to Steve. She said, "I have the sentence for you. I wrote it out. Ready? Here goes: 'God has existed forever and He created everything and He loves you and me and He made us in His image for fellowship with Him, but the bond is broken by sin which has to be punished by death so God provided His Son Jesus who became the all-sufficient sacrifice for our sins by taking on Himself, on the cross, the punishment we deserve, and substituting

His sinlessness for our guilt so that when God looks at us He sees Jesus' righteousness rather than our sins, so we simply need to believe in Jesus in order to obtain eternal life and spend forever in His presence.' There!" She folded the paper and put it back inside the envelope she was holding. "Here, you can keep it." He took it, glanced through it, and noticed a card inside too. Larry thought briefly, and responded to Coreene.

"So, the bond was broken. All our troubles come from the sin of one man? Oh, plus a woman too, I recall!"

"Yes. But it was all *solved* by one man: Jesus Christ, and our believing in Him."

"Got it. Thanks. But life is not so simple for us nonbelievers."

"It's not simple for Christians either. We live in the same world, you know!"

Steve got out of the car and joined them. Larry spoke to them both.

"Look, you two know...you're going to heaven. Right? Why should you worry about me? Why can't you just let me work out...my own destiny?"

Steve said, "Because we are concerned about you. Isn't it natural to want to share good news?"

Coreene added, "Our desire lines up with God's will that none should be lost. But we have hardly any influence in–"

"So, why would your God send a good person to hell?" demanded Larry.

"A better question might be: Why would a perfect God allow any of us sinners into His holy presence?"

"And?"

"It's only because we are covered by the righteousness of Jesus who paid the price...."

Larry had unfolded the paper and was reading part of Coreene's long sentence.

"...by taking on Himself, on the cross, the punishment we deserve."

"Yes. Exactly."

Larry said, "Look, I'm a practical man–"

"So was Jesus!"

"Oh yes. I remember. A carpenter."

"That's right," said Coreene.

"But my question is still: Why would God send a good person to hell?"

"He doesn't," Steve said.

"What, only the bad people?"

"Are you asking if the moderately naughty might get let off?"

All three smiled. Larry squinted across the compound towards a group of swaying palm trees. He was obviously thinking.

"But, Coreene, you have constant back trouble. Why doesn't your God heal you? I assume you must pray about it. And expect a miracle, eh?"

"Yes. I do pray and I do believe in miracles."

"But you're still in terrible pain."

"But I also trust God. He gives me the strength to bear the pain." Larry looked unimpressed, so Coreene added, "I could have been killed in that car accident or injured more badly. I praise Him every day for my life and the health I have, and all I am able to do. But you're right, I do pray earnestly for healing."

"Every day," added Steve. Larry gave a sympathetic nod.

"But I still don't see why you two care about me. What's in it for you?"

Coreene hesitated and then gave Larry an honest reply:

"We'd love to see you acknowledge God and His guidance in your life, and then watch you use your many gifts for His glory."

"Oh, that's heavy stuff! So, what's yer point? Keep it simple for me now."

Steve shared a thought. "Just imagine what you could accomplish – or God could accomplish through you – if you'd simply yield to His–"

"Too airy-fairy for me!" Larry scoffed. He gave a casual wave of his hand, "As I said, I'm just a practical man. I puts Number One first."

Coreene quietly said, "It all depends on who you place as Number One, doesn't it? Yourself or God."

As the conversation ended, Larry thanked Coreene for her kindness and gave them a lukewarm promise to think about what they had said.

But, as they drove away, his immediate thoughts were of his uneasy liaison with Moshi and how he could benefit or, more seriously, what it might cost him.

On the evening of Sunday the 10th of June, Larry made his routine check of the Energy Centre. The first of his usual after-dinner drinks had relaxed him and he was in a reflective mood. He was pleased with the changes he had made to N-1. The hidden storeroom door through the wall had been sealed months ago and he had strengthened the fence across the beach far out into the sea. From his second-floor window he studied the huge water tanks he had built on three levels. They stored tidal seawater to run the generators below. They were full, as the recent full moon had brought high high-tides and low low-tides, with nearly four metres variation. The wind generator was almost motionless in the slight breeze, but the bank of batteries was charged. A good thing. He had guests coming, he thought. Kuvanza had been vague about the dates, but obviously Moshi was planning something. Three days previously, after Larry had left the bar late, Kuvanza had emerged from the shadows. He informed Larry he would be entertaining some overnight visitors in the near future. The information was conveyed in a sour manner which did not suggest that the hospitality was going to be optional.

Larry stepped onto his balcony and placed his whiskey glass on the outdoor table without refilling it – as he normally did. He always needed that second drink. His upper-level position gave him a view along the eastern shoreline and the dark headland to the north. The inky sky reflected the fading colours of the long-set sun behind him. In the twilight, he sensed the activity of emerging crepuscular creatures. It was a perfect scene. But not for him. What was irking him? He couldn't pinpoint it. Then it came to him: Coreene Brandon. Steve too, but mainly Coreene.

She was kind; he had been rude. First there had been the unsatisfactory conversation when he had driven her home. Then she had brought him a gift. He remembered the card inside the envelope. It simply said 'God has wonderful plans for your life'. He had read that and asked her, Me? He clearly recalled her reply.

"Yes, but are you willing to yield your life to His Lordship?"

"I don't even believe in him!" he had retorted.

"But He believes in you. He loves you."

"How can he? The way I am, and what I believe?"

"God's divine purposes aren't dependant on your belief. But His grace and compassion can only be fully released in your life through your faith."

Larry's thoughts were interrupted by movement along the beach. He noticed a large man and two other people. In the soft glow of his front-garden ornamental lamps he saw they were all wearing police uniforms. They were walking across the sand in the shadows to the east. He remained still. Lights flashed along the fence and they began rattling the gate to the restricted eastern portion of the north beach. He could just make out their movements but they did not speak. Then he heard a metallic snap and further clicks. After a few moments, the trio walked silently back along the beach and out of sight. Larry decided that, at first light, he would investigate to see what they had done. He wondered if it could be related to Moshi's plans. *But why would the police be involved down there?*

He rested his elbow on the railing and stared into the gloom. The palm fronds rustled softly, whispering incomprehensible messages in the dying evening breeze. The empty glass on the table was invisible in the dull light. Strangely, he felt no urge for his second drink. He heard a vehicle start up and drive away. He assumed it was the police.

He thought deeply for a long time about Coreene's kind gesture and her sincere words. He still had her card in his pocket. He did not need to read it. He knew what it said: 'God has wonderful plans for your life'. Suddenly, he felt a sense of inexplicable peace and satisfaction. *She's an intelligent and gracious lady*, he thought. *And Steve obviously cares too. A lot of what they say makes sense.*

He was overwhelmed by a long-forgotten feeling which, on reflection, he identified as hope.

37

Moshi's dominant personality and fearsome reputation were so overpowering that Fatima was terrified.

At 9:15am on the 11th of June, Moshi completed a loop in his car around the Zoo, drove himself along the southern road, and pulled up outside the guesthouse. Driving was awkward with his injured right arm still supported in a sling. Earlier, he had left his bodyguard at the Energy Centre and collected two sturdy hoes, a pickaxe, and a shovel. Then he had dropped his driver to wait beside the main door through the wall in the Muslim quarter. Kuvanza was already there. They both had their instructions – two sets of directions in case Moshi's fallback plan had to be put into effect. His driver held the necessary signed documents to cover both eventualities. He told Kuvanza to find Iha. Moshi was energized by the excitement of his plan finally coming into effect. Could anything go wrong? Possibly, but not likely. He was grateful for the isolation and inaccessibility that the headland would provide.

He knew that Brett was teaching a class at the polytechnic that morning. Two students had confirmed the time frame. Moshi casually questioned a couple of children playing on the steps of the guesthouse and they told him Miss Jane was in her room. He waited in his car, keenly looking around at the passersby. He clearly visualized the type of person he wanted: someone Jane knew and would trust. He could hardly believe his luck when he saw Fatima walking across to visit the clinic. Once she had entered, his agile mind rapidly fabricated a story. He got out of the car and positioned himself so he could intercept her naturally as she left the clinic.

Fatima took a long time. Moshi kept looking at his watch as he knew he had a limited time before either Jane left the guesthouse or Brett returned. The tension was rising. Eventually, Fatima emerged. He greeted her and told her to visit Jane and invite her to the Muslim section immediately as she had something very interesting to show her. She was to explain that Mrs. Emerson had told her this, and she should stay close to Jane.

"Do not mention my name," he warned. Although Fatima did not want to get involved, Moshi's dominant personality and fearsome reputation were so overpowering that she was terrified. She had no choice but to comply. He rehearsed with her what to say and the route they should use to walk over to the big door in the wall. He would drive there and meet them.

Moshi watched from a distance as Fatima went to the guesthouse to speak to Jane. After several tense minutes, he saw them both leave and walk along the long road that would take them to the central buildings. He drove the other way around to the wall and met Kuvanza, Iha, and his driver at the heavy door below the Kismet Kantara arch. Moshi got out and instructed the men to remove the tools. Then he sent the driver with the luxurious car to wait by the Energy Centre.

He was furious when Iha told him his father had definitely lost the key. He knew Louise had a key somewhere, so he snapped his instructions to Iha.

"Keep out of sight. Wait for Fatima who will be with a white woman. Keep them here."

Moshi and Kuvanza went over to Louise's cage and roused Mjuhgiuna. Once he saw them, Mjuhgiuna became extremely cooperative and led them upstairs to get the key from the hook by Louise's front door. Back at the door, Moshi tried the key in the lock to confirm it was the correct one. Then the wait began. His contingency plan depended on Fatima following his instructions and Jane not becoming suspicious.

He was relieved when he eventually saw them both. They arrived at the wall, chatting lightheartedly. Moshi immediately sent Fatima away with a gruff word of warning to say nothing. He called Jane over to the door as he unlocked and opened it. She was surprised to see him there but before she could say anything, Kuvanza appeared. In one move, he grabbed Jane around her neck and grasped her arm with his other hand. He wrenched her arm around painfully and shoved her through the heavy door, followed by Moshi and Iha. Moshi slammed the door shut, locked it, and placed the key in his pocket. It all happened so suddenly that Jane was gasping and speechless. She tried to call out but Kuvanza clamped his hand over her mouth. She struggled and almost broke free so he hit her across the face twice, causing her nose to bleed. They pushed her along the path towards Henry's huts.

"What are you up to now, Moshi?" she demanded, wiping the blood from her face.

"Just keep quiet and cooperate, then you won't be harmed."

Jane was defiant. "What's this blood then?" Kuvanza was smirking at her. "Let go of me, I can walk on my own," she snapped at him as she tried to shake her arm free. He released his grip and she backed away from him.

"Let's go," snapped Moshi.

They walked in single file with Moshi leading. Iha was carrying a large water container in addition to some tools. He kept looking at Jane sympathetically. Kuvanza took the heavy pickaxe once he no longer needed to hold Jane. As they stumbled along, he studied Moshi. He was wearing shorts, a loose shirt, and using a heavy walking stick. He clutched his satchel awkwardly under the arm with a sling. He looked ill. It mattered little to Kuvanza; he would get paid in any case.

When they reached the compound, they immediately pushed Jane over to the southern hut where she and Brett had stayed a few months previously. Moshi spoke to the two men.

"I saw Brett James find a key for the top hut up in the roof. Look here for the key to this hut." Jane stood next to Moshi, wondering what was happening and trying to think of a way to escape. She felt she knew the area better than the men, including the paths to the beach and over to the site of the ashes. But she hesitated, wondering if Moshi had a gun, and knowing how dangerous Kuvanza was. Eventually, Iha located the key under the eaves and unlocked the hut. They pushed her inside and Moshi gave Kuvanza a sharp instruction.

"Look for the rifle."

"It's not here," Jane told him. They ignored her. After a thorough inspection, the three men stepped outside and slammed the door shut. As they left, Moshi instructed her to keep quiet. She heard the key turn in the lock. "I'll make as much noise as I like!" she yelled through the door. She shouted at him, "So, what about Christian brotherhood, Moshi?" There was silence from outside. She was alone.

She heard them move across to the naturalist's upper hut. She climbed on the bed to look out the window and saw Moshi outside the door, holding a rifle. She assumed they had found the key. Moshi and Iha were shouting in a mixture of Swahili and English.

She heard Iha say, "...no ammunition. Where is it?"

"I know...if I need..." said Moshi.

Jane knew it was in the vault. She saw there was still a little stale water left in the container from hers and Brett's visit, so she was not concerned about thirst. She washed the blood from her face and felt her bruises. She looked through the window again. The three men were still at the upper hut, looking at the sand outside and preparing to dig. She intended to retrieve the key when the men were not looking as she saw it had been left in the lock. She found a piece of thin cardboard and slid it under the door. Using a knife, she attempted to push the key through the lock, hoping it would drop onto the card which she could draw back under the door.

Unfortunately, her plan did not work because the key was twisted to the side and did not align with the keyhole. She spent a long time trying to wiggle the key to the correct position using different implements, but eventually gave up. Knowing the vault below the floor led into the tunnel, she briefly considered that as a means of escape. She immediately realized it would simply run north to where Moshi's demolition gang was hacking away at the roof of the tunnel.

Jane was not worried because she felt sure Fatima would have seen what happened and would have told someone. She was thankful, once again, for her ability to readily accept situations and make the best of them. In between watching the men through the window, she tidied up the mess they had made while looking for the rifle. Then she made herself a cup of tea using the remaining water, without milk or sugar. There was no food.

In fact, Fatima had not seen what happened to Jane at the main door because her view had been blocked by the men, but she was sufficiently worried that she spoke to Mjuhgiuna. They found Imam Faiz and told him what had happened. He immediately went to speak with the senile old *mzee*. His older son provided sufficient information that Faiz was convinced he should contact Brett or Steve. As he waved down a vehicle to take him across to the guesthouse, he did not know that Mjuhgiuna had already made his way over there. He was so distressed at Moshi having the key, and Fatima's tale, that he had told her to stay in her room and not answer the door. Then he had cadged a lift across to try to find someone to help.

When Steve heard Mjuhgiuna's report, he rushed over to the guesthouse and tried the door to the James' room. It was locked. He immediately went to the polytechnic and interrupted Brett's class. They dashed out to Steve's car and met the Imam who corroborated Mjuhgiuna's account and gave more details – all of which added urgency to the need to act. Brett checked in their room to see if Jane had left him a note. He did not see one. They asked the children playing nearby and learned that Moshi's car had been there earlier. The oldest boy described how Moshi had spoken to Fatima.

"Mrs. Jane walked away. That side, with Fatima."

"Jane's in trouble if Moshi's involved. We have to get over there," exclaimed Brett. Imam Faiz got in the car and Steve dropped him and Mjuhgiuna at the cage of one of the policemen to report what had happened. He was asleep after his night shift, but agreed to phone Sergeant Kinyanjui in Mwakindini.

Steve and Brett drove to the main door in the wall. It was locked.

"I know where there's a key," said Brett.

"I think Mjuhgiuna said Moshi took it," Steve told him.

"Let's check. There may be other keys."

They dashed across to S-33 and ran up the stairs but Louise's door was locked. "Here, let's try this," said Brett as he ran into the boardroom, dragged out the shelves, and slipped through CPZ-Store. He was dismayed to see that the key was not hanging in its usual place on the hook.

"Is there another way over the wall?" asked Steve. Brett thought about the upper door through to Kismet Kantara but realized those steps just led down into the Muslim area, not across the wall. Frantically, he thought of other possibilities. There was the door downstairs to the hidden passage, but he did not want to waste time trying to find keys into Mjuhgiuna's cage to let them through the kitchen. He did not realize that Fatima was cowering in her room down there.

"I know..." he said. He rifled through the piles of keys on the shelf. He grasped all those marked with red spots and began stuffing them in his pockets, but there were too many. "Get a towel from the bathroom," he told Steve.

Once he had all the coded keys, he wrapped them in the towel and, stuffing it down his shirt, said, "Quick! The roof."

He stepped back into the store and climbed the metal rungs set in the wall. He forced open the roof hatch and clambered out on the roof. Steve followed in amazement. Brett ripped a faded canvas cover off a pile of ropes and rungs.

"It's a rope ladder. I hope it holds." He dragged it across to the eastern parapet and threw it over. The rope was frayed and the wooden rungs looked flimsy but they remained attached at one end to the central frame. "Let's try it," Brett said as he stepped over the edge. "Wait, Steve. You'd better stay here in case I can't get through the gate. If this fails, we'll both be stuck in the passageway." As he neared the bottom, one rope snapped and he fell the last few feet. He scraped his knee and tore the slacks he had been wearing for teaching.

"You okay?" asked Steve peering over the edge.

"Yes. I'll try the gate. Wait to see if I have the right key."

After trying several keys, he found the correct one to the wrought-iron gate. He threw the others on the ground in the towel beside the door post, and called back to Steve.

"Don't risk that ladder. Go for help. See if there's a way through the fence at N-1. I'll find Jane." Without thinking of how he would get back, he pushed through the gate and dashed along the path, being as careful of snakes as he could in his panic. His heart was racing and sweat ran down every part of his body.

As he slowed down at the edge of the clearing, Brett saw the back of Moshi's stubby outline as he stood watching two other men digging. He was leaning on a thick stick and clutching a bag under his bandaged arm. There was no sign of Jane. Breathlessly, Brett called out without thinking.

"Jane, where are you?" Moshi spun around with a look of astonishment on his face. "Where's Jane?" Brett gasped.

"How did *you* get here?" said Moshi.

"Where's Jane?"

Brett heard Jane's voice: "I'm over here. In our hut."

Brett glanced over. The moment his attention was diverted, Moshi dropped his satchel and lunged at Brett with his stick raised.

"The chamber is empty. Where's the treasure?" Brett easily stepped aside. He had no fear of Moshi with his injured right arm. He looked at the scene. Several thoughts flashed through his mind. Kuvanza and another man had stopped digging. In a glance, he saw they had dug a trench along the tunnel and the tops of the two side chambers were exposed. The second vault had been broken open. As Moshi continued to demand how he got there, with his left hand clutching the stick, Brett noticed that a rifle had been placed upright beside the open door in the hut. He wondered if it was loaded or if it required the ammunition that was stored in the tunnel. Moshi had seen that. Moshi noticed Brett's glance and stepped towards him again. He was shouting at Brett.

"The treasure is mine!"

"No it isn't. It's mine! Miles gave it to me." Moshi stared in disbelief. "He bequeathed it to me. In his will," Brett added.

Moshi shook his head. "I don't believe you. Where is it? Is there another compartment in the tunnel?" Brett was defiantly silent. Moshi prompted him with a shove, "In one of the huts?"

"No."

"Where is it?" Brett was silent. Moshi repeated, "Where is it? Tell me! Where is the treasure?" He raised the stick. Brett's mind was spinning: how long would it be before Steve arrived with help? He had better play for time.

He shrugged, "In Nairobi."

"What? Nairobi?" Moshi dropped the stick and slapped Brett across his face. The force of the blow surprised Brett and sent him reeling.

"You liar!"

"No. It's in Nairobi. We took it there."

"No!"

Brett wondered about running. He hesitated because he thought Moshi may have a gun in his satchel. He was so angry that he may shoot. Also, he didn't want to leave Jane. He repeated what he had said.

"Yes, it's all in Nairobi."

"You fool!" shrieked Moshi.

"Safe in Nairobi."

"Where? With the police?" Brett grinned, which told Moshi his answer. "Not Matherton?" Brett said nothing. "With Allistair?" Again, Brett's silent expression gave Moshi the reply. "You gave it to Matherton & Son! Does anyone else know?" Brett realized he was revealing more than he should so he again said nothing, while looking over at Kuvanza and thinking of an escape plan. How could he rescue Jane? He saw Kuvanza grasp the rifle.

Moshi grabbed Brett's arm and thrust forward, trying to topple him. Brett made a rapid decision. With all his strength, he lunged sideways and pushed Moshi backwards. But as he fell, Moshi held onto Brett's arm with his left hand. Brett knew Moshi's right arm was injured, but the pull from the heavy man caught Brett by surprise and he lost his balance. Kuvanza stood, watching in amusement. Brett couldn't see the other man. Brett fell awkwardly on the ground. Moshi knelt down and again clutched his stout stick with his left hand and hit Brett viciously across his back. Brett kicked him as hard as he could from his lying position but Moshi suddenly sat all his weight on Brett's legs. Then Brett felt a heavy whack on his head. Again, he was surprised at the force of the blow. Although Moshi was gasping for breath, he was heavy and his blows were forceful. Brett sensed that another hard clout to his head could knock him unconscious, so he began to panic. He looked over at Kuvanza who was leaning on the rifle with its butt on the ground and his hand on the muzzle. In a flash, Brett reasoned he would not do that with a loaded rifle. They obviously had not found the bullets. Before Moshi could strike him again, he flipped sideways to free his leg to try to kick him a second time.

Suddenly, they all heard a shout from the beach.

"Mrs. James. Are you here?" came the voice.

"Your friends! How did they get here?" Moshi's rasping whisper reached Brett's ear. Again the voice was heard.

"Mrs. James. Jane! Are you here? Anyone here?" At the same instant, Brett and Moshi recognized that it was Inspector Ponda's voice. He was commanding them in English and Swahili to stay where they were. That was too much for Kuvanza who threw down the rifle, dashed through the trees, and headed for the pathway back to the gate. Brett then saw rapid movement in the bushes to the north as Iha disappeared into the thick foliage.

Ponda's large form emerged at the edge of the clearing. Immediately, Moshi struggled to his feet, clutched his bag and stick, and dashed towards the narrow path leading to the northern beach. His white *kofia* hat was left squashed in the sand.

38

Ponda said, "We need to find him." To Brett, his voice was more than just determined – it sounded sinister.

Inspector Ponda watched intently as Moshi fled. Behind the inspector, Brett was surprised to see a couple of fishermen he knew from the south beach, with two other policemen. Brett heard Jane shouting from the window.

"Help! Brett. I'm in our hut!" As he dashed across the sand, Brett noticed Ponda also striding towards the hut. Brett tried the door.

"It's locked!"

Then Ponda noticed that the key had been left in the lock. He opened the door and Jane rushed out and clung to Brett who held her tightly. She gasped and smiled at them.

"Thank you. All of you." She was bruised and holding her elbow. Her clothes were blood-stained.

"Are you alright?" asked Ponda.

"Yes, thank you, sir. Just a bit shocked and thirsty. And my nose was bleeding. I quickly used up the water as it was hot in the hut." They gave her a drink.

One of the policemen asked Ponda, "Should we chase those men, sir?"

Ponda shook his head. "No. They will not get far. I have officers patrolling this side of the wall."

Brett was surprised. "I thought Moshi had the door key." Ponda ignored the remark as he watched Jane splash her face, and drink again.

They all stood in the shade. Ponda was in no hurry as he looked over at the exposed tunnel, and told them what would happen next.

"One of my officers has medical training. He will accompany you to the clinic. I have four men along the north shore where that man ran. He is Iha, the younger son of the deranged *mzee.*"

Again, Brett was surprised. "But the gate in the northern fence is secure and Len told me Larry Smythe sealed the door through the store."

Ponda smiled wearily. "Last night, we inspected the gate in the fence. We used cutters to remove the padlock and install our own. My officers got through the fence this morning during the low tide so they could access the beach. Moshi will head there I am sure."

"There's no way through," stated Brett. "I climbed all along that hill, exploring–"

"Mrs. Emerson told me there is a trail through narrow paths."

One of the fishermen looked up. "It is true. I heard it. Myself, I have never been to that place."

"Why are *you* here?" Brett asked him.

Ponda answered for him: "I had arranged boats and fishermen who knew the channels in the south bay. From that direction I wanted to surprise Moshi and his men and catch them in their activities here. The tide had to be right as we needed sufficient depth to reach this place. However, Mrs. James was taken in the morning so we had to move quickly. I did not know you had another way to get here."

Brett was trying to think of an evasive answer, when Jane spoke to him.

"How are you, dear? I watched you fighting with Moshi."

"Yes, he was angry when he found the second chamber was empty. He was convinced the treasure was hidden there."

Ponda reacted silently to the word 'treasure' but he simply told the fishermen to check their boats. He directed his officers to examine the upper hut as he had noticed the open door. Once they had left, he gave Brett an explanation.

"Moshi expected to find the stash of valuables and leave the country with it. He left complicated instructions with his driver and bodyguard to deal with things after he had escaped." That surprised Brett and Jane, so Ponda added, "Our maritime personnel heard of his arrangement with two fishermen from the northern bay. When the tide was in, they planned to pick up Moshi and paddle out to a motor boat which would connect with a larger vessel beyond the headland. My officers had to get along the exposed corals to the collection point early this morning before the tide rose. They had instructions to wait for the fishermen's boat to land. Soon they will be intercepting Moshi."

"Why not pursue him now?" Brett asked.

"He won't get far. My men will be covering this narrow track to the northern beach." Ponda looked at his watch and stared west along the southern shoreline towards the Muslim sector. "I expect one of my officers will join us from there soon," he said. "He will escort you back if you wish, Mrs. James."

"No, I'll stay with Brett, thank you."

While Ponda thought, Brett said to him, "I understood you had no access through the large main door. Mrs. Emerson's key was missing and I assumed Moshi got one from the crazy old man or his son."

"We don't have a key. My men will have walked along this side of the wall from the north." As he spoke, a policeman appeared at the western edge of the compound. Ponda spoke with him and confirmed that the only way back was through the open north fence. "You return with him," Ponda told Jane.

Brett said, "Yes, she should get first-aid attention. I'll go with her."

Ponda was firm, "I told you, he has medical training. I need you to come inland with me. You have some knowledge of this area which I don't."

"Better do as he says, love," Jane told Brett. "I'm okay to walk."

"Alright then."

Ponda spoke kindly to Jane. "We have a vehicle outside the Energy Centre. My officers will help you."

As they parted, Brett added, "Go to the Brandons and get them to take you to the clinic for a check. I wish Louise was here to help."

"I'll be fine. You take care," she said, holding his arm and giving him a quick kiss on the cheek. As she walked away with the policeman, one of the fishermen appeared and spoke to Ponda.

"Is there anything else I can do to help, sir?"

"Yes. Come with us. My two officers will remain beside the huts. There may be valuables and I don't want anyone interfering."

"Will anyone come here?" asked Brett in surprise.

Ponda replied reluctantly. "Probably not. But until we have Moshi and the others in our hands, I don't want to take any chances." He was not accustomed to having to explain his instructions. He told his men to look out carefully for Kuvanza and Iha who would be trying to get back across the wall. Then he turned to the north of the clearing. The trio made their way through the bushes beyond the compound but Brett was puzzled.

"Why are we searching like this? Won't your men be able to locate Moshi?"

In a voice of flint, Ponda replied, "We need to find him. We will find him."

Brett thought of the situation. Here he was, feeling grateful for the assistance of a simple fisherman as they followed a powerful police inspector who was almost certainly carrying a gun. They were in an unfamiliar forest with Moshi, possibly armed and dangerous, in the dense bushes ahead of them. His injured wife was being escorted by police to a clinic. *Life is interesting,* he thought, as he said a silent prayer for Jane. She and the policeman were not used to the territory and some of the dangers. Brett struggled with Ponda through the bushes along an ill-defined pathway and up the hill towards the northern shore. The fisherman followed behind them.

Ponda turned to Brett and spoke in a whisper. "We need to find Moshi."

"Your staff will pick him up along with the other fellows. They can't hide for long out here."

Ponda glared at Brett and said, "We need to find him." To Brett, his voice was more than just determined – it sounded sinister. Ponda had said it three times. He was a man who seldom repeated himself. Brett was at a loss to understand the inspector's resoluteness as they scrambled along the narrow path which rose inland.

Suddenly, there was a rush of movement ahead of them. Ponda stopped and stared. Two large animals crashed away from them through the forest. Ponda reached for his concealed gun and pulled it from the holster. He took several deliberate steps forward. As they moved ahead, suddenly Brett saw a crumpled body on the ground. Approaching cautiously behind Ponda, he gasped in horror as he recognized Moshi. The sling had slipped from his shoulder, and his arm and thighs were bloodied. It looked as though his arm had been chewed. Brett stepped back in dismay. It was a terrible thing to be looking down at the man with whom, less than an hour ago, he had been fighting and who had been trying to hurt him and his wife. Now he lay crushed and torn on the ground in front of them.

Ponda turned to the fisherman. "Go and tell the officers we have found Moshi." The man dashed back along the path they had just followed. Ponda walked over to Moshi's limp body. He bent over and stared at him. He looked in silence at his dislocated shoulder and stared at the bloodied gashes and the torn flesh. Ponda put his gun away, knelt down, and checked Moshi carefully.

"He's dead," he said. He examined a puncture wound on his ankle. Brett walked over respectfully. Ponda whispered, "Snake bite. Probably a green mamba." Brett had read that mambas come out during the day, but they are normally secretive and will slither away if disturbed. Brett had experienced that.

"Could it have been a puff adder?"

Ponda examined the wound a second time. Without looking at Brett, he spoke again.

"The bite pattern is a mamba." Brett backed away because Ponda appeared troubled. Then the inspector did something that amazed Brett. He placed his large hand on Moshi's shoulder and kept it there for several moments.

"What attacked him?" Ponda was silent. "Were they bush pigs?" pressed Brett.

"Probably." His hand was still on Moshi's shoulder.

Brett said, "I once saw a large monitor lizard on the north beach."

Ponda remained kneeling beside Moshi.

"The mamba would have killed him. Then the bush pigs attacked the body."

"Mrs. Emerson warned me they are omnivorous."

Ponda nodded in silence and remained on the ground while continuing to stare at Moshi's broken body. He reached over, grasped Moshi's bag and opened it. He removed a revolver and studied it. Then he checked the safety catch, placed the gun back in the bag, and closed it. He carefully looked in all of Moshi's pockets. He motioned to Brett to help. He realized, for the first time, how difficult it is to remove objects from a dead man's pockets. They had to roll over the heavy man. They found several items. Brett recognized the main door key. Ponda removed Moshi's watch and placed it in the satchel. Brett saw Moshi's stick lying on the ground – the one he had been beaten with earlier. He picked it up, thinking it may be useful when they walked back. Brett stood to the side, holding the stick.

Ponda stood and silently walked towards the pathway back to the south beach.

As he passed Brett, in a stone-cold voice, he said, "He was my brother." Brett was speechless. Ponda stopped, turned, and looked at Brett with deep, sad eyes. He added, "My half-brother. Our mother…we had the same mother." As he continued walking towards the shore, Ponda shook his head and said, "He never knew that."

Brett heard a sound in the bushes and spun around. His immediate thought was an attacking animal had returned, but he was surprised to see the movement of several men struggling through the tangle of branches. Ponda called out as a uniformed policeman appeared. Then Brett was astonished to see his friends Hamisi and his brother emerge, both bound with ropes. They were followed by Sergeant Kinyanjui, holding a gun. Both fishermen stared in horror at Moshi's body. They looked worried, haggard, and probably in need of a cigarette. Brett was disheartened to see them and sorry to be of no help. But his mind was occupied by Ponda's dramatic revelation.

Ponda took charge. He instructed Kinyanjui and the other policeman to stay with Moshi. He spoke sharply in the local tongue to Hamisi and his brother. They walked ahead of him, with Brett following in sombre silence. As they neared the clearing, Brett boldly touched Ponda's arm, gesturing to him to hold back. He whispered to the inspector.

"They both rescued me when I had a windsurfing incident out in the northern bay." Ponda looked at Brett but did not say anything. Brett sensed that a house of cards was collapsing around them all.

They entered the clearing and walked over to the upper hut. Ponda carefully lifted up the rifle and checked that it was unloaded.

He said, almost mechanically, "The owner can collect this from our Malindi station with the proper documents." He clutched Moshi's bag close to his chest. He stood looking out at the ocean. Then his sweeping glance took in the whole compound: the door of the upper hut swinging on its hinges, the partially excavated tunnel, the lower hut, and across to Henry's secure research station. He said, "My men will stay with Moshi until we can remove the...." He stopped and swallowed, "...remove him." For Brett, it was a rare display of emotion from the cold-hearted police inspector.

The fisherman from the southern bay came over and glanced at Hamisi and his brother standing dejectedly in the shade. Ponda was the detached professional now as he spoke to him in Swahili and then to one of the policemen. Brett heard references to the Malindi Coastal Division and instructions to bring a police boat to the south shore beside Henry Emerson's station. The policeman hurried along the footpath to the west. Ponda told Brett what he planned.

"He will give instructions to my officers waiting beside the Energy Centre. I want Moshi taken to Malindi as soon as possible. If they are quick, they can land before the tide gets too low. Sergeant Kinyanjui will bring the body to the beach."

On the way back to the wall, with the two bound fishermen walking ahead, Ponda asked Brett how he got through the wall.

"Did my men on the north shore help you?"

"No. I didn't know they were there. I had to dash here as quickly as possible."

"How then?" Ponda asked again. He did not appreciate having to ask a question twice.

"There is another way. You may wish to ask Mrs. Emerson about it." He did not want to reveal Louise's secret passageway.

Suppressing his irritation at Brett's evasive answer, he said, "I will. If I need to."

The sad group reached the wall. The main door was still locked so Ponda tried the key he had retrieved from Moshi. It opened the door. A police car and a pair of officers were waiting. As they grabbed the two fishermen, Brett remembered the pile of keys he had left lying by the grilled gate. He walked along the path to the north to collect them. Ponda followed, with interest. Brett had no way of stopping him. As they stood by the small gate, they heard moaning. Brett stepped into the narrow passageway and saw Kuvanza lying on the ground.

"The rope, it broke," he wailed as he clutched his ankle. Brett saw the rope ladder had snapped and the top half hung loosely with the rest piled in a heap on the ground.

"Yes, I found it had rotted," Brett told him as he helped him up. Brett saw the towel and the pile of keys on the ground and realized he would not be able to carry Moshi's stick too, so he gave it to Kuvanza for support. Brett asked him, "What are you doing in this passage?"

"I saw the open gate. I thought I could escape this way."

During this exchange, Ponda had been looking keenly along the narrow passage and up towards the roof. He turned to Brett.

"So that is how you got here."

Brett closed the gate and locked it, adding the key to the pile he gathered up in the towel. Kuvanza limped and groaned his way along the path in front of Ponda.

"Where is Iha?" Ponda asked him.

"I don't know."

Ponda responded with, "My men will find him."

That evening, Jane and Brett were at the Brandons' cage, recovering from their ordeal. They had both received treatment at the clinic and were reviewing the day's dramatic events with Coreene. When Steve had returned from Louise's roof, he learned that Ponda had already taken his men south to arrange some boats. Coreene had heard that Iha found his way to the northern gate and was arrested by the police waiting there. They speculated on what would happen to the four men who had been taken into custody.

Brett said, "I tried to put in a good word for Hamisi and his brother, but I don't know if it'll make any difference."

Coreene gave them more information.

"The police couldn't find Fatima, but Mjuhgiuna coaxed her out by assuring her that Moshi was dead, even though she is still terrified. Louise will help everyone settle down when she returns with Shafiqah tomorrow."

Jane said, "She'll be anxious to know the whole story."

"I know I am," said Brett. "I still can't understand how it all happened."

The next morning, Fatima found Jane and apologized for deceiving her. Jane hugged and reassured her.

"That's alright. I should have been smarter and asked more questions before stepping into Moshi's trap."

Ponda played the role of a disinterested professional in the days that followed, during Moshi's funeral in Mombasa, and the later detailed investigations. He was the emotionless Inspector of Police again. Brett told no one – not even Jane – about the two half-brothers. He did not want to disclose that intimate knowledge without Ponda's permission.

39

To Brett, Ponda appeared weary of talking. Or perhaps he had simply told them all he intended to reveal.

It was neither the rifle nor the civilian clothing that surprised Louise; it was Ponda's demeanour. He entered her upper suite slowly and respectfully, and glanced around. He nodded to Brett and Jane, and then spoke gently to Louise, showing her the gun.

"This German Blaser rifle was found beside one of the huts. It has two triggers."

Louise looked at it and corrected him. "If that's the one belonging to the naturalist, it's a Merkel."

Ponda smiled. "Yes, sorry. My mistake." It was Louise's turn to smile, knowing he had been testing her. "I wanted to confirm that it belonged to the naturalist working there," he explained.

"Yes, it does," she said. He turned and placed the rifle to the right of the store curtain in the corner. He handed her the official receipt and explained that the gun would be kept for the registered owner to collect. "Thank you Mr. Ponda. I'll tell him when he returns," she said as she directed him to a chair.

He sat down and looked in silence at the trio watching him. Louise and Jane were uncertain what to expect. Brett simply hoped Ponda would disclose details that would release him from concealing what he knew about the half-brothers. Ponda had arranged the meeting through

Officer Kinyanjui following Louise's return from her hotel stay. Louise had explained her plan to the others.

"I told Kinyanjui it would be best to meet in my suite and I'd arrange tea." At the appointed time, ten days after Moshi's death, the three of them had been waiting in suspense for Ponda when they heard his car draw up outside.

Louise saw no need for the traditional social preliminaries, so she simply waited for Ponda to speak. He did, awkwardly at first.

"In the usual way, a police officer would not make a visit like this. But I felt I needed to tell you some things as, Mr. James, you were with Moshi at the end, and all three of you have been injured or attacked by my brother." Louise and Jane were clearly bewildered.

Brett said, "I have not told them."

Ponda's glance conveyed a mixture of surprise and gratitude.

"Thank you." Turning to Louise and Jane, he said, "Moshi was my half-brother. He never found out. I have to keep this a secret because I cannot be associated with such a notorious criminal." He paused and then addressed Louise and Brett: "I can trust you two because I tested you both." In response to Brett's surprised look, he explained, "On several occasions, I deliberately used wrong information and you corrected me. Also, you have both sometimes declined to supply details requested by my investigators. I assume that was to protect a confidentiality. I respect that." His tone changed as he spoke less formally: "I feel I owe you all some explanation. But first, I have two requests. You allow me to explain things in my own way even though it can be only partial revelations, and what we discuss must remain confidential." They all nodded in agreement.

Louise's innate gift for leadership surfaced. "First, may I ask why you were pursuing Moshi so vigorously? You surely didn't know he intended to kidnap Jane or flee the country."

Ponda looked uncomfortable.

"Mrs. Jane – that business – we did not know about it until it happened. But I was aware – through various contacts – that he planned to escape. Leaving the country with false passports is illegal."

"But did you have a specific charge against him?"asked Louise.

Ponda looked sheepish. "No. But there was your robbery and violent attack."

Louise was surprised. "I wasn't going to pursue that–"

"But I was! I needed to bring this Moshi case to a close."

"I had decided not to follow through–"

"Madam, the decision was not yours to make! They had forced their way in, physically attacked you, and stolen money." Ponda was the hard-nosed policemen once again. Louise tilted her head in acknowledgement as he continued, "I learned from the reliable older son of the old man that Moshi was intending to break into the tunnel in the restricted area. One of my officers in Mombasa chatted with Moshi's dimwit bodyguard – under the pretext of wanting to adopt one of his stray kittens – and learned that Moshi was armed and desperate."

"May I ask how you knew he was planning to flee the country?" asked Jane.

"Our agents in the Mombasa port found out. Simion Katana supplied additional details."

"Katana?" gasped Louise.

"Yes. Hamud Sita has been keeping him informed of any rumours he heard."

Louise was astonished. "I see." She was uncertain what else to say.

"We knew Moshi had arranged to transfer his car to another crook as a payoff. The driver was instructed what to do when Moshi had escaped overseas." Ponda adjusted his position.

"I feel I should tell you some very confidential information." They nodded, sensing his discomfort. "Our mother had a secret affair with a manager at the Mombasa oil refinery. He was a neighbour, known to the family. He was my father. It happened at a time when Moshi's father, Mr. Nasir, had separated himself from the family – virtually abandoned them – and Mama was desperate. No one else knew about the pregnancy or my birth because Mama spent time with some friends north of Mombasa at the end. That couple looked after me and raised me. I have their family name, Ponda, not Nasir."

The other three were wide-eyed. Ponda explained that someone must have found out because, as a youth, he was called names implying he was a bastard. "I was born, I think you British say, on the wrong side of the blanket." They smiled weakly. "I remember all the insults. My photographic memory allows me to recall every image and relive each moment in the past. The insults still hurt." The pain was evident in his voice. "My father secretly supported me through school and helped establish me in the police force, as he was quite influential. When I was 18 years old, he was near death, so he called for me and told me the story.

"Later, I used my investigative skills to secretly learn all I could about my mother and siblings. It was clear that Ahmed – the young Moshi's real name – was heading for a life of crime. All I could do was watch and monitor his activities from a distance. Later, I had to investigate and pursue him." Ponda paused and looked at Louise. "You will understand that it was difficult for me. He never knew. He could not know, otherwise he would have exploited the relationship. That would have jeopardized my career. Over the years, I have discreetly watched my other half-brothers who work in the government. They seem to be good people. Also, I checked on my step-sisters. By coincidence, one of them runs a successful business next to Matherton's office in Nairobi." Brett said nothing.

Louise had a further question: "Knowing he was a relative, I wonder why you didn't let an independent officer pursue the investigation?"

"That would have been the strictly correct thing to do. But I wanted to stay close to the enquiries without revealing our relationship. I was hoping to help my brother in some way."

Louise watched him with sympathy. "Yes, I see. I was away during those terrible events, so I'm still uncertain of what happened the day Jane was kidnapped."

Ponda was eager to explain. "We knew Moshi would make his move that day. He had instructed the fishermen brothers to meet him on the northern shore when the tide was in."

"Why was it related to the tide?" asked Jane.

"Hamisi and his brother needed a high tide to access the far caves in the north by boat. But that was a problem for my men as it limited their passage along the beach. They had to creep along the shore unseen at low tide and wait. Also, I had posted officers by the main south door in case Moshi returned that way, although I knew it was not his plan. He surprised me by taking Mrs. Jane as a hostage. I did not give him credit for devising a backup plan. That was my mistake. When I heard that, I knew I had a serious offence to charge him with. And I needed to act quickly."

"By approaching from the sea?" asked Louise.

"Yes. The fishermen arranged boats from the south shore for myself and my officers."

"A veritable armada!" joked Louise.

Ponda was unsmiling as he spoke to Jane.

"Moshi left the key in the lock of the lower hut. Iha informed me he and Kuvanza had been told they could release you and both bring you back through the wall once Moshi had escaped with the treasure. He would not have needed you as a hostage then." The inspector thought silently for a full minute. His next remark had a softer tone: "I will be honest. I wanted to catch Moshi on a minor offence before he did something very bad – or his enemies killed him. I thought if I had some contact, I might be able to assist him. I wanted to prevent him escaping by sea."

"Would you have revealed your relationship?" asked Louise.

"Honestly, I do not know. Once he was free of crime and no longer a threat...maybe. I do not know. I only had a hope...that...." He stopped speaking and lifted his cup.

While they all sipped their tea quietly, Louise was thinking.

"It seems to me that Fatima deserves credit for her response."

"Yes. Following her quick reaction – and Mjuhgiuna's initiative with Imam Faiz – my staff called me to the Zoo. Kinyanjui drove here to interview Fatima while I located the boats I needed. A man near the door had told the Imam he saw Moshi push Jane through. I quickly drove south to find two fishermen I know. They checked the tides and saw it was just possible to paddle over to the headland. I wanted to surprise Moshi in your late husband's compound, if possible before he headed to the north shore."

"And what was happening on that northern route?"

"I already had my men posted there to intercept Hamisi, before we heard of the kidnapping. Sita knew Moshi was planning to escape to the north."

"Hamud Sita? You mentioned him before. How did he come in on this?"

"Sita is still resentful towards Moshi about his time in prison. But he is grateful to me for helping in his release. We meet occasionally. He still has contacts in the docks who heard about the large ship planning to meet the smaller boat. I cannot reveal anything else."

"No, we understand; but how did you know Hamisi and his brother were involved with Moshi? They seemed so friendly and helpful."

"The police living in the Zoo listen for scraps of information. They were suspicious of Hamisi who had been seen talking with Moshi the previous week. Moshi's flashy car is very obvious. Also, we know of his connection with Larry Smythe and Kuvanza. My people gave me the fragments, I assembled the story."

"But, cutting the lock on the gate…?" asked Brett.

"We did that the previous evening to give us unhindered access at dawn during the low tide."

There was silence as they processed all he had told them.

Jane asked, "What will happen now? – if you are able to tell us."

"The legal process will take its course. Moshi tricked others into helping him – Iha in particular. Kuvanza is a bad man, I tell you. He is in big trouble. I will be as lenient as I can with Hamisi and his brother. They must be punished, but I will recommend fines. I do not want them to face imprisonment. I have some limited influence in these matters, but…." His shrug of deference left the thought unfinished.

"What about Larry Smythe? How was he involved?" Louise asked.

"He claims he knew nothing of Moshi's intentions and he was an innocent victim of his deception. That may be true. But he did provide safe refuge for the men. He sheltered criminals. My policemen saw Moshi's car outside his place several times. He could be an accessory after the fact. But it may be difficult to prove he was intentionally committing a crime."

"He must have known something was not right," suggested Louise, still feeling uneasy about Larry and his keen interest in the rifle.

"Moshi had a hold on him, I understand. It was somehow based on their previous association at the soda factory. I plan to drop any charges."

"Didn't he refuse to allow you access through the door in the N-1 store?"

"He did not refuse us. That has been permanently sealed. The gate in the wire fence on the beach was easier to open. He did not obstruct us doing that. I doubt if he even knew."

To Brett, Ponda appeared weary of talking. Or perhaps, he had simply told them all he intended to reveal. His head was down, looking at the newspaper on the table. He seemed to be studying the partially completed crossword puzzle as though searching for the answer to a clue. When he looked up, his eyes were moist. He blinked and rubbed them with the back of his large hand.

"Sorry. It is an emotional loss...when it is a relative. I was trying to help him, but my way was prevented...." He held his large hands out wide, palms upwards. "Now it is too late. He died alone." The others watched him in silence. Jane felt uncomfortable. Brett had never seen the big man so distressed. Ponda looked up at Louise, "Thank you for allowing me.... Thank you for understanding."

"We do understand – to some extent at least," Louise replied.

"You probably understand better than anyone." He had tears in his eyes. He grasped a tea serviette which was obviously inadequate. Louise made a gesture towards Brett and nodded in the direction of the bathroom, miming the drying of hands as she mouthed 'towel'. Brett quickly collected a small hand towel from the shelf and placed it on the chair arm next to Ponda. He lifted it gratefully and covered his face.

Louise stared at Ponda and then turned to Brett. "I expect Jane would like to see Kismet Kantara from up here," she said, nodding down the hall. Admiring her sensitivity, Jane and Brett immediately stood and walked through her apartment to the east patio. After spending ten minutes looking at the ancient construction and enjoying the view, they cautiously made their way back towards the room. They overheard Louise speaking sympathetically, "...extremely difficult for you...do not suppress it...allow yourself time to heal...." Brett motioned to Jane that they should linger in the hallway, looking at the paintings and prints on the wall.

Jane whispered, "Louise is wonderful."

Brett said, "She's a remarkable woman."

Gradually, they moved towards the seated pair so their presence would be obvious. They saw two dedicated professionals: a caring nurse and a hardened policeman.

They caught the end of Louise's words, "...appreciated all you have done to assist us. Thank you for being so gracious in coming to explain.... Ah, here are the others."

They took their seats again.

Jane said, "I hope you don't mind, but may I say a prayer?"

Ponda looked surprised, but Louise said, "Why not?"

Brett said, "Yes please." Ponda nodded.

Jane and Brett bowed their heads and individually clasped their hands together. Louise and Ponda noticed this and did the same.

Jane prayed, "Heavenly Father, we do not understand all that is happening, but we trust that you are working out your higher purpose in it all. We pray for the deceased, Mr. Moshi, and comfort for his family at this tragic time. Please be with Mr. Ponda and his staff as they continue to protect everyone in this community. Amen."

Brett said, "Amen."

Louise intoned, "Mmm."

Ponda sat in silence. Then he looked at Jane.

"Thank you. No one has prayed for me like that before."

Jane smiled and said, "Your grandmother probably did."

"My grandmother?"

Brett explained. "Yes. On your mother's side. She was a Christian. She prayed for all her grandchildren. Your brother told us. He remembered some of her teaching." Ponda looked at them both and his eyes conveyed a profound understanding that needed no words.

After a respectful pause, Louise spoke to the inspector.

"Mr. Ponda, we won't delay you any...." At that cue, he eased himself up out of the chair, placed the crumpled towel on the seat, and towered over her. In silence, he reached down and grasped her hand. As he did, Brett noticed an expression which suddenly reminded him of Moshi. He saw the likeness in a characteristic tilt of the head with the eyebrows raised slightly. Brett wondered why he had not noticed the resemblance before.

Turning to shake hands with Brett, Ponda addressed him formally.

"The Kenyan police are grateful for your assistance. Thank you for being with me when we discovered...when we discovered my brother."

He stretched his hand towards Jane. She noticed his firm grip.

"Thank you for rescuing me, Mr. Ponda."

He nodded diffidently. "I am sorry you were treated badly by...by... one of my countrymen." Brett stepped beside him as he moved slowly to the door. Ponda's dignified composure was restored as he lifted the rifle from the corner. Brett noticed his alert eyes sweep across the shelving unit and into the CPZ-Store. Ponda stared into the opening a moment longer than a cursory peep warranted and his eyes revealed a flicker of comprehension. He swung his gaze up, across the ceiling, and back down to Louise. The faint crease on his lips and a gentle nod were imperceptible to the women but Brett saw them.

Brett escorted him down the stairs and out the front door. As he left, the Inspector of Police resumed his official stance in spite of his civilian clothing. He carried the rifle in his right hand with the barrel pointing downwards. He walked uprightly and with authority through the curious group standing outside. They parted respectfully to make way for him. He strode over to his car and climbed in the rear seat, saying nothing. The police vehicle drove away quickly. A trail of exhaust fumes mingled with puffs of dust from the tyres grinding on the *murram* road. Brett thought it resembled smoke.

Brett returned upstairs and closed the door. Jane sat next to Louise who looked extremely tired. Louise glanced up.

"Now I see a likeness between the two brothers that I had never noticed before."

"You saw it too? I wonder if Miles made the connection," Brett asked

"I doubt it. But I'm sure Heinrick would have done. That's just the sort of thing he'd notice. Oh, I do miss Heinrick." She sat quietly and then said, "Jane, I think your prayer was wonderful. Thank you. Ponda was affected by it. So was I."

Jane smiled, "When Christians pray, something always happens. Even when we don't see it, results happen all the time from God's standpoint."

Louise asked, "Do you think God loved someone like Moshi?"

Jane replied thoughtfully. "I know He does! He loved a sinner like me when I was rebellious! God doesn't love us because we're good. He loves us unconditionally – everyone – even while we're bad. Jesus offers everyone a path of redemption. We simply need to accept that in faith."

"Yes. Acceptance in faith, I know." Louise sighed, "Poor Moshi. May a peaceful rest attend him."

40

Brett asked himself if there were repercussions from all the illegal goods they had transported. Should they have handed them over to the police immediately?

The tension of the last few weeks had exhausted Brett and Jane but as their departure neared, they took opportunities to say farewell to people when they saw them. A few of their friends arranged a small teatime party to say goodbye. Louise offered her advice.

"You're bound to get a delayed reaction to all the trauma you experienced. Allow time to deal with it, won't you?"

Brett said, "I'll try. But usually I like to get on with something practical. I call it the Therapy of Action."

"Nowadays, I prefer the therapy of inaction!"

Jane laughed. "Yes, I think resting would be more conducive to the healing of my wounds."

On their last evening, Coreene joined them in Louise's lower suite to pray for Brett and Jane's safe journey home and the healing of Louise's cancer. Louise told them the Board of Governors had decided that the whole complex of the central buildings should be named the Emerson Centre. Louise felt honoured but said recognition should go to others too. She said how much she appreciated Coreene and Steve's continuing work to build up the Zoo community.

Coreene gave a small gesture of appreciation and said, "The work goes on. Many Kenyan people are working hard to make a positive difference. We are thankful to God for the opportunity to serve alongside them."

Brett had sent a message to Imam Faiz asking if he could call in to visit them before they left. Brett had a gift he wanted to give him – a pair of craftsman's tools. When he purchased them, Brett had described them to Jane.

"It's a Warrington hammer and a ball-peen hammer. It links back to the time we worked together on a carpentry project."

As they emerged from Louise's cage, Mjuhgiuna told Brett that Faiz would visit them at the guesthouse within an hour. They were pleased with the opportunity to thank Faiz once more for his decisive actions upon learning that Jane had been captured. Brett was surprised when Faiz handed over a gift he had crafted himself: a pair of carved white rhinos. They were sculptured from mahogany.

Faiz joked, "I thought white rhinos carved from black wood is a nice symbol. You white people have become the friends of us black people. We are bonded together now."

On the fourth Sunday in June, Brett and Jane loaded their cases in the back of the pickup and drove across the Zoo to say goodbye to Louise. She had told Brett at their previous meeting that she could only manage a quick farewell. She was waiting by the front door of her cage. They shook hands and hugged her. Louise spoke seriously.

"It's been a joy to have known you both. We had some adventures, didn't we?" Jane and Louise had tears in their eyes. So did Fatima and Shafiqah, and even Mjuhgiuna's eyes were moist as Jane thanked him again for his part in rescuing her. Brett simply shook hands and smiled.

Louise told Brett, "I said my final farewell to you last time! Two and a half years ago. No more sad goodbyes." Then she added, "But thanks for coming back, with your lovely bride. It completes things for me. I will write. Go well, both of you."

Those were Louise's final words as they got in the vehicle. When Brett glanced in the rearview mirror he saw Louise standing alone, waving. He felt a lump in his throat.

"This is the last time we'll see her." he told Jane.

As Louise watched the retreating vehicle, she felt both sadness and a sense of fulfilment. She watched the pickup until it was out of sight and then turned away.

The next stop was at the Brandons' cage where, once again with some tears, they said goodbye. Both their maids and Khadijah were there and wished Brett and Jane well on their journey. Just as they approached the main gate, Larry Smythe drove into the compound. He stopped his car and got out.

"I'm glad I caught you. I wanted to apologize to you both about what happened. I think I was partly to blame. I'm sorry if I may have contributed... to you getting hurt." As they shook hands, Brett and Jane thanked him and told him not to worry. Larry said, "I don't wish to speak ill of the dead, but Moshi fooled me. I have a lot to think about. Some deep...spiritual things, actually. Safe journey."

As Brett drove south along the familiar road, Jane opened a package that Louise had thrust in her hand as she left. Louise had given instructions.

"Take care of this. The details are inside. May it bless you." Inside the wrapping was a small package and a note.

Jane read it aloud. "It says 'Please keep this safe. Hold onto it to open in the future when you receive good news or when you have something significant to celebrate. Love, Louise. Z'. How sweet of her."

"We've been given some lovely gifts, haven't we? Including that amazing hand-embroidered tablecloth from Khadijah."

"Gifts are important to reinforce friendships, aren't they?" said Jane, clutching Louise's package.

"But, even more than practical presents, I value the deep relationships we made. The Kenyans in particular shared part of their lives and culture with us."

They appreciated the cooling temperature on the long drive up to Nairobi. The journey went well, although they were tired by the time they arrived at the Gossards. They were distressed to see how distorted Mary's finger was from the attack, although she said it was healing well. After a brief chat and a bite to eat, they collapsed in their guest room.

Before leaving Kenya, Jane and Brett gave their spare clothes and shoes to Mary to distribute to some of the needy people she worked with. They returned the Datsun pickup, and Brett and Jim calculated a fair payment for the extended rental time. Brett phoned Allistair Matherton, but there was no news on the valuation or disposal of the assets. Allistair confirmed he had their correct UK address and promised to write.

At the airport, Brett and Jane were queuing for customs when a serious-looking man wearing a suit and tie approached them and politely asked to see their passports. After leafing through them, he silently motioned to them to step out of the line and wait at the side. They felt embarrassed at the attention they received in front of the other passengers.

"Come this way please. Bring your cases." He held onto their documents. He directed them through a small door into a quiet hallway, away from the crowds. As they followed him, Brett observed his athletic and muscular frame. Obviously he was a tough and well-trained individual.

Jane was worried; Brett felt apprehensive. His pulse was racing as a tumble of thoughts rushed through his mind: they had paid the departure tax, but had they overrun their visa date? They walked slowly, pulling their cases. Jane wondered what was wrong. Was there a problem with their documents? Surely Brett knew the system well enough to take care of those formalities. Brett asked himself if there were repercussions from all the illegal goods they had transported. Should they have handed them over to the police immediately rather than giving them to the lawyer?

Sensing Jane's concern, Brett gently placed his hand on her shoulder. They were shown along a narrow corridor into a softly lit room. The official spoke at last.

"Leave your bags with me. Please, you take a seat and the attendant will speak to you about your wishes for drinks."

"What's happening?" Brett asked him.

"Oh, this is the VIP lounge. You may relax here until your flight." Seeing Brett's puzzled look, he added, "An officer will be here very soon to explain."

Brett and Jane smiled at each other and sat down in the comfortable chairs.

"What's all this about?" whispered Jane.

"I don't know. I entered Kenya all those years ago as a rascal and now I'm leaving as a VIP!"

"Except that you're still a rascal!" A uniformed lady with a notepad asked what drinks they would like. She indicated where the toilets were.

After ten minutes, another fit-looking young man approached.

"Mr. James, I am a police officer. I have a message for you." He handed Brett an envelope. Opening it, Brett read the handwritten note:

> Dear Mr. and Mrs. James,
>
> Thank you for your assistance to the Kenyan Police Service.
>
> I am sorry I am unable to say goodbye in person.
>
> Please relax now and enjoy my expression of appreciation.
>
> I wish you both a pleasant flight.
>
> Sincerely, Inspector Ponda.

A uniformed policeman came up to them.

"Excuse me, sir, madam. Here are your passports. Everything is in order. Your luggage has been cleared and delivered to the airline. It will be on your flight. Have an enjoyable journey. *Safari njema.*"

"*Asante sana.* Thank you," replied Brett. Jane smiled.

"Do you have any questions?" the officer asked.

"When do we board?"

"In about forty minutes. I will return to escort you to the plane. Please relax during your final moments in Kenya."

They thanked him as he left. Alone again, Jane sighed in appreciation for the release of tension. She closed her eyes and relaxed as she thought about their amazing holiday. She rested her hand on Brett's arm.

"I'm overwhelmed by the total experience of Kenya: the people and their faith, the mystery, the drama...oh, and the colours, textures, and aromas. Thank you for sharing it all with me." She sighed, "But the relaxing holiday we planned turned out to be quite an adventure, didn't it?"

Brett had to admit, "Fulfilling Miles' final wishes resulted in a risky adventure. But risk with a purpose?"

Jane hesitated. Then she squeezed Brett's arm. "Yes, risk with a purpose."

Epilogue

In the hectic months following their return to England, Brett and Jane heard occasional news of the Zoo community through letters from Louise and the Brandons. Steve had been reassigned to a church in Malindi to work in partnership with a Kenyan priest. They would train counterparts and build a team to develop a joint commitment to all that Steve and Bishop Onyango held close to their hearts. It was easier to take the children to school, although they missed the familiar community at the Zoo. Coreene explained that their oldest daughter, Ruth, was working as a teaching assistant at her former school for the next year until deciding which university courses to pursue. Louise wrote with news that she now lived full time in a Malindi nursing home. She was content and felt safe there. After her first letter, however, she wrote less frequently.

Jane picked up her previous duties at the church and Brett, after several months looking for employment, secured a two-year contract with an engineering company in Reading. They both felt blessed to have full-time employment again.

They also exchanged letters and news with Julie Lancaster in Kent. She was always interested to hear details of life in Kenya and developments at the Zoo. She mentioned her desire to return for a visit there one day and see where her father had spent his last years. It had been several decades since she left Kenya as a teenager.

A letter with American stamps arrived in September 1990. Kelsey wrote, describing how her wrist was healing and the plans that were in place for her and Shane to meet in Savannah over American Thanksgiving. They would go through their Kenyan photos and share copies of prints. At the end she wrote 'Shane said it was neat the way you both forgave Moshi and that guy who attacked you. He said he only found peace after he had forgiven the drunk driver who killed his wife and son. Remember him telling us that?' Jane read those words several times and smiled at Brett.

"I like Kelsey. She's a lovely, thoughtful girl." Brett also smiled – in silence.

In October, the Jameses saw that the postman had delivered a letter from Matherton & Son in Nairobi. They were anxious to read the news it brought.

> Dear Brett,
>
> In a recent conversation, Mrs. Louise Emerson authorized me to tell you the following news as she finds writing difficult these days. She also asked me to send her best wishes.
>
> Mrs. Emerson will be receiving a substantial sum for the diamonds. I am not at liberty to disclose the amount, but I can assure you it is considerable. You can feel satisfied that all of your efforts – and risks – were worth it. We are processing the bank transfers now.
>
> You may be interested in the few details that I am permitted to convey to you. Mrs. Emerson has established a trust fund at the Mwakindini bank, with three accounts. A third of the monies will fund the continuing research into the relationship between the monkeys on the headland and similar groups in the Kenya/Uganda border region, with a high conservation component.
>
> A quarter of the amount will be invested in developing the potential of ecotourism based in the Zoo; and the remainder is to be used to expand the residential accommodation and the associated infrastructure. This will also improve the Zoo's water supply, including a

water treatment plant and rainwater collection facilities throughout the complex.

Concerning the two gold bars and the coins you found, the police are still analysing those and have undertaken to notify us when they have concluded their investigations. I should warn you that these items may be confiscated by the authorities, although we are cognizant of the fact that Mrs. Emerson and you desire that the Zoo community benefit from those assets. We will do our best to present that case.

On a separate matter, we believe we are very close to receiving official clearance to allocate all of the currency that you discovered in the form of cash (Kenyan and foreign funds) to finance an experimental desalination plant. Mrs. Emerson was delighted when she heard this news. In our files, we have your written authorization to proceed with this. As far as can be determined, you were the recipient (by means of bequeathment) of those funds from the late Mr. Miles Jolly. No doubt, the beneficiaries of your generous donation will be contacting you in due course, with details of the disbursement of the monies.

Yours sincerely, Allistair Matherton

Two weeks before Christmas, they received word that Vi Ridge-Taylor had died in Shropshire. For Brett particularly, this news brought back many memories. However, Jane's thoughts were focused on another development. She had started a poem.

Baby, stir within me!
Stir in me belief that you are there.
Never such affinity
As between us two, for everything we share.

Baby, quicken in me!
Quicken my slow body with your kick.
Waiting is eternity!
Or is it all part of a cruel trick?

Baby, reassure me;
Push away my tired doubts with your small limbs;
Remove my fearing
As you move your tiny body deep within.

In January 1991, Jane's appointment with the doctor came a year – almost to the day – after they had flown into Kenya. Brett was also present to hear the doctor confirm the wonderful news that Jane was pregnant. At her age, there was some concern, but the doctor assured her of the good care she would receive in the next few months. The ecstatic couple quickly shared the news with their families by telephone.

On the way home from the appointment, Brett had to try three florists before he found a bunch of freesias for Jane. She wondered what he was doing as he dashed into different shops, but was delighted at his uxorious persistence.

"That's so sweet of you to try so hard to find my favourite flowers. Bless you."

"Hey Jane, do you think this is the right occasion to open that mysterious package from Louise we've been saving?"

"Yes!" she said. "Let's do that. I've been dying to know what's in it." When they got home, Jane opened it and saw the brooch that Louise wore. She read the letter inside:

Dear Jane,

You admired this brooch, so I would like you to have it. It holds significant memories in the gems and silver filigree. It was crafted in Nairobi many decades ago. The deep blue stones are lapis lazuli from Afghanistan. The emerald-green gemstones are Tsavorit, a variety of garnet mined here in Kenya and named after the Tsavo National

> Park that you visited. I feel certain that the centre stone is a genuine diamond. That seems appropriate!
>
> The brooch was a gift to me from Heinrick in 1949 just after our son died. You will understand that it has always been precious to me. I have sometimes thought that Brett was sent to me as a replacement son. I never had a daughter. Knowing you will have the brooch brings me joy and, perhaps, the promise of future life to compensate me for my loss.
>
> I can honestly say that you two dear people have been like family to me. For that I am deeply grateful.
>
> Love to you both, Louise, Z

Brett said, "That's really special. I saw her wearing it but I never knew its significance."

Some time after that, Jane completed her poem. The last verse read:

> Baby, what's that I feel?
> I hold my breath; I feel another writhe.
> Now I know you're real.
> My prayers were heard: you are alive!

It was a late-February day of gale-force winds and driving rain when Brett and Jane received another letter from the lawyers in Nairobi. Together, they glanced at the outside of the envelope with its row of familiar, colourful Kenyan stamps. With considerable apprehension, Brett opened it. He saw two letters. He took a deep breath before reading the first one.

Dear Mr. James,

It is with deep regret that I inform you of the passing of Mrs. Louise Emerson. This sad event occurred in the Malindi hospital on the 8th of February, 1991.

My father, who has known the Emerson family for a long time, is saddened. He asked me to convey his sympathy to you.

We will be communicating further details in due course, but Mrs. Emerson left specific instructions that you be notified as soon as possible.

Yours sincerely, Allistair Matherton

Brett opened the second envelope and found a long, handwritten note. He read it with sadness.

Dear Brett,

I felt that our official letter was rather formal, so I wanted to enclose a note expressing my sorrow at the sad news. I imagine you will be distressed, as you and Mrs. Emerson were close neighbours and friends for several years. She appreciated all the assistance you gave her, I know.

We will be communicating with you officially, but I feel at liberty to tell you (informally, as a friend) that Louise has left you and Jane a large gift in her will. Keep this information under your hat for now, but you can expect to receive a transfer of 8,000 UK pounds from her London bank. In order to process this, I will need your bank details as soon as possible, please.

Brett and Jane stared at each other in astonishment.

> "That's incredible," Brett managed to say.
>
> "How could she have…?" wondered Jane. "I hope she received our news about the baby and my letter thanking her for the brooch." Brett returned to the note.
>
> You may be interested to learn that we have moved into smarter offices. I think you and Jane would approve. But, we have maintained our humble demeanour – even though (as I once told you) we are, indeed, brilliant lawyers!
>
> I trust that all is going well with you and Jane in Berkshire. It's been good to have known you.
>
> Best wishes, Allistair.
>
> P.S. I forgot to mention that Louise told me she was delighted to hear that you two will be parents. Congratulations.

Brett gave a rueful grin and sighed. Jane experienced a surge of mixed emotions. She was overwhelmed by the promised gift but remained melancholy for several hours. That evening, they were both pensive. They sat on the sofa together. He had his arm around Jane's shoulder as he stared for a long time at the rhino carvings on the shelf below the painting he had given to Miles. Jane worked on her next poem. She suddenly turned to Brett.

"As the baby is probably a boy, what would you like to call him?"

"I don't know. Do you have any ideas?"

"I thought his name could be linked to Kenya. What about giving him the name Miles?"

Brett tilted his head and squinted in reservation. "Miles would have liked that. But he was a bit of a rogue."

"What about naming him after Henry?" Jane asked.

Again, Brett was ambivalent. "Although I heard a lot about him, I never knew Henry. It's strange because he was so pivotal in the Zoo and his presence pervaded everything. Yet he remains an enigma, like his code name Cypher."

"Well, we can't call our son Cypher!" Jane joked. "But calling him Henry would keep alive the Emerson family connections that Louise mentioned in her note. The doctor told us it will be a boy. He has a reputation for always knowing ahead of time."

"Yes, but when he told us it would be a boy, I saw him write GIRL in his notes. I can read upside down."

"Aha, that's why he's known for always being right! He's got it covered both ways."

"So, we should think about a girl's name. I also wondered about a name from Africa," he said.

"Louise?"

"No, a Kenyan name."

"Do you have one in mind?"

"Chania."

"Oh, I remember the lovely river and Chania Falls at Thika."

"Rivers are significant. They mean life, continuity, and hope."

"That would be appropriate."

"Perhaps more than you realize. The Chania River joins the mighty Tana River which eventually flows into the Indian Ocean. It reaches the East African coast just north of the Zoo."

The End

Other Books by the Author

BOOK 1: THE ZOO

Just as he starts his new teaching job in Kenya, Brett James discovers that things are not as they appear on the surface. He bravely confronts the mysteries of the cross-cultural, multi-religious community called The Zoo. His faith is deepened as he deals with unexpected and stunning revelations.

Follow our hero, Brett, as he battles through a fog of mystery, deception, and violence. He challenges the impenetrable wall, constructed by the elusive founder who controls access to the isolated Monkey Island.

Will the residents reveal their sinister histories and complex relationships to this naive outsider? And will Brett be sympathetic as the surviving leaders strive for reconciliation and truth that parallel their spiritual longings?

What readers say about The Zoo

Keith Brown is clearly a most astute observer of characters as he drew those who are diverse, yet fully real and believable. I commend most heartily this book, and I look forward to the next instalment of the trilogy.

What's not to like in this book? I love history. I greatly enjoy a mystery. Who doesn't like the humorous side of cultural differences? Now, mix in a cast of diverse but very real characters and you have a book which quickly drew me from one end to the other. I start reading many books, but precious few are ever read to the last page.

The Zoo effortlessly carried me to the end, and now I am eagerly looking for the next book from Keith Brown. I need to know what happens next!

Jim Barber

I read this novel last night in two sittings – it's very readable! It's a stellar example of popular fiction, enhanced by erudition throughout, covering so many fields of knowledge, from African history, culture, and politics, to interfaith dialogue, to an array of European cultural references. The nuanced assessment of pluralism conveys tact and wisdom.

The main character, Brett, is a likeable and intellectually and spiritually vibrant character whose consciousness gives the novel a moral soundness and good horse sense. The prose is beautifully clear. I don't think I had to reread anything for lack of clarity.

This work represents a great achievement as a first novel, and I believe it outshines much of the popular fiction that occupies privileged space in bookstores.

Dr. David Anonby, Assistant Professor of English

The Zoo is a quintessential mini-series for the heart and mind. The setting is staged with deliberate care and fine descriptions as the players enter the scenes slowly and deliberately. Each person and group are carefully juxtaposed to create the undercurrent of tensions. We see Brett James sense that all is not peace and harmony in the Zoo, and the reader is invited along to see him navigate and sometimes blunder through his days and ways, to a greater perception of his self and his place in this corner of Kenya. Brett comments: "It seems we've had a crisis every week." Yes, a crisis in every chapter.

The adolescent reader will be enthralled at the prospects of venturing into the unknown. Brown's elaborate attention to details heightens the anticipation of the adventures while at the same time educating his audience in survival gear and thinking. The novel is captivating and a pleasant read. I am so glad there is a Book 2 coming.

Ted V., former English teacher

I have read *The Zoo* by Keith Brown and I recommend it on several levels. It is a well written book. The plot is both clever and unique. Although I am not an avid reader of fiction, in this book the author's knowledge of the setting, the people and their customs give it an authenticity that could be real. The description of the characters has the ability to draw you into the story.

It is refreshing to read a novel that is not laced with profanities like so many books written today. This fact is highlighted, albeit with humour, that even the word "heck" draws admonition against its use!

I look forward to the next book which the author has assured us will give us a dramatic conclusion to the plot.

Rev. C.R.M.

An awesome book cover, great font and writing style. A very professionally written adventure book. It was extremely easy for me to read and follow from start to finish and never a dull moment. There were no repetitive or out-of-line sequence sentences. Lots of exciting scenarios, with several twists and turns and a huge description list of unique characters, settings, and facts.

This could also make another great adventure movie, or better yet a mini TV series. There is no doubt in my mind this is an extremely easy rating of 5 stars.

Tony P.

This fast-paced, easy-read novel gives a wonderful glimpse of life in Kenya in the 1980s. There are many intriguing characters interwoven between the different nationalities, customs, and morals. The mystery of *The Zoo* is set in a very strange village near Monkey island.

The back section of the Zoo is blocked by a huge stone wall, like a fortress, to keep everyone out. What is beyond this wall? Is it really a top-secret African wildlife research project?

The author describes in detail the natural beauty of Kenya, its foliage, the ocean, the towns, the scary roads, the dangers. This novel is a real page-turner, but it ends as a cliffhanger. I can't wait to read the second volume to discover what happens to some very shady characters and the Zoo village - does it survive?

Ted G.

Brett James is the newest - and probably the most headstrong - member of the unusual and exotic microcosm of a human society living in the community.

Like in many other books and life itself, the main protagonist is disciplined enough to follow the rules and, simultaneously, to break them. This type of behaviour is not paradoxical and is often both punished and rewarded, and the author expresses this beautifully. His language is very cinematographic, his vocabulary is beyond rich, and the actions chosen in the chapters flow effortlessly.

Marin D.

BOOK 2: THE ZOO REVEALED

What lies behind the persistent police enquiries? Will the leaders of the small coastal community reveal any more mysteries to Brett James, the inquisitive teacher? And at what further cost to him? Will he suffer any more attacks if he pursues his enquiries?

Brett hopes the eccentric characters will continue to accept him. But, beyond that, what are the chances that the diverse residents can restore their relationships and experience a deepening faith?

Perhaps Brett would be wise to simply appreciate the beauty of The Zoo, continue to relish the satisfaction of his teaching work, and stop asking questions! But that is not in his nature.

What readers say about The Zoo Revealed

Keith Brown has once again hit the middle of the bulls-eye with Book 2 of his Zoo trilogy. Having so loved Book 1 for all of the many connections which I made, and Brown's characters, I was eager to get my hands on Book 2.

The unfolding of many of the dilemmas stirred up in the first book were addressed in a way that kept the pages quickly flying by (all too quickly). Excited as I was for Book 2, I am now even more eager for Book 3 to appear.

Jim Barber

Keith Brown's second novel, *The Zoo Revealed,* will take you on a wild ride into the covert inner workings of an experimental multi-ethnic, multi-faith community in the fictional town of Mwakindini, Kenya. You will discover the hidden pasts of an array of characters who will excite your sympathy, despite their scandalous activities.

You will be taken on a safari through Kenya in the late 1980s, visiting world famous evolutionary digs, teeming game reserves, urban sprawls, and rustic tea plantations, all under the looming threat of danger and intrigue. Your guide will be the protagonist Brett James, an adventurous, idealistic young English engineer who finds himself making friends with the long-term members of The Zoo. His disarming, nonjudgmental attitude has the effect of making even criminals confide in him. What will Brett do with this burden of knowledge?

The much anticipated second instalment in Brown's trilogy, *The Zoo Revealed,* is charged with suspense, as unexpected shocks and escapes are delivered at every turn. The novel's fast-paced action is supported by a sophisticated philosophical meta-structure that challenges the trajectory of Western culture and its impact on an unsuspecting paradise on the shores of the Indian Ocean. Brown's insights into cross-cultural relationships, interfaith dialogue, personal ethics, and geopolitics are astonishing.

Dr. David Anonby, Assistant Professor of English

For more information,
please visit keithbrownauthor.com
or email keithbrownauthor@gmail.com
facebook.com/thezootrilogy

Manufactured by Amazon.ca
Bolton, ON

19518696R00203